STEPHEN COONTS

THE MINOTAUR

"ONE OF THE PREMIER WRITERS OF THIS GENRE ALONG WITH DALE BROWN AND TOM CLANCY."
—*The Milwaukee Journal*

"STEPHEN COONTS HAS WRITTEN HIS MOST IN-VOLVED AND ENGAGING BOOK. COMBINING THE GEE-WHIZ TECHNOLOGY OF TOM CLANCY WITH THE INTRICATE PLOTTING OF ROBERT LUDLUM HAS MADE FOR A STORY THAT THRILLER FANS WON'T WANT TO MISS."
—*Rocky Mountain News*

"THE FLYING EPISODES RING TRUE. THERE ARE ALSO A FEW THINGS NOT NORMALLY ENCOUNTERED IN BIG BOOKS . . . IT MAKES ONE THINK."
—Newgate Callendar,
The New York Times Book Review

"ACTION AND PLENTY OF IT . . . clever twists of plot, es-pecially in the spy end of the storyline, abound. . . . Like an Aga-tha Christie mystery, *The Minotaur* achieves that rare balance be-tween plot and characterization that keeps the reader hooked from beginning to end."
—*San Diego Tribune*

RAVE REVIEWS FOR

STEPHEN COONTS'S
FINAL FLIGHT

"Coonts goes back to putting the reader in the cockpit and describes the sights and sounds of an aircraft carrier. He is a master of that art." —*The Washington Post Book World*

"A new high in adventure stories . . . a superlative thriller . . . a new masterpiece." —*The West Coast Review of Books*

"Coonts describes with force . . . the camaraderie of rare and honorable men . . . [his] gripping first-person narration of aerial combat is the best I've ever read."
—John Lehman, former Secretary of the Navy,
The Wall Street Journal

"Coonts has brought to naval air warfare the intimacy and quiet thoughtfulness that Stephen Crane gave to *The Red Badge of Courage.*" —*San Diego Union*

FLIGHT OF THE INTRUDER

"Packed with action, emotion, suspense and tragedy, *Flight of the Intruder* offers profound and gripping insight into the lives and loves of naval carrier pilots." —Clive Cussler, author of *Cyclops*

"Coonts makes us care deeply about the fate of Jake Grafton, his decent, sensitive hero. . . . The action scenes are vivid and authentic: Coonts makes us see, smell, hear, taste and feel battle. The final chapter becomes especially exciting."
—*The Plain Dealer,* Cleveland

Also by Stephen Coonts

Flight of the Intruder
Final Flight

THE
MINOTAUR

STEPHEN COONTS

A DELL BOOK

Published by
Dell Publishing
a division of
Bantam Doubleday Dell Publishing Group, Inc.
666 Fifth Avenue
New York, New York 10103

This novel is a work of fiction. The characters, names, incidents, dialogue, and plot are the products of the author's imagination or are used fictitiously. Any resemblance to actual persons or events is purely coincidental.

Epigram reprinted from *Jomini's Art of War*, by Brig. Gen. James D. Hittle, USMC Ret., with permission of Stackpole Books.

Lines of poetry quoted in Chapters 19 and 31 are from *Darius Green and His Flying Machine* by J. T. Trowbridge, a humorous poem written in the mid-nineteenth century about a young bumpkin who tried to fly from his father's hayloft.

ISBN: 0-440-20742-8

Reprinted by arrangement with Doubleday

Printed in the United States of America

October 1990

10 9 8 7 6 5 4

RAD

ACKNOWLEDGMENTS

The author received invaluable unclassified technical advice from numerous individuals who volunteered to assist in his education. Some of them wished to remain anonymous. Those who forgot to request anonymity are: Commander Robert Day, Commander Doug Hargrave, Captain Michael E. Kearney, Fred Kleinberg, Captain Richard E. "Dick" Koehler, Captain Wayne Savage, Captain Karl Volland and Dr. Edward Walsh. The author also referred extensively to Bill Sweetman's excellent works on low-observable technology aircraft. To all of these people the author extends his thanks.

Knowledgeable readers are advised that the intricacies and eccentricities of the bureaucratic maze within the Department of Defense forced the author to take liberties within this novel in the interest of readability. Some of the mind-boggling complexities of modern military hardware have been simplified for the same reason.

You've heard the story—it's old, they say—
how the queen of Crete took a bull for a lover
and in her time delivered the Minotaur.
Contriving to hide his shame, to banish
the hideous man-bull from the sight of men,
King Minos ordered Daedalus to construct a labyrinth.
The artist set the stone, captured conflict
in aisles and passages of confusion and deceit,
devious ways that twisted the mind and eye
of all who entered that prison of no escape,
wherein was placed the Minotaur.
Thus did Daedalus build his monument
to the betrayal of the king.

The means of destruction are approaching perfection with frightful rapidity.

—BARON ANTOINE HENRI JOMINI, 1838

1

       Terry Franklin was a spy. This afternoon in February, in a small cubbyhole in the basement of the Pentagon, he was practicing his trade. It was tedious work.

He adjusted the screen brightness on his computer monitor and tapped the secret access code of the user he was pretending to be tonight. Now the file name, also special access, a classification higher than top secret. He had to be careful, since the letters and numerals he was typing did not appear on the screen. A mistake here meant the computer would lock him out and deny him the file. And he was not a good typist. He worked with just two fingers.

Voilà! There it was. The ATA File, the Advanced Tactical Aircraft. He tapped some more and began examining the document list. Number 23.241, that's the first one. He slid one of his high-density, 5.25-inch floppies into the slot and hit the keys again. The little red light came on above the disk drive and the drive began to whir. Franklin smiled when he saw the light.

It was quiet here in the computer service shop. The only noise was the whirring of the disk drive and the tiny clicks of the keyboard. And the sound of Terry Franklin's breathing. It was ironic, he mused, how the computer silently and effortlessly reveals the deepest secrets of its owners. Without remorse, without a twinge of emotion of any kind, the screen lays bare the insights gained from man-years of research by highly educated, gifted scientists and the cunning application of that research by extraordinarily talented engineers. Pouring onto the floppy disk was a treasure more valuable than gold, more precious than diamonds, a treasure beyond the reach of most of the human race, still struggling as it was with basic survival. Only here, in America, where a significant percentage of the best brains on the planet were actively engaged in fundamental research into the secrets of creation, were these intangible jewels being created in significant quantity, gushing forth, almost too fast to steal.

Terry Franklin grinned to himself as he worked. He would do his best. He called up the document list again, then changed floppies as he listened to the silence.

These three little floppy disks would earn him thirty thousand dollars. He had bargained hard. Ten thousand dollars a disk, whether full or partially full. Cash.

He had figured out a way to make computers pay. He grinned happily at this thought and stroked the keyboard again.

Terry Franklin had become a spy for the money. He had volunteered. He had made his decision after reading everything he could lay his hands on about espionage. Only then had he devised a plan to market the classified material to which he had access as a navy enlisted computer specialist. He had thought about the plan for months, looking for holes and weighing the risks. There were risks, he knew, huge ones, but that was the reason the compensation would be so high. And, he assured himself repeatedly, he enjoyed taking risks. It would add spice to his life, make a boring marriage and a boring job tolerable. So he recruited himself.

One Saturday morning five years ago Terry Franklin walked into the Soviet embassy in Washington. He had read that the FBI kept the embassy under constant surveillance and photographed everyone who entered. So he wore a wig, false mustache and heavy, mirrorlike sunglasses. He told the receptionist he wanted to see an intelligence officer. After a forty-five minute wait, he was shown into a small, windowless room and carefully searched by the receptionist, a muscular, trim man in his early thirties. A half hour later —he was convinced he was photographed during this period by an unseen camera—a nondescript man in his fifties wearing a baggy suit had entered and occupied the only other chair. Without a word, Franklin displayed his green navy ID card, then handed the man a roll of film. The man weighed it in his hand as Franklin removed the sunglasses, wig and mustache. The Russian left the room without speaking. Another half hour passed, then another. No doubt he was again photographed.

It was almost noon when baggy-suit returned. He smiled as he entered and shook Franklin's hand. Could he examine the ID card? Where was Franklin stationed? When had he exposed the film? Why? The Russian's English was good but slightly accented.

Money, Terry Franklin had said. "I want money. I have something to sell and I brought you a free sample, hoping you might want to buy more."

Now, as Franklin worked the computer keyboard, he thought back to that day at the embassy. It had been the most momentous day of his life. Five years and two months after that day he had $540,000 in cash in a storage locker in McLean, Virginia, under an assumed name and no one was the wiser. He was going to quit spying when that figure reached a million. And when his enlistment was up, he was going to walk out on Lucy and the kids and fly to South America.

It was typical of Terry Franklin that he intended to delay his departure until he received his discharge. When he entered his new life he would go free, clean and legal, with no arrest warrants anywhere. He would go in his fake identity. Petty Officer First Class Terry Franklin, the college kid from Bakersfield who had knocked up Lucy Southworth in the back seat of her father's station wagon at a drive-in movie, married her, then joined the navy —that Terry Franklin would cease to exist.

It was a nice bundle: $540,000, plus $30,000 for these three disks. A lot of money. But not enough. He wasn't greedy, but he had to have a stake big enough so that he could live on the interest.

He had been very, very careful. He had made no mistakes. He had never spent a penny of the money. The spying was going smooth as clockwork. These Russians, they were damn good. You had to take your hat off to them. They had never called or spoken to him after that last meeting in Miami almost three years ago, right after he received orders to the Pentagon.

The operation was slick, almost foolproof, he reflected as he inserted the third disk. The calls always came on an evening when his wife was out, sometimes with her bowling league, sometimes at a friend's house. The phone rang once, and if he picked it up there was no one there, merely a dial tone. One minute later it rang again, once. Then a minute after that it rang one, two, three or four times. The number of rings that third time was the message. He was to check dead drop one, two, three or four, and he was to do it as soon as possible. He usually left the house immediately, cruised for at least an hour in his car to ensure he wasn't being followed, then headed for the dead drop. And the information would be there. Spelled out in block letters on the back of an empty, torn cigarette pack would be the file name he was to photograph, the classified computer codes necessary to gain access and a telephone number to call the evening he was ready to transfer the disks, when the whole sequence would begin again. No one saw him, he saw no one, all very slick.

He chuckled. The cigarette packs on which he received his instructions were always Marlboro Gold 100s, and it had occurred to Terry Franklin that someone had a subtle sense of humor. As he worked now and thought about the money, he savored that sardonic twist.

They must be watching the house to see when he was home alone. Of course someone was servicing the drops. But how were they getting the computer codes and file names? Oh well, he was getting his piece of the pie and he wasn't greedy.

"Ask me no questions and I'll tell you no lies," Terry Franklin muttered as he removed the final disk from its slot and tucked it into its own little envelope. He grinned at the monitor screen, then tapped keys to exit the file.

Now came the tricky part. Three years ago, when he had first been told by the Soviets that they wanted copies of documents from the computer system, he had written a trapdoor program for the software of the main computer. The job had taken him six months; it had to be right the first time—he would get no second chance. This program accomplished several things: it allowed Franklin to access any file in central memory from this terminal here in the repair shop, a permanent secret "doorway," thereby defeating the built-in safeguards that gave access to classified files only from certain specific terminals; it erased the record of his access from the 3-W file, which was a security program that automatically recorded who, what and when; and finally, it allowed him to access the 3-W file to see that his footprints were indeed not there.

This trapdoor program was his crowning achievement. He had once seen a written promise from the software designer that unrecorded access was an impossibility. What a load! It had been damn tough—he would give them that—but he had figured out a way in the end. There's *always* a way if you know enough. That contractor, he really sold the brass a sow's ear when he told that fib. Ah well, the contractor had gotten his and now Terry Franklin was making his own score.

He had loaded the trapdoor program in the main computer one day while fifteen technicians loafed and sipped coffee and watched him work on a sticky tape drive. Not a one of them saw what he was doing. Nor, he told himself with glee, would they have understood what he was doing even if they had noticed. Most of them were as ignorant as they were trusting.

Tonight the 3-W file looked clean as a virgin's conscience. Franklin exited the program and turned off his terminal. He stood and stretched. He felt good. Very, very good. The adrenal excitement was almost like a cocaine high, but better since there was no comedown. He was living on the edge and it felt terrific.

After straightening up the office, he turned off the coffeepot and put on his coat. With a last glance around, he snapped off the lights and locked the door behind him.

Getting past the guards at the building exits carrying the disks was a risk, though a small one. The civilian guards occasionally selected people for a spot search and sooner or later he would be chosen. He knew several of the guards on sight and made it a habit to speak to them, but inevitably, sooner or later . . . It didn't happen this evening, but he was clean just now anyway. The disks were still back in the office, carefully hidden. He would bring them out some evening next week at the height of the rush-hour exodus when the probability of being searched was the smallest. Minimize the risk, maximize the gain.

As he rode the escalator up to the bus stop for Virginia suburban buses, Terry Franklin buttoned his coat tightly and turned the collar up behind his neck. From a pocket he extracted his white sailor's cap and placed it carefully on his head, exactly one finger width above his eyebrows.

The cold, wet wind at the top of the mechanical stairs made him cringe. He quickly climbed aboard the Annandale bus and made his way to an empty window seat. He stared through the gathering dusk at the looming building. People in uniform and civilian clothes kept pouring from the escalator exit, trying to hide their faces from the wind, scurrying for buses. These poor snooks. What they didn't know!

Vastly content, Terry Franklin pursed his lips and began to whistle silently.

As the bus bearing Terry Franklin pulled away from the loading area, a senior naval officer, a captain, leaned into the wind as he crossed the lighted parking lot. He paid no attention to the buses queued for the freeway entrance and it was probable no one on the buses paid any attention to him. Terry Franklin was opening the sports section of a newspaper he had purchased during his lunch break. Franklin wouldn't have recognized the captain out there in the rapidly emptying parking lot anyway, not even if they had passed in a corridor. They had never met. But Franklin would have recognized the officer's computer security access password, for he had just finished using it.

Tonight the captain grimaced as the wind tore at his unprotected face and took the time to open the hatchback of his Toyota Corolla and toss his attaché case in. Then he fumbled with the key to the driver's door. Snuggled in with the engine running and waiting for the heater to warm up, Captain Harold Strong tried to relax. It had been another long week, as each and every one of them were in this gargantuan paper factory by the Potomac. He cast a bleak eye on the cars creeping toward the exit. Not too many now, well after quitting time. And he had wanted to get an early start this evening! God, he was tired.

He put the car in gear and threaded it toward the exit. He checked his watch. It was twenty-two minutes past six. At least the timing was right. He would reach the interstate just as the car pool restrictions ended.

On the freeway he headed north along the river, past the Arlington Memorial Bridge, under the ramps of the Teddy Roosevelt Bridge and out into the traffic snarl on I-66 westbound. Here at the tail end of rush hour the traffic moved along fairly well at about forty miles per hour, only occasionally coming to a complete stop. Captain Strong listened carefully to an airborne traffic reporter tally the evening's casualties. I-66 westbound wasn't mentioned.

Nearing Falls Church he stopped beside the road for a moment and removed his bridge coat. With the car back in motion and the radio tuned to a soft-rock FM station, Strong chewed over the week's frustrations and disasters again. Oh crap, he thought, it's Friday night and you have the cabin all to yourself for an entire weekend, so forget it. It'll all keep until Monday, God knows.

Since the divorce he had spent most of his weekends in the cabin. His son was a junior in college this year, busy with school and girls. The captain wasn't interested in female companionship, which was perhaps a good thing since he lacked both the finances and the time.

They want too much from that airframe, he told himself as he drove, reviewing the arguments of the week yet one more time. You can't build a plane that will drop bombs, shoot missiles, hassle with MiGs, have a radar cross section so small it can't be detected —haul the President back and forth to Camp David on weekends when it isn't being used to save the free world—and still expect the goddamn thing to take a cat shot and make an arrested carrier landing. With so many design compromises it can't possibly do any mission well.

A fucking flying Edsel, assuming that one way or the other it can be made to fly. He had used precisely those words this afternoon to that simple sonuvabitch from SECNAV and that slimy political hack looked like his wallet was being snatched. And what had he said to Vice Admiral Henry after the meeting? "It's almost as if those idiots want to buy just one ultimate do-everything flying machine and park it in the Rose Garden of the White House to scare the shit out of the Russian ambassador when he comes to call." Henry wasn't happy with his blunt assessment. Well, he was right, whether Henry liked it or not. Those political clowns want to build something straight out of a Hollywood special-effects shop, a suborbital battlestar that will automatically zap anybody who isn't wearing olive-drab underwear.

Why is it, over eighty-five years after Orville and Wilbur showed the world how to build an airplane, that we have to keep explaining the basic laws of aerodynamics to these used-car salesmen in mufti?

Strong was still stewing when he reached the outskirts of Winchester. Raindrops began to splatter on the windshield. He turned on the wipers. The road looked slick and the wet night seemed to soak up his headlights, so he slowed down.

He was hungry. He turned into the drive-through lane of a Mc-Donald's and was soon back on the road mechanically munching a burger as he headed west. The coffee was hot and black.

Passing through Gore he noticed headlights behind him. Not too close, but glued there. How long had that guy been back there? A cop clocking him? Well, he wasn't speeding, not on a night like this.

The road was a twisty two-lane and empty. Almost no traffic. That was one of the charms of coming up here. The glare of his headlights illuminated the black trunks of wet, naked trees as he cranked the wheel back and forth around the switchbacks up the mountain. The sign at the top said: "Welcome to Wild, Wonderful West Virginia." And the radio reception would go on the other side of the sign! Sure enough, on the second curve down the music faded to static. He switched off the radio. The headlights were still in the rearview mirror.

At the foot of the mountain he went through the village of Capon Bridge. Almost there, just a few more miles. He checked the mirror as they went by a sodium light on a pole by the little Texaco station, which was dark and deserted at this hour of the evening. It was some kind of pickup with a huge steel bumper welded to the front. Not too new. Mid-seventies maybe.

Impossible to make out the color. Then a camper passed him headed east and, curious, he glanced in the mirror again. The guy behind—blue, I think. Maybe blue.

Leaving the village the road began to climb and he was again in switchbacks at twenty-five miles per hour. The glare of the headlights from the pickup behind him swept across the mirror going into and coming out of every curve, and he squinted. He turned the mirror so the lights wouldn't blind him. Should've got the day-night mirror, he told himself, but he had saved twenty bucks passing on that option.

Above the noise of his engine he could hear the rhythmic slap-slap of the wipers and the protests of his tires on the wet macadam.

He was almost at the top of this low mountain. He would build a fire in the fireplace when he reached the cabin in a few minutes. Maybe a shot of Irish whiskey while the fire was driving out the chill. Tomorrow he would—

He could hear the engine of the pickup behind roaring and the headlights spotlighted his dash and windshield. He squinted. What was that damn fool doing? Did he want to pass? We're right at that overlook—

The truck behind smashed into his rear bumper and pushed him. Strong fought the wheel. His vehicle was accelerating. He applied the brakes. Wheel lock-up. He released the brakes and jammed the throttle down. He was trying to steer but the wheels wouldn't bite on the slick pavement. Goddamn—the car was going across the road, straight for the overlook pullout!

In the gravel the car skidded sideways and Strong glanced over his shoulder, straight into the pickup's headlights. Then he felt the lurch as the pickup slammed on its brakes.

Panicked, he looked forward but saw nothing, still blinded from the headlights' glare. He felt the car's nose go down, then it began to roll, over and over and over.

The motion stopped suddenly with a terrific, smashing impact.

When he came out of his daze he was in darkness and the engine was silent. There was a little light, but it seemed to come from above and behind, from the road. Jesus . . . Something black and wet beside him. A tree trunk, where the passenger seat used to be.

The car was half wrapped around a tree. He had gone down over the edge and rolled several times and smashed into a tree. That asshole in the pickup . . . trying to *kill* him.

He wasn't hurt too bad. Thank God for seat belts. Blood on his face, minute pieces of glass everywhere. He was still groggy. What's that smell? *Gasoline!* A leak. He fumbled for the seat-belt release.

Someone was beside him, reaching in through the smashed window. "Hey—"

He was being splashed with something wet. "What—" Gas! It was *gas!* "Please, you gotta—"

Out of the corner of his eye he saw the lighted match come floating through the broken window. The roar of the gasoline igniting was the last sound he heard.

2

The airplanes were shiny and brilliant in their bright colors of red, yellow and blue. They hung in the window suspended on wires, frozen in flight, the spring sunlight firing the wings and fuselages and emphasizing the sleek perfection of their forms.

Jake Grafton stood on the sidewalk and stared. He examined each one carefully, letting his eyes roam from tail to prop to gull-like wingtip. After a moment he pushed the door open and went into the warm shop, out of the weak sunshine and the cool breeze coming off the ocean.

As he stood and gazed at another dozen or so planes hanging from the ceiling, the shop proprietor behind the glass counter laid aside his newspaper and cleared his throat. "Good morning."

"Hi." Jake glanced at the man. He was balding and bearlike and perched on a stool. "You've got some nice airplanes here."

"Sure do. You have a son interested in radio control?"

Jake let his eyes find the swooping, soaring forms above his head. "No," he said thoughtfully. "Just looking."

The proprietor began turning the pages of his newspaper as Jake moved deeper into the shop. He wandered slowly, examining the counter displays, fingering balsa from a wire bin, scanning the rack of X-acto knives and miniature drills, looking at the rows and rows of boxes with airplanes and cars on the covers that stood on shelves behind the counter. Finally, back at the door, he muttered his thanks to the shopkeeper and went out onto the sidewalk.

The sea breeze was brisk this morning and tangy with salt. Not many people on the street. This Delaware beach town lived on tourists and summer was a long way off. At least the sun was out after a week of low, scuddy clouds and intermittent drizzle. Standing there, Jake could faintly hear the gulls crying as they soared above the beach and boardwalk a half block away. He looked again at the airplanes in the window, then went back into the shop.

"Sell me an airplane," he said as the proprietor looked up from his newspaper.

"Delighted to. Which one you want?"

Jake scanned the planes hanging from the ceiling. He began to examine them critically.

"You ever build an RC plane before?"

"Build? You mean I can't buy one already made?"

"Not any of these, you can't. My son built all these years ago, before he went to the air force. They're his."

"Build one," Jake said softly, weighing it. He hadn't figured on that. Oh well, the decision was already made. Now he wanted a plane. "Let me see what you have."

Forty minutes later, with a yellow credit card invoice for $349.52 tucked into his wallet, Jake Grafton left the hobby store carrying two large sacks and walked the block to his car. He walked purposefully, quickly. For the first time in months he had a task ahead that would be worth doing.

Fifteen minutes later he parked the car in the sand-and-crushed-seashell parking area in front of his house. He could hear the faint ringing of the telephone as he climbed the steps to the little wooden porch. He unlocked the front door, sat one of the paper sacks on the floor and strode across the living room for the phone on the wall by the kitchen table. The ringing stopped just as he reached for the receiver. He went back to the car for the other sack.

The airplane on the lid of the box looked gorgeous, mouth-wateringly gorgeous, but inside the box was sheet after sheet of raw balsa wood. At least the aircraft parts were impressed, stamped, into the wood. All you would have to do was pick them out and maybe trim the pieces. The instruction booklet looked devilishly complicated, with photos and line drawings. Jake studied the pictures. After a bit he began laying out the balsa pieces from the box on the kitchen table, referring frequently to the pictures in the booklet. When the box was empty he surveyed the mess and rubbed his temples. This was going to be a big job, even bigger than he thought.

He put coffee and water in the brewer and was waiting for the Pyrex pot to fill when the phone rang again. "Hello."

"Jake. How are you feeling this morning?" Callie, his wife, called twice a day to check on him, even though she knew it irritated him.

"Fine. How's your morning going?"

"Did you go out?"

"Downtown."

"Jake," she said, tension creeping into her voice as she pronounced his name firmly. "We need to talk. When are you going to call that admiral?"

"I dunno."

"You can't keep loafing like this. You're well. You're going to have to go back to work, or retire and find something to do. You can't just keep loafing like this. It isn't you. It isn't good for you, Jake."

She emphasized the word "good," Jake noticed listlessly. That's Callie, instinctively dividing the world into good and evil. "We'll talk about it this weekend." She was driving over from Washington when she got off work this evening. Jake had driven over to the beach house two days ago.

"That's what you said last weekend, and Monday and Tuesday evenings. And then you avoid the subject." Her voice was firm. "The only way I can get your undivided attention is to call you on the phone. So that's what I'm doing. When, Jake?"

"This weekend. We'll discuss it this weekend. I promise."

They muttered their goodbyes. Jake poured a cup of coffee and sipped it as he sorted through the piles of balsa again. What had he gotten himself into?

Coffee cup in hand, he went through the front door and walked past the car to the street. He turned toward the beach, which was about a hundred yards away. The house beside his was empty, a summer place that belonged to some doctor in Baltimore. The next house belonged to a local, a pharmacist whose wife worked nights down at the drugstore. He had seen their son on the beach flying a radio-controlled airplane, and didn't Callie say this week was spring break for the kids? He went to the door and knocked.

"Captain Grafton. What a pleasant surprise."

"Hi, Mrs. Brown. Is David around?"

"Sure." She turned away. "David," she called, "you have a visitor." She turned back toward him, "Won't you come in?"

The boy appeared behind her. "Hey, David," Jake said. He explained his errand. "I need some of your expert advice, if you can come over for a little while."

Mrs. Brown nodded her approval and told her son to be back for lunch.

As they walked down the street, Jake explained about the plane. The boy smiled broadly when he saw the pile on Jake's kitchen table. "The Gentle Lady," David read from the cover of the instruction booklet. "That's an excellent airplane for a beginner. Easy to build and fly. You chose a good one, Captain."

"Yeah, but I can't tell which parts are which. They aren't labeled, as far as I can tell."

"Hmmm." David sat at the table and examined the pile. He was about twelve, still elbows and angles, with medium-length brown hair full of cowlicks. His fingers moved swiftly and surely among the parts, identifying each one. "Did you get an engine for this plane?"

"Nope."

"A glider is more difficult to fly, of course, more challenging, but you'll get more satisfaction from mastering it."

"Right," Jake said, eyeing the youngster at the table.

"Let's see. You have a knife, and the man at the store—Mr. Swoze, right?—recommended you buy these pins to hold the parts in place while you glue them. This is a good glue, cyanoacrylate. You're all set, except for a board to spread the diagram on and pin the parts to, and a drill."

"What kind of board?"

"Oh, I'll loan you one. I've built three airplanes on mine. You spread the diagram on it and position the parts over the diagram, then pin them right to the board. And I'll loan you my drill if you don't have one." Jake nodded. The youngster continued, his fingers still moving restlessly through the parts, "The most important aspect of assembling this aircraft is getting the same dihedral and washout on the right and left wing components, both inner and outer panels. Be very careful and work slowly."

"Okay."

"I'll run home and get my board and drill. You won't need the drill for several days, but I might as well bring it over." He bolted out the door, leaving Jake to refill his coffee cup and stare at the actual-size diagram.

The house was quiet, with only the background murmur of the surf on the beach and the occasional burble of a passing car to break the solitude. The task assumed a life of its own; breaking the pieces out of the balsa boards, assembling them on the diagram, occasionally sanding or trimming with the razor-sharp hobby knife before pinning them into place. As he worked he occasionally glanced at the picture on the box, visualizing how the airplane would look soaring back and forth above the sand, trying to imagine how it would feel to fly it. This would be real flying, he knew. Even though his feet would not leave the ground, the plane would be flying free, and since he would be flying it, so would he. He carefully glued the rudder and vertical stabilizer parts together and began assembling the horizontal stabilizer.

The knock on the door startled him. He had been so intent on his task he had paid no attention to the sound of the car driving up. "Yeah. Come on in."

He heard the door open. "Captain Grafton."

"Yep." Jake looked up.

The man standing there was in his late twenties, slightly above medium height, with short brown hair. "Toad Tarkington! Come on in! What a surprise!"

The man's face split in a wide grin and he crossed the room and pumped Jake's hand. "It's great to see you again, CAG. I thought for a while there you were dead."

Grafton nodded and studied Lieutenant Toad Tarkington, today clad in jeans and rugby shirt and windbreaker. He looked . . . just the same as he did the morning they went after Colonel Qazi in an F-14 five months ago. Last September. And here he was with that grin . . . quick, energetic, nervous. He was ready to laugh or fly, ready for a prank in the ready room or a night cat shot, fully alive. That's what Toad Tarkington projected—vibrant, energetic, enthusiastic life.

"I'm not a CAG now, Toad. I'm just a plain ol' sick-leave captain." CAG was the title bestowed on an air wing commander, and was pronounced to rhyme with "rag."

Toad grabbed his hand and held it, that grin splitting his face. "Have we got a lot to talk about! I tried to call you, sir, but your phone wasn't listed."

"Yeah. Had to have the number changed. The reporters were driving me nuts."

Toad pulled one of the kitchen chairs around and sat down. "I was pretty damn happy last fall when I heard you were alive. What happened to you anyway, after we rammed that transport?"

"Some Greek fishermen pulled me out of the water. I don't remember a thing. Had a concussion. Lucky for me the life vests inflate automatically nowadays. Anyway, they pulled me out and I made it."

"How come they didn't radio someone or head for port?"

"Their radio was broken and they were there to fish." Jake looked away from Toad. He was back among the ordinary, everyday things. For a moment there . . . but he was *here*, at the beach house. "They thought I was gonna die on them any minute and they needed the fish. I was in a coma." His shoulders moved up and down. "Too damned many Gs. Messed up my eyes. That's why I wear these glasses now."

Jake removed the glasses and examined the lenses, as if seeing them for the first time. "It's 20/100 now. It was 20/500. The Gs almost ripped my eyeballs out." He placed the glasses back on the bridge of his nose and stared at the pieces of balsa on the kitchen table. "I don't remember much about it. The docs say some blood vessels popped in the front part of my brain and I had some memory loss."

"By God, sir, I sure as hell can fill you in." Toad leaned forward and seized his arm. Jake refocused on that excited, expressive face. "The Gs were something else and I couldn't get to the ejection handles, and I guess you couldn't either. Man, our bacon was well and truly fried when she broke up and spit us out. The left wing was gone and I figure most of the left vertical stab, because we were getting pushed around screwy. I—" He continued his tale, his hands automatically moving to show the plane's position in space. Jake stopped listening to the voice and watched the hands, those practiced, expressive hands.

Tarkington—he was the past turned into a living, breathing person. He was every youngster Jake had shared a ready room with for the past twenty years, all those guys now middle-aged . . . or dead.

Toad was still talking when Jake turned back to the pile of balsa on the table. When he eventually paused for air, Jake said mildly,

"So what are you up to these days?" as he used the X-acto knife to trim a protruding sliver from a balsa rib piece.

"My squadron tour was up," Toad said slowly. "And when you get a Silver Star you can pretty well call your next set of orders. So I talked it over with the detailer." He looked around the room, then swiveled back to Jake. "And I told him I wanted to go where you were going."

Jake laid the knife down and scooted his chair back. "I'm still on convalescent leave."

"Yessir. I heard. And I hear you're going to the Pentagon as a division director or something. So I'm reporting there this coming Monday. I'll be working for you."

Jake smiled again. "I seem to recall you had had enough of this warrior shit."

"Yeah. Well, what the hell! I decided to stay around for another set of orders. I can always pull the plug. And I've got nothing better to do right now anyway."

Jake snorted and rubbed his fingertips together. The glue had coated his fingertips and wouldn't come off. "I don't either. So we'll go shuffle paper for a while, eh?"

"Yessir," Toad said, and stood. "Maybe we won't get underway, but we'll still be in the navy. That's something, isn't it?" He stuck out his hand again, like a cowboy drawing a pistol. "I'll be seeing you in the office, when you get there," he said as Jake pumped the outstretched hand. "Say hello to Mrs. Grafton for me."

Jake accompanied Toad to the door, then out onto the porch. There was a young woman in the car, and she looked at him curiously. He nodded at her, then put a hand on Toad's shoulder and squared around to face him. "Take care of yourself, y'hear?"

"Sure, CAG. Sure."

"Thanks for coming by."

As Toad drove away Jake waved, then went back into the house. The place was depressing. It was as if Tarkington brought all the life and energy with him, then took it away when he left. But he was of Jake's past. Everything was past. The flying, the ready rooms, the sun on the sea as you manned up to fly, all of it was over, gone, finished.

It was after four o'clock. He had forgotten to eat lunch. Oh well, Callie wasn't going to get here until nine o'clock or so. The Chesapeake Bay Bridge shouldn't be crowded on Friday evenings this time of year. He could get some more of this plane assembled, then fix a sandwich or something. Maybe run over to Burger King.

He scratched at the glue caked on his fingertips. The stuff came off in flakes if you peeled it right. This plane—it was going to be a nice one. It was going to be good to fly it. When flying was all you knew and all you had been, you needed a plane around.

Oh, shit! As he looked at the pieces he felt like a fool. A fucking toy plane! He threw himself on the couch and lay there staring at the ceiling.

Toad Tarkington was silent as he drove from stoplight to stoplight on the main highway through Rehoboth Beach. The woman beside him finally asked, "So how is he?"

"He's changed," Toad said. "The official report said he was in a coma for two weeks. It was a week before that Greek fishing boat even made port. It's a miracle he didn't die on the boat. He said the fishermen expected him to and kept fishing."

"I would have liked to meet him."

"Well, I was going to mention you were in the car, but he was busy working on a model airplane and he was . . . Anyway, you can always meet him later."

The woman reached for the knob to turn the stereo on, then thought better of it. "This new assignment—asking for it just because you like him . . ."

"It's not that I like him," Toad said. "I respect him. He's . . . different. There aren't many men like him left in this day and age. If Congress hadn't jumped into that incident with both feet and voted him the Medal of Honor, he would probably have been forced to retire. Maybe even a court-martial." Toad smacked the steering wheel with his hand. "He's a national hero and he doesn't give a damn. I've never met anyone like him before." He thought about it. "Maybe there aren't any more like him."

The woman reached for the knob again and turned the stereo on. She had known Toad Tarkington for three weeks and she was still trying to figure him out. He was the first military man she had dated and he was modestly famous after the attack last fall on *United States*. Her friends thought it was so exciting. Still, he was a little weird. Oh well, he made a decent salary and bathed and shaved and looked marvelous at parties. And he was a fine lover. A girl could do a lot worse.

"Where do you want to eat tonight?" she asked.

* * *

It was dark and spattering rain when Jake heard Callie's car pull in. He had completed assembly of the vertical and horizontal stabilizers, the rudder, and the wings, and had placed them on top of the bookcase and credenza to cure and was cleaning up the mess on the kitchen table. He raked the rest of it into the box the airplane had come in and slid the box up on top of the kitchen cabinets, then went outside to meet her. She was opening the trunk of her car.

"Hey, good-looking. Welcome home." He pecked her cheek and lifted her overnight bag out of the trunk.

"Hello." She followed him into the house, hugging herself against the evening chill. He closed the door behind her and climbed the stairs toward the bedrooms. "What's this?" Callie called.

"I'm building an airplane," he boomed as he dropped the bag on the bed. When he reached the foot of the stairs she was examining the wing structure without touching it. "It's dry enough to pick up. How about coffee?"

"Sure." Callie walked slowly around the living/dining area, her purse still over her shoulder, looking. She opened the door to the screened-in porch and was shivering in the wind, looking at the wicker furniture, when he handed her the coffee cup. "This stuff needs to be painted again." She slid the door closed and leaned back against it as she sipped the hot liquid.

"What kind of week did you have?"

"So-so." She was halfway through her first semester as a language instructor at Georgetown University. "They asked me to teach this summer."

"What did you say?"

"That I'd think about it." She had been planning on spending the summer here at the beach. Kicking her pumps off, she sat on the sofa with her legs under her. "It all depends."

Jake poured himself coffee and sat down at the kitchen table where he could face her.

"I went to see Dr. Arnold this afternoon."

"Uh-huh." Jake had refused to go back to the psychologist.

"He says if you don't get your act together I should leave you."

"Just what does the soul slicer think my act is?"

"Oh, cut the crap, Jake." She averted her face. She finished her coffee in silence, then rinsed the cup in the sink. Retrieving her shoes, she went upstairs.

The sound of water running in the shower was audible all over the downstairs. Jake spread the airplane diagram on the table and opened the instruction manual. Finally he threw the manual down in disgust.

He needed a drink. The doctors had told him not to, but fuck them. He rummaged under the sink and found that old bottle of bourbon with several inches of liquid remaining. He poured some in a glass and added ice.

The problem was that he didn't want to do anything. He didn't want to retire and sit here and vegetate or find a civilian job. He didn't want to go to the Pentagon and immerse himself in the bureaucracy. The Pentagon job had been the only one offered him when he was finally ready to be discharged from Bethesda Naval Hospital. The politicians had made him a hero and checkmated the naval establishment, but the powers that be had still been smarting from the way the official investigation had been derailed. Luckily he had been damn near comatose in the hospital and everyone in uniform knew he had nothing to do with the political maneuvering. So he was still in the navy. But his shot at flag rank had vaporized like a drop of water on a hot stove. Not that he really ever hoped to make admiral or even cared.

He lay down on the couch and sipped at the drink. Maybe the whole problem was that he just didn't care about any of it anymore. Let the other guys do the sweating. Let them dance on the tightrope. Let someone else pick up the bodies of those who fell. He put the glass on the floor and rolled over on his side. Maybe he was depressed—that soul doctor . . . Yes, depression, that was probably . . .

When he awoke it was two in the morning and the lights were off. Callie had covered him with a blanket. He went upstairs, undressed, and crawled into bed with her.

The wind whipped the occasional raindrops at a steep angle and drove the gray clouds at a furious pace as Jake and Callie strolled the beach. They were out for their usual morning walk, which they took rain or shine, fair weather or foul. Both wore shorts and were barefoot; they carried the flip-flops they had worn to traverse the crushed-seashell mix that covered the street in front of their house that led to the beach. Both were wearing old sweatshirts over sweaters. Callie's hair whipped in the wind.

Jake critically examined the contours of sand around the piles that supported a huge house some ignorant optimist had constructed on the dune facing the beach. The first hurricane, Jake suspected, would have the owner tearing his hair. The sand looked firm now. Shades obscured all the windows. The house was empty. Only three or four other people were visible on the beach.

Birds scurried along the sand, racing after retreating waves and probing furiously for their breakfast. Gulls rode the air currents with their noses pointed out to sea. He watched the gulls and tried to decide if the Gentle Lady could soar with them. The moving air had to have some kind of an upward vector over the sand. Perhaps if he kept the plane above the dune. The dune was low, though. He would see.

Callie's hand found his and he gave it a squeeze. He led her down into the surf, where the ice-cold water swirled about their feet. "Toad Tarkington said to say hi."

"He called?"

"Stopped by yesterday afternoon. He's going to the Pentagon too."

"Oh."

"If you teach summer school, we'll see more of each other this summer," he said. "We'll be together every evening at the apartment in Washington as well as every weekend here."

Her hand gripped his fiercely and she turned to face him.

He grinned. "Monday morning, off I go, wearing my uniform, vacation over—"

She hugged him and her lips made it impossible to continue to speak. Her hair played across his cheeks as the ebbing surf tugged at the sand under him.

3

It was almost 9 A.M. when the subway train—the Metro—ground to a halt at the Pentagon station. Jake Grafton joined the civilian and military personnel exiting and followed the thin crowd along the platform. Rush hour for the 23,000 people who worked in this sprawling five-story building was long over. The little handful that Jake accompanied seemed to be made up of stragglers and visiting civilians.

Just ahead of Jake a man and a woman in casual clothes led two small children. When they came to the long escalator, the kids squealed joyfully and started to run up the moving stair. Each parent grabbed a small arm, then a hand.

The sloping staircase was poorly lighted. As he looked at the dim lights, Jake noticed the plaster on the ceiling was peeling away in spots.

At the head of the escalator two corridors led in, one from either side, and more people joined the procession, which trudged ever upward on a long, wide staircase toward the lights above.

At the head of the stair was a large hall, and the stream of people broke up, some heading for the main entrance, some moving cautiously toward the visitors' tour area. The couple that Jake had followed led their progeny in that direction with an admonition to behave. Jake approached the two Department of Defense policemen scrutinizing passes at the security booth. "I have an appointment with Vice Admiral Henry."

"Do you have a building pass, sir?"

"No."

"Use those phones right over there"—he pointed at telephones by the tour windows—"and someone will come down to escort you."

"Thanks." Jake called and a yeoman answered. Five minutes, the yeoman said.

Jake stood and watched the people. Men and women wearing the uniforms of all four services came and went, most walking quickly, carrying briefcases, folders, gym bags and small brown paper bags that must have contained their lunches. People leaving the interior of the building walked by the security desk without a glance from the two armed DOD policemen.

"Captain Grafton?"

A small black woman in civilian clothes stood at his elbow. "Yes?" he said.

"I'm your escort." She smiled and flashed her pass at the guards and motioned Jake toward the metal detector that stood to the left of the security booth. He walked through it, nothing beeped, and the woman led him through the open doors into another huge hallway, this one lined with shops. Directly across from the entrance was a large gedunk—a store selling snacks, magazines and other sundries.

"I was expecting a yeoman."

"The phone started ringing and he sent me down."

As she led him along the corridor, he asked, "How long did it take you to learn your way around in here?"

"Oh, I'm still learning. I've only been here five years. It's confusing at times."

They went up a long ramp that opened onto the A-Ring, the central corridor that overlooked the five-acre interior courtyard. As they proceeded around the ring, Jake glanced through the windows at the grass and huge trees and the snack bar in the center.

"Have you ever been here before?" she asked.

"Nope," said Jake Grafton. "I've always managed to avoid it."

After she had gone what seemed like a hundred yards or so, she turned right and ascended a staircase with a ninety-degree bend in it and at the top turned right. They were still on the A-Ring, but on the fourth level. After another fifty feet she veered left down a corridor, then right onto another corridor that zagged away at an angle. "Now we're walking back toward the outside of the building," she said. "There are five concentric rings in the Pentagon. The inner is the A-Ring, and next is B, and so forth, with the outer being E. They are connected by ten radial corridors like the spokes of a wagon wheel. It's supposed to be efficient but it does confuse newcomers." She grinned.

This corridor had little to commend it. It was lit by fluorescent lights, and over half the tubes were dark. The walls were bare. Not a picture or a poster. Dusty, tied-down furniture was stacked along one wall. It looked as if it had been there since the Eisenhower administration. Catching Jake's glance, the guide said, "It's been there for three months. Some of the offices got new furniture. This is the old stuff." The piles were composed of sofas and chairs and scarred and battered gunmetal-gray desks. "These places on the ceiling where the plywood is?" Jake looked. "The plaster was falling off from water seepage from the roof and asbestos was being released."

At the end of the corridor stood a magnificent large painting of Admiral Dewey's flagship, *Olympia,* entering Manila Bay. Spots illuminated it. The guide turned right and Jake followed. The overhead blue mantel proclaimed: "Naval Aviation." Here the hallway was well lit, painted a yellowish pastel and decorated with pictures of past and present naval and marine aircraft. This straight stretch was long, a third as long as the outside of the building. Almost at the end, his guide turned left into a large office. The sign over the door said: "Assistant, Chief of Naval Operations, Air Warfare." Beside the door was a blue sign that read: "OP-05." This was the office of the senior U.S. Naval Aviator, Mr. Naval Aviation.

The room was large and contained numerous windows facing south across the huge parking lot toward Arlington. Wooden desks, blue drapes, wainscoting on the walls.

A commander greeted Jake. "I'm a little early," Jake said, glancing at his watch.

"I'll see if the admiral's free." He was. Jake was escorted in through a swinging double saloon door.

Vice Admiral Tyler Henry rose from his chair and came around his desk wearing a warm smile to greet Jake.

"Good to see you again, Captain." The men had met on several occasions in the past, but Jake was unsure if Henry would remember. After he pumped Jake's hand the admiral motioned to a chair. "Please, be seated. Have any trouble getting here this morning?"

"I rode the Metro this morning, sir," Jake said as the admiral seated himself behind his desk. It was dark wood, perhaps mahogany. A matching table extended outward from the main desk, forming the leg of a T. It was at this table Jake sat.

"Good idea. Parking places are all for car pools and flag officers." He pushed the button on his intercom box. "Chief, did Commander Gadd sweep the office this morning?"

"Yessir," was the tinny reply.

"Are the window buzzers on?"

"Yessir."

"Please close my door. . . . Window buzzers are little security gizmos to vibrate the glass. Supposed to foil parabolic mikes, but who knows?" the admiral explained. "The damn things play waiting room music, and I can't hear noises like that anymore." Jake listened hard. He could just hear the beat and a trumpet.

The admiral leaned back comfortably in his chair as the door to the office closed behind Jake. "Soundproof," he muttered, then smiled. "You look surprised."

Jake smiled, his embarrassment showing. "Seems like a lot of trouble to go to just to talk to the guy who's going to be designing the new officer fitness report form."

The admiral smiled broadly. "That job has been floating around with no takers. No, we have another project for you that is going to demand expertise of a different sort."

Jake was having trouble holding his eyebrows still. "I thought," he said softly, "that I was a pariah around here."

The smile disappeared from Admiral Henry's face. "I'm not going to bullshit you, Captain. Last fall when you disobeyed a direct order from a vice admiral, you may have torpedoed any chance you had of ever getting promoted again. Now with hindsight and all, most people can see you did the right thing. But the military won't work if people go around telling flag officers to get fucked. For any reason, justified or not. And the congressmen and politicos from SECDEF's office who interfered with a navy investigation of that incident made you no friends."

He raised his hand when Jake opened his mouth to speak. "I know, I know, you had nothing whatever to do with that and you couldn't control the politicians even if you tried. No one can. They go any damn place they want with hobnail boots. Still, they raised hackles when they implied the navy couldn't or wouldn't be fair in its treatment of a naval officer."

"I understand."

The admiral nodded. "I suspect you do. Your record says you're one of our best, which is why I asked for you. We need a shit-hot attack pilot with a ton of smarts and a gilt-edge reputation who can waltz a little project through the minefields. You're him."

Jake flexed his hands and rearranged his bottom in his chair. "I didn't think my reputation was quite that shiny. And I've never had any Pentagon duty before."

Henry pretended not to have heard. "Do you want to hear about the job?"

"I'm just a little surprised, sir. Shocked might be a better word. I'd thought . . ." He punched the air. "What's the job?"

"You'll be working for Vice Admiral Roger Dunedin. He's NAVAIR." NAVAIR was Naval Air Systems Command, the procurement arm of naval aviation. "He needs a new program manager for the Advanced Tactical Aircraft, also known as the ATA. If and when we get it, it'll be the A-12."

Jake Grafton couldn't suppress a grin.

The admiral laughed. "The fact we have this project is unclassified. ATA, A-12, those are the only two things unclass in the whole program, and those two terms were just recently declassified. The project is black." Jake had heard about "black" programs, so highly classified that even the existence of the program was sometimes a secret.

The admiral rapped a knuckle on the desk. "So far, it *appears* to be one of our best-kept military secrets." His voice fell to a murmur. "No way of being sure, of course."

Henry fixed his eyes on Jake. "The A-12 is our follow-on airplane for the A-6." The A-6 Intruder was the aircraft carriers' main offensive weapon, an all-weather medium attack plane.

"But I thought the A-6 was going to remain in the inventory into the next century. That was the justification for the A-6G project—new graphite-composite wings and updated avionics."

"The A-6 had to have the new wings just to stay in the air, and the A-6G avionics are going into the A-12. We were trying the new gee-whiz gizmos out in the A-6G, until they canceled it." The A-6G had died under the budget cutters' knives. Henry smiled wickedly. "The A-12 will have something even better. Athena. Do you know Greek mythology?"

"A smattering. Wasn't Athena the goddess of war, the protector of warriors?"

"Yep, and she had a quality that we are going to give to our new plane." He paused and raised one finger aloft. When he grinned like that his eyebrows matched the curve of his lips. "She could make herself invisible."

Jake just stared.

"Stealth technology. The air force built a land-based fighter: that's first-generation stealth technology. Then came new paint and radar-absorbent materials and the flying-wing shape—that's second-generation." His voice dropped conspiratorially. "We're building an all-weather, go-anywhere anytime carrier-based attack plane that will equal or exceed the A-6 in range, speed and payload, and carry advanced sensors that will make the A-6 look blind as a cornfield scarecrow. These sensors—anyway, they're a whole new generation beyond the A-6. *And* the A-12 will have third-generation stealth technology—Athena—which will make it truly invisible to radar. A stealth Super-Intruder, if you will. That's the A-12." Henry's eyebrows danced.

"And that, my friend, is the secret."

The admiral smacked his hand on the desk. The gold rings encircling his sleeve attracted Jake's eye. "The Russians don't know about it. Yet. If we can get this thing to sea before they steal the technology and figure out how to counter it, we've pretty well guaranteed that there won't be a conventional war with the Soviets for at least the next ten years. Their ships would be defenseless against a stealth Intruder."

Admiral Henry sighed. "We're trying to build one of these things, anyway. You're replacing Captain Harold Strong, who was killed in a car wreck a month ago. We had to wait to get you, but now, by God, your ass is ours."

Jake Grafton sat stunned. "But how—all the weapons will have to be carried externally and they'll reflect energy—how will you get around that?"

The corners of Henry's lips turned up until his mouth formed a V and his eyebrows danced. "You're going to enjoy this job, Captain."

"A real job," Jake said, his relief obvious. "And I thought I was just going to be designing fitness report forms."

"Oh," Henry boomed. "If you want you can work on that in your spare time. Don't know when you'd sleep, though." He turned serious. "Things are really starting to move. We've got two prototypes about ready to fly—constructed by two different manufacturers—and we must get them evaluated and award the production contract. We've got to quit noodling and get this show on the road. We need airplanes. That's why you're here."

After a glance at his watch, Henry reached for his intercom. His hand hovered near it. "Start checking in," he said hurriedly. "Go get your paperwork done. They've got some orders for you someplace; you'll have to find them. Maybe at NAVAIR, which is over at Crystal City. Then you might go around the corner and introduce yourself to the project coordinator, Commander Rob Knight. He's here today, I think. I'll see you at nine tomorrow morning. And then I want to hear all about the attack on *United States* and how you started El Hakim on the road to Paradise."

He keyed the intercom and started talking as he shooed Jake out with his left hand. Jake didn't even get a chance to say thanks.

Crystal City, Jake was informed by Henry's aide, was across the Pentagon's south parking lot, on the other side of the highway, southeast of the Pentagon. NAVAIR was in buildings JP-1 and JP-2, in the northern portion of the Crystal City office complex. He wandered out into the corridors and walked along slightly dazed. A real job! A *big* job!

Although the aide had suggested the shuttle bus, Jake decided to walk. After asking an air force officer in the parking lot which set of tall buildings was which and getting a careful sighting across a pointing finger, Jake began walking. The wind was chilly, but not intolerably so. Under I-395, across a four-lane boulevard dodging traffic, under U.S. Route 1, the hike took about ten minutes. He accosted a pedestrian and building Jefferson Plaza 1 was pointed out. In he went, punched the elevator button and after waiting what seemed to be an inordinately long time, rode to the twelfth floor, the top one.

They did have a set of orders. It took the civilian secretary five minutes to find them, and in the interim Jake visited with three officers he knew from his shipboard days. With the orders in his hand, the secretary called a yeoman, who put the captain to work filling out forms.

Jake was eating lunch in Gus's Place, a commercial cafeteria on the ground floor of the complex, when Toad Tarkington spotted him. Toad came over, tray in hand. "Saw you sitting over here by yourself, CAG. May I join you?"

Jake moved his tray and Toad off-loaded his food onto the table.

A group of junior officers twenty feet away began to whisper and glance in their direction.

"How has your morning gone?"

"Same old stuff," Toad announced as he placed his large brown manila envelope full of orders and forms on his chair and carefully sat on it. "Got my picture taken for my permanent building pass, which I'm supposed to pick up this afternoon. I must have signed my name fifty times this morning. Every naval activity between here and Diego Garcia will soon receive notification in triplicate that I can be found sitting on the bull's-eye at this critical nerve center of the nation's defenses, ready to save the free world from the forces of evil." Toad made a gesture of modesty and slowly unfolded his napkin.

"I hear we're going to be putting that new officer fitness report form together, though just why the heck they got the two greatest aerial warriors of the age over here at NAVAIR to do that sort of beats me. Ours not to reason why . . ." He glanced at Jake to get his reaction as he smoothed the napkin on his lap.

Grafton sipped his coffee, then took another bite of tuna salad.

"But what the hey," Toad continued cheerfully. "Flying, walking, or sitting on my ass, they pay me just the same. Do you know there are 3.4 women in Washington for every man? This is *the* place. Bachelor city. Sodom on the Potomac. A studly young lad ought to be able to do pretty well with all these lonely females seeking to satisfy their social and sexual needs. Mr. Accommodation, that's me. I figure with my salary—"

"The sexual revolution is over," Jake muttered as he forked more tuna salad. "You missed it."

"I'm carrying on a guerrilla campaign, sir. Indomitable and unconquerable, that's the ol' Horny Toad, even in the age of latex. I just dress up like the Michelin man and go for it. A fellow could always spring a leak, I guess, but the bee must go from flower to flower. That's the natural order of things." He chewed thoughtfully. "Have you noticed how those people over there keep sneaking looks at us?"

"Yeah." Jake didn't look around. Although the room was filled with civilians and uniformed men and women eating and carrying trays and visiting over coffee, the four junior officers two tables away had been glancing over and speaking softly since Jake sat down.

"It's been like that all day with me," Toad said with a hint of despair in his voice, then sent another mouthful of food down behind his belt buckle. "At first I thought I had forgotten my pants, but now I think it's the hero bit. Asked two admirers for dates this morning and got two yeses. Not bad for a Monday."

"It'll pass. Next week you'll have to spell your name twice just to get into the men's head. How's your leg?"

"Got a couple girders in it, sir. One of them is a metal rod about a foot long. But I passed my flight physical. Those Israeli doctors did a good job. Aches some occasionally."

"We were damned lucky."

"That's an understatement," Toad said, and proceeded to fill Jake in on how he had spent the last five months.

After lunch Jake hiked back across the streets and parking lots to the Pentagon. His temporary pass so excited the security cop that he nodded his head a quarter inch as Jake walked by.

Commander Rob Knight was several years younger than Jake and had more hair, although it was salt-and-pepper. He wore steel-rimmed glasses and beamed when Jake introduced himself.

"Heard about your little adventure in the Med last year, Captain. It's been pretty dull without El Hakim to kick around." Knight grinned easily. He had an air of quiet confidence that Jake found reassuring. Like all career officers getting acquainted, Knight and Jake told each other in broad terms of their past tours. Knight had spent most of his operational career in A-6 outfits, and had been ordered to this billet after a tour as commanding officer of an A-6 squadron.

"I came by to find out everything you know about the A-12," Jake said lightly.

Knight chuckled. "A real kidder, you are. I've been soaking up info for a year and a half and I haven't even scratched the surface. And you see I'm only one guy. The A-6 coordinator sits here beside me, and on the other side of the room we have the F-14 and F/A-18 guys. One for each airplane. We don't have a secretary or a yeoman. We do our own mail. We make our own coffee. I spend about a third of my time in this office, which is where I do the unclass stuff and confidential. Another third of my time is spent upstairs in the vault working on classified stuff. I have a desk up there with another computer and safes. The rest of my time is spent over at NAVAIR, in your shop, trying to see what you guys are up to."

"Just one guy." Jake was disappointed, and it showed. He felt a little like the kid who met Santa for the first time and found he was old and fat and smelled of reindeer shit. "One guy! Just exactly what is your job?"

"I'm the man with the money. I get it from Rear Admiral Costello. He's the Aviation Plans and Programs honcho. He tells me what we want the plane to do. We draw up the requirements. You build the plane we say we want, you sell it to me, and I write the checks. That's it in a nutshell."

"Sounds simple enough."

"Simple as brain surgery. There's an auditor that comes around from time to time, and he's going to cuff me and take me away one of these days. I can see it in his eyes."

They talked for an hour, or rather Knight talked and Jake listened, with his hands on his thighs. Knight had a habit of tapping aimlessly on the computer terminal on his desk, striking keys at random. When Jake wasn't looking at Knight he was looking at the *Sports Illustrated* swimsuit girl over Knight's desk (April 1988 was a *very* good month), or the three airplane pictures, or the Farrah Fawcett pinup over the A-6 guru's desk. Between the two desks sat a filing cabinet with combination locks on every drawer. Similar cabinets filled the room. Twice Knight rooted through an open cabinet drawer and handed Jake classified memos to read, but not to keep. Each was replaced in its proper file as soon as Jake handed it back.

Then Knight took Jake up a floor to the vault, where he signed a special form acknowledging the security regulations associated with black programs. In this chamber, surrounded by safes and locks and steel doors, Commander Knight briefed him on the technical details of the prototypes, the program schedules and so on.

At three o'clock Jake was back on the twelfth floor of the Crystal City complex to meet with Vice Admiral Dunedin. His office was not quite as plush as Henry's but it was every bit as large. Out the large windows airliners were landing and taking off from National airport.

"Do you have any idea what you're getting into?" Dunedin asked. He was soft-spoken, with short gray hair and workman's hands, thick, strong fingers that even now showed traces of oil and grease. Jake remembered hearing that his hobby was restoring old cars.

"In a vague, hazy way."

"Normally we assign Aeronautical Engineering Duty Officers, AEDOs, to be program managers. By definition, an AEDO's specialty is the procurement business. Harold Strong was an AEDO. But, considering the status of the A-12, we figured that we needed a war fighter with credibility on the Hill." The Hill, Jake knew, was Capitol Hill, Congress. But who, he wondered, were the "we" of whom the admiral spoke? "You're our warrior. There's not enough time to send you to the five-month program manager school, so we've waived it. You're going to have to hit the ground running. Your deputy is a GS-15 civilian, Dr. Helmut Fritsche. He's only been here three years or so but he knows the ropes. And you've got some AEDOs on your staff. Use them, but remember, you're in charge."

"I won't forget," Jake Grafton said.

Dunedin's secretary, Mrs. Forsythe, gave him a list of the officers who would be under his supervision. She was a warm, motherly lady with silver-gray hair and pictures of children on her desk. Jake asked. Her grandchildren. She offered him a brownie she had baked last night, which he accepted and munched with approving comments while she placed a call to the Personnel Support Detachment. She gave him detailed directions on how to find PSD, which was, she explained, six buildings south. When Jake arrived fifteen minutes later a secretary was busy pulling the service records for him to examine.

He found an empty desk and settled in.

The civilian files stood out from the others. Helmut Fritsche, Ph.D. in electrical engineering, formerly professor at Caltech, before that on the research staff of NASA. Publications; wow! Thirty or forty scientific papers. Jake ran his eye down the list. All were about radar: wave propagation, Doppler effect, numerical determination of three-dimensional electromagnetic scattering, and so on.

George Wilson was a professor of aeronautical engineering at MIT on a one-year sabbatical. He had apparently been recruited by Admiral Henry and came aboard the first of the year. He would be leaving at the end of December. Like Fritsche's, Wilson's list of professional publications was long and complicated. He had co-authored at least one textbook, but the title that caught Jake's eye was an article for a scientific journal: "Aerodynamic Challenges in Low Radar Cross Section Platforms."

Jake laid the civilians' files aside and began to flip through the naval officers'. Halfway through he found one that he slowed down

to examine with care. Lieutenant Rita Moravia, Naval Academy
Class of '82. Second in her class at the Academy, first in her class
in flight school and winner of an outstanding achievement award.
Went through A-7 training, then transferred to F/A-18s, where she
became an instructor pilot in the West Coast replacement squadron. Next came a year at the Naval Postgraduate School in Monte-
rey, California, for a master's in aeronautical engineering, and another year at Test Pilot School at NAS Patuxent River, Maryland,
where she graduated first in her class.

There were three line commanders: an A-6 bombardier-navigator, an F-14 pilot and an EA-6B Electronic Countermeasures Officer—ECMO. Jake knew the A-6 BN and the Prowler ECMO.
There was an aircraft maintenance specialist, whom Jake knew,
and five AEDOs, all of whom wore pilot or naval flight officer
wings. Except for the A-6 BN and the Prowler ECMO, the rest
had fighter backgrounds, including Tarkington, who was one of
only two lieutenants. The rest were commanders and lieutenant
commanders.

If the navy wanted a stealth attack plane, why so many fighter
types? The air force called all their tactical drivers fighter pilots,
but the navy had long ago divided the tactical fraternity into attack
and fighter. The missions and the aircraft were completely different, so the training and tactics were also different. And according
to the amateur psychologists in uniform who thought about these
things and announced their conclusions at Happy Hour, the men
were different too. Either their personalities were altered by the
training or the missions attracted men of certain types. According
to the attack community, fighter pukes were devil-may-care, kiss-
tomorrow-goodbye romantics who lived and lusted for the dubious
glory of individual combat in the skies. The fighter crowd said the
attack pukes were phlegmatic plodders with brass balls—and no
imaginations—who dropped bombs because they didn't know any
better. Most of it was good, clean fun, but with a tinge of truth.

When Jake finished going through the records he stacked them
carefully and stared thoughtfully at the pile. Dunedin and Strong
had assembled a good group, he concluded, officers with excellent
though varied backgrounds, from all over tactical naval aviation.
The test pilot was the only real question mark. Moravia certainly
had her tickets punched and was probably smarter than Einstein,
but she had no actual experience in flight-testing new designs. He
would ask Dunedin about her.

Tomorrow he would meet them. That was soon enough. First he had to find out what was really happening from Henry or Dunedin.

Henry spoke of minefields—a grotesque understatement. The problems inherent in overcoming the inertia of the bureaucracy to produce a new state-of-the-art weapons system were nothing short of mind-boggling. Dunedin must feel like he's been ordered to build the Great Pyramid armed with nothing but a used condom and a flyswatter. And for God's sake, do it quietly, top secret and all. Aye aye, sir.

In the Crystal City underground mall he found a toy store and purchased a plastic model of the air force's new stealth fighter, the F-117. He also bought a tube of glue. Then he boarded the Metro blue train for the ride to Rosslyn.

When the subway surfaced near the Key Bridge, Jake stared gloomily at the raindrops smearing the dirt on the windows as the train rocked along under a dark gray sky, then it raced noisily back into another hole in the ground and like his fellow passengers, he refocused his eyes vacantly on nothing as he instinctively created his own little private space.

He felt relieved when the doors finally opened and he joined the other passengers surging across the platform, through the turnstiles, then onto the world's longest escalator. The moving stair ascended slowly up the gloomy, slanting shaft bearing its veterans of purgatory. Amid the jostling, pushing, hustling throng, he was carried along as part of the flow. This morning he had been a tourist. Now he was as much a part of this human river as any of them. Morning and evening he would be an anonymous face in the mob: hurry along, hurry, push and shove gently, persistently, insistently, demanding equal vigor and speed from every set of legs, equal privacy from every set of blank, unfocused eyes. Hurry, hurry along.

Rain was still falling when he reached the sidewalk. He paused and turned his collar up against the damp and chill, then set off for the giant condo complex four blocks away.

Most of the people scurrying past him on the sidewalk had done this every working day for years. They were moles, he told himself glumly, blind creatures of the dark, damp places where the sun and wind never reached, unaware that the universe held anything but the dismal corridors where they lived out their pathetic lives. And now he was one of them.

He stopped at the corner, the model in the box under his arm. People swirled around him, their heads down, their eyes on the concrete. Callie wouldn't get home to the flat for another hour.

He turned and walked back against the flow of the crowd toward the station exit. Right across the street from the exit was a Roy Rogers. He paid for a cup of coffee and found a seat near the atrium window where he could watch the gray people bent against the wind and the raindrops sliding down the glass.

The euphoria he had felt when he talked to Vice Admiral Henry this morning was completely gone. Now he had a job . . . a paperwork job, going to endless meetings and listening to reports and writing recommendations and trying to keep from going crazy. A job in the bureaucracy. A staff job, the one he had fought against, refused to take, pulled every string to avoid, all these years. In the puzzle palace, the place where good ideas go to die.

It could have been worse, of course. He could have been assigned to design the new officer fitness report form.

Like many officers who spent their careers in operational billets, Jake Grafton loathed the bureaucrats, held them in a secret contempt which he tried to suppress with varying degrees of success. In the years since World War II, the bureaucracy had grown lush and verdant here in Washington. Every member of Congress had twenty aides. Every social problem had a staff of paper pushers "managing" it. The military was just as bad. Joint commands with a staff of a thousand to fifteen hundred people were common.

Perhaps it happens because we are human. The people in the military endlessly analyze and train for the last war because no one knows what the next one will be like. New equipment and technologies deepen the gloom which always cloaks the future. Yesterday's warriors retire and new ones inherit the stars and the offices, and so it goes through generations, until at last every office is filled with men who have never heard a shot fired in anger or known a single problem that good, sound staff work, carefully couched in bureaucratese, could not "manage" satisfactorily. Inevitably the gloom becomes stygian. Future war becomes a profound enigma that workaday admirals and generals and congressmen cannot penetrate. So the staffs proliferate as each responsible person seeks expert help with his day-to-day duties and the insoluble policy conundrums.

Another war would be necessary to teach the new generation the ancient truths. But in the Pax Americana following World War II, Vietnam accelerated the damage rather than arrested it.

In its aftermath Vietnam appeared to many as the first inadvertent, incautious step toward the nuclear inferno that would destroy life on this planet. Frightened by the new technologies and fearful of the incomprehensible political forces at work throughout the world, citizens and soldiers sought—demanded—quantifiable truths and controls that would prevent the war that had become unthinkable, the future war that had become, for the generations that had known only peace, the ultimate obscenity. Laws and regulations and incomprehensible organizational charts multiplied like bacteria in a petri dish. Engineers with pocket calculators became soothsayers to the terrified.

All of this Jake Grafton knew, and knowing it, was powerless to change. And now he was one of *them,* one of the faceless savants charged with creating salvation on his desk and placing it in the out basket.

Over on the beach it was probably raining like this. The wind would be moaning around the house and leaking around the windowpanes. The surf would be pounding on the sand. It would be a great evening for a walk along the beach under a gray sky, by that gray sea. Suddenly he felt an overpowering longing to feel the wind in his hair and the salt air in his nostrils.

Oh, to be there and not here! Not *here* with the problems and the hassles and the responsibilities.

His eye fell upon the bag that the clerk had placed the F-117 model in. He ripped out the staple and slid the box from the bag. The artist had painted the plane black. It had twin vertical stabilizers, slanted in at the bottom, and flat sides all over the place, all of which he suspected were devilishly expensive to manufacture. The intakes were on top of the fuselage, behind the canopy. How would the engines get air when the pilot was pulling Gs, maneuvering? He stared at the picture. No doubt this plane was fly-by-wire with a flight control computer stabilizing the machine and automatically trimming. But what would it feel like to fly it? What would be the weight and performance penalty to get this thing aboard ship? How much were they going to cost? Could these machines ever be worth the astronomical sums the manufacturers would want to charge? The politicians would decide.

Jake drained his coffee and threw the cup in the trash can by the door. He pulled the bag up over the box and rolled the excess tightly, then pushed the door open and stepped out into the evening.

"Hi, darling," Callie said brightly when she came home and found Jake assembling the model on the kitchen table.

"Hey, beautiful." Jake looked up and grinned at her, then resumed his chore of gluing the landing gear into the wheel wells.

"So how was the first day back at the office?"

Jake laid the plastic model on the diagram and leaned back in his chair. He stretched. "Okay, I guess. They didn't tie me to the wooden post where they shoot traitors, and nobody said anything about a court-martial, so I guess I'm still in the navy." He winked at her. "It's going to be all right. Don't sweat it."

She poured a cup of coffee and blew across it gently, then took an experimental sip. She stood looking at him over the rim of the cup. "Where will you be working?"

"It's a little shop, some cubbyhole that belongs to NAVAIR. I'll be working on the new Advanced Tactical Aircraft."

"Oh, Jake." She took the seat beside him. "That's terrific." For the first time in months, her voice carried genuine enthusiasm.

"That's about all I can tell you. The project is classified up the wazoo. But it's a real job and it needs doing, which is a lot more than you can say for a lot of the jobs they have over there."

He shouldn't have added that last phrase. The muscles around her eyes tightened as she caught the edge in his voice. "After all you've done for the navy, they owed you a good job."

"Hey, Callie, it doesn't work like that. You get paid twice a month and that's all they owe you. But this is a navy job and Lord knows how it'll all turn out." Perhaps he could repair the damage. "I'd rather have a navy job than be president of a bank. You know me, Callie."

Her lips twisted into a lopsided smile. "Yes, I guess I do." She put her cup on the coffee table and stood.

Uh-oh! Here we go again! Jake took out his shirttail and used it to clean his glasses as she walked into the kitchen. You'd better be cool now, he decided. Help her along. He called out, "What say we go get some dinner? I'm hungry. How about you?"

4

The ringing of the telephone woke Jake Grafton. As he groped for the receiver on the stand by the bed he blinked mightily to make out the luminous hands of the alarm clock: 5 A.M. "Grafton."

"Good morning, Captain. Admiral Henry. I wanted to catch you before you got started this morning."

"You did, sir."

"How about meeting me on the steps of the Lincoln Memorial about oh-seven-hundred in civilian clothes."

"Aye aye, sir."

"Thanks." The connection broke.

"Who was that?" Callie asked as Jake cradled the phone and closed his eyes. The alarm wouldn't ring for half an hour.

"One of my many bosses."

"Oh," she muttered. In less than a minute he heard her breathing deepen with sleep. He wondered what Tyler Henry wanted to talk about that couldn't be said at the office. After five minutes he gave up trying to sleep and got out of bed. He tiptoed for the bathroom.

By the time the alarm went off he had showered and shaved and dressed. He had picked out dark gray slacks and a long-sleeved yellow shirt. Over this he had added a tie, an old sweater and a blue blazer.

"Good morning," he said as he pushed the lever in on the back of the clock to silence it.

"Come hug me." She smelled of warm woman and sleep. "It's so nice having you here to give me my morning hug." She pushed him back so she could see his face.

"I love you, woman." He cradled her head in his hands. "You're going to have to quit trying to analyze it and just accept it. It's true."

"Hmmm." She flashed a smile and became all business as she moved away from him and got up. "Why the civilian clothes?"

"I'm playing hooky with the boss."

"And it's only your second day on the job. Lucky you," she said as she headed for the bathroom. With the door closed she called, "How about turning on the coffeepot and toasting some English muffins?"

"Yeah." He headed toward the kitchen, snapping on the lights as he went. "You're a real lover, ace. One look at your sincere puss and they tighten up like an IRS agent offered a ten-dollar bribe."

Vice Admiral Henry was sitting on the steps of the Lincoln Memorial when the taxi deposited Jake in front. He came down the steps as Jake approached and joined him on the wide sidewalk. "Morning, sir."

The admiral flashed a smile and strolled to the curb. As he reached it a gray Ford Fairmont sedan sporting navy numbers on the door pulled to a stop. Henry jerked open the rear door without fanfare and maneuvered his six-foot-three-inch frame in. Jake followed him. When the door closed the sailor at the wheel got the car in motion.

"Why the cloak and dagger?"

"I don't know who all the players are," the admiral said without humor.

Jake watched the occasional pedestrians braving the blustery wind under a raw sky until he became aware that the admiral's attention was on the vehicles on the street behind them. Jake glanced over his shoulder once or twice, then decided to leave the spy stuff to Henry. He watched the sailor handle the car. The man was good. No wasted motion. The car glided gently through the traffic, changing lanes at the last moment and gliding around corners without the application of the brake, all quite effortlessly. It was a show and Jake watched it in silence.

"Could have picked you up at your place," Henry muttered, "but I wanted to visit the Wall." The Wall was the Vietnam Memorial, just across the street from the Lincoln Memorial. "It's been too long and I never seem to have any time."

"I understand."

"Turn left here," Henry said to the driver, who complied. The car headed east on Independence Avenue. Henry ordered another left turn on Fourteenth Street and directed the driver to go by the Jefferson Memorial. "I think we're clean," he muttered to Jake after yet another careful look through the rear window. At the Jefferson Memorial, Henry asked the driver to pull over. "Come back for us at nine."

He led Jake toward the walkway around the Tidal Basin. Across the basin the Washington Monument rose toward the low clouds. Beyond it, Jake knew, but not visible from here, was the White House.

Jake broke the silence first. "Does Admiral Dunedin know we're having this talk this morning, sir?"

"Yeah. I told him. You work for him. But I wanted to brief you personally. What do you know about stealth?"

"The usual," Jake said, snuggling into his coat against the chill wind. "What's in the papers. Not much."

"The air force contracted for two prototype stealth fighters under a blanket of absolute secrecy. Lockheed got the production contract. They call the thing the F-117A. It's a fighter in name only; it's really an attack plane—performance roughly equivalent to the A-7 without afterburner but carries less than half the A-7 weapons load. Primary weapons are Maverick missiles. It's a little ridiculous to call a subsonic minibomber a fighter, but if they can keep the performance figures low-key they might get away with it."

"I thought that thing was supposed to be a warp-three killing machine."

"Yeah. I suspect the congressmen who agreed to vote for a huge multibillion-buck project with no public debate probably did too. But even supersonic ain't possible. The thing doesn't even have afterburners. Might go supersonic in a dive—I don't know. Anyway, the air force got more bang for their buck with the stealth bomber, the B-2, which Northrop is building. It's also subsonic, a flying wing, but big and capable with a good fuel load. The only problem is the B-2s cost $516 million a pop, so unless you're sending them to Moscow to save the human race, you can't justify risking them on anything else. A B-2 isn't a battlefield weapon."

"How are these gizmos going to find their targets?" Conventional bombers used radar to navigate and locate their targets, but the transmission of a radar beam from a stealth bomber would reveal its location, thereby negating all the expensive technology used to hide it.

Admiral Henry settled onto a park bench with his back to the Tidal Basin. His eyes roamed the sidewalks, which were deserted on this early-spring morning. "You're not going to believe this, but the air force hasn't solved that problem yet. They're waiting for technology that's under development."

Jake Grafton looked at Henry to see if he was serious. He appeared to be. "How about a satellite rig like the A-6G was going to have? The Navstar Global Positioning System?"

"That's part of the plan, but the trouble with satellites is that you can't count on them to last longer than forty-eight hours into a major East-West confrontation. And there's only eight satellites aloft—the system needs twenty-eight. If they ever get all the birds aloft it should tell you your position to within sixteen meters anywhere on earth, but that's a big if what with NASA's shuttle and budget problems. No, I think the answer is going to be a system made up of a solid-state, ring-laser gyro inertial nav system, passive infrared sensors and a stealthy radar, one that powers up only enough to see what's necessary, has automatic frequency agility, that sort of thing. That's basically the A-6G and B-2 system. We'll use it on the A-12. It's still under development."

Henry snorted and wiggled his buttocks to get comfortable. "Congress isn't going to fund any significant B-2 buy. The way the whole budget process screwed up the buy, with inflation and predictable overruns and underbuys, the last plane in the program is going to cost over a billion bucks. The manned strategic bomber is going the way of the giant panda and the California condor. We want to avoid the mistakes the air force made."

"SAC will have more generals than airplanes."

"The stealth concept has been around since World War II," Henry continued, "more as a curio than anything else. It really became a driving force in aircraft design after Vietnam when it became apparent that conventional aircraft were going to have a very rough time surviving in the dense electronic environment over a Western European battlefield. Conventional electronic warfare can only do so much. The spooks say there'll be too many frequencies and too many sensors. That's the conventional wisdom, so it's probably wrong." He shrugged. "But any way you cut it, the attrition rate over that battlefield would be high, which favors the Soviets. They have lots of planes and we can't match them in quantity. So we would lose. Ergo, stealth."

"But we *could* match them in quantity," Jake said. "At least the air force could build a lot of cheap airplanes optimized for one mission, like fighter or attack. No room on carriers for that kind of plane, of course."

"The air force doesn't want that. Their institutional ethic is for more complex, advanced aircraft with greater and greater capability. That's the whole irony of the stealth fighter. They've billed this technology as a big advance but in reality they got a brand-new tactical bomber with 1950s performance. But, they argue, it's survivable. Now. For the immediate future. Until and only until the Russians come up with a way to find these planes—or someone else figures out a way and the Russians steal it. Even so, the only thing that made first-generation stealth technology feasible was smart weapons, assuming the crew can find the target. These planes have little or no capability with air-to-mud dumb bombs." Henry stared at his toes and wriggled them experimentally. "Can you imagine risking a five-hundred-million buck airplane to dump a load of thousand-pounders on a bridge?"

"Does stealth ensure survivability?" Jake prompted, too interested to notice his continuing discomfort from the breeze off the river.

"Well, it all boils down to whether or not you think fixed air bases are survivable in the war the air force is building their planes to fight, and that is a war in Europe against the Soviets *which has escalated to a nuclear exchange.* If I were a Russian I wouldn't worry much about these airplanes—neither of which has any off-concrete capability—I'd just knock out their bases at the beginning of hostilities and forget about them."

"What about a conventional war with the Soviets?"

"If anyone has figured out a way to keep it from going nuclear, I haven't heard about it."

"How many Maverick missiles are there? A couple thousand?"

"Twice that."

"That's still no more than a week or two's supply. It'd better be a damn short war."

The admiral grunted. "The basic dilemma: without stealth technology the air force says planes can't survive over a modern battlefield; with stealth they must use only sophisticated weapons that are too expensive to buy in quantity. And they're not as reliable as cheap weapons. And if the airplanes truly are a threat, the Soviets have a tremendous stimulus to escalate the war to a nuclear strike to eliminate their bases." He chopped the air with the cutting edge of his hand. "This stuff is grotesquely expensive."

"Sounds like we've priced ourselves out of the war business."

"I fucking wish! But enough philosophy. Stealth technology certainly deserves a lot of thought. It's basically just techniques to lower an aircraft's electromagnetic signature in the military wavelengths: radio—which is radar—and heat—infrared. And they're trying to minimize the distance the plane can be detected by ear and by eye. Minimizing the RCS—the Radar Cross Section—and the heat signature are the two most important factors and end up driving the design process. But it's tough. For example, to half the radar detection range you must lower the RCS by a factor of sixteen—the fourth root. To lower the IR signature in any meaningful manner you must give up afterburners for your engines and bury the engines inside the airplane to cool the exhaust gases, the sum total of which is less thrust. Consequently we are led kicking and screaming into the world of design compromises, which is a handy catchall for mission compromises, performance and range and payload compromises, bang-and-buck compromises. That's where you come in."

Admiral Henry rose from the bench and sauntered along the walk discussing the various methods and techniques that lowered, little by little, the radar and heat signatures of an aircraft. He talked about wing and fuselage shape, special materials, paint, engine and inlet duct design and placement, every aspect of aircraft construction. Stealth, he said, involved them all. Finally he fell silent and walked along with his shoulders rounded, his hands thrust deep into his pockets.

Jake spoke. "If the best the air force could get out of their stealth attack plane was A-7 performance, is it a good idea for the navy to spend billions on one? We can't go buying airplanes to fight just one war, and we need a sufficient quantity of planes to equip the carriers. Five gee-whiz killing machines a year won't do us any good at all."

The admiral stopped dead and scrutinized Jake. Slowly a grin lifted the corners of his mouth. "I *knew* you were the right guy for this job."

He resumed walking, his step firmer, more confident. "The first question is what kind of fights are we going to get into in the future. And the answer, I suspect, is more of the same. I think the likelihood of an all-out war with the Soviets in Western Europe is pretty small—no way to prevent it from going nuclear and the Russians don't want that any more than we do. But we must prepare to fight it, prepare to some degree, or we can't deter it. I'd say it's a lot more likely we'll end up with more limited wars, like Korea or Vietnam or Afghanistan or the Persian Gulf or the Middle East or South Africa. So the capability to fight those wars is critical. We need planes that can fly five hundred miles through a high-density electronic environment, deliver a devastating conventional punch, and return to the carrier to fly again, and again and again. Without *that* capability our carrier battle groups are an expensive liability and not an asset. We need that plane by 1995, at the latest."

"You're implying that our plane can't rely on pinpoint missiles for weapons."

"Precisely. The air force has a lot of concrete to park their specialized planes on; carrier deck space is damn precious. We can't build planes that can only shoot missiles that cost a million bucks each, then push them into the drink when we run out of missiles. We have to be able to hit hard in any foreseeable conflict with simple, cheap weapons, like laser-guided bombs."

"So we can do something the air force couldn't with the F-117?"

Henry threw his head back and grinned, obviously enjoying himself. "We aren't going to trade away our plane's performance or mission capability."

"But how—"

"Better design—we learned a lot from the F-117—plus Athena. *Active* stealth technology." His mood was gloomy again. "I think the fucking Russians have gotten everything there was to get out of the F-117 and B-2. Every single technical breakthrough, they've stolen it. They don't appear to be using that knowledge and they may not ever be able to do so. This stuff involves manufacturing capabilities they don't have and costs they can't afford to incur. But what they can do is figure out defenses to a stealthed-up airplane, and you can bet your left nut they're working their asses off on that right this very minute."

He looked carefully around. "There's a Russian mole in the Pentagon." His voice was almost a whisper, although the nearest pedestrian was a hundred yards away. "He gave them the stealth secrets. The son of a bitch is buried in there someplace and he's ripping us off. He's even been given a top secret code name— Minotaur." He scuffed his toe at a pebble on the sidewalk. "I'm not supposed to know this. It goes without saying that if I'm not, you sure as hell aren't."

"How'd—"

"Don't ask. I don't want you to know. But if I know the Minotaur's there, you can lay money *he* knows we know he's there. So the bastard is dug in with his defenses up. We may never get him. Probably won't."

"How do we know he gave them stealth?"

"We know. Trust me. We know."

"So we have a mole in the Kremlin."

"I didn't say that," Henry said fiercely, "and you had damn well better not. No shit, Grafton, don't even whisper that to a living fucking soul."

They walked along in silence, each man occupied with his own thoughts. Finally Jake said, "So how are we gonna do it?"

"Huh?"

"How are we going to build a stealth Intruder and keep the technology in our pocket?"

"I haven't figured that one out yet," Henry said slowly. "You see, everything the Russians have gotten so far is passive—techniques to minimize the radar cross section and heat signature. To build a mission-capable airplane like we want we're going to have to use active techniques, Project Athena. They haven't stolen Athena yet and we don't want them to get it."

"Active techniques?" Jake prompted, unable to contain his curiosity.

"We're going to cancel the bad guys' radar signal when it reaches our plane. We'll automatically generate a signal that nullifies the echo, mutes it, cancels it out. The plane will then be truly invisible to the enemy. They'll never see it on their scope. They'll never receive the echo." He thought about it. "It's the biggest technological breakthrough since the Manhattan Project. Biggest by a mile."

"I've heard speculation about canceling radar signals for years.

The guys who were supposed to know all laughed. Can it be done?"

"The party line is no. Impossible. But there's a crazed genius who wants to be filthy rich that has done it. That technology is the living, beating heart of the ATA. Now all we have to do is get an airplane built and keep the Minotaur from stealing the secret."

Jake whistled. "Can't we put this on all our ships?"

"No doubt we will," Henry said sourly, "and the Russians will steal it before our first ship gets out of the harbor. For now let's just see if we can get it in one airplane without someone stealing it. That'll be plenty for you and Roger Dunedin to chew."

"Existing aircraft? How about retrofitting them?"

"Right now, as the technology exists, the best approach is to design the plane for it. The power output required to hide a stealthy plane would be very small. The device would be easy enough to put on a ship, when we get the bugs worked out. As usual there are bugs. Expensive, though."

Admiral Henry glanced at his watch. "Our work's cut out for us. The air force will want this technology when they get wind of it, and right now everything they see winds up in the Kremlin. It's not their fault, of course, but that's the way it is. The manufacturer of our plane will see it and from there it may end up in the Minotaur's clutches. Ditto the ship drivers. And the politicians who have been trick-fucked on the F-117 won't sit still for more stealth hocus-pocus; they're gonna want justification for the four or five billion dollars the ATA will require just to develop, and there it goes again. So right now I'm sitting on a volcano that's about to erupt and my ass is getting damn warm. You see why I wanted you on board."

"Not really," Jake said, wondering how far he should push this. After all, who the hell was Jake Grafton? What could an over-the-hill attack pilot in glasses with four stripes on his sleeve do for a three-star admiral? Bomb the Pentagon? "So what's your plan? How are you going to do this?"

Henry was so nervous he couldn't hold still. "I'm going to hold the cards real close to my chest and catch the Minotaur peeking over my shoulder. Or that's what I'm going to try to do, anyway."

"Admiral, with all respect, sir, what does CNO say about all this?" CNO was the Chief of Naval Operations, the senior uniformed naval officer.

Henry squared off in front of Jake. "I'm not stupid enough to try to run my own private navy, Captain. CNO knows exactly what I'm doing. So does SECNAV and SECDEF. But you sure as hell didn't get it all in this little conversation."

"Admiral, I'll lay it on the line for you. I'm not going to do anything illegal or tell even one solitary little lie. I'm not a very good liar."

Admiral Henry grinned. "You just haven't had the experience it takes. I've been single for ten years, so I've done a good bit of it. Seriously, all I want you to do is play it straight. Do your job for NAVAIR. Just keep it under your hat that we have an active system we're going to put into this bird. Roger will tell you the same."

"How many people know about this active system?"

"Here in Washington? Eight now. The Secretary of the Navy, CNO, SECDEF, NAVAIR, OP-50—which is Rear Admiral Costello—me, you and Helmut Fritsche. And let's keep it that way for a while."

"Have you tested this system? Does it work?"

Henry made a face. "Fritsche's seen it work on a test bench. Your first job, after you look at the prototypes, is to put part of it into an A-6 and test it on the ground and in flight."

Jake eyed the older man. He had this sinking feeling in the pit of his stomach. There was a hell of a lot he wasn't being told. "So how do you know Fritsche?"

"He was a professor at Caltech when I was there for a master's. We became good friends. He did some consulting work for the inventor on some theoretical problems. He saw what the guy had and came to me. That was three years ago. It was coincidence that there was a deputy project manager job opening in the ATA program. I talked Fritsche into taking it. He wants to be a part of Athena. The theoretical problems intrigue him."

"You said you didn't know all the players."

Henry took this opportunity to look around again. "Yeah. I don't. Your predecessor, Harold Strong? Great guy, knew naval aviation from catapult to tailhook, everything there is to know, but he wasn't a politician, not a diplomat. He was a blunt, brilliant, take-no-prisoners kind of guy. Somebody killed him."

"Why?"

"I wish I knew." Henry described how he personally drove to West Virginia on Saturday morning after the Friday-night automobile accident. He summarized the conversation he had had with the West Virginia state trooper who investigated the accident. The trooper had served four years in the marine corps and by a stroke of fortune Henry had been in uniform. The trooper had been good; he knew murder when he saw it. He had taken the admiral to see the local prosecuting attorney, who had been splitting firewood in his backyard when the two of them arrived in the police cruiser. After two hours of talking, Henry induced the prosecutor and the trooper to agree to a wording of the accident report that did not mention homicide and yet would not preclude a homicide prosecution if the identity of the murderer could ever be established.

"My theory"—Henry shrugged—"I got no evidence, you understand—my theory is Harold found out something, learned something somebody didn't want him to know—so he got rubbed out."

The navy Ford pulled up to the curb, but Henry put a hand on Jake's arm. "This is big, Jake. Real big. You don't understand how big. The Russians will figure out we're going to do something different and wonderful with the A-12 and they'll pull out all the stops to get Athena. And five billion dollars in development money is on the line, plus twenty to thirty billion in production money—that much shit will draw every blowfly and bloodsucker in the country. A lot of these people would kill for this technology."

"Maybe someone already has."

"Just don't trust anybody."

"I've figured that out, sir. I think there's a hell of a lot here you haven't told me. So I don't trust you."

Henry threw back his head and guffawed. "I *knew* you were the right man for this job." He became instantly serious. "I don't give a damn whether you trust me or not. Just do your job and keep your mouth shut and we'll get the navy a good airplane."

"By the way, did Strong know about the active system?"

"Yes."

The admiral's driver dropped Jake at his office building. One of the few benefits of working a black program was that he could come to work in civilian clothes.

Vice Admiral Dunedin was finishing a conference, so Jake visited with Mrs. Forsythe. In fifteen minutes the door opened and people streamed out, in a hurry.

"Good morning, Admiral," Jake said.

"How'd your talk go with Admiral Henry?"

"Very well, sir."

"Don't lie to me, Captain. I'm your boss."

"Yessir." Jake found a seat and looked straight at the blue-eyed

Scotsman behind the desk. "He told me what he wanted me to know and that was that."

"How long you been in the navy?"

Long enough to know how to take orders, Jake thought. "Yessir."

"Let's talk about the A-12. It's now your baby."

An hour later the admiral rose from his chair. "Let's go meet the crew."

Jake mentioned to the admiral that he had been looking at the personnel folders. "Lieutenant Moravia. She's got platinum credentials but no experience. How'd she get on the team?"

"Strong wanted her. He was down at Pax River when she went through as a student. He said she's one of a kind. Since he was a test pilot himself, I figured he had the experience even if she didn't, so I said okay."

"I'm not a test pilot," Jake said.

"I know. These people work for you. If you want someone else, just say so. That goes for any of them, except for Fritsche. If they stay it's because you think they can do the job and you trust them."

"I read you loud and clear, sir."

"Anybody doesn't pull his weight, or you get goosey about any of them, I'll have them sitting on the ice cap in the Antarctic so quick they won't have time to pack their long johns."

The office in Crystal City where the A-12 program team worked was a square space with twenty metal desks jammed in. Five-drawer filing cabinets with combination locks on the drawers had been arranged to divide the room into work areas. The scarred tops and askew drawers of the desks proclaimed them veterans of other offices, other bureaucratic struggles now forgotten. Office equipment was scattered all over the room: a dozen computer terminals, four printers, a copy machine, a paper shredder, and a fax machine linked to an encryption device. Jake's office would be one of the two small private offices. These two small offices each had an outside window and a blackboard, plus the usual filing cabinets with combination locks on the drawers.

But the security—wow! There were two entry doors, each with cipher locks, and a closed-circuit television that monitored the dead space between the doors. An armed security team was on duty inside twenty-four hours a day. Their business was to check each person entering the space against a master list and log them in and out. The windows had the music sound vibrators and could not be opened. The shades were permanently closed. The fire extinguisher system in the ceiling had plastic cutouts installed in the pipes so that they would not conduct sound.

"Every sheet of paper is numbered and accounted for," the admiral told Jake. "The phone numbers are unlisted and changed monthly. I can never find my number sheet, so I end up walking down here."

After a quick tour, Jake stood in the middle of the room with the admiral. "Where'd they get this carpet?"

"Stole it someplace. I never asked."

"Sure would be nice to get a little bigger space. Thirty people?"

"This is all the space I have to give you. It takes the signature of an Assistant Secretary of the Navy to get space not assigned to NAVAIR. I haven't had time to kiss his ass. But if you can get his scrawl, go for it."

"Nothing's too good for the boys in navy blue," Toad Tarkington chirped cheerfully from his little desk against one wall, loud enough to draw a frosty glance from the admiral.

"You're Tarkington?" Dunedin said.

"Yessir."

"I hear you suffer from a mouth problem from time to time. If it's incurable your naval career is about to hit the wall. You read me?"

"Yessir."

Dunedin raised his voice. "Okay, folks. Gather around. I want you to meet Captain Jake Grafton, the new program manager. He's your new boss." Dunedin launched into a traditional "welcome aboard" speech. When he was finished Jake told the attentive faces how pleased he was to be there, then he and the admiral shook hands. After a quick whispered word with Fritsche, Dunedin left the office.

Jake invited the commanders and civilian experts into his new cubbyhole. It was a very tight fit. Folding chairs were packed in and the place became stuffy in minutes. They filled him in on the state of the project and their roles in it. Jake said nothing about his visits with the admirals and gave no hint that he knew anything about the project.

He looked over Helmut Fritsche first, the radar expert from Caltech. About fifty, he was heavyset, of medium height, and sported a Hemingway beard which he liked to stroke when he talked. He had alert, intelligent eyes that roamed constantly, even when he was addressing someone. He spoke slowly, carefully, choosing his words. He struck Jake as an intelligent, learned man who had long ago resigned himself to spending most of his life in the company of fools.

George Wilson was at least five years younger than Fritsche and much leaner. He spoke slowly, in cadenced phrases, automatically allowing his listeners to take notes if they wished. When he used his third pun Jake finally noticed. Listening more carefully, he picked up two double entendres and another pun. At first blush Wilson seemed a man in love with the sound of his own voice, but Jake decided that impression didn't do justice to the fertile, active mind of the professor of aeronautical engineering.

The A-6 bombardier, Commander Les Richards, looked as old as Fritsche although he couldn't have been a day over forty-two or forty-three. Jake had met him years ago at NAS Oceana. They had never been in the same squadron together but had a speaking acquaintance. Richards' tired face contained tired eyes. Jake remembered that just a year or so ago Richards had commanded an A-6 squadron, so this assignment was his post-command tour. His eyes told whoever looked that the navy was no longer an adventure, if indeed it ever had been. The navy and perhaps life itself were experiences to be endured on this long, joyless journey toward the grave. If he caught any of Wilson's wordplay his face gave no hint. In spite of his demeanor, Jake knew, Richards had the reputation of being an aggressive, competent manager, a man who got things done.

Commander "Smoke" Judy was an F-14 pilot. Like all the commanders, he had had a squadron command tour. Smoke was short and feisty. He looked like a man who would rather fight than eat. The joyous competitive spirit of the fighter pilot seemed incarnate in him. A fire-eater—no doubt that was the origin of his nickname, which had probably ceased to be a nickname long ago. Jake suspected that his wife and even his mother now called him Smoke.

Dalton Harris was an extrovert, a man with a ready smile. He grinned nervously at George Wilson's humor and glanced at him expectantly every time it seemed Wilson might become inspired. He was a lithe, compact man, as full of nervous energy as Judy. An alumnus of the EA-6B Prowler community, he was an expert in electronic warfare. He even had a master's in electrical engineering from the Naval Postgraduate School.

The other two commanders, Aeronautical Engineering Duty Officers, were equally interesting. Technical competence was their stock-in-trade.

An excellent group, Jake decided as the conversation wound down, good shipmates. Harold Strong and Admiral Dunedin had chosen well. He glanced at his watch with a start; they had been talking about the A-12 for two hours. In parting he told them, "I want a complete inventory of the accountable classified material started tomorrow. Every document will be sighted by two officers and they'll both sign the list."

"We did an inventory after Captain Strong died. Took two weeks."

"You'd better hope I don't kick the bucket any time soon or you'll be doing it a couple more times."

Jake spent five minutes with each of the other officers, saving Moravia and Tarkington for last. He saw them together. After the preliminaries he said, "Miss Moravia, I'm going to be blunt. You don't seem to have any test-flying experience other than Test Pilot School."

"That's right, sir. But I can do the job. Try me and see."

Moravia was of medium height, with an excellent figure and a face to match. Subtle makeup, every hair in place. Her gold naval aviator wings gleamed above the left breast pocket of her blue uniform. Try me and see—that fierce self-confidence separated those who could from those who never would.

Tarkington seemed to treat her with deference and respect, Jake noted wryly. "Ever flown an A-6?"

"About two hours or so at Pax River, sir." Jake knew how that worked. During the course of his training at Test Pilot School—TPS—each student flew anywhere from twelve to seventeen different kinds of aircraft. The final examination to qualify for graduation consisted of writing a complete flying qualities and performance evaluation of an airplane the student had not flown before. The student was handed a manual, and after studying it, was allowed to fly the airplane for four flights or six hours' flight time, whichever came first. On the basis of this short exposure the student then wrote the report. Rita Moravia was an honors graduate of that program.

Try me and see!

"I want you and Tarkington to leave for Whidbey Island tomorrow morning. The folks at VA-128 are expecting you." VA-128 was the replacement training squadron for A-6 Intruders on the West Coast. "They're going to give you a crash course on how to fly an A-6. Report directly to the squadron skipper when you get there tomorrow. Mrs. Forsythe in the admiral's office is getting you orders and plane tickets." He looked again at his watch. "She should have them for you now."

"Aye aye, sir," Moravia said and stood up. "Is there anything else, sir?"

"Remember that nobody at Whidbey has a need to know anything. You'll be asked no questions by the senior people. The junior ones will be curious, so just say the Pentagon sent you to fly. That's it. Learn everything you can about the plane and its mission. And don't crash one."

Miss Moravia nodded and left, but Toad lingered.

"Uh, CAG," Toad said, "I'm a fighter type and this attack puke stuff—"

"The admiral says that anyone I want to get rid of can winter over in Antarctica. You want to go all the way south?"

"I'll take Whidbey, sir."

"I thought you would." He picked up some paper on his desk and looked at it, signaling the end of the interview. "Oh," he added, looking up again, "by the way, you stay the hell away from Moravia. Absolutely no romance. Keep it strictly business. You'd mope around here like a whipped puppy after she ditched you. I haven't got the stomach for another sorry spectacle like that."

The office emptied at 5:30. Jake stayed, sorting through the paper that had accumulated in Strong's in basket. Most of it he threw in the waste can under his desk. Memos and letters and position papers that looked important he saved for later scrutiny.

When he finished with the in-basket pile he began rooting through the desk drawers. Unbelievable! Here at the back of the wide, shallow drawer above his knees was an old memo on army stationery, dated 1956. Where had they gotten these desks? And what else was in here? Maybe he would find an announcement from the War Department that Japan had surrendered.

Alas, nothing so extraordinary. A two-year old date book, most of the pages blank. Some matchbooks from a restaurant—perhaps Strong liked to drop in there for a cup of coffee. Three envelopes addressed to Strong in a feminine hand: empty envelopes with the stamp canceled, no return address. One broken shoelace, a button that didn't look like it came from a uniform, two rubber bands, a collection of government pens and #2 lead pencils. He tried the pens on scrap paper. Most of them still worked. Some of the erasers on the pencils were pretty worn.

So Harold Strong had been murdered.

And Admiral Henry had throttled the investigation even before it started. Or so he said.

He shook his head in annoyance. Those problems were not his concern. His job was to run this project. With the A-12 still in the prototype stage, many major decisions remained to be made. Jake already knew where he would throw his weight, what little he had. For too long, in his opinion, the military had been stuck with airplanes designed to accomplish so many disparate missions that they were unable to do any of them well. If they wanted an attack plane, then by God he would argue like hell for a capable attack plane.

Every aircraft design involved inevitable trade-offs: fuel capacity was traded for strength and maneuverability, weapons-carrying capacity sacrificed for speed, maneuverability surrendered for stability, and so on, because every aircraft had to have all of these things, yet it needed these things in degrees that varied with its mission. But with stealth literally everything was being compromised in varying degrees to achieve invisibility, or in the jargon of the trade, survivability.

For two hours this afternoon the commanders and experts had argued that a plane that could not survive over the modern battlefield was not worth having. Yet a plane that did survive but could not fight was equally worthless. Somewhere between these two extremes was a balance.

The other major consideration that had been tossed around this afternoon was a conundrum that baffled politicians and generals as well as aircraft designers. What war do you build your airplane to fight? World War III nuclear? World War III conventional? Vietnam? Anti-terrorist raids against Libya? The answer, Jake believed, had to be all of them. Yet achieving survivability over the European battlefield might well mean trading away conventional iron-bomb-carrying capacity that would be essential in future brushfire wars, like Vietnam. Megabuck smart missiles were currently in vogue but the nation could never afford enough of them to fight any war that lasted longer than two weeks.

This job was not going to be easy, or dull.

"She-it," Jake Grafton said aloud, drawing the word out slowly. When you looked at Tyler Henry and listened to him he seemed okay. But if all you did was listen to the words—well, it sure did make you wonder. Spies? Murder investigations put on hold? Was Henry some paranoid wacko, some coconut schizo on the naked edge who ought to be locked in the bowels of St. Elizabeth's without his belt and shoelaces?

The first thing I ought to do, Jake told himself, before I go see the ultimate war machine manufactured by some greedy Gyro Gearloose in a garage in California, is check out Henry. It would be nice to know that the big boss has all his marbles. It would be damn nice to know if he doesn't. Dunedin wanted Jake to salute and march.

"A fellow never gets very far marching in the dark, anyhow," Jake said aloud. "Too much stuff out there to trip over."

He used one of the black government pens from Strong's hoard to write a note for the senior secretary's desk. What was her name? Mrs. Pulliam. There were just two secretaries, both civilians.

The note informed all and sundry he would be in late tomorrow, after lunch. He had a moment of doubt. There was so much to be done here. Yet they had gotten along without a project manager for two months now: they could suffer through another day.

5

Toad Tarkington lowered himself into a seat against the window on the left side of the airplane, a Boeing 727. Three engines, he noted with satisfaction. Airliners made him nervous these days. He couldn't see the guys flying or monitor the instruments and he had no ejection seat, so he couldn't boogy on out if the clowns up front hamburgered it, which, from what he read in the newspapers, they had been doing lately with distressing frequency. Luckily this flight to Seattle was almost empty, so after the crash there wouldn't be any unsightly mob ripping out hair and eyeballs scrambling for the emergency exits.

He glanced across the four empty seats and the aisle at Rita Moravia sitting against the window on the right side. Now there was one cold, cold woman. She hadn't yet smiled in his presence or given any indication she ever would. The old Tarkington charm rolled right over her as if it had gone bad in the winter of '85, turned sour and rotten and gave off an evil odor.

The plane began to move. Backwards. They were pushing it out. Toad glanced at his watch. Twenty minutes late. They were always late. He tried to get comfortable in his seat. Reluctantly he picked up the copy of *The Washington Post* he had purchased at a news counter and scanned the headlines. Same old crap—it's absolutely uncanny how politicians can be relied upon to do or say something every single day that even Charlie Manson would think bizarre.

He sneaked a glance at Moravia. She was reading a paperback.

He squinted. My God—it's a Jackie Collins novel! How about that? The ice queen deep into sex among the rich and stupid. Maybe her hormones are okay after all.

Toad leaned back and closed his eyes. He needed to work out some kind of approach, a line. First he needed to know more about her. This was going to take some time, but she looked like she'd be worth it and Jake Grafton had implied that they were going to be spending plenty of time together. That Grafton, he didn't just fall off a turnip truck. He knew the score.

Toad opened one eye and aimed it her way. Yep, a nice tight unit. Reading a romance novel. Who'd have guessed?

When the plane was safely airborne he reclined his seat and drifted off to sleep wearing a satisfied little smile.

Jake Grafton found a place to park the Chevy right on Main Street a block from the courthouse intersection, which sported the only stoplights in town. Actually there were three empty parking places all in a row and he took one on the end. Romney, West Virginia, was not a bustling place on a cold, breezy March morning.

The interior of the courthouse was massive and calm. The ceilings were at least fifteen high. Even the interior walls were thick, substantial, built to last. He examined the signs on the wooden doors and settled on the circuit clerk's office. Inside he asked, "Where do I find the prosecuting attorney?"

"Across the street on the left end of the block. He has an office above the liquor store. Cookman's his name." The lady smiled.

"And the state police?"

"Out of the courthouse, turn right and go three blocks, then another right and down about a half mile. The barracks is a nice little brick building. You can't miss it."

Standing in front of the courthouse beside the statue of a World War I doughboy, Jake decided to walk to the state police barracks first. The first three blocks were along the main drag, by stores and empty display windows. The decay of the American Main Street had reached this little community too. When he turned right he left the commercial district and found himself in a quiet residential area. As he passed modest houses with trees in the lawns and pickups and motorcycles in the drive, he could hear dogs barking and occasionally a snatch of talk show from an open door.

The police barracks had American and West Virginia flags flying on large poles in front, beside an empty parking area festooned with signs and plastic barriers for driving tests. Inside there wasn't a cop in sight. The girl behind the desk looked like she was barely out of high school.

"Hi, I'd like to get a copy of an accident report from a couple months ago."

"Did it happen in the city or out in the county?"

"Outside the city."

"You've come to the right place." She smiled. "I need the names of the parties involved, or at least one of them."

"Harold Strong."

"Just a moment." She selected a drawer in a large file cabinet and began looking. "All we have are copies, of course. The originals go to DMV in Charleston. We're not even required to keep copies but we do because the lawyers and insurance adjusters always want to see them. Are you a lawyer?"

"Uh, no. I was a friend of Captain Strong's."

"Here it is." She looked at it as she walked toward the counter. "He was in the navy, wasn't he."

Her comment was a statement, not a question, but he responded anyway. "Yes, he was."

She laid the report on the counter in front of him. "That's our office copy and our copy machine is out of order. There's one up in the county clerk's office, where they keep the deeds and all?" He nodded. "But you need to leave your driver's license with me." She smiled apologetically. "So many people forget to bring our copy back."

He dug out his wallet and extracted his license. She didn't even look at it. "Thanks. I'll be back in a bit."

Very nicely done, he thought as he walked the half mile back toward the main street. No doubt before he got out of Romney he would be talking to a state trooper. He looked at the name on the report. Trooper Keadle.

There was an unpadded bench in the corridor outside the county clerk's office and he settled there. The report consisted of three pages. The first was a form with blanks to be filled in and a diagram where the investigating officer drew little cars and arrows to show what he believed happened. The next two pages were merely handwritten comments of the investigating office. Keadle had a neat hand—he obviously hadn't ruined his penmanship with years of furious note-taking.

The report was straightforward, devoid of bureaucratese. Jake

read it a second time slowly, studying the words. According to
Admiral Henry the prosecuting attorney had had a hand in this
report, which "would not preclude a homicide prosecution." That
could only mean that none of the critical facts were omitted. A
half-smart defense lawyer would raise holy hell if the prosecutor
asked the trooper to testify about facts that he had "forgotten" to
put in the official report.

What was in the report? Marks on the highway where it appeared tires may have broken their regular grip with the pavement
and spun under power. No skid marks: wet pavement prevented
that. Deep trenches in the gravel, some of which went all the way
to the edge, presumably from skidding tires. Marks in the earth
where the Corolla went over the edge. Wooden guardrails had been
chain-sawed several days before the accident, presumably by van-
dals or parties unknown; see previous report of sheriff's deputy.
Fire in Corolla passenger compartment very intense, body burned
beyond recognition and identified with help of FBI forensic lab. No
mention of why or when the FBI was notified. Dents and scrape
marks all over the vehicle. Finally, Corolla still structurally intact
but gutted by fire.

No mention of the Corolla's fuel tank. But the trooper could
certainly testify that the fuel tank, like the car's frame, was intact.
No speculation on or estimate of how fast the Corolla would have
had to be going up that mountain to slide all the way across the
overlook area. Did he explain that the Corolla was ascending the
grade? Yes, on page one.

No speculation about the cause of this single-car accident and no
speculation anywhere that another vehicle might be involved.

He took the report into the office beside him and had it copied.
They charged him thirty cents. He was tempted to use the car to
return the original report but decided the exercise would be good
for him. As he approached the police building, a trooper was parking his car in a reserved spot.

"Thanks," he told the girl at the desk. She handed him his driver's license, which had been lying on the counter beside the police
radio microphone.

The door behind Jake opened. "Hi, Susie." Jake turned. The
trooper was clad in a green uniform and wore a short green nylon
jacket. He was somewhere between thirty and thirty-five years of
age, with a tanned, clean-shaven face and short military haircut.
He stood several inches taller than Jake and was built heavier. On

the left breast of his coat was a silver name tag: Keadle. "Hello," he said, addressing the greeting to Jake.

"Hi."

"This is Mr. Jacob L. Grafton of Arlington, Virginia," the girl said. "He was a friend of Captain Strong's."

"Izzatso?" The trooper's eyes swept him again, more carefully. "Why don'tcha step into this other room here for a minute. Susie, how about getting us both coffee. White or black?" he said to Jake.

"Black."

"Black it is," he said, and led the way behind the counter and through a door into an adjoining office. His big revolver swung freely below his jacket in a brown holster that hung halfway down his right leg.

"Captain Strong had a little cabin a few miles east of here for weekends and all," the trooper said. "I knew him to speak to. Helluva nice guy. Too bad about that wreck."

Jake nodded and sank onto an old sofa with the stuffing coming through the cracks in the vinyl.

"You in the navy too?" the trooper asked.

Jake took out his wallet and extracted his green ID card. He passed it across. The trooper looked it over, both sides, then handed it back. "Why'd you come up here, Captain Grafton?"

"Were you ever in the service?"

"Marines, four years. Why?"

"Just curious."

The door opened and Susie came in with coffee in Styrofoam cups. Both men thanked her and she pulled the door shut on her way out.

"Let's try it again. Why'd you come up here, Captain Grafton?"

"To get a copy of this report."

Keadle thought about that for a bit, then said, "Well, you got one. What do you think of it?"

"It was a strange accident."

"How so?"

"Car going up a steep, curvy road on a rainy evening goes skidding off the pavement and across a fifty-foot-wide gravel turnout. Right over the edge. Then there's a furious fire in the passenger compartment."

"What's strange about that?"

"He must have been flying low that night. Or else somebody pushed him over the edge. And an interior fire—I thought that stuff only happened in movies. Wrecked cars rarely explode or catch fire."

"You don't say. If it wasn't an accident, who wanted Captain Strong dead?"

"I don't know. I dropped in to see if you did."

"I'm just a rural peace officer, not some big-city detective. This county don't have much real crime. Seems that most of the scumbags just do their thing over in Washington. I'm not—"

"Let's cut the bullshit. Why aren't you investigating an apparent homicide?"

"Who says I'm not? I'm sitting here chinning with you, ain't I?"

Jake sipped on his coffee. Finally he said, "Well, you got any more questions?"

"Gimme your address and phone number." Keadle picked up a pad of paper and a pen from the desk. "If I think of any I'll give you a call."

Jake told him the number. "Susie already gave you my address from my driver's license." He stood and drained his coffee. "Thanks for the coffee. I hope you catch him."

Keadle looked at him with pursed lips.

Jake opened the door and walked out. He nodded at Susie as he went by.

The red flag was up on the Main Street parking meter but no ticket yet. It was almost noon. Perhaps he should stop and see if the prosecutor was in his office. But what good would that do?

There was no way he could make it back to the office before everyone left for the day. Perhaps a hamburger. He fed the meter another quarter and walked down Main Street toward a cafe that he had noticed near the courthouse. Before he got there Trooper Keadle went by in a state police cruiser.

When he finished his lunch Jake drove east on the road back to Washington. Somewhere off one of these side roads, between here and the accident site, Harold Strong had had a cabin. He wished he had thought of finding the cabin and stopping by before he went to town.

Who are you kidding, Jake? What would you look for? A long golden hair on the bedspread? Perhaps a sterling silver cigarette case bearing Mata Hari's initials? You're no murder investigator. Keadle has undoubtedly been through that cabin with a fine-tooth comb. If there were clues he has them.

Thoroughly disgruntled, Jake drove at forty miles an hour along the two-lane highway toward Virginia. He didn't want to see Trooper Keadle in the rearview mirror with his red light flashing. Not too likely, of course. The odds were that Keadle was sitting in his cruiser right now in sight of Strong's cabin, hoping against hope that Jake would drop by and enter without using a key.

Keadle was no hick cop, even if he liked to play the role. He undoubtedly knew a murder when he tripped over one, and then the very next morning a man appeared—by the Lord Harry a vice admiral in the U.S. Navy—who wanted the investigation of the very recent death of a captain in that very same navy put on the back burner. And Keadle and the prosecutor went along. Or did they? And how did the FBI get involved?

But if it didn't happen like that, why did Henry tell that fairy story?

He glanced at the map he had jammed over the passenger's sun visor. The report said the accident happened four miles west of Capon Bridge, that little village Jake had stopped in this morning to get gas. The Shell station.

When he topped the mountain west of Capon Bridge he slowed and looked for the scenic overlook. There. On a whim he parked his car beside the trees so he could examine whatever marks remained after two months. As he got out of his car and surveyed the muddy gravel he knew it was hopeless. Two months of rain and snow and traffic pulling off to look at the valley had totally obliterated the marks that Keadle's report said were here after Strong's wreck.

He walked over to the edge. Some of the guardrails were obviously newer than the others. He looked down the embankment. Beer cans, trash, bare dirt, washed-out furrows. Well, it sure looked like a car might have been dragged up that slope some time back. The ground was soft and no plants had yet had a chance to hide the scars. No sense going down there and getting muddy.

Harold Strong died here. Jake had lied to the office girl—he had never met Strong. He stood now feeling foolishly morbid and half listening to a car laboring up the grade from Capon Bridge. The engine noise carried through the trees budding with spring green and echoed off the mountainside.

Henry had been telling the truth about one thing anyway: Harold Strong had been murdered. Not even a race car could come up that grade and around that curve fast enough to skid completely across this pullout and go over the edge. Not without help.

Jake glanced up as the car climbing the mountain went by. It was going about thirty miles per hour. The driver was watching the road. And the driver was Smoke Judy.

The commanding officer of Attack Squadron 128 (VA-128) nodded at Rita Moravia and Toad Tarkington, then picked up his phone. A yeoman appeared almost immediately to collect their orders for processing and a lieutenant commander was right behind. He led them into another office and gave each of them a manual on the A-6E and introduced them to their personal mentors, two lieutenants. "These two gentlemen are going to teach you to be credible A-6 crewmen in one week, starting right now. We'll get your luggage over to the BOQ and these guys will drop you there when they get finished tonight."

Toad's teacher was a prematurely bald extrovert from New England named Jenks, who began talking about the A-6E's electronic weapons system—radar, computers, inertial nav, forward-looking infrared and laser ranger-designator—in the car on the three-block trip to the building that housed the simulators. Toad listened silently with growing dread.

Jenks continued his monologue as he led Toad across the parking lot, lectured on at the security desk while Toad filled out a form to obtain a temporary visitor's pass, and didn't pause for breath as they climbed the stairs and went through a control room and across a catwalk inside a huge room to the simulator, a cockpit mounted on hydraulic rams. "So just make yourself comfortable here in the hot seat," Jenks said in summary, "and we'll move right on into the hardware."

Toad looked slowly around the cavernous room at the three other simulators. Then he looked into the cockpit. Like every military cockpit in the electronic age, it was filled with display screens, computer controls and information readouts in addition to all the usual gauges, dials, knobs, switches and warning lights. "I have a question."

"Shoot."

"How long is the normal syllabus to train a bombardier-navigator?"

"Eight months."

"And you're going to cram all that info into me in *one week*?"

"You look like a bright guy. That captain in Washington said you were motivated as hell."

"Grafton?"

"I didn't talk to him. The skipper did. Sit down and let's get at it." Jenks turned and shouted to the technician in the control room; "Okay, Art, fire it up."

People were streaming out of Jefferson Plaza at 4:30 when Jake passed through the main entrance on the way in. He was still in civilian clothes. He waited impatiently for the tardy elevator.

The secretary was still in the office along with several officers. What was her name? "Hi. What's happening?"

"Hello, Captain. Didn't expect to see you today."

"Yeah. Didn't think I'd make it back. Seen Commander Judy?"

"Oh, he was in for a little while this morning, then he said he had a meeting. Said he'd probably be gone the rest of the day."

Jake paused near the woman's desk. "Did he say where the meeting was?"

"No, sir."

"Was he here when you arrived this morning?"

She tried to remember. "Yessir, I think so. Oh, by the way, the computer wizard stopped by this afternoon to give you your brief on the office system. He said he was going to be working late, so if you're going to be around a while, I'll call him now and see if he can come over and do the brief."

"Sure. Call him."

Jake greeted the other officers and walked across the room to his office door. Two of his new subordinates stuck their heads in for a few pleasantries, then shoved off.

A pile of documents sat in the in basket. Jake flipped through the stuff listlessly. There was enough work here to keep him chained to this desk for a week, or maybe a month since he didn't know anything about most of the matters the letters and memos referred to. He would have to use the staff heavily.

The secretary appeared in his door. "The computer man will be here in a little while. His name is Kleinberg. Good night, Captain."

"Did you lock up everything?"

"No, sir. I thought you might want to look through some files."

"Sure. Good night."

Jake waited for the door to click shut, then went out into the room. He found Judy's desk and sat down. He stirred through a small pile of phone messages, just names and numbers. A thin appointment book with a black cover. He flipped through it slowly.

The days up until now were heavily annotated. Today's page was blank. He held the book at arm's length over the desk and dropped it. It fell with a splat.

Damn! He felt so frustrated.

Well, at least he knew most of Henry's once-upon-a-time story was true, though where that got him he had no idea. And he knew that Judy made a trip to West Virginia today. Why? To see Trooper Keadle or the prosecutor? To search Strong's cabin? Well, Judy was certainly going to be surprised to hear that Jake knew he was there. Or was he? Maybe he would tell Jake himself in the morning.

Jake turned on the office copy machine and while it was warming up stood and read the entries in Judy's calendar again carefully. Smoke seemed to have made a lot of notes about Karen. Karen who? Karen 472-3656, that's who. Why did he write her phone number down so often? Aha, because she had different phone numbers—at least four of them. And this guy Bob—lunch, tennis on Saturday, reminders that he called, to call Bob. Call DE. Call from RM. Drop car at garage. Commode broke. Smoke Judy seemed to jot down everything out of the ordinary. He was a detail man in a detail business.

When he had his copies Jake put the appointment book back on Judy's desk and went back to his little office. In a few moments he heard a knock on the door, so he heaved himself up and walked across the room to admit the visitor.

The man in civilian clothes who came in was slighty below medium height, built like a fireplug and just as bald. "Hi. Name's Kleinberg. From NSA. Computers." His voice boomed. Here was a man who could never whisper. In his left hand he carried a leather valise.

"I'm Grafton."

"Beg pardon," the man said as he reached out and tilted the bottom of Jake's security tag. He stared at it a few seconds, then glanced again at Jake's face. "Yep, you're Grafton, all right. Can't be too careful, y'know."

"Uh-huh."

"Let's look at the patient."

Jake led the way to his desk. "I don't know much about computers."

"No sweat. I know enough for both of us. When we're through, you're going to be able to make this thing sing and dance." Kleinberg turned on the computer. "See this prompt here? That's the sign-on prompt and you have to type in your secret password. This is a code that identifies you to the machine, which allows you access to certain files and only certain files. Security, y'know. Here's your password." He used a pencil on a sheet of paper and wrote, "Reverberation."

"How come I can't pick my own word?"

"We tried that on the second go-around. Everyone wanted to come up with something cute, except for the aviators, who all wanted to use their nicknames. You'd have thought they were ordering vanity license plates. So . . . Now type in your password."

Jake did so. The computer prompt moved from left to right, but the letters failed to appear.

"Now hit 'enter.' Uh-oh, the computer won't take it. So type it again and spell it right." This time the computer blinked to the next screen. "You only get two tries," Kleinberg advised. "If you are wrong both times, the computer will lock you out and you'll have to see me about getting back in."

"How can it lock me out if I haven't told it exactly who I am?"

"It locks out everyone who has access from the bank of monitors in this office." Kleinberg wrote another password on the paper: "Fallacy."

"This is the password that allows you access to files relating to the ATA, which is what I understand you are working on here in this shop. Type it in and hit 'enter.' " Jake obeyed. "Now, to call up the directory of the files you have access to due to your security clearance and job title, you have to type one more password." He wrote it down. "Matriarch."

After Jake entered this code, a long list of documents appeared on the screen. "Of course, if you already have the document number, you can type it right in and not bother calling up the directory with the matriarch code word. Got it?"

" 'Reverberation,' 'fallacy' and 'matriarch.' What was the first go-around on the code words?"

Kleinberg laughed. "Well, we used computer-generated random series of letters. They weren't words, just a series of letters. But people couldn't remember them and took to writing them down in notebooks, checkbooks and so forth. So we tried plan two. This is plan three."

Kleinberg took a lighter from his pocket and held the flame under the piece of paper on which he had written the code words.

It flared. Just before the fire reached his fingers, he dropped the paper on the plastic carpet protector under the chair and watched the remnant turn to ash, which he crushed with his shoe. Kleinberg rubbed his hands and smiled. "Now we begin." He spent the next hour showing Jake how to create, edit and access documents on this list. When he had finished answering Jake's questions, he flipped the machine off and gave Jake one of his cards. "Call me when you have questions, or ask one of the guys here who's been around a while."

"Uh-huh."

"Welcome to Washington." Kleinberg shook hands, hoisted his leather bag and left.

Jake began to lock away the papers on his desk. While he was here he might as well look again at that two-year-old book of Harold Strong's.

He opened the upper left drawer. The matchbooks and rubber bands and other stuff were still there, but the book wasn't. He looked in every drawer in the desk. Nope. It was gone.

Henry Jenks dropped Toad at the BOQ at 11 P.M. After he filled out the paperwork at the desk, Toad went up to his room and crashed.

The following day was a copy of the previous afternoon: an hour in the simulator, an hour at the blackboard, then back to the simulator. By noon he was navigating from one large radar-reflective target to another. In midafternoon he ran his first attack.

During all his hours in the simulator the canopy remained open and Jenks stood there beside him talking continuously, prompting him, pointing out errors. Running the system in the simulator wasn't too difficult with Jenks right there.

Toad wasn't fooled.

At five hundred feet above hostile terrain on a stormy night with the tracers streaking over the canopy and the missile warning lights flashing, this bombardier-navigator business was going to be a whole different ball game. The pilot would be slamming the plane around, pulling on that stick like it was the lever to open heaven's gate. And the BN had to sit here delicately tweaking the radar and infrared and nursing the computer and laser while trying not to vomit into his oxygen mask. Toad knew. He had been there in the backseat of an F-14. The best way to learn this stuff was by repetition. Every task, every adjustment, the correction for every failure

—it all had to be automatic. If you had to think about it you didn't know it and you sure as hell wouldn't remember it when you were riding this bucking pig up the devil's asshole.

At five in the evening Jenks drove him back to the BOQ. "Tonight you study the NATOPS." NATOPS—Naval Air Training and Operating Procedures—was the Book on the airplane, the navy equivalent to the air force Dash One manual. "Learn the emergency procedures. Tomorrow you and Moravia will be in the simulator together. We'll run some attacks and pop some emergencies and failures. The next day you fly the real airplane. Study hard."

"Thanks, sadist."

"You're all right, Tarkington, even if you are a fighter puke."

Toad slammed the car door and stomped into the BOQ. He was whipped, drained. Maybe he ought to go jogging to clean the pipes. In his room he changed into his sweat togs. The wind coming in off Puget Sound had a pronounced bite and the sun was already setting, so he added a second heavy sweatshirt.

He was leaning into a post supporting the roof over the walkway leading to the officers' club when a gray navy pickup pulled up in front of the BOQ and dropped Rita Moravia. She was wearing an olive-drab flight suit and flight boots.

"If you're going running," she called, "will you wait for me?"

"Sure." Toad continued to stretch his right leg, the one with the pins in it. He hopped around and trotted in place a few steps. The leg was ready. On the grass was a bronze bust: Lieutenant Mike McCormick, A-6 pilot killed over North Vietnam. The BOQ and officers' club were named for him.

Toad was standing beside the bust watching the A-6s in the landing pattern overhead and listening to the throaty roar of their engines when Moravia came out. She had her hair pulled back into a ponytail. "Which way do you want to run?" she asked.

"I dunno. How about north along the beach?" They started off. "Were you flying today?"

"Yes. Twice." She picked up the pace to a fast trot.

"How'd you like it?"

"Old airframe, not as fast and agile as the Hornet, of course, but with better range and more lifting capacity. More complex." An A-6 went over and she waited for the roar to fade. "It's a nice plane to fly."

On the western side of the road was a beach littered with driftwood and, beyond, the placid surface of the sound. Just visible in the fading glow of the sunset was an island five or six miles away— it was hard to tell. Silhouettes of mountains stood against the sky to the southwest. "It's pretty here, isn't it?"

"Oh yes. Wait till you see it from the air."

"Why'd you get into flying anyway?"

She shot him a hard glance and picked up the pace. He stayed with her. She was going too fast for conversation. The paved road ended and they were on gravel when she said, "Four miles be enough?"

"Yep." Well, he had stepped on it that time, got it out and dragged it in the dirt and tromped all over it. What's a pretty girl like you doing in this dirty, sweaty business anyway, sweetie? Ye gods, Toad, next you'll be asking about her sign.

On the inbound leg they stopped running several blocks short of the BOQ and walked to cool down. "I got into flying because I thought it would be a challenge," Rita said, watching him.

Toad just nodded. In the lobby she asked, "Want to change and get some dinner?"

"Thanks anyway. I gotta study."

As he showered Toad realized that somewhere on the run he had jettisoned his nascent plan to bed Rita Moravia. The Good Lord just doesn't have any mercy for you, Toad, my man. Not the tiniest pinch.

6

The admiral can see you in thirty minutes, sir."

"Thanks." Jake Grafton cradled the phone and doodled on his legal pad. It was almost 10:30 and Smoke Judy was at his desk. He had said good morning to Jake and spent an hour on the phone, and now seemed to be busy on the computer with a report, but he hadn't mentioned his sojourns of yesterday. Jake had toyed with the idea of questioning Judy about where he was yesterday, then decided against it. Whatever answer Judy gave, truth or lie, what would that prove? Would a lie incriminate him? In what? A murder? Espionage? If Judy told the truth, what would the truth be? That he went to West Virginia yesterday—so what? And if he denied it—what then? No, Jake didn't know enough to even ask an intelligent question.

Vice Admiral Henry, however, was in a more interesting position. His fairy tale about deflecting a murder investigation left him vulnerable. Vulnerable to what? To more questions. He would have to answer reasonable questions or . . . ? Or?

I can't recognize truth when I hear it, Jake mused. What the hell kind of job is this? Can I trust the admiral?

Do I have a choice? He tossed the pencil on the desk and rubbed his eyes. He knew the answer to that one. He had no choice at all. He stood and stretched. His doodles caught his eye. Airplanes. Gliders. Long wings.

In front of the breezeway between JP-1 and JP-2, he caught the shuttle bus and rode it over to the Pentagon. The chief offered him a cup of coffee, which he accepted. Then he waved him in to see Henry, who was busy locking his desk and office safe.

"Good morning, sir."

"Morning. Don't sit. We're going to a meeting with SECNAV."

"Okay." Jake had never met F. George Ludlow, but he had heard a lot about him. Scion of an old New England family—was there any other kind?—Ludlow was in his early forties, a Vietnam vet with a B.S. from Yale and a business doctorate from Harvard. He had spent ten years knocking around the gray-suit defense think tanks before being tapped as Secretary of the Navy three years ago by his father-in-law, Royce Caplinger, the Secretary of Defense. Nepotism, fumed the Senate Democrats, but they confirmed the nomination anyway: Ludlow's credentials were as bluechip as his family connections and dividends from the family investment trusts.

"What this meeting about, sir?" Jake asked as he and the admiral walked the outer ring of the Pentagon—the E-ring—toward Ludlow's office.

"Don't know. When Ludlow wants you, he summons you—now."

It was common knowledge that Ludlow had vigorous hands on the throttle and helm of the navy. He had firm ideas about what ships and weapons systems the navy needed, how they should be acquired, how they should be employed. With his insider's knowledge of Washington and the upper reaches of the defense establishment he outargued most admirals. Those he couldn't win over he shuffled off to sinecures or retirement. Unlike the usual dilettante who spent a year or two as a service secretary on his way to a bright political future or the vice presidency of a major defense contractor, Ludlow behaved exactly like a man whose present job was the fulfillment of a lifelong quest. If Ludlow had any other political or business ambitions, no hint of them had percolated down to Jake's level. His saving grace, or so it appeared to the rank and file, was his strong commitment to the navy as an institution, to its people and its traditions. This was probably one of the reasons for unease at the flag level, since the admirals were unwilling to defer to anyone as keeper of the faith, the role in which they cast themselves.

The corridor in which the secretary's office was located was decorated for the general public. Large oil portraits of naval heroes of the past were prominently displayed; Farragut, Dewey, Halsey and many others. The old admirals stared dourly at Jake and Vice Admiral Henry as they went to their appointment to discuss the navy of the future.

Ludlow's large office was paneled in dark wood, the real thing, not veneer, Jake noticed as he took his first, curious look—and nautical memorabilia were everywhere, on the desk, the credenza, the little sitting desk. Oil paintings of famous naval scenes—also original, Jake noted—adorned the walls. The chairs were black leather. One of them was occupied by a fat gent in his mid-sixties whose skin looked as tough as the chair covering. Jake recognized him from his picture—Senator Hiram Duquesne, chairman of the Senate Armed Services Committee. Ludlow was behind his desk and didn't rise from his chair.

"You gentlemen know the senator," Ludlow said after Admiral Henry had introduced Jake.

Duquesne eyed Jake speculatively. "Aren't you the pilot that strapped on El Hakim last year?"

"Yessir."

"Sit down, gentlemen. Please." Ludlow gestured to the chairs. Jake ended up on Henry's left, Duquesne on the admiral's right. Ludlow's executive assistant sat on the sofa with a legal pad on his lap, ready to take notes.

The senator and the two naval officers faced the secretary across his massive mahogany desk strewn with paper. Ludlow had one leg draped over his chair arm, revealing hairy skin in the gap between the top of his sock and his trouser leg. In his hands he held a rifle cartridge that still contained a bullet. He worked the cartridge back and forth between his fingers as he spoke to Jake. "Senator Duquesne wanted to meet you when I informed him you would be doing the testing and evaluation of the ATA prototypes."

"Now, as I understand it, George, you people are not going to do your usual T and E routine," Senator Duquesne said. T and E was Test and Evaluation.

"No way to keep the lid on or meet our time goals if we did it the usual way."

"You a test pilot?" Duquesne shot at Jake.

"No, sir."

Ludlow's leg came off the arm of his chair. "He's an attack

pilot," the secretary said mildly, "one of the very best we have. He knows carrier aviation as well as anyone in uniform."

"What d'ya know about stealth?" the senator demanded.

"Very little, sir, but I'm learning."

"Horse puckey! What does the navy need for an attack plane at the turn of the century? What about range, payload, survivability, maintainability? How much should the navy pay?"

"I—" Jake began, but Ludlow was also talking: "Senator, *policy* is my—"

Senator Duquesne raised his voice. He thundered at Ludlow: "I'll say this again with these gentlemen present. I'm not happy about this whole thing, George. Not happy. You have a program here that you will want funded for three hundred and fifty airplanes at about fifty million each, seventeen and a half billion dollars' worth, and you intend to make the decision on which prototype to buy based on Captain Grafton's quick and dirty recommendation?"

"You overstate it, Senator. We—being me, CNO, Vice Admirals Henry and Dunedin—we propose to make a recommendation to SECDEF based on the needs of the navy. We will look closely at Captain Grafton's evaluation to help us determine which of the two prototypes best meets those needs. And his evaluation will be quick but it won't be dirty." The senator twisted in his chair. The secretary continued, relentless. "No captain determines the needs of the navy, Senator. I do that. The President and SECDEF—"

Duquesne stopped him with an upraised palm. "Don't lecture me, George. And don't patronize me! Major weapons systems procurement gets shrouded in secrecy, taken out of the normal channels where Congress can look things over, and major decisions get made on the basis of one document generated by one of your junior subordinates which no one can confirm or refute. And you tell me to *relax*? Seventeen *billion* dollars for a plane that may or may not be adequately tested, that may or may not do what we're buying it to do? Plus ten more billion for spare parts and simulators and all the rest of it. No dirt, huh? Goddamnit, Ludlow, I don't trust you any further than I could throw a scalded cat! You're trying to make Congress a goddamn rubber stamp!"

Ludlow leaned forward in his chair. "I never said for you to relax! You people *agreed* to the classification level of these black stealth projects! You people *understood* the problems involved and approved the administrative shortcuts! Now you—"

"I said *don't patronize me!* And quit *pointing* that fucking bullet at me!"

Henry rose hastily and Jake followed. "Talk to you later, Mr. Secretary," he said, and Ludlow nodded as he fired another volley at the senator.

"Jesus," Jake muttered when they reached the hallway and the door closed behind them.

"Yeah," the admiral agreed.

"How come Duquesne is so upset when the decision hasn't been made?"

"That's just it. One of the prototypes was manufactured in his home state. He's fought hard on the Hill for stealth and he wants his plane to be chosen and the air force didn't buy it. Now, if the navy doesn't . . . Well, you get the idea."

"Uh-huh," Jake said as the full dimensions of his new position came into much better focus. So Henry had asked for him to run the ATA project, eh? No doubt his name had been discussed with Ludlow and the Chief of Naval Operations as well as Vice Admiral Dunedin—NAVAIR. They could praise him to the skies for his report or ease him right out of the navy. They needed a man they could dispose of if necessary. And they found me, Jake thought bitterly. A gilt-edge reputation, my ass!

In Henry's office, Jake said calmly, "Better make sure your anti-bugging devices are on."

The admiral did so while eyeing Jake. When he was seated, Jake said, "I took a little drive yesterday, sir. Saw a state trooper up in West Virginia named Keadle. Read an accident report."

"So?"

"Passed one of the guys from my shop on my way back here yesterday afternoon. He was on his way to West Virginia."

"Oh?"

"Admiral, why don't you tell me what really happened in West Virginia after Harold Strong was killed?"

"Are you suggesting I haven't?"

"I can't do my job, sir, unless you play straight with me. I play straight with you, you have to play straight with me."

Admiral Henry looked out his window a while, examined his fingernails and finally directed his gaze back to Jake. "I think you had better discuss any concerns you have with Admiral Dunedin." He picked up a sheet of paper and began to scan it. The interview was over.

"Aye aye, sir," Jake said, and left the room. He retrieved his hat in the outer office and caught the shuttle back to Crystal City.

As the little bus wound its way from the parking lot, Jake looked back at the Pentagon. It appeared low and massive from this perspective. Endless rows of windows. It also looked gray under this overcast.

Admiral Dunedin was in conference. Jake didn't get in to see him until almost 3 P.M. He got right to it. "I went to West Virginia yesterday to see what I could find out about Harold Strong's death. On the way back here I passed one of the people from my shop heading the other way."

"Who?" said Dunedin, apparently genuinely curious.

"Smoke Judy."

"How about that," Dunedin muttered.

"Admiral, I'm a little baffled. Vice Admiral Henry briefed me on some of the events surrounding Strong's death, but this morning when I mentioned this incident to him, he didn't even ask who it was from my office that passed me. I get the distinct impression I'm being mushroomed."

Dunedin lifted an eyebrow, then apparently thought better of it and went back to deadpan. He apparently knew about mushrooms: you kept them in the dark and fed them shit. "I guess everyone is a little baffled," he said carefully. "Strong's death was a tragedy. Nothing *we* can do about it, though."

"Well, I could sure use a little more infor—"

"Who couldn't? But I don't have any information I can share with you. Sorry." His tone made the apology a mere pleasantry. Before Jake could reply, he said, "There's a meeting at sixteen-thirty hours in the Under Secretary of the Navy's office on next year's budget. We've got a billion dollars for ATA buried in there under carrier modernization and enhancement. You go to the meeting and represent me. If they try to cut that line item or slice it down in any way, you call me."

"Yessir." The admiral selected a report from his in basket and began to read. Jake left.

After he told the secretary that he was going to a meeting, he walked to the officer personnel office, where he had to wait until two other officers had finished before he could talk to the chief petty officer. "Do you have my service record in here?"

"Last four digits of your social security number, sir?"

"Oh-six-oh-seven."

It took the chief just half a minute to pull it from the drawer.

"Chief, how about you ginning up a request for retirement for my signature?"

The chief yeoman's eyes showed his surprise. "Okay, sir, if that's what you want. It's gotta be effective on the first day of a month between four and six months from now."

Jake eyed the wall calendar. "September first. When can I sign it?"

"Monday okay?"

"See you then."

"Any particular reason you want stated, sir?"

"The usual. Whatever you usually say."

Dashing the four blocks to Dr. Arnold's office after her eleven o'clock class on Friday was always a hassle for Callie. A student or two usually buttonholed her to clarify a point or comment made during class and it took several minutes to satisfy them without being rude. Then came the four-block march which crossed two avenues hub to hub with noon traffic.

She was perspiring slightly when Arnold's receptionist nodded at her. Two minutes early. Of course, a few minutes late wouldn't hurt, but Arnold ended the sessions precisely at ten minutes before the hour and the fee was $105 regardless. She sank onto the couch and once again tried to decide if the fifty minutes was worth the cost.

Forget the money. What are the important things to discuss during this session? She was trying to arrange her thoughts when the door opened and Dr. Arnold beckoned. He was of medium height, in his late thirties, and wore a neat brown beard. "He looks like Sigmund Freud before he got old and twisted," Jake had grumped once. Above the beard this morning was a small, thoughtful smile.

"Good morning, Callie." He held the door open for her.

"Hello." She sank into the stuffed armchair across from him, the middle of the three "guest" chairs. When he used to come Jake always sat on her left, near the window, while she always used this chair. For a brief moment she wondered what Arnold made of her continued use of this chair although Jake wasn't here.

After a few preliminary comments, she stated, "Jake went back to work this Monday," and paused, waiting for his reaction.

Arnold prompted, "How has that gone this week?"

"He seems enthusiastic, and somewhat relieved. They have him working on a new airplane project and he hasn't said much about it. If that's what he's working on. I think he's disappointed, but it doesn't show. He's hiding it well." She thought about it. "That's unusual. He's always been stoic at work—his colleagues have told me that he usually shows little emotion at the office—but he's never been like that at home. I can read him very well."

Dr. Arnold, Benny to all his patients, looked up from his notes. "Last weekend, did you threaten him?"

Callie's head bobbed. "I suppose." She swallowed hard and felt her eyes tearing up. She bit her lower lip. "I never did that before. Never again!" She moved to the chair near the window, Jake's chair, and looked out. Trees just budding stood expectantly in the pale spring sun. Jake had sat here all winter and looked at the black, bare, upthrusted limbs. And now spring was finally here.

She should never have said those things, about leaving him. She could never do it. She loved him too much to even consider it. But it was so hard last fall, after she thought him dead and her life in ashes. When she heard he was still alive the euphoria swept her to heights she didn't believe possible. The subsequent descent from rapture to reality had been torturous.

An officer from the CNO's office had escorted her to Bethesda Naval Hospital the morning after Jake was flown back from Greece. She had expected—thinking about it now, she didn't know just what she expected. But her hopes were so high and the officer who drove her tried gently to prepare her.

His face was still swollen and mottled, his eyes mere slits, his tongue raw from where he had chewed on it. His eyes—those piercing gray eyes that had melted her a thousand times—they lay unfocused in the shapeless mass of flesh that was his face as IVs dripped their solution into his arms. A severe concussion, the doctor said gently. Jake had taken a lot of Gs, more Gs than any man could be expected to survive. Capillaries had burst under the tremendous strain. And he was grossly dehydrated, unable to take water. Slowly Callie began to understand. Brain damage. Bleeding in the frontal lobe, where memory and personality resided. Oh, she assured herself a hundred times that he would be the same—that life would never play them a dirty, filthy trick like that, that God was in his heaven, that the man who loved her and she loved with all her soul would get well and . . . He had gotten well. Almost—

He's quieter, more subdued, as if he's someplace else . . . or thinking of something he can't share.

"Do you think he has forgotten?"

The words startled her. She had been musing aloud.

"I don't know. He says he can't remember much about it, and that's probably true. But he stops there and doesn't say what he does remember."

Arnold nodded. For three months in this office Jake had said nothing of the flight that led to his injury. "What of his decision to die?"

Callie stared at the psychologist. "You think he made that decision?"

"You know he did." Arnold's eyes held her. "He decided to ram the transport. The odds of surviving such a collision were very small. Jake knew that. He's a professional military aviator; he had to know the probably outcome of a ramming." The doctor's shoulders moved ever so slightly. "He was willing to die to kill his enemies."

After a moment Callie nodded.

"*You* must come to grips with that. It was a profound moment in his life, one he apparently doesn't wish to dwell on or try to remember. The complex human being that he is, that's how he chooses to live with it. Now you must come to grips with his decision and you must learn to live with it."

"Don't many men in combat come to that moment?"

"I think not." Benny tugged at his beard. "The literature—it's hard to say. Most men—I suspect—most men facing a situation that may cause their death who do go forward probably do so without thought. The situation draws them onward, the situation and their training and their own private concept of manhood. But in that cockpit—Jake evaluated the danger and saw no other alternative and decided to go forward. Willingly. To accept the inevitable consequences, one of which would be his death." He continued to worry the strands of hair on his chin.

"There's a verse in the Bible," Callie said, her chin quivering. " 'Greater love has no man than this, that a man lay down his life for his friends.' "

"Aha! If only you believed that!"

"I do," she said, trying to convince herself, and turned back to the window. Other husbands went off to work every morning, they had regular jobs, they came home nights and weekends and life was safe and sane. Of course, people die in car wrecks and you read about airliner crashes. But those things don't happen to people like me!

Why couldn't Jake have found a safe, sane, regular job, with an office and a company car and a nice, predictable future? Damn him, she had waited all these years for the sword to drop. Those memorial services whenever someone was killed—she always went with Jake to those. The widow, the kids, the condolences, the organ music. But it wouldn't happen to Jake—oh no! He's a good pilot, real good, the other men say, *too good* to ever smear himself all over some farmer's potato field, *too good* to ever leave her sitting alone in the chapel with the organ wheezing and some fat preacher spouting platitudes and everyone filing past and muttering well-meaning nonsense. Damn you, Jake. *Damn you!*

Arnold passed her a Kleenex and she used it on her eyes. He held out the box and she took several and blew her nose.

"Next week, perhaps we can talk about that little girl you want to adopt?"

Callie nodded and tried to arrange her face.

"Thank you for coming today." He smiled gravely. She rose and he held the door for her, then eased it shut as she paused at the receptionist's desk to write a check.

He opened her file and made some notes. After a glance at his watch, he picked up his phone and dialed. On the third ring a man answered. One word: "Yes."

"She was here today," Arnold said without preliminaries. "He's going to be working on a new airplane project, she says." He continued, reading from his notes.

It wasn't until the A-6 was taxiing toward the duty runway for takeoff that the incongruity of the whole situation struck Toad Tarkington. The plane thumped and wheezed and swayed like a drunken dowager as it rolled over the expansion joints in the concrete. He had been so busy with the computer and Inertial Navigation System while they sat in the chocks that he had had no time to look around and become accustomed to this new cockpit. Now as he took it all in a wry grin twisted his lips under his oxygen mask.

Rita Moravia sat in the pilot's seat on his left in the side-by-side cockpit. Her seat was slightly higher than his and several inches further forward, but due to her size her head was on the same level as his. Not an inch of her skin was exposed. Her helmet, green visor and oxygen mask encased her head, and her body and arms were sheathed in a green flight suit, gloves, steel-toed black boots. Over all this she wore a G suit, torso harness and survival vest, to which was attached an inflatable life vest. Toad wore exactly the same outfit, but the thought that the beautiful Rita Moravia was hidden somewhere under the flight gear in the pilot's seat struck him as amusing. One would never even know she was a woman except for the sound of her voice on the intercom system, the ICS. "Takeoff checklist," she said crisply, her voice all business.

Toad read the items one by one and she gave the response to each after checking the appropriate switch or lever or gauge as the plane rolled along. The taxiway seemed like a little highway going nowhere in particular; the concrete runways on the right were hidden by the grassy swell of a low hill. To the left was a gravel road, and paralleling that the beach, where the Puget Sound waves lapped at the land. The water in the sound appeared glassy today. Above them was blue sky, a pleasant change from the clouds that had moved restlessly from west to east since Toad and Rita arrived on the island. Even Mother Nature was cooperating. The background noise of the two idling engines, a not unpleasant drone, murmured of latent power. They promised flight. Toad breathed deeply and exhaled slowly. He had been on the ground too long.

Clearance copied and read back, Toad asked the tower for clearance to take off. It was readily granted. The traffic pattern was momentarily empty. Rita Moravia rolled the A-6 onto the runway and braked to a stop. With her left hand she advanced the throttles to the stops as Toad flipped the IFF to transmit. The IFF encoded the plane's radar blip on all air control radars.

The engines wound up slowly at first, then quickened to a full-throated roar that was loud even in the cockpit. The nose of the machine dipped as the thrust compressed the nose-gear oleo, almost as if the plane were crouching, gathering strength for its leap into the sky. Moravia waggled the stick gently, testing the controls one more time, while she waited for the engine temperatures to peak. Outside the plane, Toad knew, the roar of the two engines could be heard for several miles. No doubt the flight crewmen on the ramps near the hangars were pausing, listening as the roar reached them, their attention momentarily captured by the bird announcing its readiness for flight. Finally satisfied, Rita Moravia released the brakes.

The nose oleo rebounded and the A-6 began to roll, gathering

speed, faster and faster and faster. The needle on the airspeed indicator came off the peg . . . 80 . . . 100 . . . faster and faster as
the wheels thumped and the machine swayed gently over the uneven concrete . . . 130 . . . 140 . . . the nose came off the
ground and Moravia stopped the stick's rearward movement with
a gentle nudge.

As the broad, swept wings bit into the air the main wheels left
the ground and the thumps and bumps ceased.

Moravia slapped the gear handle up and, passing 170 knots,
raised the flaps and slats. Climbing and accelerating, the Intruder
shot over the little town of Oak Harbor bellowing its song. Upward
they flew, upward, into the smooth gentle sky.

He was flying again. It seemed—somehow it was strange and bittersweet all at once. He hadn't thought about his last flight in
months, but now as the engines moaned and the plane swam
through the air, memories of his last flight with Jake Grafton in an
F-14 over the Med flooded over Toad Tarkington. There was fear
in those memories. He fought to push them out of his mind as he
twiddled the knobs to optimize the radar presentation and checked
the computer readouts. He glanced outside. The peaks of the Cas-
cade Mountains were sliding by beneath the plane. The steep crags
were gray in those places where the clouds and snow didn't hide
their naked slopes.

Rita Moravia had the Intruder level at Flight Level 230—23,000
feet. Toad concentrated on the equipment on the panel in front of
him. As he tried desperately to remember all that his instructor
had told him, he sneaked a glance at Moravia. She sat in her seat
calmly scanning the sky and the instrument panel. She had engaged the autopilot and was watching it fly the plane. Now she
adjusted the bug on the HSI, the rotating compass ring. She had
the Yakima TACAN dialed in. Now she toggled the switch that
moved her seat up a millimeter and stretched lazily. "Nice plane,
huh?" she said when her left hand once more came to rest on the
throttles, where her ICS button was.

Toad fumbled with his ICS button, which he keyed with his left
foot. "Yeah. Fucking super."

"How's the system?"

"Looks okay to me, as if I knew."

"Found Yakima yet?"

He ignored the question as he studied the radar. The city was still seventy miles away according to the TACAN. There it was on the radar, right under the cursor cross hairs, just a blob of solid return amid a whole scopeful of return from hills and ridges and houses and barns.

Yeah, Toad, you better figure out how to find a city in all this mess or this little flight is gonna be a disaster. The whole essence of the bombardier's art was interpreting this jumble of return on the radar scope. And Jake Grafton and those other A-6 perverts demanded he pick it up in just a week! Well, he'd show them! If those attack weenies can figure out this shit in eight months, a week will be about right for the old Horny Toad. After all, this worn-out flying dump truck—

Moravia was asking Seattle Center if they could proceed direct to the start of the low-level route. Toad cycled the steering to that point and examined the radar carefully. Thank God the guys at VA-128 had picked a town on the Columbia River to start the route. Even a blind fighter RIO—Radar Intercept Officer—could find that. Or should be able to find it with the aid of the radarscope photographs that were included in the navigation package for this route. He arranged the stack of photographs on his kneeboard and compared the first one to the live presentation on the radar scope. Yep!

They had passed the third checkpoint on the navigation route and were somewhere in central Oregon flying at 360 knots true, 335 indicated, 500 feet above the ground, when Toad's savage mood began to improve. He was identifying the checkpoints without difficulty, no doubt because they were ridiculously prominent features in the landscape ahead, but he was finding them. The system seemed to be working as advertised and the INS was tight, tight as a virgin's . . .

For the first time he became aware of Moravia's smooth, confident touch on the controls. She flew the plane with a skill that belied her inexperience. Toad watched her handle the plane. The stick barely moved as the plane rose and fell to follow the ground contour and her thumb flicked the trim button automatically. She was good. The airspeed needle seemed glued to the 335-knot tic on the dial. "You're a pretty good pilot," he said on the ICS.

"Just navigate," she replied, not even glancing at him.

Another casual slap in the chops. Goddamn women! He placed his face against the black hood that shielded the radar scope and studiously ignored her.

The plane approached the Columbia River again from the south down a long, jagged canyon that ran almost straight north out of central Oregon. Stealing glances from the radar, out the right side of the airplane Toad saw a harsh, arid landscape of cliffs and stone pillars, spectacular monuments to the power of wind and water and the vastness of time. The almost vertical rock surfaces produced crisp, sharp images on the radar screen. He examined the infrared display. The infrared images were from a sensor mounted on a turret on the bottom of the aircraft's nose, immediately in front of the nose-gear door. The sides of the rock toward the sun looked almost white on the IR scope, which was mounted above the radar scope and was also shielded from extraneous light by the black flexible hood projecting from the instrument panel.

The navigation checkpoint to enter the navy's target range at Boardman, Oregon, was a grain silo and barn on top of a cliff near the lower reaches of this canyon. The cursors—cross hairs positioned by the computer on the radar screen—rested near a prominent blip. Toad turned up the magnification on the infrared as he moved the cursors to the blip. Yep. That was the barn all right.

Over the barn he cycled the steering to the initial point for the run-in to the target and called the range on radio.

"November Julie 832, you're cleared in."

Rita let the plane drift up to 1,500 feet above the ground. They had left the cliffs and canyons behind them and flew now over almost flat, gently rolling terrain that was used for dry-land farming. Following a printed checklist on his kneeboard, Toad set the switches in the cockpit for bombing. Six blue twenty-five-pound Mark 76 practice bombs hung on a rack under the right wing, Station Four. Each of these little bombs contained a smoke charge that would mark the spot of impact. The A-6 crossed the initial point, the IP, and Rita swung it toward the target ten miles east.

The target lay on the south side of the Columbia River in flat, dry, treeless country. The run-in line was marked by a dirt road on the ground, but neither Toad nor Rita paid any attention. During the minute and forty seconds it took the Intruder to traverse the ten miles from the IP to the target, Toad was absorbed in getting the cursors precisely on the radar reflector that marked the target bull's-eye, checking the computer and inertial readouts, using the infrared for visual ID, locking up the target with the laser ranger-designator, then checking the information the computer received to make sure it was valid. Finally he put the system into attack.

Even though the practice bombs lacked laser seekers, the laser in the nose turret would give the computer more precise range and angular information than the radar could. Rita was equally busy flying the plane and centering the steering commands on the Analog Display Indicator, the ADI, immediately in front of her.

The infrared and laser stayed locked to the radar reflector on the little tower that constituted the target bull's-eye even after bomb release as the nose turret rotated. In the cockpit Toad watched the picture on the infrared display change as the plane passed over the target. He was looking at an inverted picture of the tower when he saw the puff of smoke near the base sent up by the practice bomb. An excellent hit.

On the downwind leg Toad raised his helmet visor and swabbed his face with his gloved hands. This was work. The plane was headed west parallel to the Columbia River. Rita scanned the sky for light aircraft.

"832, your hit twenty-five feet at six o'clock."

"Roger." Toad made a note on his kneeboard. "On the next run," he said to Rita, "let's do 500 knots."

"Okay."

At the increased speed Toad had only about sixty-five seconds from the IP to bomb release, so he had to work faster. The plane bounced in the warm afternoon thermals. In wartime the plane would race in toward its target at full throttle. The air could be full of flak and enemy radar signals probing the darkness to lock them up for a missile shot. Today over this Oregon prairie under a brilliant sun, Toad could visualize how it would be. Sweat trickled down his forehead and into his eyes as he manipulated the switches and knobs of the equipment. He got the bomb off but he was struggling. He would need a lot of practice to gain real proficiency, and today the equipment was working perfectly, no one was shooting.

"A thousand feet this time, as fast as she'll go."

"Roger," Rita said.

As fast as she'll go turned out to be 512 knots indicated. On the next run they came in at five hundred feet, then four hundred, then three.

On the downwind leg before their last run, Toad flipped the radar switch from transmit to standby. The picture disappeared from the scope. A stealth bomber that beaconed its position with radar emissions would have a short life and fiery end. The infrared was passive, emitting nothing.

As they crossed the IP inbound, Toad found the infrared was still on the bull's-eye tower. With the help of the inertial, the computer had kept the cursors there and the infrared was slaved to the cursors. He turned the laser on early and stepped the computer into attack.

Yes, it could be done, and with practice, done well. Moisture in the air would degrade the IR, of course, but you couldn't have everything.

As they crossed the Columbia climbing northwest, the spotting tower gave them a call. "We didn't spot your last hit. Maybe the smoke charge didn't go off."

Toad checked the computer readouts. Rita had been eleven mils off on steering at the moment of weapon release. Toad couldn't resist. He informed her of that fact. She said nothing. "Still," Toad added magnanimously, "an okay job." He was feeling rather pleased with himself.

"For a woman."

"I didn't say that, Miss Thin Skin. I said an okay job."

"Look at the ordnance panel, ace." Toad did so. He had inadvertently selected Station Three instead of Station Four for the last bomb run. The practice bombs were on Station Four, and the last bomb was undoubtedly still there. Station Three—the belly station —had been empty, thank God! Oh damn. And good ol' Rita had sat there and watched him do it and hadn't squeaked a word! "Call Center and get our clearance back to Whidbey," she said now, her voice deadpan.

Toad reached for the radio panel.

Terry Franklin was watching television when he heard the telephone ring. He listened for the second ring, but it didn't come. He sat staring at the TV screen, no longer hearing the words or seeing the picture.

His wife had taken the kids to the mall. She had left only a half hour ago. How long would she be?

He was trying to decide just how much time he had when the phone rang again. He felt his muscles tense. Only one ring.

He turned off the TV and got his coat from the closet. He felt in his pocket for the keys to the old Datsun. They were there. He snapped off the living-room lights and peered between the curtains at the street. No one out there.

Ring, pause, ring, pause, ring . . .

Three rings. The drop on G Street. He would have to hurry to beat Lucy and the kids home. He remembered to lock the door behind him.

Matilda Jackson was sixty-seven years old and she was fed up. Five years ago she retired from the law firm where she had worked as a clerk-typist for twenty-six years. Seventeen months ago she had made the last payment on her mortgage. The house wasn't much—a run-down row house in a run-down neighborhood—but by God it was hers. And it was all she could afford on her social security income and the $93.57 she got every month from the law firm's pension plan.

The house had been something when she and Charlie bought it in 1958, and Charlie had been a good worker inside and outside, keeping everything painted and nice and the sidewalk swept. But he had died of diabetes—had it really been sixteen years ago?—after they amputated his feet and his liver got bad.

Poor Charlie, thank God he can't see this neighborhood now, it'd break his heart. Everything gone to rack and ruin, trash everywhere, and those kids selling dope in the house right across the street, the house where ol' lady Melvin, the preacher's widow, used to live. Some old man from New Orleans was in there now: she didn't know his name.

Mrs. Jackson heard a car stop outside and peered through the window. Four young men dressed fit to kill stood on the sidewalk looking around. Mrs. Jackson reached for her camera, an ancient Brownie, but she had loaded it with some of that new film the man at the drugstore said would take pictures without a flash. When she got the camera ready and pointed through the gap in the drapes she could see only two men. The other two must have gone inside.

Damn those cops anyway.

She had told those detectives that Melvin's was a crack house and nothing had happened. They weren't going to pay much attention to a fat old black lady, no way. She had seen that in their hard eyes as they looked up and down the street at the boarded-up windows and the trash and that worthless, shiftless Arnold Spivey sitting on Wilson's stoop drinking from a bottle in a paper bag.

She was going to get pictures. They would have to do something if she had pictures. And if they didn't do anything, she would send the photos to that neighborhood watch group or maybe even the newspapers. Leaving old people to watch their neighborhood rot and the dope peddlers take over—they would have to do something about pictures.

She snapped the camera at the two men on the sidewalk, slick loose-jointed dudes with sports coats and pimp hats with wide brims and flashy hatbands. The license plate of that big car would be in both photos.

Here comes someone. A white man, walking bold as brass after dark in a neighborhood as black as printer's ink, a neighborhood where the kids would rip off your arm to get your Timex watch. She squinted. Late fifties or early sixties, chunky, wearing a full-length raincoat and a little trilby hat. Oh yes, he went by earlier this evening, just walking and looking. She hadn't paid much attention then, but here he is, back again. She pointed the camera and clicked the shutter. The two dudes on the opposite sidewalk by the big car were watching him, but he was ignoring them.

Now what did he just do? Stuffed something in that hollow iron fence post as he walked by.

Why did he do that? My God, the street is full of trash; why didn't he just throw it down like everyone else does?

The two men who had gone into the crack house came out and they and their compatriots piled in the car and left, laughing and peeling rubber. Mrs. Jackson got more photos of them, then busied herself in the kitchen making tea since the street seemed quiet now.

She was sipping tea in the darkened living room and looking through the curtain gap when a haggard black woman in dilapidated blue jeans and a torn sweatshirt staggered around the corner and along the sidewalk to the crack house. She struggled up the steps to the stoop. The door opened before she even knocked. Mrs. Jackson didn't bother taking her picture; she was one of the regulars, a crack addict who Mrs. Jackson suspected didn't have long to live. Mrs. Blue next door had said her name was Mandy and she had heard she was doing tricks under the Southeast Freeway.

Nobody gave a damn. About Mandy or Mrs. Jackson or Mrs. Blue or any of them. Just a bunch of poor niggers down in the sewer.

Wonder what that white man stuffed in that fence post? Something to do with that crack house, no doubt. Maybe he's a judge or police on the take. Not getting enough. Maybe it's money, a payoff for someone.

Well, we'll just see. We've got some rights too.

She pulled her sweater around her shoulders and got her cane. Her arthritis was bothering her pretty badly but there was no help for it. She unbolted the door and lowered herself down the steps. As she approached the hollow iron post two houses down she glanced around guiltily. Her frustration was fast evaporating into fear. No one looking. Quick! She reached into the post. Only a crushed cigarette pack. Disappointed, she felt around in the hollow cavity. There was nothing else. With the cigarette pack in her pocket, she slowly made her way back to her house, steeling herself to look straight ahead. Oh God, why had she done this?

She locked and bolted her doors and sat at the kitchen table examining her find. Writing on the back, block letters. Numbers and such. Code of some sort. Payoffs, most likely. We'll see what the police make of all this. Not that they'd ever tell an old black woman what it's all about. No matter, if they'd just close that crack house, that'd be something.

But should she go to the police? They've been told about that crack house and they've done nothing. What if the police have been paid off? What if they tell the dopers about her?

Mrs. Jackson had lived too long in the ghetto not to know the dangers associated with interfering in someone else's illegal enterprise. As she stared at the cigarette pack she realized she had crossed that invisible line between officious nuisance and enemy. And she knew exactly what happened to enemies of dope dealers. They died. Fast and bloody. Those four punks on the sidewalk in their fancy clothes would smile as they cut off her ears, nose and tongue, then her arms.

She turned off the kitchen light and sat in the darkness, trying to think. What should she do? My God, what had she *done*?

Mrs. Jackson was still sitting in the darkness of her kitchen thirty minutes later when Terry Franklin walked past the front of her house toward the hollow post. He had parked the car three blocks away. Normally he was very circumspect and drove around for at least an hour to make sure that he had lost any possible tails, but tonight he was in a hurry. He had to get home before Lucy and the kids got back from the mall. So he had driven straight from Annandale to G Street.

The block appeared empty. No, there was someone sitting in a doorway, across the street. Some black guy with a brown bag. A wino. No sweat. What a shitty neighborhood! He had never understood why the Russians had picked a drop in a run-down black neighborhood, but since he hadn't talked to them after he had found the described drops, he had had no opportunity to ask.

It would be just his luck to get mugged down here some night.

He walked at a regular pace toward the post, not too fast and not too slow. Just a man who knows where he's going. He would just reach in while barely breaking stride, get the cigarette pack and keep on walking, right on around the block and back to his car. Piece of cake.

He slowed his pace as he reached into the post.

It was empty!

Dumbfounded, he stopped and looked in. There was just enough light coming from the streetlight up on the corner and the windows of the houses to see into the hole. It was about four inches deep. *Empty!*

He walked on. What had happened? This had never happened before. What in hell was going on?

He turned and walked back to the post. He looked in again. The hole was still empty. He looked around on the sidewalk and the grass behind the fence for anything that might be an empty cigarette pack.

Nothing!

It *must* be here, somewhere, and he just wasn't seeing it.

He was living one of those cold-sweat gibbering nightmares where you are stuck in quicksand and going to die and the rope is forever just inches out of reach. Finally he realized the cigarette pack truly wasn't there.

Maybe he was being set up. Maybe the FBI was going to grab him.

Franklin looked around wildly, trying to see who was watching. Just blank windows. The wino—still there, sucking from his bottle. He reached into the hole again, trying to understand. Someone had gotten it. God, it must be the FBI. They *must* be on to him. Even now, they're *watching* from somewhere, ready to pounce. Prison—he would go to *prison*. The *wino*—an agent—watching and laughing and ready to arrest him.

Terry Franklin panicked.

He ran for the car, a staggering hell-bent gallop down the sidewalk as he tried to look in every direction for the agents closing in. To *arrest* him.

He careened into a garbage can and it fell over with a loud clang and the lid flew off and garbage went everywhere. He kept running. At the intersection a car slammed on its brakes to the screeching of tires, barely missing him. He bounced off a parked car but he didn't slow.

He almost broke the key getting it into the door lock. The engine ground mercilessly and refused to start.

He smacked his head against the steering wheel in rage and frustration. He tried the ignition again as he scanned the sidewalks, searching for the agents that must be coming.

The engine caught. Franklin slammed the shift lever into drive and mashed on the accelerator.

Bang! Into the car ahead. *Holy . . . !* Reverse. Then forward, out of the parking space.

Cranking the wheel over at the corner, he slewed around with tires squalling and stomped on the gas.

Toad Tarkington stared glumly at the remains of a beer in the glass in front of him. Across the table Rita Moravia was chattering away with the peckerhead attack pilot who had spent the last three days initiating her into the mysteries of the A-6. Beside Toad sat the bombardier who had been coaching him, ol' Henry Jenks. Both these mental giants were hanging on every word from Moravia's gorgeous lips. There she sat, smiling and joking and behaving like a real live normal woman-type female, as she never did around him, damn her! And these two attack weenies were eating it with a spoon!

The pilot, Toad decided, had a rather high opinion of himself. He looked and acted like a lifelong miser who has just decided to spend a quarter on a piece of pussy that he knows will be worth two dollars. His smile widened every time Moravia glanced into his little pig eyes. If he wasn't careful his face would crack.

This BN, Jenks, wasn't any better. He obviously hadn't had a good piece of ass since his junior year of high school. Jenks was telling a funny to the pilot as he watched Rita's reaction out of the corner of his eyes. "Do you know a fighter puke's definition of foreplay?" After the obligatory negative from his listeners, Jenks continued. "Six hours of begging." Rita joined in the ha-ha-has.

Watching these two cheap masturbators in action was a thirsty

business. The waitress caught Toad's hi sign and came over. "Four
double tequilas, neat," Toad said, and looked around to see if there
were any other orders. The attack weenies were still drooling down
Moravia's cleavage as she told an anecdote about something or
other. "That's it," he told the waitress, who regarded him incredulously.

"Four?" she asked.

"Yeah."

She shrugged and turned away.

The club was still crowded with the remnants of the Friday-
night Happy Hour gang. The married guys had left some time back
and a bunch of reservists were drifting in. Altogether forty or fifty
people, ten or twelve of them women, three of whom were still in
uniform. Canned rock music blared from loudspeakers that Toad
didn't see. Only one couple was dancing.

When the waitress brought the drinks she sat them in the center
of the table. Jenks looked at the drinks with raised eyebrows. "I'll
have another beer," he said. "Perrier with a twist," Moravia
chirped. "Diet Coke," intoned the lecher beside her.

Toad drank one of the tequilas in two gulps. The liquor burned
all the way down. Ah baby!

Another song started on the loudspeakers, a fast number. Toad
tossed off a second drink, then climbed up on his chair. He
straightened and filled his lungs with air. *"Hey, fat girl,"* he roared.

Every eye in the place turned his way. Toad picked the nearest
female and leaped toward her with a shout: "Let's dance!" Behind
him his chair flew over with a crash.

And oh, that woman could dance.

7

The bedroom lights were on in the second story of the town house when Terry Franklin parked the car. He turned off the ignition and headlights and sat behind the wheel, trying to think.

He had driven around for an hour and a half after his panicked departure from the drop, craning to spot the agents he felt sure were tailing him. At one point he had pulled over and looked at the damage to the front of his car. The left front headlight was smashed and the bumper bent from smacking into that car when he tried to get out of that parking space too quickly.

A dozen times he thought he spotted a tail, but the trailing vehicle usually went its own way at the next corner or the one after. A blue Ford with Pennsylvania plates followed along for half a mile until he could stand it no longer and ran a red light. His panicky wanderings back and forth through the avenues and traffic circles of downtown Washington seemed like something from a drug-induced nightmare, a horrible descent into a paranoid hell of traffic and stoplights and police cars that refused to chase him.

Franklin sat now behind the wheel smelling his own foul body odor. His clothes were sodden with sweat.

Lucy and the kids were home. He tried to come up with a lie for Lucy as he scanned the street for mysterious watchers and people sitting in cars.

How long could he live like this? Should he take the money he had and run? Where could he run with the FBI and CIA looking for him? He didn't have enough money to evade them forever. Should he go to Russia? The very thought nauseated him. Freezing in some gray workers' paradise for the rest of his days was about as far from the good life as a man could get this side of the grave.

He wasn't feeling well and went to the dispensary, that was what he would tell Lucy. God knows he must look like he was in the terminal stages of AIDS. No good. No prescription. A beer. Yeah, he went out for a beer. He got out of the car wishing he had really stopped for one. After another look at the broken headlight and grille, he plodded toward the front door.

She came out of the kitchen when she heard the door open. "Where have *you* been?" She stood rigid, her face pale.

Uh-oh. He kept his voice calm. "Hey, babe. I went out for a beer. Did you all get anything at the mall?"

"I *know* where you've been. Cindy across the street has told me all about your little expeditions when I'm out for the evening. I know *all* about you, you son of a bitch."

He stared, thunderstruck. This isn't happening. No, not to me. For the love of— "How?"

"Who is she? I want to know. Who is she?"

"Who is who?"

"Who is the goddamn bitch you're tomcatting around with, you son of a fucking bitch. Who *is* she?"

At last he understood. As the relief washed over him he was suddenly too weak to stand. He sank into a chair. "Lucy, there's no other wo—"

"*Don't* give me that *shit!* I *know!* Cindy *told* me!" She was a quivering, shouting pillar of hysterical righteousness. "You're *cheating* on me." Tears were flowing now. "Oh God. I tried so hard . . ."

"Lucy, calm down. Please, for the love of— The kids will hear. Honest to God, there's no other woman." He got to his feet and approached her. "Babe, I love you. There's nobody—"

"Don't you touch me, *liar*. I'm getting a divorce." She spun and made for the stairs. "I'm locking the bedroom door. If you try to get in, I'll call the police. Liar. Cheat. Bastard."

He lost it. It had been that kind of evening. "You crazy cunt," he roared. "You don't know shit. I went down to the corner for a goddamn beer and when I get home you're fucking *loony* crazy. I haven't cheated on you! I haven't fucked another woman since that night I knocked you up at the drive-in. You don't have any god-damn evidence at all, you crazy lunatic."

He heard the bedroom door slam and the kids sobbing. He threw himself onto the living-room couch. Some days—it's absolutely crazy how some days just go bug-fuck nuts. You almost get arrested, smash up the front of the car, your wife demands a divorce because you're cheating on her when you're not. What else? What else can fucking happen before midnight?

The drop was empty. He stretched out on the couch and contemplated that fact. He closed his eyes and tried to relax. He could hear Lucy putting the kids to bed upstairs. Finally the noises stopped.

He would have to call them. In Miami they had given him an emergency telephone number that he had memorized and a verification code. He would call. He looked around for the evening paper. On top of the TV. He flipped to the sports section. The code was simple; the location and opponent in the next scheduled game of the Bullets, Orioles or Redskins, whichever was in season. They had been insistent; he was never to call except in an emergency and then only from a pay phone. Well, this was sure as hell an emergency. But he wasn't going back out onto those streets tonight, no way. Even if he could work up the courage, Lucy would use a butcher knife on his crotch when he got back.

He went into the kitchen and dialed the phone. On the third ring a man's voice answered with a recitation of the telephone number. The voice was tired, the English perfect. "Six-six-five, oh-one-oh-five."

"This is Poor Richard." He had picked his code name himself. Easier for him to remember, they said. "It wasn't there. It wasn't at the dr—"

"Verify please." The voice was hard, exasperated.

"The Bullets play the Celtics tomorrow night at Capital Centre."

"I'll call you back. Where are you?"

"Seven-two-nine, seven-four-oh-one."

"You're at *home*?" The voice was incredulous, outraged.

"Yeah, I—" He stopped when he realized he was talking to a dead instrument.

Shit. He would have to call again. He had to find out what the hell was going on. A pay phone. Lucy was going to come sweet-

Jesus holy-hell screaming unglued. What a night! He picked up his jacket and eased the front door shut behind him.

From her seat on the top of the stairs, Lucy heard the door close. She had started to come down earlier but stopped when she heard him enter the kitchen and pick up the phone. She had heard his side of the conversation and she sat now trying to figure it out. "Poor Richard" he had called himself. It wasn't there. The Bullets play the Celtics? A code of some sort?

What is he into? she asked herself, her horror growing. He had looked so stunned when she said she knew. That look was the verification she needed that he was cheating on her. But how did that fit with a code and nonsense sentences? Was he placing bets with a bookie? No, he wasn't spending money she didn't know about. Something to do with his job at the Pentagon? Could he be spying, like those Walkers several years ago? No, that wasn't possible. Or was it? He would do it if he could get away with it, she decided. In their eleven years of marriage she had found him a man who always put himself first.

What else could it be? My God, what other possibilities were there?

The sun was still embedded in the gray scud over the ocean on Saturday morning when Jake and Callie walked through the gap in the low dune on their way to the beach. Callie trailed along behind him on the narrow path, her hands tucked into the pockets of her windbreaker.

He strolled as he always did, his eyes moving restlessly across the sky and the sea and the naked sand and coming to rest often on her. Whenever she was with him she drew his eyes. It had been that way since they first met, one of the little unconscious things he did that told her without words what she meant to him. This morning walking beside him she was acutely aware of his glances.

"How did your little interview with the soul stripper go yesterday?"

"He says I have to come to grips with your decision to ram that transport in the Med last fall."

Jake stopped and turned to face her. He looked bewildered. "What the hell are you worrying about that for?"

"For a week I was a widow."

He turned away and looked out to sea. It was a moment before he spoke. "You may be again someday." He faced her. "Women live longer than men these days. I don't have a crystal ball, Callie. *Jesus,* we can't stop living because we're mortal." He gestured angrily. "I may get hit by a meteor ten seconds from now. I may get run over by some drunk when I step off the curb at—"

He stopped because she was walking away from him, along the beach, her arms wrapped around her chest.

He hurried after her. "Hey—"

"For a whole week you were *dead*! You had killed yourself chasing those damned Arabs and I was left here all alone!" He put his hand on her arm and she jerked away, whirling to face him. "You *knew* how much I loved you and . . . and . . . when they called and said you were alive, the memorial service was scheduled for the *next* morning. *I* was going to *bury* you. You were *dead*!" He enveloped her in his arms and she pressed her face against his shoulder.

After a while she stopped trembling and he murmured, "Still love me?"

"Yes."

"A little bit or a whole lot?"

"I haven't decided."

With his arm around her shoulder, he started them walking north again. In a moment he paused and kissed her, then they resumed their journey with their arms locked together.

Something white. Whatever it was that blocked Toad's gaze, it was white. He closed his eyes and the pain and nausea washed over him, enveloping him. Ye gods . . . Something hard and cold against his cheek—he opened his eyes again—and white. Lotta light . . . He moved. Shit! He was lying in a fucking bathtub.

He raised himself slowly. His head felt like it was coming off. He was still dressed in his khaki uniform, but it was wrinkled and had vomit on it. He still had his shoes on. Oh God, he felt worse than he had ever felt in his entire twenty-eight years, felt like he had been dead for a week or two. He sat up slowly. His head was being hammered on by an angry King Kong. After a moment he grasped the shower handles and faucet and hauled himself erect. He swayed as the blood pounded in his temples with every beat of his heart. Then he tried to step out of the tub. He tripped and sprawled heavily on the floor, striking his head against the bottom of the sink cabinet. He lay there, too sick and dazed to move.

Amid the pain he heard the door open. "Good morning." A woman's voice.

Toad flopped over and squinted against the ceiling light. Rita Moravia!

What had he done to deserve this? It's true, life is all misery and pain.

"I'd appreciate it if you would transport yourself to your own room, Tarkington. Now. I don't want anybody to get the wrong idea about you and me."

He tried to speak. His mouth was dry and tasted of sour vomit. He cleared his throat and licked his lips. "How'd I get here?"

"Four men carried you in here last night. We thought someone should keep an eye on you during the night. I volunteered."

"Aren't you a sweetie."

"I want you out of here, Tarkington."

He hoisted himself up and staggered past her. He was going to have to find another bathroom pretty damn quick. He went through the little sitting room and got the door open and was hustling down the hall when he heard her voice behind him. "We're flying at two this afternoon. Meet you in the lobby at ten till twelve."

Jake sat on the crest of the low dune and watched the glider moving north, away from him above the dune. He had its nose pointed obliquely forty-five degrees out to sea, but the velocity of the incoming wind was such that the plane stayed more or less over the dune. He was holding her low, only eight or ten feet up, to take advantage of the upward vector of the breeze as it crossed the low sand hill.

"Better turn her back this way," advised the eleven-year-old aviation expert from up the street.

Jake banked the plane. "Keep the nose up," David urged, his voice rising. Jake fed in back stick. Too late. The right wingtip kissed the sand and she cartwheeled. David was up and running instantly.

The boy was examining the wreckage when Jake reached him. The rubber bands that held the wings to the fuselage had popped off, which undoubtedly minimized the damage. "A hole in the wing Monokote and a busted spar in the right horizontal stabilizer," the youngster advised cheerfully. "Not bad. Yippy-skippy! You gotta remember to feed in a little back stick on the turns."

"Yeah. Let's take it over to my house and fix it."

"What kind of planes do you fly in the navy?" David asked as they walked down the beach with the pieces of the glider in their arms.

"A-6s mostly. Last year I flew the F-14 some."

"Wow, those fighters! Did you see *Top Gun*?"

"Uh-huh."

"My dad bought that movie for me. I must have watched it a couple dozen times. When I grow up I'm gonna fly fighters." He paused, apparently considering the implications of this bold statement. "What's it really like?" he asked, not quite so confident.

Jake was still trying to explain when they rounded the corner and he saw the strange car in the driveway. When he saw the blue Department of Defense bumper sticker with the three stars on it, he knew. Vice Admiral Henry. He led the boy inside.

The admiral was wearing jeans and a heavy jacket today. He and another man in a coat sat at the dining room table with Callie drinking coffee. David marched over to her and held the wing so she could see it. "He let the nose fall in a turn and crashed. We can fix it, though."

"Good morning, Admiral."

"Jake, I'd like you to meet Luis Camacho."

"Hi." Jake leaned across the table and shook hands. Camacho was in his early fifties with no tan, a man who spent his life indoors. Even though he wore a jacket his spare tire was evident, but his handshake was firm and quick. He didn't smile. Jake got the impression that he was not a man who smiled often.

"Nice place you have here," Camacho said.

"We like it," Callie said. "Would you all like a quiet place to talk?"

The admiral stood. "I thought we could take a walk along the beach. Be a shame to drive all the way over here from Washington and not walk on the beach."

The three men left David working on the glider at the kitchen table. He was telling Callie about servos and receivers when they went out the door.

"Nice day," Admiral Henry muttered as they walked toward the beach trail at the end of the street.

"They're all nice here," Jake said. "Raw and rainy at times, but nice."

"Luis is from the FBI."

"Got credentials?" Camacho produced them from a pocket and passed them to Jake, who looked the ID card and badge over carefully and returned them without comment.

Henry stopped at the end of the little path that led through the waist-high dune and looked right and left, up and down the beach. He turned right, south, and walked with his hands in his pockets toward the area with the fewest people. He didn't even glance toward the ocean. Out on the horizon a large containership was making its way north, perhaps to round Cape Henlopen and go up the Delaware.

"Yesterday you wanted to know what really happened in West Virginia after Harold Strong was killed."

"Yessir."

"I told you the truth, but I left a few things out. Camacho here was with me that morning. We met with Trooper Keadle and the local prosecutor, guy named Don Cookman. They weren't happy campers. They knew murder when they saw it and cooperation smacked of cover-up. So Luis got on the phone to Washington and the director of the FBI drove up along with the forensic team. We got cooperation with a capital C from then on."

"Go on," Jake prompted when the admiral fell silent.

The admiral turned to face him. "You're asking too damn much, Jake."

"I'm not asking for anything other than what I need to know to do my job."

"Like shit."

"Would you let yourself be led along by the nose if you were me? Jesus Christ, Admiral, my predecessor was murdered! I got a wife over there"—he pointed back toward his house—"who would like to have me alive for—"

"What do you want to know?"

"Why was Strong killed? What did you tell those people in West Virginia? Why the silence on a murder? Who and what are you investigating?" He looked at Camacho. "Who the hell *are* you?"

Camacho spoke first. "I'm special agent in charge of the Washington-area FBI group that handles counterespionage. *That's* why the locals in West Virginia cooperated. That's why Trooper Keadle called me when you left his office Thursday. That's why he called me when Commander Judy showed up that afternoon to search Harold Strong's cabin." He turned and started down the beach, still talking. Admiral Henry and Jake Grafton trailed along. "Why was Strong killed? If we knew that we would be almost there. It wasn't personal or domestic. No way. It was a hit, a contract. He got taken out by someone who knew precisely what they were doing, a cool customer. So the hypothesis that seems most likely is that he knew something he shouldn't. That leads us to his job—the ATA program."

"That sea story about a Minotaur—that was true?"

"Yeah, that's the code name. But we don't know if it's one guy or several," the agent said, with a glance at Tyler Henry, who picked that moment to look out to sea.

"I thought," Jake said, "that these spy things usually get broken when you get somebody to talk."

"That's the history. It'd be nice if we knew who to put the screws to to clean up this little mess. But we don't. So right now we're busy doing it the hard way." He led the two naval officers along the beach as he talked and answered questions. When Jake remembered to glance out to sea, the containership was no longer in sight.

"Let's transfer Smoke Judy," Jake suggested to the admiral.

Henry just stared at him.

"Dunedin said if I got goosey, I could get rid of him."

"I'd rather you left him in place," Camacho said. "I've already made that request to Admiral Henry and now I'll make it to you."

"Going to be real tough to pretend I don't know anything."

"You don't *know* anything," Henry growled. He jerked his thumb at Camacho. "If he talked to you for a week, you still wouldn't know anything. I sure as hell don't."

An hour later, as they came single file through the dune trail, Henry said, "Now you know as much as I do, which is precious little. On Monday you tell that chief in officer personnel to tear up your retirement papers."

"Yessir."

"Don't ever pull that stunt on me again, Grafton."

"Or . . . ?"

"Don't you abandon ship and leave me and Dunedin up to our necks alone in this sack of shit."

After the two men had departed in the admiral's car, Jake went back into the house. Callie was sitting on the couch reading a book. "David got your plane fixed, but his mother called and he went home for lunch. He said he would come back later and help you fly it."

Jake nodded and poured a cup of coffee.

"Want to tell me about it?"

"Huh?"

"Jake . . ." Her voice had that time-to-come-clean, no-more-nonsense tone. That tone in her voice always got his attention, perhaps because his mother had used it so effectively some years ago.

"Admiral Henry's my boss's boss. Camacho's a civilian. They drove over here to talk about a problem at the office. A classified problem. That's all I can say. You want coffee?"

She nodded yes. When he handed it to her she said, "So you *are* working on the ATA program?"

"Callie, for Christ's sake. I told you I was. I don't lie to you."

She sipped her coffee for a bit. "David likes you," she said.

It made him nervous when she shifted subjects like that. "He's a great kid," he said noncommittally. "Honest, Callie. I tell you the truth. If something's classified and I can't talk about it, I just say so. You know that! You know me!"

She nodded her agreement and picked up the book. He waited a moment, slightly baffled, then wandered outside with his coffee cup in his hand. Women! Any man who thinks he's got them figured out should be declared incompetent and incarcerated to protect himself.

The cursors were running all over the scope when it occurred to Toad to check the velocities in the inertial. They were all gone to hell. "Hold this heading," he growled at Rita as he consulted his kneeboard cards. He pushed the buttons to take the inertial out of the system, then typed in a wind he thought would work.

"Okay," he told her. "This run, no inertial and no radar. Computer dead reckoning and the IR—that's all we'll use. We'll even leave the laser off. Go in at a hundred feet and let's see if we can hit anything." Below two hundred feet system deliveries in the A-6 were degraded, probably, Toad suspected, due to the trigonometry of low grazing angles.

She lowered the left wing and let the nose sag down into the turn. When she leveled the wings they were on the run-in line at a hundred feet, throttles against the stops, bouncing moderately in the turbulence as the engines moaned through their helmets.

He got the reticle, or cross hair, on the IR display onto the tower. The cross hairs started drifting. The wind he typed into the computer was wrong. He pushed the velocity correct switch, then held the cross hairs on the tower bull's-eye.

"Master Arm on, in attack, and in range."

"I'm committed," she said. This meant she had squeezed the commit trigger on the stick, authorizing the computer to release the weapon.

Toad glanced out his side window. The desert was right there, close enough to touch, racing by beneath them. He came back to the IR scope. All okay. If Moravia got distracted and let the nose fall just a smidgen, they would be a fireball rolling across the desert so quickly they would never even know what happened. "Release coming," he advised. The cursors started to drift in close and he held them on the base of the tower.

When the release came she eased back on the stick and Toad felt the G press him down even as he watched the tower on the IR scope—now going inverted—for the hit. Pop. There it was! Almost dead-on.

That was the last bomb. He glanced at the panel in front of her. They were climbing and heading north for Yakima. He flipped the radar to transmit and began to adjust the picture.

"Your hit forty feet at seven-thirty."

"Boardman, thanks a lot. We're switching to Center."

"Have a safe flight."

"Yo." Toad dialed in the Seattle Center frequency.

"Pretty good bombing for a fighter puke," Moravia said.

"Yep. It was that," he agreed smugly, relishing the role and willing today to play it to the hilt. Moravia had had her fun last night. His head was still thumping like a toothache. "Ain't anybody better than the ol' Horny Toad."

"Or anyone more humble."

"Humble is for folks that can't," he shot back. "I *can.*"

Rita called Center and asked for a clearance to the military operating area over Okanogan. She leveled the plane at Flight Level 220. Toad played with the scope.

Entering the area, Rita disengaged the autopilot and looked about expectantly. She and her pilot instructor of the previous week, Lieutenant Clyde "Duke" Degan, had agreed to and briefed an ACM engagement. She was right on time. Now if she could just find him first. She dialed in the squadron tactical frequency and gave him a call.

"I'm here," Degan replied.

Toad caught the first glimpse of the other A-6. It was high, near the sun. Ol' Duke didn't intend to give Moravia any break at all. "All right," Toad enthused. "Now, by God, we're playing my game!" Toad pointed over her left shoulder. "Up there. Better turn under him and get the nose down for some airspeed."

Rita knew Toad had just recently finished a three-year tour in the backseat of F-14 Tomcats. He had ridden through literally hundreds of practice dogfights. Fighter crews lived for Air Combat Maneuvering (ACM), the orgiastic climax of their training and their existence. So she knew Toad Tarkington undoubtedly knew a thing or two about dogfighting. She took his advice. "Think he's seen us?" The A-6's radar had no air-to-air capability.

Toad kept the other plane in sight. Immediately above them— maybe two miles above—it rolled inverted, preparatory to a split S. "Looks like it," Toad murmured. "Already you're at a serious disadvantage, assuming he's smart enough to cash in."

With the throttles on the stops, she began a climbing right turn holding 340 knots indicated, the best climb speed. Toad glanced across the panel, then cranked his neck to keep the other plane in sight. "He's coming down like a ruptured duck," Toad advised. "If you had guns you could get a low-percentage deflection shot here. Shake him up some."

The other plane came rocketing down with vapor pouring off its wingtips. Now his wingtip speed brakes—boards—came open. "He's trying to minimize his overshoot." The other Intruder went dropping through their altitude with the boards still open, vapor swirling from his wings. "Work the angles," Toad advised. "Turn into him and get the nose down."

Rita Moravia did just that in a workmanlike four-G pull. "Not too much nose-down," Toad grunted against the G. Duke Degan would undoubtedly use his energy advantage to zoom again and try to turn in behind her, but he should not have left the boards out as long as he did. That was his second mistake. His first was the split S; he should have spiraled down to convert his energy advantage to a lethal position advantage.

Degan zoomed. Moravia smartly lifted her nose into a climb, still closing, then eased it to hold 340 indicated. "Very nice," Toad commented. Inexperienced pilots would just yank on the stick until they had squandered all their airspeed. Moravia had better sense. Patience, Toad decided. She was patient.

Degan was above them now, spread-eagled against the sky,

maybe a mile ahead and four thousand feet above. And he was running out of airspeed.

"You got him now," Toad said, excitement creeping into his voice.

Apparently Degan thought so too. He continued over the top of his loop and let the nose fall through as he half-rolled. He was going to try to go out underneath with a speed advantage and run away from her, then turn and come back into the fray on his own terms. Moravia anticipated him; as he committed with his nose she dumped hers and slammed down the left wing and honked her plane around.

"You get another deflection shot here," Toad advised. "You're kicking this guy's *ass*! What a clown! He should never have come back at you out of the loop."

She was dead behind him now, both diving, but Degan lacked the speed advantage to pull away cleanly.

"Fox Two," Toad whispered over the radio. Fox Two was the call when you were putting a heat-seeking missile in the air. "You're dead meat."

"Bull." Degan's voice did not sound happy.

"Go ahead, try something wonderful and Rita will get a guns solution."

"I have enough gas for one more series of turns," Rita told the instructor.

A long pause. Degan wasn't liking this a bit. Part of the pain, Toad suspected, was Rita's well-modulated feminine voice on the radio and the ribbing Duke knew he would have to take in the ready room about getting whipped by a woman. Toad would have wagered a paycheck the guys back in the ready room at Whidbey were crowded around the duty officer's radio this very minute. Toad whacked Rita playfully on the right arm with his fist. He was having a hell of a good time. "Okay," Degan said at last, "break off and we'll start again with a head-on pass at twenty-two grand. I'll run out to the west."

Rita dropped her wing to turn east. Toad cackled for her benefit over the ICS. Then he keyed his radio mike switch. "Hey, Duke, this is Toad. I got ten bucks to put on ol' Rita if you can spare it."

"You're on, asshole."

Toad chuckled over the radio. On the ICS he said, "We got him now, Rita baby. He's mad, the sucker."

"Don't *Rita-baby* me, you—you—"

"Goddamn, cool off, willya?" Toad roared. "I don't give a damn if you're the lesbo queen of Xanadu—but right fucking now you're a fighter pilot. This ain't for fun." He paused for air, then muttered, " 'Fight to fly, fly to fight, fight to win.' There ain't no other way."

"You didn't just make that up."

"That's the Top Gun motto. Now what're you gonna do on this high-speed pass?"

"I thought a turn in the same direction he turns."

"He'll probably make a horizontal turn as hard as he can pull. No imagination. Wait to see which way he turns, then nose up about forty degrees and roll hard into him, the rolling scissors. If he's not too sharp you'll get a winning position advantage, and this guy hasn't impressed me."

The two Intruders came together out of the emptiness at a combined speed of a thousand knots. At first the other plane was just a speck, but it grew larger quickly until it seemed to fill the windshield. Toad had been there before, in a head-on pass with Jake Grafton in an F-14 that resulted in a collision. Involuntarily he closed his eyes.

His head snapped down and the floor came up at him. She had the G on. He opened his eyes and used the steel handgrip on the canopy rail to pull himself around to look behind. "Which way?"

"Left. I got him." She was holding herself forward in the seat with her left hand on her handgrip as she craned back over her shoulder and applied the G.

"Get the nose up higher." Enough advice. Either she could hack it or she couldn't.

The left wing sagged to the vertical and the nose fell toward the horizon. G off as she slammed the stick all the way to the right and the plane rolled two hundred degrees in the blink of an eye. Back on the stick with the nose coming down. Pull, pull, pull that nose around.

Degan was in front of them now and below, but Rita was on the inside of his turn going down at him. Relax the stick and build up your speed, close on him; Toad silently urged her on.

"Degan lost sight," Toad said as he fought the vomit back in his throat. The hangover had caught up with him. He ripped off a glove and jerked the mask aside. His stomach heaved once. She was set up perfectly for a downhill Sidewinder shot.

"Fox Two," he called over the radio. "You owe me ten bucks, Degan." Then he puked into the glove again.

Rita lifted the nose and reversed her turn until she was headed west. "Fuel's going to be a little skosh," she murmured to Toad, then called Degan and told him she was leaving this frequency for Seattle Center.

After the debrief the duty van dropped them at the BOQ. "Thanks," Rita said.

"For what?"

"Coaching me during the ACM."

"No sweat. They're attack guys. ACM ain't their bag."

"Are you going to get some dinner?" she asked.

"Naw. I'm going to bed."

"I hope you aren't coming down with something," she called after him.

Jake Grafton sat in the attic beside the pile of boxes that contained the miscellaneous junk he had collected through the years and had never been able to throw away. Everything from high school year-books to souvenirs from half the world's seaports was tucked away in some box or other. He examined the boxes and tried to remember which was which. Perhaps this one. He opened it. Shoe trees, almost empty bottles of after-shave, buttons, spools of thread and some paperback novels. Three worn-out shirts.

It was in the fourth box. He removed the pistol from the holster and flipped the cylinder out. The chambers were empty. He held the weapon up so the light from the bare forty-watt bulb on the rafter shone full upon it. No rust. Good thing he had oiled it before he put it away. He looked into the box to see if there was any ammo. Yep, one box of .357 magnum, a couple dozen shells still in the box. He closed the cylinder, worked the action several times, then loaded the weapon.

With his back against one of the boxes, he extended his legs, crossed his ankles and thoughtfully stared at the holstered pistol on the floor beside him. Camacho said it had probably been a professional hit. Harold Strong would be just as dead if he had had a pistol. Still, a pistol nearby would make a nervous man feel better, sort of like an aspirin. Or a beer.

A large-frame revolver like this couldn't be hidden under a uniform. Perhaps in an attaché case? Then he would be the slowest draw in the East. In the car it could go in the glove compartment or under the seat, but it would be too far away if someone opened fire while he was sitting at a traffic light or driving along the freeway. And he rode the Metro to and from work anyhow. Maybe he should keep the gun in the bedroom or kitchen here at the beach and in the apartment in Arlington.

How would he explain the gun to Callie?

The hit man nailed Strong as he was driving to his weekend cabin. Probably the same route every Friday night. Predictable. Predictability was vulnerability. Okay. So what do I do routinely every day, every week? He reviewed his schedule in light of his new job. Boarding the Metro, driving to and from the beach, what else?

Strong was divorced, lived alone. What about Callie? Would she be a target?

Smoke Judy—had he put out the contract on Strong?

George Ludlow . . . Admiral Henry . . . Senator Duquesne was the tip of the congressional iceberg . . . Seventeen billion dollars, how many jobs did that mean, how many people supporting families and raising children? Seventeen . . .

"Jake." Her voice seemed distant. "Jake, are you still up here?"

He shook himself awake. "Hmmm."

Her head appeared in the attic access hole. She was standing on the ladder. "What are you doing up here?"

"Drifted off." He stirred himself. Rain was smacking against the roof, a steady drumming sound. He glanced at his watch: 1 A.M.

She came on up the ladder and sat down beside him. She touched the leather of the pistol holster. "Why do you have this out?"

"Looking through the boxes." He laid the holstered pistol in the nearest open box.

They sat holding hands, listening to the rain. "Jake," she said, "I want to adopt that little girl."

"Won't be easy, Callie. An eleven-year-old veteran of how many foster homes? She's had more rocky experiences and picked up more scars in her short life than you have in yours. Won't be easy."

"You're having problems at work, aren't you?"

"Yes."

"Bad?"

"I suppose." He picked up her hand and examined it carefully, then looked her straight in the eye. "I may be in over my head."

"Won't be the first time."

"That's true."

"You've always managed to come out in one piece before."

"That's the spirit. Good of you to point that out. I see you've taken our talk this morning to heart." He tried to keep the sarcasm out of his voice, but some crept in anyway.

She took her hand back. "Jake. Our lives are slipping by. I want that little girl. I want her now."

"Okay, Callie."

"You're doing what you want to do. I want that little girl."

"I said okay."

"Thursday. Thursday morning we see her, then that afternoon we go to the Department of Social Services for an interview."

"Okay. I'm leaving town Monday, but I should be back Wednesday. I'll take Thursday off. Just for the record, though, last week I asked the personnel people to fill out retirement papers for me. I'm going to tell them to forget it before I leave on Monday."

"Retirement? Is that what the admiral's visit today was about."

"Not really. The retirement thing was the catalyst, maybe. No kidding, Callie, this may be the worst mess I've ever been in. Worse than Vietnam, worse than the Med last year."

"You haven't done anything wrong, have you?"

"Not that I know of. Not yet."

She got up and moved toward the ladder. "I'm not going to wait any longer. I want that little girl," she said, then went down.

Toad Tarkington was sound asleep when the phone rang. He was still groggy when he picked it up. "Yeah."

"Tarkington, this is Grafton."

The cobwebs began to clear. "Yessir."

"How're you doing on the flying?"

"Pretty good, sir."

"Flown any full-system hops yet?"

"Yessir."

"How's Moravia doing?"

Toad checked his watch: 12:15 in the morning. It was 3:15 in Washington. "She's doing great, sir. Good stick."

"You doing okay dropping the bombs?"

"Yessir. It's a little different, but—"

"How many more hops are you going to get?"

"Six, I think. Two each Sunday, Monday and Tuesday. We come home Wednesday."

"Stay Wednesday and fly two more hops. Do eight. And Toad, leave the radar off. I want you to fly all eight without the radar. Use the IR and the laser and nothing else. You understand?"

"Yessir. Leave the radar off."

"See you this Friday in the office. And give me a written recommendation Friday on what we can do to the system to make it easier to use without the radar. Night." The connection broke.

Toad cradled the dead instrument. He was wide awake. He got out of bed and went to the window. Raindrops were smearing the glass. What was that all about? Grafton didn't seem to be getting much sleep these days. Shore duty sure wasn't cracking up right.

He cranked the window open a couple inches. The wind whistled though the crack and chilled him. It would be a miserable night to try to get aboard the ship. The meatball would be dancing like a crazed dervish while the fuel gauge told its sad tale. "Thank you, Lord, that I ain't at sea flying tonight," he muttered, and went back to bed.

The phone rang again. Toad picked it up. "Tarkington, sir."

"Grafton again, Toad. Leave the Doppler off too. It radiates."

"Aye aye, sir."

"Good night, Toad."

"Good night, Captain."

8

The plane carrying Jake and Helmut Fritsche landed at San Francisco International Airport, where the two men rented a car and ventured forth upon the freeways. Fritsche drove since he had made this trip several dozen times.

"I guess a fair appraisal of Samuel Dodgers would include the word 'crackpot,'" Fritsche said as they rolled south toward San Jose. "Also 'religious fanatic,' 'sports fanatic' and a few more."

Jake eyed Fritsche, with his graying beard and bushy eyebrows. "Crackpot?"

"Well, he's a man of outrageous enthusiasms. Got a Ph.D. in physics from MIT in one of his prior incarnations, before he got religion or changed his name to that of his favorite baseball team. He grew up in Brooklyn, you know."

"No," said Jake Grafton through clenched teeth. "I didn't."

"Yeah. Anyway, he's dabbled in computers and radar for years and patented this technology for suppressing reflected radiation. He came to me with some technical problems. I used my influence with the navy to get him a good radar to work with. Had it delivered in a moving van." He chuckled. "I'll tell you that story sometime."

"Henry says he's a genius."

Fritsche nodded his agreement between drags on his cigar. Smoke filled the interior of the car. Jake cracked his window an inch to exhaust the thick fumes. "He'll probably be in the running for a Nobel when his achievements get declassified."

"Somebody said he's greedy."

"Samuel wants some bucks, all right. I can't condemn him for that, not after a few years of reading about the pirates of Wall Street. Dodgers is the founder and only benefactor of his church and he wants to take it nationwide, with TV and radio and a hallelujah choir, the whole schmear. I think he realizes that since he's so heavy into hellfire and damnation, contributions are going to be light. The feel-good, be-happy ministries are the ones rolling in the dough. Dodgers is going to have to keep his afloat out of his own pocket."

Jake Grafton arranged the collar of his civilian jacket around his neck and lowered the window another inch. "What did George Ludlow say when he heard about Dr. Dodgers?"

"Amen," Fritsche said lightly.

"I believe it," Jake muttered. His companion tittered good-naturedly.

The car rolled on into the farm district south of San Jose. Eventually Fritsche turned up a dirt driveway and parked in front of a ramshackle wooden structure. A large sign amid the weeds proclaimed: "Faith Apostolic Gospel Tabernacle."

"I think we ought to get down on our knees inside and pray the GAO never gets wind of this," Jake said as he surveyed the weeds and the fading whitewash on the old structure. The last coat of thin whitewash had been applied over a still legible Grange hall sign.

"You'll see," Fritsche assured him.

Samuel Dodgers was a stringy man in constant motion. He stood in the small, dusty chapel and tugged at this, gestured at that, reset the Dodgers baseball cap on his balding dome for the hundredth time, pulled at his trousers or ear or nose or lower lip, moving, always moving. "So you fellows wanta see it again, huh, and see what progress looks like in the late twentieth century? When do I get some money?"

"You got your last check two weeks ago."

"I mean the next one." He hitched up his pants and reset his cap and looked from face to face expectantly. The sunlight coming through a dirty windowpane fell on a long, lean face. His chin jutted outward from almost nonexistent lips. Above the grim mouth was a sharp nose and two restless black eyes. "The next check—when?"

"I think it's a couple months away," Fritsche replied gently.

"If I weren't a Christian I'd cuss you government people. Your tax people squeeze the juice right out of a man—a man who's sitting on the biggest advancement in military technology since the horseshoe—but the giving hand is so all-fired parsimonious, stingy, miserly. You people are just *cheap!*"

"You're being paid according to the contract you agreed to, Dr. Dodgers."

"Get a man over a barrel and squeeze him. It's a sin to take advantage of a man trying to do the Lord's work like I am. A *sin.*"

Jake glanced at Helmut Fritsche. He appeared unperturbed.

Dodgers led them between a dozen or so folding chairs toward the door near the altar. "Praise the Lord and pass the ammunition," Fritsche muttered just loud enough for Jake to hear above the tramping and scraping of heavy feet on the wooden floor.

The back half of the old Grange hall was a well-lit workshop. Several strings of naked hundred-watt bulbs were woven through the joists and cast their light on a crowded jumble of workbenches, tools and junk. The visitors picked their way through it behind Dodgers, who approached the only person in the place, a young man of about twenty with carrot-red hair and acne to match.

"My boy Harold," Dodgers said to Jake, who shook the offered hand and introduced himself. "Harold was at Stanford, but they weren't teaching him anything, so he came back here to work with me. Learn more here with me than he would in that Sodom of little minds. Those fools with their calculators, always saying that something won't work . . ." He continued to fulminate as he opened the large doors at the back end of the building and began stringing electrical cords. "Well, Helmut, you seen this done before. Don't just stand there like a tourist."

Dodgers drew Jake aside as Fritsche and Harold hooked up electrical cords and moved a workbench outside. "Okay." He cleared his throat. "Over there on that little bench below those trees"—he pointed at the side of a hill about a half mile away—"is the radar. Harold will run that. That's the radar the navy loaned me. Got it up there in an old two-holer that used to be here behind the tabernacle." He stopped and showed Harold exactly how he wanted the power cables connected.

Jake joined him at a workbench. "Now this little radar suppressor—it picks up the incoming signal on these three antennas here and feeds it into this computer over there. Got four of the fastest chips made in this thing—Harold did most of the computer design. Computers are his bag. Little hobby of mine too. Anyway, the computer analyzes the incoming signal: strength, frequency, direction, PRF—that's Pulse Repetition Frequency—and so forth, and generates a signal that goes out through these companion antennas to muffle out future signals. That's why these antennas are twins. You have a receiver and a transmitter."

"But you can't suppress the first signal coming in?"

"Nope. They get one free look. The very first incoming pulse will not be muffled. Nor, in this generation of this device, will the second. See, you can't get a pulse repetition frequency until you have received at least two pulses, which you must have to time your outgoing pulses, the muffling pulses. But with existing radars, the return from one pulse will be treated like static. The cathode-ray tubes need a lot more pulses than that."

"And when the guy painting you stops transmitting, you beacon one more time?"

"That's the problem Harold and I are working on right now. You see, after the first pulse comes in, and the second, the computer then has to figure it all out and start transmitting. Right now we've got the computing time down to about ten billionths of a second. That's not enough of a clean chirp to let any existing radar get a definable return. If the next pulse doesn't arrive right on time, we'll stop the muffling pulses ten nanoseconds later. Just need to fix the software, the XY dipole and . . ." His voice fell to an incoherent mumble.

"Why wouldn't a second radar that is in a receive-only mode see you beaconing to the first radar?"

"Bistatic radar? It would," said the genius in jeans, "if all we were doing was pulsing straight back at the transmitter. But we aren't. We're pulsing from a series of antennas all over the plane to neutralize the reflected signal. Knowing how much to radiate, precisely enough yet not too much, that's where the computer really makes this thing work. First you must know the exact reflective characteristics of the object you are trying to protect—that's your airplane—and put that data into the computer's memory. Then the computer calculates the scatter characteristics of the incoming signal and tells each of the two hundred transmitters positioned over the fuselage and wings and tail just how much to radiate. All of the transmitters have to radiate in all directions. And this whole thing has to work very, very quickly. No computer was fast enough to handle this until superconductivity came along. See, to make the electrical signals move along fast enough to make this work, I've had to super-cool my computer in a tank of liquid hydrogen and encase the wires to each of the antennas in this special sheathing. That lowers the resistance just enough." He gestured to a row of pressure bottles that stood in one corner of his workshop. "Still, there's so much computing involved we had to go to a distributed system with multiple CPUs."

Jake felt like a schoolboy who hadn't done his homework. "But how does the outgoing radar signal cancel the incoming one?"

Dodgers stepped over to a blackboard standing in the corner. He looked around—"Where's the rag?"—then used his shirt sleeve to erase a spot. "Harold, where's that blasted chalk?"

"Here, Dad." The young man picked up a piece from a nearby bench.

Dr. Dodgers drew a sine wave on the board. "Do you know *anything* about radiation?" he asked Jake gruffly.

Jake nodded hesitantly as he traced a sine wave in the air with his finger. He knew from experience that claiming knowledge in the presence of a physicist was not a good idea.

"It moves in waves," Dodgers agreed dubiously. He drew another sine wave over the first, yet the peaks of the second were where the valleys of the first one were, and vice versa. "The first line is the reflected signal. The second line is our outgoing signal. They cancel each other."

Jake turned to Fritsche with raised eyebrows. Fritsche nodded affirmatively. "This principle has been known for a century. Dr. Dodgers' real contribution—breakthrough—has been in the area of superconductivity at higher temperatures than anyone else has been able to achieve. So he asked himself what computer applications were now possible that had been impossible before."

"And came up with this one," Jake muttered, for the first time seeing the intelligence and determination in that face under the bill of the cap.

"Let's fire it up," Dodgers suggested. "Helmut, if you will be good enough to take Captain Grafton and Harold up to the outhouse, I'll do the magic down here."

As Harold drove the rental car along a dirt track through a field, Jake asked, "How's security out here?"

"Security?" the young man said, his puzzlement showing. "The neighbors are all Presbyterians and Methodists and they think

Dad's a harmless loony. Their kids get curious and come around occasionally when they're out of school or in the evenings, but we don't tell them anything and they wander off after a while. Just got to keep them away when we're radiating. Been having some troubles with the power company from time to time. We sure pull a lot of juice when we're cooling down that hydrogen and they've dropped the load hereabouts a time or two."

"We had the head of the Federal Power Commission call the president of Pacific Gas and Electric," Fritsche told Jake.

"The district engineer still comes around occasionally, though," Harold continued. "I think he's harmless. Dad's been feeding him a line about experimentation with electromagnetism, and he bought it 'cause he's local and knows Dad's a dingbat." The youngster goosed the accelerator to take them through a mudhole in the road. "Nice car. I'd sure like to have a car, but Dad—with the church and all . . ."

The radar was mounted in the old outhouse on the bench where the seats once were. It radiated right through the open door. Harold Dodgers removed a padlock from a flap door at the back of the structure to gain access to the control panel and scope. "This is an Owl Screech radar," Fritsche told Jake. "We borrowed it from the EW range at Fallon." The Electronic Warfare range at NAS Fallon, Nevada, provided realistic training for fleet aircrews.

"Wonder where the U.S. Navy got this thing." Owl Screech was a Soviet-made gunfire-control radar.

"From the Israelis, I think. They had a few to spare after the 1973 war."

The drone of a jet somewhere overhead caused Jake to scan the blue sky. It was high, conning. An airliner or a bomber. A row of trees higher on the hill waved their leaves to the gentle breeze. So warm and pleasant here. Jake sat down in the grass while the redheaded youngster worked at the control panel and Helmut Fritsche observed.

"We're not getting any power," Harold announced. "Can I borrow the car and run back to the shop?"

"Sure. You have the keys." Harold eased the car around and went bumping down the dirt road. Fritsche joined Jake in the grass.

Jake tossed a pebble at the outhouse. The stone made a satisfying thunk. "What's the plan to get this gizmo into production?"

"Normally we would do engineering drawings and blueprints

and take bids, but due to the time constraints and secrecy requirements, we'll have to select a contractor on a cost-plus basis. The government will retain title to the technology and we'll pay Dodgers royalties."

"What contractor will get it?"

"One with the staff and manufacturing capacity to do it right and do it quickly. Probably an existing radar manufacturer."

"Cost-plus. Isn't that beltway French for 'can't lose'? And the contractor's engineers will see all the technology and have a leg up on bids for second- and third-generation gear."

"Yep."

"And if they can dream up ways to do it better, they can get some patents of their own." Jake tossed another pebble at the outhouse. "Gonna be a nice little plum for somebody."

"Yep."

"Good thing all the guys in our shop are honest."

Fritsche sat silently, weighing that remark, Jake supposed. "I guess our people are like everyone else," Fritsche said at last, without inflection. "People are pretty generally alike all over."

"Why was Strong killed?"

"Don't know."

"Any ideas?"

"Some. But I keep them to myself. I try not to gossip. There are laws against slander."

Jake Grafton stood and brushed off the seat of his trousers. "A river of money flowing along in front of a bunch of guys on middle-class salaries, a bunch of guys all humping to keep their bills paid until they get middle-class pensions and form letters of appreciation from the government. Everybody's honest. Nobody's tempted. Makes me want to salute the fucking flag and hum a march." He looked down at Fritsche.

"I have no facts, Captain," the scientist said. "None."

Jake looked around, trying to think of something to say. He gave up and strolled up the hill to the trees, where he relieved himself. Somehow aboard ship things had been simpler, more clear. On his way back to the wooden building he saw the car returning with Harold at the wheel.

The redhead had the radar fired up in less than a minute. With Fritsche and Jake looking over his shoulder, he flipped switches. "This is its target-acquisition—its search—mode. And that blip right there is the tabernacle." He pointed. Jake stared at the return

a moment, then stepped a few paces to his right and looked around
the shed at the scene. The radar in the shed made a variety of
mechanical noises and he could hear the antenna banging back and
forth against its stops. Now he referred again to the radar scope,
which was American, not Soviet. Okay, there was the tabernacle,
the house beyond and to the right, the trees on the left . . .

"Now," said the young Dodgers, "step over there again and
wave your arms at my dad. Then he'll fire up the suppressor." Jake
did as requested and returned to the scope. Even as he watched,
the blip that was the tabernacle faded from the screen, along with
the ground return in the area beyond. Where the blip had been was
merely a blank spot with no return at all.

"Try the frequency agility," Fritsche suggested. Harold flipped
another switch and then turned a dial. The tabernacle became
faintly visible as a ghost image. "As he changes frequency on the
Owl Screech, the computer on the suppressor is trying to keep up,"
Fritsche explained to Jake, "so he sees this ghost image, which is
not enough to lock on to. And remember, this is an American
scope, more sensitive than Soviet scopes."

"I'm impressed."

"Go to a higher PRF and try to lock on the spot where we know
the tabernacle is," Fritsche said to Harold. "Try the expanded display."

Nothing. The radar failed to lock. The center of the presentation
was an empty black spot.

After a long silence, Fritsche spoke softly, almost as if he were
afraid of his own thoughts. "If we could implement this technique
at optical wavelengths you wouldn't even be able to see that building down there with the naked eye."

"You mean you could see right through it?"

"No, it would look like a black hole. Nothing would come back
from it. But no one is going to have that kind of technology until
well into the next century."

"For heaven's sake," said a stunned Jake Grafton, "let's just get
the bugs worked out of this and get it to sea. That's more than
enough for you and me."

The phone on Luis Camacho's desk rang at noon on Tuesday as he
was eating a tuna salad sandwich. He had mayonnaise on his fingers and managed to smear it on the telephone. "Camacho."

"Luis, this is Bob Pickering. Could you take a few minutes now and come down to my office? I have some folks here I would like you to meet."

Camacho wrapped the half sandwich that remained and stuck it in his lower desk drawer, which he locked without thinking. Every drawer and cabinet in his office was always locked unless he was taking something out or putting something in. It was a habit.

Camacho knew Pickering, but not well. Pickering worked the District of Columbia and routinely handled walk-ins. "Luis, this is Mrs. Matilda Jackson and Mr. Ralph Barber. Luis Camacho." As they shook hands, Pickering added, "Mr. Barber's an attorney with Ferguson and Waithe." Ferguson and Waithe was one of the District's larger firms, almost two hundred lawyers, and specialized in federal regulatory matters.

Pickering summarized Mrs. Jackson's adventures of the previous Friday evening while Camacho glanced at the visitors. He concluded, "Based on past experience, Mrs. Jackson felt that the District police may not be sympathetic to a complaint from her, so she went to Mr. Barber, her former boss, yesterday, and he thought she should come see us."

Barber was in his fifties, still wearing his topcoat and white silk scarf. Apparently he hoped this interview would be brief. Mrs. Jackson still had her coat around her too, but its faded cloth contrasted sharply with the blue mohair that kept the spring winds from the lawyer's plump frame.

"The neighborhood used to be someplace a person could be proud of," Mrs. Jackson said slowly. "But those crack houses and dealers on the corners . . . The police have *got* to do something!"

"We felt that the information and evidence Mrs. Jackson has would probably receive a more dispassionate look from the FBI." The counselor gestured toward the edge of Pickering's desk, upon which lay a roll of film and a clear plastic Baggie containing a crumpled cigarette pack.

"I thought you might want to send these to the lab," Pickering told Luis. "I'll do the report and send you a copy. We'll get back to you in a few days, Mrs. Jackson. One of us will. Right now we need to get a set of your fingerprints to compare with whatever is on that cigarette pack. Just in case, you understand."

Camacho jotted the report number on a piece of paper from Pickering's desk, then excused himself. Curious about the two items he carried, he walked them straight to the lab and logged them in. Tomorrow afternoon, he was told. After three.

* * *

The Consolidated Technologies prototype had a hangar all to itself in Palmdale. As Jake stood and looked about the cavernous interior, he was surrounded by engineers and vice presidents, at least twenty people all told. The vice presidents all wore business suits, but the engineers seemed fond of short-sleeved white shirts with dark ties. If that garb didn't announce their profession, they all sported nerd buckets—plastic shirt-pocket protectors full of pens and pencils, from which dangled their building passes. Solar-powered calculators rested in belt holsters on engineers and vice presidents alike.

The black airplane had a conventional dual nose wheel with the nose tow bar that enabled it to be launched by catapult, but that was about the only feature Jake found familiar. The rounded wings were situated well back on the fuselage and a canard protruded under each side of the canopy. Two vertical stabilizers canted inboard rose from the rear of the fuselage. The engine air intakes were on top of the plane, behind the cockpit, which seated two crewmen in tandem.

The senior vice president, a tall woman in her late forties whom Wilson had said rose from the accounting department to her present position on sheer raw talent, led the group toward the machine and explained major features to Jake. "The aircraft's shape is optimized to reduce the aircraft's Radar Cross Section. We've used radar-absorbent materials in all the leading and trailing edges—laminated layers of glass fiber and plastic with carbon coating . . ."

"Uh-huh," said Jake Grafton.

"For low frequencies that put the plane into the Rayleigh region, we've tried to lower the overall electromagnetic susceptibility . . . carbon-epoxy laminate for wing skin, coatings of multilayer absorbers—mainly Schiff base salts and honeycomb composites. The goal was to reduce resonant microwave frequency scattering, magnetic waves and even surface waves before they escape from the edges."

"I see," he lied. The canopy was open and the boarding ladder down, so Jake climbed up and peered into the forward cockpit. The control stick was a small vertical handle on the right side of the cockpit. Two power levers were installed on the left console. The forward panel contained two Multifunction Displays, MFDs, arranged on either side of the control panel for a Heads-Up Display, a HUD, which sat on top of the forward panel so as he flew the pilot could look straight ahead through the tilted glass. Under the HUD control panel was another screen, similar to the MFDs, but without the frame of buttons that circled the upper two. All of the screens looked like eleven-inch color television screens with the power off: they were larger than the five-inch displays to which Jake was accustomed. But the weirdest thing—there were no engine instruments. Oh, the panel had a conventional gear lever, a standby gyro and even a G meter, but of engine instruments there were none.

"Go ahead. Climb in and sit down," the woman urged. Jake glanced again at her name tag. Adele DeCrescentis.

"Okay." As he arranged himself in the pilot's seat, Ms. DeCrescentis mounted the ladder. "Where's the ashtray?" he asked.

"Captain, I don't think—"

"Sorry. Just kidding." The look on her face implied that levity was inappropriate. Here in the high-tech cathedral, Jake thought. Or the new-car showroom.

Down below, the entourage was making small talk among themselves and casting many glances at the cockpit and vice president DeCrescentis, who probably didn't look very vice presidential perched on the boarding ladder. "What's going to happen to engine airflow in high-angle-of-attack maneuvers?"

"That was one of the trade-offs," said DeCrescentis, shifting her weight gingerly. Even the medium heels she was wearing must be mighty uncomfortable on the rungs of that ladder. "Each intake has a flap that is raised hydraulically to funnel more air into the intake when the FCC—Flight Control Computer—senses an increase in G or angle of attack which correlates with a decrease in compressor inlet pressure, but those flaps can only do so much. The concept is angle-of-attack-limited, so it made sense to design to a five-G limit. That enabled us to lighten the airframe and increase the use of honeycomb composites, which made it even more stealthy. And we achieved better fuel economy."

"I bet spins will be exciting."

"The engines will compressor-stall in an upright spin and have to be shut down, but they can be restarted once a normal angle of attack is achieved. Inverted spins shouldn't be a problem."

"Hmmm." Jake moved the control handle experimentally. It looked like the joystick for a computer game. "Fly by wire?"

"Of course."

"Ms. DeCrescentis, I appreciate all you folks taking the time this morning to show me this plane, but what say I sort of look it over with my staff? They've been involved in this project for quite a while and no doubt can answer any questions I know enough to ask."

"I suppose," she said reluctantly, glancing again at the crowd below. She maneuvered her way down the ladder and two men below reached up to help her to the floor.

Fritsche scrambled up and seated himself on the cockpit coaming. Commander Rob Knight, the project coordinator, came up behind him and stood on the ladder. "What d'ya think?" Dr. Fritsche asked.

"Pretty stealthy, I guess."

"About the same RCS as a bird."

"How big a bird?"

"You aren't impressed, are you?"

Jake Grafton took his time answering. He examined the panels on each side of the seat, then fingered the switches experimentally. "You guys tell me if I'm wrong: what we have here is one of the air force stealth-fighter prototypes, a version the blue-sky boys decided not to buy. It's subsonic, shoots only smart weapons, has limited maneuverability and carries a nonstealthy belly tank for training purposes that can't be carried in combat. Combat radius unrefueled is about six hundred nautical miles. Now, that is. To make this plane carrier-suitable it needs a beefed-up structure, tail-hook and folding wings, all of which will add at least a thousand pounds of weight—probably fifteen hundred pounds—and cost us speed and range. This killing machine will lighten Uncle Sugar's wallet to the tune of about sixty-two million bucks a pop. *If,* and only *if,* it can be acquired on the most economic—the optimum—production schedule. Is that right?"

"Well, the cost factors are a lot more complicated than you've indicated, but your summary is fair."

"Due to the likelihood that the five-G limit will be routinely exceeded by fleet aircrews in training situations, the design needs further modification to prevent compressor stalls. That involves more structural strengthening, computer-operated secondary intakes, loss of some stealthiness. That will cost an additional . . . ?"

"Five million a plane, assuming an optimum production schedule. Ten million more per plane if we buy new engines."

"Five million a plane," Jake continued. "And if we don't buy that mod, we'll have the compressor-stall problem that plagued the F-14 the first ten years of its life, which will mean a higher attrition rate than we would experience otherwise." Attrition meant crashes, planes lost in training accidents. "Yet to go the new-engine route will take ten years because the engines don't even exist; all we have is an engineers' proposal saying they could build them sooner or later for about so many dollars apiece, subject to all the usual caveats about buy rates, research, inflation, etc."

"Hiram Duquesne likes this plane."

"Ah yes, Senator Duquesne. Another great American."

"We didn't get the senior vice president this morning because she likes your nose," Knight shot back. "Consolidated has about two hundred million dollars of their own funds tied up in this prototype. They employ twenty thousand people. Consolidated is *big* business. They've bet their company on getting a stealth contract."

"Yeah. Stock options and bonuses and company cars for the executives, jobs for the little people, and votes for the big people in Washington. I got the picture."

"Don't be so damned cynical," Rob Knight said. "Listen, Jake, it may well come down to buying this plane to replace the A-6 or doing without. Ludlow and Royce Caplinger have to be goddamn sure they have the votes in Congress before they go up to Capitol Hill with their hats in their hands."

"That's their problem, not mine. I'm just a worn-out, washed-up attack pilot. I didn't understand two words that DeCrescentis woman said." He twiddled some knobs. "I didn't ask for *this* job," he roared. "I'm not going to be responsible for whether twenty thousand people keep *their* jobs! Don't lay that *crap* on *me!*"

Knight retreated down the ladder. Fritsche followed, his face averted. Jake sat alone in the cockpit. He tried to imagine how this plane would feel to fly. With his right arm in the rest and his hand on the stick and his left curved over the throttles, he thought about how it would feel to look through the HUD at a Soviet ship. This plane had to be able to take on Soviet ships in the Med and the Indian Ocean and the Arctic in winter. But it also had to be able to fight in brushfire wars in places like Lebanon and North Africa,

Afghanistan, Iran, Korea, Vietnam. Maybe China. Could it? With million-dollar missiles and a five-G restriction?

When he had recovered his temper, he motioned to Knight and Fritsche, who ascended the ladder again. "What would Sam Dodgers' gizmo do for this plane?"

"Lower the RCS from a bird to a June bug." Fritsche frowned. "It's so stealthy now that making it more so wouldn't be cost-effective, at least not in the lifetime of this machine. That's just my opinion, of course."

"On the other hand," Knight said, "this plane wouldn't be junk if Dodgers' suppressor can't be made to work in a real airplane. Dodgers knows the reflective characteristics of that tabernacle wall precisely when viewed from the old outhouse by one radar. Protecting a shape as complex as an aircraft from numerous transmitters and God knows how many receivers situated in all three dimensions—that's another thing altogether."

"Tell me what all this stuff is," Jake said. "This doesn't look like any cockpit I ever saw."

"Both prototypes have exactly the same layout. This is all the stuff that was going into the A-6G. What these television-screen things are are Multifunction Displays. This lower middle one is a map that moves as the plane moves. The plane always stays in the center. This should do away with the necessity for the crew to always carry awkward charts in the cockpit.

"Now these upper two MFDs present literally all the information the pilot might wish to know, or the info can be presented on the HUD. A touch of the button calls up engine information, another button calls up the radar presentation from the rear cockpit, still another the presentation from either one of the two IR sensors, and so on. Then there's a variety of tactical displays . . ." He droned on.

Jake was astounded. This was several generations beyond the A-6 cockpit. It was technically as far beyond an A-6 as an A-6 was from a World War II B-17. "I had no idea," he muttered, awed.

Knight showed him the rear cockpit. It was equally futuristic. Instead of the HUD control panel, it possessed a third MFD, so three of them were arranged in a row right across the panel. Under the center one was the map display. "This moving map—didn't James Bond have one like this in one of the movies?"

"Yep. But this is better."

"Mamma Mia!"

The BN in an A-6 had one cursor control stick. The BN in this plane had two, one on each side panel, and instead of just a couple of buttons sticking out, each stick was festooned with buttons, like warts. "The idea is that the BN won't have to reach for controls. Everything he needs is on those control sticks."

After Jake spent another half hour walking around the airplane and looking at every inch, he asked each of the commanders what they thought. One complained about range and payload, another about the intake problems, a third about the difficulty of maintenance. All were aghast at the cost. "But five years from now we'll all probably think sixty-two million dollars for a plane was a hell of a buy," Smoke Judy commented.

"You know," Jake said later as he stood in the doorway with Helmut Fritsche and looked back at the all-black airplane, "I had an uncle who went to the car dealer one morning to buy a station wagon for the family, and that evening he went home with a little red convertible coupe."

"High tech *is* sexy."

Jake thought about it. "It's so damn neat that you try to convince yourself that you need it. All the bells and whistles and doohickeys and thingamajigs. And the day you have to bet your ass on these gadgets, they don't work."

"Shapes and absorbers work."

"I suppose. But how is Sam Dodgers' superconductive computer with multiple CPUs going to work after five hundred catapult shots and five hundred arrested landings when some kid racks the plane through a six-G pull to evade an optically aimed missile? How are all these MFDs and IR sensors and ring-laser gyros going to hold up? Is this techno-junk gonna work then?"

9

       Terry Franklin stood with his back against a pillar and tried to keep his face pointed at Lincoln's Second Inaugural Address. The pillar was the second one on the right after you came through the main entrance. The man on the phone had been very precise about that. Second pillar on the right, on the side toward the Inaugural Address.

His eyes kept moving. He was nervous, so nervous. He had vomited up his breakfast an hour ago . . . Not that person, a teenage girl. Not that old fat woman with the cane and the two kids. Maybe that man in the suit over there . . . *he* could be FBI. Was he looking this way? Why was he turning? That long-haired guy in jeans . . .

He had been here ten minutes and had already spotted five men who could be FBI. Maybe they all were. What if they had him staked out, like a goat? Maybe he should just leave, walk away and forget all of this. He had plenty of money. Enough. He had enough. If they weren't on to him he could live carefully and comfortably for years with no one the wiser. But what if they *knew*?

"It's one of the world's great speeches, isn't it?"

He turned and stared. A man, in his fifties with a tan face, stocky, wearing a short jacket, looking at the speech carved in the marble. On his head a brimmed hat. What's the response? Holy . . . *think!* "Yeah . . . uh, but I think the Gettysburg Address is better."

"Stay twenty feet or so behind me." The man turned and walked for the entrance, not fast, not slow, just walking. After he had gone three paces Terry Franklin could wait no longer and followed.

The man was only ten feet ahead going down the wide, broad steps in front of the Memorial. Franklin forced himself to slow down and lag behind. The distance had increased to fifteen feet by the time they reached the sidewalk, but it narrowed again as Franklin strode along. He stood right behind the man as he waited for a tour bus to roll by.

On the other side of the street the man said, "Walk beside me." He led Terry along the north side of the Reflecting Pool until he found an empty bench. "Here," he said.

"Can't we go somewhere private?" Franklin asked, still on his feet and looking around in all directions.

"This is private. Sit!" The petty officer obeyed. "Look at me. Stop looking around. You're as nervous as a schoolboy smoking his first cigarette."

"Something went wrong. Really wrong. Why in hell did you people have a drop in a black ghetto? Some nigger doper could have torn my head off over there."

"The drops were selected in Moscow, from a list. That drop was originally chosen for another agent." The man shrugged, resigned. "Bureaucrats. These things happen."

"So who got the message? Answer me that! Who saw me there? The cops? The FBI? NIS?" The pitch of his voice started rising. "What am I supposed to do now? Wait until—"

"No one saw you. Some child or derelict probably removed the cigarette pack, or it was blown out of the hole by the wind. If you had been observed they would be tailing you now."

Franklin couldn't help himself. He turned his head quickly, scanning.

"Sit still! You only call attention to yourself by doing that, and believe me, there is nothing to see. You are clean. I wouldn't be here if you weren't."

Franklin stared at his feet. He was so miserable. "I called in sick today."

"And you rode the subways just as we instructed, and we checked you all the way. No one followed. No one pulled up to Metro stations to see if you got off. No one made phone calls or ran for a car after you passed by. You are clean. You are not being watched."

"So who are you?"

"You don't need—" He took a deep breath and exhaled slowly. "My name is Yuri." The man extracted a pack of cigarettes from an inside jacket pocket and lit one. Marlboro Gold 100s, Franklin noticed. The fingers that held the cigarette were thick, the nails short. No rings.

"So what do you want me to do?"

"I'm here to evaluate you, to see if you are capable of going on, of continuing to serve."

Franklin thought about it. Lucy hadn't spoken to him for four days now. God only knows what that bitch will do. Still, ten thousand bucks a disk was damn good money. And if . . .

"If you wish to continue, you must calm down. You must get a grip on yourself." Yuri's voice was low and steady. "Your greatest asset is that no one suspects you, and if you become nervous, irrational, irritable, not your usual self, then you call attention to yourself and *make* yourself suspect. Do you understand?"

"Yes." He glanced at the man, who was looking at him carefully with inquisitive, knowing eyes. Franklin averted his gaze.

"We'll give you a rest," Yuri said. "We'll wait a few months before we give you another assignment. Will that help?"

Terry Franklin was torn. He wanted the money, quickly, but as he sat here on this bench knowing *they* could be watching he knew just how close he was to the end of his emotional rope. For the first time in his life he realized how little real courage he had. But for this kind of money maybe he could screw up enough stuff to keep going, for a while at least. If he had some time. He rubbed his eyes, trying to quell the tic in his left eyelid. "Yes," he said slowly, "perhaps it would be better to let things cool off, settle down."

"Okay. So tomorrow you go back to work as usual. Do all the usual things, all the things you normally do. Keep to your routine. Do nothing out of the ordinary. Be pleasant to your colleagues. Can you manage that?"

He considered it, visions of the office and the chief flashing before his eyes, fear welling up.

"Yes?"

"Yes." He got it out.

"Do you want to talk about anything else?"

He shook his head no.

"You are doing important work. You have made a great contribution. Your work is known in Moscow."

Terry Franklin said nothing. Of course his work was known in Moscow. Just as long as no one here found out about it, everything would be fine. Ensuring that that didn't happen was the whole problem.

"To show you how valuable your work is, we are raising your pay. To eleven thousand a disk."

Franklin just nodded. The enormity of the risks he was running to earn that money had finally sunk in the last four days. He no longer thought of it as easy money. He was earning every goddamn dime.

"You may leave now. Walk up Twenty-third Street to the Foggy Bottom Metro station and board there. Goodbye."

Terry Franklin rose and walked away without a backward glance.

"How long you guys gonna be in town?" the driver of the rental car shuttle bus asked George Wilson as they circled Terminal C at Dallas–Fort Worth to pick up more people.

"Oh, a day or so."

"Going home then?"

"No. We've got a couple more cities to visit." Inquisitive devil, Jake thought, sitting beside George and watching people board.

"Did you come here from home?" Maybe the driver was working for a tip. Or maybe he was just bored. He got the bus in motion again as the people who had just boarded tried to store their bags in the bin and hold on too.

"Nope. Came from L.A. Been on the road a while."

"I knew it! You're a traveling salesman, huh?"

"Yep."

"I can always tell."

At TRX Industries the six men were passed from person to person until they reached the program manager. His ample gut hung over a wide leather belt secured with a Budweiser buckle. At least it appeared to be a Budweiser buckle, but it would be impossible to know for sure unless you checked while you were shining his cowboy boots. His name was Harry Franks.

After the introductions and how-are-yous, he said, "Do you guys want to see it right now, or go to the conference room and watch the video presentation first?" He eyed Jake.

"I'd just as soon see the plane now."

"For sure. Maybe see the presento during lunch. We worked real hard on it. You fellas follow me."

As they strolled along he bantered with Wilson and the commanders, whom he called by name. Just a bunch of good ol' boys.

The plane was in the hangar. The design seemed to Jake Grafton to be more conventional than Consolidated's. This plane had a tandem cockpit and twin vertical stabilizers canted in at the top, toward each other, but there the similarity to the other prototype stopped. This bird was tactical navy gray, with engine intakes in the wing roots and no canards. Instead of a plenum chamber and fairings to cool the exhaust, the tailpipes were arranged above a fairing that might shield the worst of the heat signature from a ground observer. There were no afterburners. "The Soviets are doing a lot of work on air-to-air IR sensors for their latest generation MiGs," Smoke Judy said.

"Yeah, probably stole ours," somebody grumbled.

Jake walked slowly around the plane, the chief engineer at his elbow. On the left side of the fuselage, just behind the nose radome, was a place from which a twenty-millimeter-cannon barrel peeked out. "Vulcan?"

"Yep. Six hundred fifty rounds capacity, five hard points for missiles and bombs faired in underneath. This baby'll carry, shoot or drop anything in the U.S. inventory or anything any NATO country's got."

"Ranger?"

"Combat radius is projected at six hundred nautical miles unrefueled."

"How stealthy is this thing?"

"Well," said Harry Franks with his thumbs in his belt, "it's got a head-on RCS of about a half of a square meter. That reduces its detection range compared with an A-6 Intruder by about forty-five percent. That's naked, as she sits. Hang bombs and a belly tank and the RCS rises, though it's still down about sixty percent from an A-6 loaded for bear. Our design concept was to be as stealthy as possible and still come up with a mission-capable attack plane with good range and flying characteristics. This prototype was optimized for aircraft-carrier operations. It seemed to us that if you guys couldn't get it aboard ship and keep it there for a reasonable cost, it didn't matter how stealthy it was." He sighed and scratched his head and checked the shine on the toe of his boots. "That logic didn't impress the air force, of course. Not stealthy enough for them by a long shot."

"What's this thing gonna cost Uncle Sam?" Jake already knew this answer, but he wanted to hear Franks say it.

"Well, there're a ton of variables." Franks's hands went into his pockets and he looked Jake straight in the eyes. "Optimum production rates, as is, fifty-three mil."

"When did you stop selling used cars and go to work for TRX?" Franks chuckled good-naturedly.

"If it were something under fifty, I could probably bring my wife over and let her drive it."

The engineer's grin disappeared. "I hear you. You'll get some votes in Congress under fifty that you won't get over that number. But we already scraped and cut and chopped like hell to get down to fifty-three."

"Uh-huh. Just a suggestion—we're a long way from a decision—but were I you, I'd be sweating that number again and trying to shrink it. Sweating it real hard."

Later Jake managed to draw Dalton Harris aside. Harris had spent most of his career in electronic warfare. By definition he was an expert on Soviet radars, their capabilities and their usage. "Tell me," Jake asked, "what a forty-five percent reduction in the detection range of an A-6 means to the Soviets. Over fifty percent reduction carrying weapons."

"It means that all the Soviet fire-control radars are obsolete." He shrugged. "They would have to redesign and replace everything they have. Or—and this is a big or—they would have to double the number of existing radars."

"At what cost?"

"Replacement would be astronomical. Their whole system involves using proven technology that can be manufactured in quantity at low cost by low-skilled workers with inexpensive equipment and techniques. They need a lot of everything since the Soviet military is so big. Has to be big because the country is; distances are mind-boggling. So they rarely declare anything obsolete until it's worn out completely. Yet in a mass obsolescence like this low-observable technology threatens, they have to come up with new cutting-edge designs or fixes for over a dozen types of front-line radars, manufacture huge quantities and get them all in service quickly." Harris raised his hands and dropped them in a gesture of defeat. "I don't think they can do it. It'll cost too much. Their best

bet is to merely make a lot more of what they have, but that will
cost them the farm and the family cow. All of which is why
Gorbachev has become a good guy."

"You think?"

"Look at it this way. The Soviet economy is on its ass. They
don't even have money over there. The ruble is non-convertible.
They've been spending at least an eighth of their gross national
product on defense. The barrel is empty. They hate Star Wars
because the research and development costs to match or counter it
are prohibitive. Now comes stealth: the B-2, the F-117. Those are
threats against land-based targets. If that wasn't enough bad news,
now the U.S. Navy wants a stealth bird to threaten their fleet—the
A-12. I'll bet if we were on the Politburo and heard what coun-
tering this low-observable technology was going to cost, we'd think
about converting to Christianity."

"They must be looking hard for a way to do it on the cheap,"
Jake suggested.

"Wouldn't surprise me," Dalton Harris replied.

"Why not build their own stealth birds?"

"They will someday. Right now they can't afford it. When they
do, though, we'll have to upgrade all our radars."

"Hell, we can't afford it either," Jake Grafton said. Franks was
walking this way. When he was close enough Jake said to him,
"Let's sit down and talk about the flight-test schedule."

"Oh, Mom," Lucy Franklin sobbed into the telephone, "I didn't
want to call you, but I've got no place else to turn."

"You did the right thing, lucy. Has he hit you?"

"Oh, no. It's nothing like that. It's . . ." She bit her lip. It was
all so bizarre. Her neighbor, Melanie, hadn't believed her and neither had the minister. Her mother was her last hope. "I think
Terry is a spy."

Silence on the other end of the phone. Finally: "Tell me about
it."

Lucy explained. She went over the events of last Friday night in
great detail.

"Well," her mother said. "*Something* is going on. He's probably
cheating on you."

"*Mother!* Please! This is more serious. I'm scared stiff. I can't
eat. I can't talk to him. I'm afraid of what he'll do to the kids.

Mother, I'm petrified. I'm at the end of my rope." She began to sob.

"Do you want me to come out there?"

"Oh, I don't know. What good would that do?"

"He wouldn't hurt you while I was there. We could confront him." More silence. "Let me talk to your father and call you back."

"Not Daddy!" Lucy wailed. "He won't *understand.*"

"I know you and he don't see eye to eye. He didn't think Terry was the right man for you."

"He's never let me forget it."

"Do you want to come home? Bring the kids?"

If she went home her father would be there. She was genuinely afraid of her father. He just had never been able to cope with a daughter . . . "Can you come out here?"

"I'll call your dad at work, then call you back. Okay?"

"Mom, I really need you to help me through this one."

They said their goodbyes and hung up. Lucy drank more coffee and chewed her fingernails. Mom would be such a help. Terry wouldn't do anything with her here. Oh, please, Daddy, let her come.

"Looks like gibberish, of course. What it is is two computer access code words and a file name." The man from the lab laid an eight-by-ten color photo of the inside of the cigarette pack on Camacho's desk. "No prints on the pack except for Mrs. Jackson's."

Camacho studied the print. The words and numbers were:

Interest Golden.TS 849329.002EB

"And the photos?"

"They didn't come out so good. She used a miserable camera with a fixed focus." The lab man handed Camacho the stack. He looked at each one and laid them across the desk. He stood and bent over to study them, moving slowly.

"This one." He selected a photo of a man in a trilby hat wearing a full-length coat. Only the bottom half of his face was visible, and it was fuzzy. Yet obviously a white man. The other men in the pictures were black. "Blow up the face and see what you can do with computer enhancement."

The lab man checked the back of the photo for the number of the negative. He excused himself and left. Camacho sat in his chair and stared at the face. Thick cheeks, rounded chin, the suggestion of a fleshy nose. He had seen that face before. He picked up the phone: "Dreyfus, bring in the mug book of Soviet embassy personnel."

It took twenty minutes, but Camacho and Dreyfus finally agreed. The man in Mrs. Jackson's photo was Vasily Pochinkov, assistant agricultural officer at the Soviet embassy.

"These black dudes." Camacho tapped the stack. "Take these over to the D.C. police and go through the mug books. They'll be in there."

"Your father agreed that under the circumstances I should come."

"Thank you, Mother. Thank you," Lucy said.

"You should thank your father too. He was going to use this money for a down payment on a new car."

"Yes," Lucy said, trying to hold back the tears.

"He loves you too, Lucy. He always wanted what was best for you."

"I know, Mom."

"I'll be there day after tomorrow at one o'clock. Dulles." She gave Lucy the flight number. "Can you meet me?"

"The kids and I'll be there. Thanks so much, Mom. I really need you."

"I know, baby. I know. Just don't tell Terry I'm coming."

From his window seat Jake stared at the mountains and forests through the gaps in the cloud cover as the Boeing 727 descended into the twilight. The mountain ridges ran off to the northeast between valleys now dark and murky, enlivened only by the twinkling jewels of towns and villages.

Over the Shenandoah Valley the 727 pilot broke his descent. Jake felt the gentle adjustment in nose attitude and the power addition. Now the left wing rose and the pilot eased to a new heading, still in a descent. This long glide back to earth was the best part, Jake decided, the best part of the flight after hours in the stratosphere. He closed his eyes and became one with the plane as the pilot leveled the wings and made another power adjustment. He could feel the controls, the stick and throttles in his hands, the—

"Is your seat belt fastened, sir?"

"Oh yes." Jake moved the newspaper on his lap so the stewardess could visually check. She smiled automatically and moved on.

Your return from the sky should be gentle and slow so that all the bittersweet flavor can be savored. The airspeed and altitude that held you so high above the earth should be surrendered gradually, not— Argh! What's the use? Why long for things that cannot be again? Stop it, Grafton! Stop wishing and longing and tasting the things of the past.

Power back, almost to idle. He heard the high-pitched whine of the flap motor and checked the wing. The pilot was milking them out as he turned yet again, no doubt following instructions from Air Traffic Control. The earth was only three or four thousand feet below and headlights of cars and trucks were visible. Farmhouses, towns, highways, dark woodlots, all slipped past beneath as the pilot in the cockpit of the airliner milked the flaps out further and eased left in a long sweeping turn that would probably line him up for the approach into Dulles. Jake waited. He was rewarded with a thunk and hum as the gear doors opened and the main mounts were lowered into the slipstream.

You miss it too much, he told himself. Too much.

Callie was waiting when Jake stepped out of the shuttle bus onto the concourse. He saw her and grinned, and walked right into the fat lady ahead of him. She had stopped dead and bent over to scoop two children into her arms. The children piped their welcome to their grandmother as the line of people behind came to a jerky halt. Callie watched with a wide grin on her face.

"Hi, Mom," Jake said as he put his arm over her shoulder.

The grin got even wider and her eyes sparkled. "Hi, Dad."

"We're not really going to do that, are we? Call each other Mom and Dad?"

"Maybe. Every now and then."

"Miss me?"

"A teeny tiny little bit. I'm getting used to having you around."

10

The plane to Washington was full. By some quirk, Toad was assigned a window seat and Rita was given the middle seat beside him. She asked about an aisle or window seat and was told by the harried agent that there were no more seats. Rita looked up and down the counter at the lines of people waiting to check baggage and get seat assignments, then turned back to the clerk and grinned. "That'll be fine, thank you."

Moravia had her hair pulled back and rolled tightly. Her white boater hat sat squarely, primly on the top of her head. She had used some makeup this morning, Toad noticed, and a glob of it showed on her right cheek where she had failed to feather it in. It was the only imperfection he could see. Her navy-blue blouse and skirt showed off a healthy figure in a modest yet sexy way. Toad took a deep breath and trailed along as they left the ticket counter. He had to stride to get up beside her.

"Let's get something to read," he suggested. "We have time."

She was agreeable. At the newsstand Toad looked longingly at the *Playboy* and *Penthouse* magazines with their covers hidden under a piece of black plastic to keep from titillating schoolboys or heating up old ladies. Maybe he should buy one and read it on the plane. That would get Moravia all twitchy. He glanced over to where she stood looking at newsmagazines and slicks for upscale women. No. He devoted his attention to the rack of paperbacks and finally selected one by Kurt Vonnegut. *Slaughterhouse-Five* was Toad's favorite book. Vonnegut knew life was insanity, just as Toad did, deep down, in the place where he lived. Today he chose one called *Galápagos*.

When the boarding announcement came, the seats near the gate emptied as everyone surged toward the stewardess guarding the entrance to the jetway. Toad took his time and held back. Two people sandwiched themselves between him and Moravia as they ambled toward the door; a guy in a business suit with shoulder-length hair and a woman in her fifties with bad knees. Yet somehow when Toad turned in his boarding pass he ended up right behind Moravia going down the jetway. There was another line waiting to get through the airplane's door. He queued behind her. The people behind him pressed forward. His nose was almost in her hair. She was wearing a delicate, heavenly scent. He inhaled it clear to his toenails.

They inched down the crowded aisle toward their seats. The air was stifling; too may people. Toad felt the walls closing in on him. There was a woman already in the aisle seat in their row, and when Toad finished stuffing his attaché case and hat into the overhead bin, he found Moravia was already in her seat. The woman on the aisle ignored him. Toad muttered his excuses and edged in front of their knees. Rita looked up from the operation of removing her hat and for the first time since he had known her gave him a warm smile. "Sorry."

"No problem," Toad said as he settled in beside her, acutely aware of her physical presence. Too aware. He adjusted the air nozzle in the overhead and turned hers on too. "Is this okay?"

"Thank you. That helps a lot." She smiled again, beautiful white teeth framed by lips that . . . Toad looked at his novel a while, couldn't get interested, then scanned the airline magazine from the seat pocket. Her skirt had inched up, revealing her knees. He obliquely examined her hands. Nails painted and trimmed, fingers long and slim. God! He caught her glancing at him and they both grinned nervously and looked away. He turned the overhead air vent full on and glued his face to the window.

They were somewhere over Montana and Toad was deep into Vonnegut's vision of humans evolving into seals in the millennia to come when Rita spoke again. "Toad," she said softly.

"Yeah." She was looking straight into his eyes.

"Why can't you and I be friends?"

He was thunderstruck. "Uh . . . aren't we?"

"You know what I mean."

Toad Tarkington glanced around desperately. No one was apparently paying any attention. Those eyes were looking straight at him. Just what does she mean? There are friends and there are *friends*. He had been floating along footloose and free and—whap! —suddenly here he was, smack in the middle of one of those delicious ambiguities that women work so hard to snare men in. For the first time he noticed that her right eye was brown and her left was hazel, a brownish green. Why not just tell her the truth? One good reason, of course, is that truth rarely works with women. Ah . . . the hell with it! Pay the money and see all the cards.

He leaned into the aura of her. "Because I like you too much to ever just be your friend, Rita Moravia. You are a beautiful woman and—" He reached up and smoothed the makeup in the caked buildup near her right ear. Then he lightly kissed her cheek. "That's why."

Those eyes were inches from his. "I thought you didn't like me."

"I like you too damn much."

Her hands closed around his. "Do you really mean that?"

He mumbled something inane.

Her lips glided into his. Her tongue was warm and slippery and the breath from her nostrils hot upon his cheek. Her hair brushed softly against his forehead. When she broke away he was breathing heavily. She had a trace of moisture on her upper lip. Out of the corner of his eye Toad saw the woman in the aisle seat scowling at them. "Rita . . ."

She glanced over her left shoulder, then back at Toad. She straightened in her seat while holding tightly to his hand with her right. She gave the woman beside her a frozen smile. She gripped his hand fiercely.

"Will you excuse us?" she said, and stood, still holding his hand as she moved past the knees that guarded the aisle, dragging Toad along in her wake.

She marched aft, past the kitchen and the stews loading the lunch cart, and got behind a girl in jeans waiting for the rest rooms. She turned and flashed Toad a nervous smile, then stood nonchalantly, still gripping his hand with hers. He squeezed and got a quick grin over her shoulder.

They made room for a woman who came out of one lavatory and then stood between the little doors shoulder to shoulder. A boy of eleven or twelve joined them. He examined their uniforms like they were dummies in a store window. Rita studiously ignored the inspection, but Toad gave him a friendly wink. Meanwhile the stews maneuvered the luncheon cart into the aisle.

When the other lavatory door opened and the occupant was clear, Rita stepped in and pulled Toad along. "Better get your mom to help you too," Toad told the wide-eyed boy. As he got the door closed Rita slammed the lock over and wrapped herself around him.

When they finally broke for air, she whispered, "I really thought you didn't like me."

"Fool."

"I wanted you to like me so much, but you were so distant, as if you didn't care at all." Her arms were locked behind his back, crushing them together. With his hands against the side of her head, he eased her head back. Her lipstick was smeared. He kissed her again, slowly and deeply.

Matilda Jackson peered through the peephole in the door. A man. "Luis Camacho, Mrs. Jackson. We met yesterday. Don't you remember?"

Oh yes. One of the FBI agents. She unfastened the chain lock and shot the dead bolt. When she opened the door, he said in a low voice, barely audible, "Special Agent Camacho, Mrs. Jackson. May I come in?"

"Please." She looked across the street at the crack house. No one in sight, though Lord knows, the lookout was probably watching out the window. Sometimes she caught a glimpse of him. She shut the door quickly.

Now he produced his credentials. "I have a few follow-up questions and—"

"Let's talk in the kitchen." She led the way. "Would you like a cup of coffee?"

"That would be nice."

The kitchen was warmer than the living room, and well lit. This was her favorite room in the house. Charlie had enjoyed sitting here watching her cook, the smell of baking things heavy in the air.

Camacho sat at the table and waited until she had poured coffee for both of them and sat down across from him. "Perhaps we can go over the whole thing again, if you don't mind?"

"Oh, not at all." She explained again about the crack house, about Mandy and Mrs. Blue and the dudes who delivered the crack and picked up the money. He led her into the events of last Friday night, the photos and the man who left the cigarette pack in the iron post two doors up the street.

"So you never saw anyone reach into that post?"

"No. I didn't. God, I didn't even think about that. If I had thought that somebody was going to come along any second and look for that thing I probably wouldn't have gone out there and gotten it. No. I know I shouldn't have done it, but I just wasn't thinking."

"We're pleased that you did. It's concerned citizens like you that enable law enforcement to function. When the time comes, and it's months—even years—away, would you be willing to testify?"

"Well . . ." Those dopers, if they knew who she was . . .

"We'll need your testimony to get the photos introduced as evidence."

"I'll . . ." She swallowed hard. She would be risking her life. "I'll think about— Can't you do it without me? You don't know what you're asking."

"We'll try, Mrs. Jackson. We won't ask unless we really need you." He sipped his coffee. "How long has the crack house been there?"

"Three, maybe four months. I called the police—"

"Have you been watching the place since it opened?"

"Yes. On and off. You know how it is. I just look over there occasionally. Try and keep an eye on what's going on."

"Have you seen the black men there before?"

"Oh yes." She thought about it. "At least a dozen times, I guess. I think they come almost every day to collect the money and such, but a lot of times I miss them. They don't come at the same time every day. And sometimes I think they skip a day."

"Have they seen you watching?"

"I don't think so. My God, I hope not." She sat back and smoothed her hair. "I've tried to stay out of sight . . . I've seen them so often . . ."

"How about the man who put the cigarette pack in the hollow fence post? Have you seen him before?"

She thought about it. "I—I don't think so. But really, I just can't remember."

"Have you ever seen anyone retrieve anything from the post?"

"Well, I—I just can't remember. Maybe I saw somebody and didn't pay much attention. Is it important?"

"At this point I don't know."

"Would he be white?"

"Probably."

She thought about it. There were so many people, up and down the street, all day long, week in, week out. Yet not that many were white. "I'll have to try and remember."

"Okay." He scooted his chair back and stood. "I appreciate your taking the time to talk to me. Is there anything else you think we should know?"

"Oh, I guess not. But when are you all going to get that crack house closed down?"

"We'll talk to the District police. I hope it's soon."

She accompanied him to the door and carefully locked it behind him. If only they would shut those people down. Get them out of the neighborhood.

"I got lipstick all over you," Rita Moravia said, and used a wet paper towel to wipe Toad's face. This lavatory was certainly not designed for two adults. He perched on the commode with the top down and she sat on his lap, humming softly as she worked on his face and he swabbed hers.

He carefully wiped away all the mascara and makeup. "You shouldn't use this stuff," he said. "You don't need it."

"Why did you get drunk last Friday?"

"I wanted you and couldn't have you." He lifted his shoulders and lowered them. "It seemed like a good idea at the time."

She laid her forehead against his and ran her fingers through his hair.

Someone pounded on the door.

"Maybe we should get back to our seats," he suggested.

"I suppose," she murmured, but she didn't move.

More knocking. "Hey, in there!"

Toad helped her to her feet and straightened her uniform. He ran his hands across her buttocks and hips as he stood. She kissed him again to the accompaniment of the pounding on the door.

She stepped out first, her head up, still holding his hand. Three stews stood in the kitchen area staring at them. Rita Moravia smiled. "We're newlyweds," she announced simply, and stepped past.

The women applauded wildly and the passengers joined in.

* * *

They parked the cars in the lot outside of Rita's apartment complex and Toad carried her bags in. He had followed her home from Dulles. They kissed in the elevator and they kissed in front of the door. A giggling, happy Rita used her key.

When the door swung open a young woman on the couch in front of the television shrieked. She had her hair in curlers and was wearing only bra and panties. Toad got an eyeful of skin as she scurried for the bedroom.

"Don't mind Harriet," Rita said. "I do the same for her on alternate Saturdays when she brings her boyfriend by."

Toad grinned and nodded. He stood in the center of the living room and glanced about while Rita lugged her bags toward the bedroom. "Need any help?"

"No, I'll manage. Make yourself comfortable." In a moment she called from the bedroom, "There's probably Coke in the fridge."

Toad sagged comfortably into the couch the roommate had recently vacated. Aha, a remote control for the TV. He flipped around the dial until he found a basketball game and settled his feet upon the settee. Knowing women as he did, he knew he had a while to wait.

"Who's the hunk?" Harriet demanded of Rita in the bedroom.

"A friend."

"What about Ogden? He's called twice this week wanting to know when you'd be home. I told him you'd call him this evening." Ogden was an attorney at a large Washington law firm whom Rita had been dating.

Rita opened her suitcase on the bed and began to empty it. She separated her dirty clothes from the clean ones, working quickly. "I'll call Ogden tomorrow."

Harriet eased the bedroom door open and peeked at Toad sprawled on the couch. "He's a live one, all right," she said after she had eased the door shut again. "Navy?"

"Yep."

Harriet sat cross-legged on her bed. "Are you sure about this, Rita? Ogden's a pretty great guy. He's athletic, rich parents, good future, madly in—"

"He wasn't the one. I'm sure."

Harriet pounced. "And this guy? Is he the one?"

"Maybe." Rita removed the pins that held her hair against the back of her head and shook it out. "He might be. He almost got away." She grinned and attacked her hair with a brush. "Reeled him in on the plane this afternoon."

"*This* afternoon?"

"And I'm going over to his apartment to spend the night."

Harriet flopped back on her bed and pointed her legs at the ceiling, toes extended. "Well, no one can say you're just jumping right into bed with him. My God, you've stifled your hormones and female appetites for an entire afternoon . . . it's positively Victorian. This will set the sexual revolution back a hundred years if it gets out." She lowered her legs and propped her head on one arm. "Why not let it cool off a quarter of a degree, Rita? A week . . ."

Rita Moravia shook her head.

"You've got it bad, huh?"

"Yep."

"Luis," his wife called from the top of the stairs. "Harlan is here."

"Send him down."

Mrs. Camacho smiled at her next-door neighbor and said, "He's in the basement watching a basketball game. As usual."

"I thought he might be," Harlan said, smiled and descended the staircase.

"Hey, Harlan. Great game. Boston College and West Virginia. BC's ahead by a bucket."

"Do you men want a beer?" Mrs. Camacho calling down from the kitchen.

"Thanks anyway, honey." They heard her close the door at the top of the stairs.

Harlan Albright sank into a chair near Camacho. He extracted a pack of Marlboros from his pocket and lit one. "Catching any spies?"

"Got Matilda Jackson's photos back from the lab yesterday afternoon. She's got one of Vasily Pochinkov, the assistant agricultural whosis at the embassy. So we've burned him. I'm trying to get surveillance approved. And sure enough, Mrs. Jackson had Franklin's drop message. The computer guys should decide it's the Pentagon by tomorrow."

"Better tell me all of it." Albright stared at the television as Camacho went through the initial interview with Mrs. Jackson and her attorney, the lab report, the interview with Mrs. Jackson today at her house. When Camacho was finished, Albright lit another cigarette. "Is there a crack house across the street?"

"Apparently. One of my men was going to check the D.C. police mug books. We'll have names and rap sheets by tomorrow, probably."

"But there's no way to tie this in with the crack gang?"

"You know there isn't."

"Did Mrs. Jackson ever see Franklin?"

Luis Camacho rubbed his chin thoughtfully. "I'm not sure. She may have and doesn't remember. She said she'd think about it."

"What do you think?"

"How many times has he been to that drop?"

"Five."

He considered. "I think she's probably seen him," he said at last. "Whether she could pick him out of a lineup or mug book, I don't know."

"Where will you be if your boss asks you why you haven't tried that, once the Pentagon angle is nailed down?"

"I'll look like an incompetent. I'll have to bring her in to go over the photo books to cover myself."

"When?"

"Maybe next week. Maybe the week after. They'll want to evaluate. At first they're going to be interested in Pochinkov. For a day or two. Then they'll get interested in Mrs. Jackson again."

"Pochinkov is a dead end."

"They'll come to that conclusion. Bigelow, my boss, has no background in counterespionage, but he's a smart man. He'll drool over Pochinkov for a day or two, toy with the idea of trapping and turning him, then eventually decide that we can't spare the manpower to watch him day and night forever. Of course, the National Security Council could decide to try to catch him servicing a drop just so we can kick him out of the country, but you probably have a better feel for that than I."

A wry grin twisted Albright's lips. The implication was that Albright knew whether or not the Soviets were going to pick up an American diplomat in Moscow anytime soon, knowledge that Camacho well knew Albright would never have. So even here, in the safety and comfort of his own den, Camacho was stroking the ego of his control. He did it unconsciously, without even thinking. No wonder Luis Camacho had done so well in the FBI.

"How come you guys had a drop in that neighborhood anyway?"

"It was on the approved list." Albright shrugged. The paper pushers in Moscow had no appreciation of the dynamics of an American neighborhood, how fast it could evolve or erode. The approval of drop sites was one method Soviet intelligence bureaucrats used to justify their salaries, but Albright wasn't going to explain that to Camacho. He had learned early in his career that a wise man never complains about things he can't change, especially to an agent he needed to keep loyal and motivated.

Still, Luis Camacho wasn't like other agents. Albright had been running him now for over ten years, but it was only in the last few years, when the source the Americans called the Minotaur had surfaced and within months Camacho had had the serendipitous good fortune to be assigned to head the Washington, D.C., FBI counterespionage department, that Camacho had become a Soviet treasure.

Tonight as he stared at the ballet of black men on the television screen, Albright reflected again on that chain of events. After a high-profile black-tie affair in the ballroom of a Washington hotel, the Soviet ambassador had discovered a picture postcard in his coat pocket as his limousine returned him to the embassy. On the front of the card was a photo of the Pentagon at night. On the back were two words and a series of numbers and letters—a computer file name—all written in block letters. Below that were ten words; not a message, just words. Nothing else. No fingerprints except the ambassador's.

It had been enough. Using Terry Franklin, the Soviets had obtained engineering and performance data on the new U.S. Air Force stealth fighter, the F-117A, from the Pentagon computer system. The information appeared genuine. So who was the source? Unmasking the source would undoubtedly reveal why the information was passed and enable the Soviet intelligence community to properly evaluate its authenticity. But the official guest list for the black-tie reception ran to over three hundred names and was almost a Who's Who of official Washington. The names of spouses and girlfriends in attendance were not on the list, nor were the names of at least a dozen officials who had been seen there. The lists of hotel and caterer personnel were also inaccurate and incomplete.

The upper echelons of the Soviet intelligence community were stymied. The first rule of intelligence gathering—know your source —had been violated. Yet the information appeared genuine and revealed just how far ahead of the Soviets the Americans were with stealth technology.

Three months after the ambassador had received the postcard, an unsigned letter in a plain white envelope arrived at the Soviet embassy addressed to the ambassador. The letter, in neat block letters, was a commentary on the rights of minorities in the Soviet Union. In accordance with standard procedure for unsolicited mail, the letter was sent to Moscow. There the code was broken. The writer had constructed a matrix using the first random word on the original postcard as the key word. The message was three random words, the first two of which proved to be computer access words. The third word wasn't a word at all, but a series of numbers and letters. From the bowels of the Pentagon, Terry Franklin produced a fascinating document concerning the development of a land-based anti-satellite laser about which Soviet intelligence had known absolutely nothing.

Further letters followed, each encoded on the basis of a key word which appeared on the original postcard, the ambassador's. The information was golden: more stealth, Trident missile updates, SDI research breakthroughs, laser optics for artillery, satellite navigation systems . . . the list was breathtaking. The Soviets were seeing hard data on America's most precious defense secrets. And they didn't know who was giving it to them. Or why.

So Harlan Albright was told to use Mother Russia's most precious agent to find out. And here he sat, Luis Camacho, FBI special agent in charge, Washington, D.C., office of counterespionage. Camacho hadn't found a sniff.

Damn, it was frustrating. And now the Terry Franklin tool to exploit the unknown source was unraveling.

"Do you believe in the entropy principle?" Camacho asked. There was a commercial on the television.

Albright shifted his gaze and tried to clear his thoughts. "Entropy?"

"Disorder always increases in a closed system."

"I suppose."

"Will Franklin hold up?"

"I don't know. I doubt it. And he knows too much." He felt a chill as he contemplated the wrath of his superiors if Franklin should ever list his thefts for the Americans.

"Can you get him to the Soviet Union?"

Albright shrugged and stood. "I'd better go home and get some sleep."

"Yeah."

"Drop over tomorrow evening."

"Sure."

Rita Moravia's worst moment came when she preceded Toad into his apartment. "I've only been here a month or so," Toad said behind her. Open cardboard boxes brimming with books and towels and bric-a-brac sat everywhere. She stepped into the kitchen. The sink was full of dishes. Something hideous was growing in a saucepan on the stove. The refrigerator contained half a case of beer and a six-pack of Coke—nothing else. At least it was clean. But how in the world had this man managed to get all these dishes dirty? Aha, the freezer was chock-full of frozen vegetables and TV dinners. Even some meat.

She dumped the contents of the saucepan into the sink and ran the pan full of water, then let the water from the faucet flush the putrid mixture past the trap.

Toad was fidgety. "I'm not much of a housekeeper," he mumbled. "Been trying to get unpacked and all but I've been so busy."

Rita went into the bedroom and snapped on the lights. The bed was a rumpled mess. She ripped away the spread and blanket and tossed them on the floor, then began stripping the sheets. "Get out clean sheets."

"Uh . . . y'see, that's the only set I have. Why waste money on extra sheets when you can only use one set at a . . ." He ran out of words when she glanced at him as she removed the pillows from their cases. "Why don't I take the sheets and pillowcases down to the basement and run them through the washer." He grabbed them from the floor where Rita had thrown them and charged for the door. It closed behind him with a bang. Rita Moravia smiled and shook her head.

She tackled the bedroom first. Dirty clothes were piled in one corner of the closet. She used a T-shirt for a dustrag. No cleanser in the bathroom. He had never cleaned the commode. She was swabbing it when she heard the apartment door open. In seconds he appeared.

"Hey, Rita, you don't—"

"Is there a convenience store nearby that's still open?"

"I suppose . . ."

"I want cleanser, dishwashing liquid, something to clean these floors with . . . a mop and some sponges. And an air freshener."

"Tomorrow I—"

"Now, Tarkington."

He turned and left without a word.

In twenty minutes he was back with a bag full of supplies. She handed him the laundry from the closet. "You go wash these and then clean up the living room and kitchen."

When she got the sheets back on the bed she locked the bedroom door. Toad was making noises in the kitchen. She washed her face, brushed her teeth and hung up her clothes from the overnight bag. She put on a frilly negligee Harriet had given her for Christmas when it looked as if her anemic romance with Ogden might finally blossom.

Poor Ogden. His town house always looked as if the maid just left five minutes before you arrived. Appearances were so important to him. He would be devastated if he could see her in this slum. Oh well. Toad had something that Ogden would never have. She thought about it as she brushed out her hair again. Tarkington had guts as well as brains, and he knew what was important and what wasn't. He believed in himself and his abilities with a profound, unshakable faith, so he wasn't threatened by what she was, what she accomplished. Any way you looked at it, Toad Tarkington was a man.

And a man was precisely what Rita Moravia wanted in her life.

She turned off all the lights except the one on the nightstand, then opened the bedroom door.

Toad was up to his elbows in soapsuds in the sink. He had used too much dishwashing liquid. Too much water too. Water and suds were slopped over half the counter. Damn. He shouldn't have brought Rita here with the apartment in such a mess. He had been meaning to unpack and clean it up, but the chore always seemed one that could wait. He had been seeing that secretary over in Alexandria but they always went to her place. It just hadn't occurred to him how Rita might react until it was too late—like when he was fishing for the key to open the door.

Doggone, Toad, you find a really nice girl for a change and you screw it up right at the start. More water slopped over the edge of the sink. He felt it soaking the front of his pants. Oh poop.

He heard a laugh and turned. Rita was standing in the kitchen door laughing with her hand over her mouth. He grinned at her and worked blindly on the dishes. He couldn't take his eyes off her.

"You used too much water," she said.

"Uh-huh." With her hair down around her shoulders she looked like a completely different woman—softer, more feminine. And that frilly little nothing she was wearing!

"Do you have any dish towels?"

"Of course I have—"

"Where?"

"Where?" He forced his eyes to look at the likely places while he considered. "Oh yeah, in that box over there behind the table."

She swabbed the counter while he hurriedly finished the dishes and stacked them in the drainer. He pulled the plug in the sink and she wiped his hands and arms.

"I'm sorry this place is such a mess. I—"

She put her arms around his neck and kissed him. He never did get to finish that apology.

"What's your first name?"

"Robert."

"Why do they call you Toad?"

"Because I'm horny all the time."

"Umm," Rita Moravia said. "Oh yes, I see. Lucky me."

11

We got something," Dreyfus said with a grin as he leaned in Luis Camacho's office door.

"Well, don't keep me waiting."

After entering and closing the door, Dreyfus approached the desk and handed Camacho a photocopy of the message from the cigarette pack that Mrs. Jackson had supplied. "Interest Golden. TS 849329.002EB."

"What I did," Dreyfus said, "was to have the computer wizards in the basement assume this message came from one of those letters that have been going to the Soviet embassy." Camacho nodded. All mail addressed to the Soviet embassy was routinely examined and interesting items photocopied. So the FBI had copies of messages from sixty-three letters that looked suspicious.

"And sho nuff, it did. This little dilly right here." From a file he pulled another photocopy. The message was a vitriolic screed on Soviet support of the Afghan puppet regime.

"What's the code word?"

"Luteinizing."

"What the heck kind of word is that?"

"Some medical word."

"Will that break any of the other messages?"

"These four." Dreyfus laid four more photocopies on the desk before his boss. On the bottom of each was penciled the code word and the message, and the initials of the computer technician.

"How about that?" Camacho said. "Very nicely done, Dreyfus."

Dreyfus sagged into a seat across the desk. He was tall and angular and liked his pipe, which he extracted from a sweater pocket and charged. "We're still short a whole bunch of code words."

Camacho eyed his colleague as he drew deeply on the pipe and exhaled clouds of smoke. "So now we know how the code is constructed?" he prompted.

"Yeah. It's a matrix."

"And?"

"And if we could tie up the mainframe for a couple weeks, we could construct a matrix for each and every word in the dictionary and compare them with every message. Given enough time on the computer, we can crack them all."

"And then we'll know what was stolen." Camacho turned to the window. There was little to see. It was a windy, cold day out there. "Two weeks? Jesus, that's a hell of a lot of computing time. You should be able to find the Grand Unified Theory with two weeks on a Cray computer."

"Well, from looking at this word he used—'luteinizing'—it's obvious that some of the words are probably verb participles, past tense, etc. It's possible—probable, since this guy's pretty damn cute—that some of the code words are the names of persons or places. The number of possible English codewords is in the millions, and the computer must construct a matrix for each and every one of them and test each matrix against all the suspected messages. So what is that—a couple million repetitions of the program times sixty? Assuming he used real words or names. But if he made up random combinations of letters, say a dozen letters . . ." Dreyfus shrugged.

On a scratch pad Camacho wrote, "26^{12}." "Point made," he muttered.

"Oh, I know, I know. Even after we have all the messages cracked, we won't have the Minotaur. But we'll have his scent. Once we know which files he's been in, we can trot over to the Pentagon and glom on to the access sheets for those files. Our boy has seen them all."

"Maybe. But not very likely. Probably he got the access codes during an unauthorized peek in the main security files. But the document key words and numbers—" He sighed. "I would bet my last penny he hasn't seen all the files he's given away. I'll bet there isn't a man alive who's had authorized access to all those files."

"It's worth a try."

"Agreed. But we'll never get the Cray mainframe for two weeks. The fingerprint guys would cry a river. So let's get started with what we have. Get the access sheets for these five files we know about and let's see who's on them. And for Christ's sake, keep your head down. Don't let anyone know what you're after. We don't want to spook our man."

"Okay," Dreyfus agreed. "While we're at it, why don't we just pick up Terry Franklin and sweat the little bastard?"

"Not yet."

Dreyfus' pipe was dead. He sucked audibly, then got out his lighter. When he was exhaling smoke again, he said, "I think we're making a mistake not keeping Franklin under surveillance."

"What if the little shit bolts? What then? Is Franklin the only mole Ivan has over there? Is he?"

Dreyfus threw up his hands and gathered up his papers.

"Get somebody to tackle this decoding project with the mainframe when it's not in use. The front office will never give us two weeks, but let's see what we can do with a couple hours here and there."

"Sure, Luis."

"Again, nice work, Dreyfus."

Camacho stared at the door after Dreyfus left. He had slipped and made a mistake; he had lied to Dreyfus. The only way to keep two separate lives completely, safely separate was to never tell a lie. Never. You often had to leave out part of the truth, but that wasn't a lie. A lie was a booby trap, a land mine that could explode at any time with fatal results. And this lie had been a big one. He sat now staring at the objects on his desk with unseeing eyes as he examined the dimensions of the lie and its possible implications. Stupid! A stupid, idiotic lie.

He rubbed his forehead again and found he couldn't sit still. He paced, back and forth and back and forth, until finally he was standing in front of the Pentagon organization chart. If there were forty files or sixty-three or any number, there would be a small group of people who would have access to all of them, if you constructed just one more hypothesis—that all the files concerned classified projects in research or development. Tyler Henry the admiral suspected they did. Albright the spy already knew and had told him so. Camacho the spy catcher must verify or refute that hypothesis soon, or Dreyfus and Henry and Albright and a lot of the others are going to think him incompetent, or worse.

He stood staring at one box on the complex chart. Inside the box was printed: "Under Secretary of Defense for Acquisition."

He sat at his desk and unlocked the lower right drawer and removed a file. Inside were photocopies of all sixty-three letters. They were in chronological order. All had been written on plain white copy machine paper in #2 lead pencil, which had been a wise precaution on the part of the person or persons who wrote them. Ink could be analyzed chemically and the sellers of pens could be interviewed, but a #2 lead pencil was a #2 lead pencil. And copy machine paper—the stuff was everywhere, in every office of the nation.

On an average day the Soviet embassy received several dozen casual cards and letters mailed from all over the United States. Most of the messages were short and to the point. Many were crude. "Eat shit, Ivan," seemed to be popular. The Chernobyl disaster and the Armenian earthquake had elicited thousands of pieces of mail, much to the chagrin of the postal inspectors and FBI agents assigned to screen it.

Over the last three years these letters in this file had been culled for further scrutiny. All the messages were printed in small block letters, all were long enough to contain an internal code and all of them had been written in English by someone with a fairly decent education. Some were signed and some weren't. Interestingly, about 80 percent of these letters had been mailed in the Washington metropolitan area. Not a one had been mailed from over a hundred miles away. All had been enclosed in cheap, plain white envelopes available in hundreds of bookstores, convenience stores, supermarkets, etc., all over town.

Camacho looked closely. It was easy to see that the same person had written them all; the penmanship was so careful and neat, the style of the writer so consistent from letter to letter. And every now and then, maybe once in every other letter, the syntax was tortuous, not quite right. It was as if the writer purposefully chose a difficult sentence construction. The conclusion that these letters, or at least some of them, contained an internal code was inescapable.

The mechanics of the matrix demanded a reasonably long letter if one were going to encrypt a long message, say three dozen characters. If it took an average of three words to signal one character, then the message must run to at least nine dozen words, too many for a postcard.

The sheer number of letters was daunting. Some of them were probably dross. The Minotaur knew these letters would arouse suspicion, so he wrote lots of them. And it was impossible to tell which contained a code and which didn't. He was hiding in plain sight.

Maybe that was the key. Maybe the Minotaur wasn't just some career civil servant, some clerk. Maybe he was a man in plain sight, out in the open, known to one and all. But why? Why was he committing treason? That's what the Soviets wanted to know.

Camacho picked up the phone and punched numbers. "Dreyfus, pull the files on all the political people in the Defense Department and put them in the conference room."

"All of them? Again?"

"All."

"Yessir," Dreyfus said without enthusiasm.

Even a blind hog finds an acorn occasionally, Camacho told himself as he cradled the phone. And if there's an acorn in those files, this time I'm going to find it.

The youngest child, a four-year-old boy, threw a fit as Lucy Franklin drove toward Dulles. The nine-year old, Karen, had been deviling him all morning, and apparently he decided he had had enough. He wailed at the top of his lungs and punched at his sister. One of his swings connected with her nose. Blood spouted and she screamed too. Lucy pulled off the freeway and put the car in neutral.

"Shut up!" she roared. "Both you kids, *stop it!*"

Satisfied with the outcome of the battle, the boy sat back and stared at the blood dripping on his sister's dress as she sobbed uncontrollably.

"Look at you two. Fighting again. Now Karen's hurt. Aren't you sorry, Kevin?"

He didn't look a bit sorry, which made Karen cry harder. Lucy got her into the front seat and held a tissue on her nose until the bleeding stopped. She cuddled the child. Karen had vomited twice during the night, so this morning Lucy had kept her home from school.

The traffic roared by. "Say you're sorry, Kevin."

"I'm sorry." His hand came over the seat and touched Karen's hair. The sobbing gradually eased. Holding a tissue against Karen's nose with her left hand, Lucy leaned over the seat and cuddled the boy. This week had been tough on them. Terry was so distant, saying little, shouting at the children as they ran through the house and made their usual noise.

He was a volcano about to erupt. His tension and fear were tangible, visible, frightening to the children, terrifying to Lucy. Even as she sat here on the freeway, the unreasoning panic that Terry caused washed over her again. What had he done? What would he do? Would he hurt the children? Would he hurt her?

"Mommy, don't cry."

"I'm not crying, sweetheart. I just have something in my eye."

"I'm okay now," Karen said, casting an evil glance across the seat back at her brother.

"No more fighting. You two love each other. No more fighting. It makes me sad to see you two trying to irritate each other."

Now Kevin's hand touched her hair. "Let's go get Grandma."

"Yes. Let's do." She started the engine and slipped out into traffic.

At lunch Toad and Rita shared a table, just the two of them. From a table fifty feet away Jake Grafton watched the body language and gestures as he listened to George Wilson and Dalton Harris talk baseball. So Toad Tarkington had fallen in love again! That guy went over that precipice with awe-inspiring regularity. The impact at the bottom was also spectacular.

You really had to tip your hat to the guy. He arrives, takes in the female situation at a glance, then immediately makes a fool of himself over the best-looking woman in sight. Jake allowed himself a grin. The ol' Horny Toad.

Back in the office after lunch, Jake called Tarkington over to his desk. "I've been looking over this memo about the A-6 system. How did it go when you turned off the radar and Doppler?"

"Well, sir, without the Doppler to dampen the velocities, the inertial tends to drift somewhat. But without the radar all you have is the IR and it's tough. When it isn't raining or snowing you can run attacks okay once you've found the target. The nav system just isn't right enough to let you find the targets without the radar. The IR doesn't have enough field of view. With a global positioning system to stabilize the inertial you might have a chance, but not now."

"It looks to me like you've got a handle on the major problems. This evening how about jumping a plane and flying up to Calverton, New York? With Commander Richards. The guys at Grumman are expecting you two. I want you to look over the A-6G system and play with it and let me know what you think. Come back Monday. Tuesday you and I are going to take a little trip out West."

The lieutenant's face reflected his dismay.

"That's not going to put you out or interfere with anything, is it?" Jake tried to appear solicitous.

"Geez, CAG. The whole weekend—"

"You didn't have anything going, did you? I mean, you haven't been around here long enough to—"

"Oh no, sir. I just thought I'd do my laundry and all. Maybe take in a movie. Write a letter to my mom."

Jake couldn't hold back a smile. "Running out of clean underwear, huh?"

Toad nodded, trying to maintain a straight face.

"Buy some more. See you Monday, Toad."

"Yessir. Monday."

At four o'clock Jake received a call from Commander Rob Knight. "Could you come over to my office?"

"Well, I was getting ready to go home."

"On your way?"

"Sure."

Jake locked the files, turned off the lights and snagged his hat on the way out. Smoke Judy was still there. "Lock up, will you, Smoke?"

"Sure, Captain. Have a good weekend."

"You too."

Jake walked to the Pentagon. He was getting very familiar with this route. The parking lot was emptying as he crossed it and he had to do some dodging.

On the fourth-level corridor the pile of used furniture was still gathering dust. Jake turned right on the D-Ring and walked down three doors. He knocked.

Rear Admiral Costello opened the door. "Ah, Captain, please come in."

The room was packed. People were sitting on desks. Everyone had a beer can in his hand. Vice Admiral Henry was there, Costello's three aides—all captains fresh from carrier commands and waiting for the flag list or new orders—together with the four office regulars and two admirals Jake didn't know. He accepted a beer and found himself talking to Henry. "Glad you could join us, Captain."

"Delighted, sir."

It was Happy Hour. These men who had spent their lives in the camaraderie of ready rooms needed two hours at the end of the week to review the week's frustrations and reduce them to manageable proportions. Soon the subject turned from shop to mutual friends, ships, ports, and planes they had flown.

Just before six Jake excused himself. He and Callie were going to the beach this evening. Tyler Henry grabbed his hat and started with Jake for the door. As Jake opened it, Henry paused and took a long, smiling look at the bulletin board. He was looking at a photo. It was a black-and-white eight-by-ten of singer Ann-Margret holding a microphone in her hand and singing her heart out, wearing a sleeveless shorty blouse and no pants at all.

"I was there," Henry said. *"Kitty Hawk,* '67 or '68. That woman . . ." He pointed at the picture. "She's *all* lady. She's my favorite entertainer."

The photo was autographed and signed. "To the guys of OP-506." Yes, thought Jake Grafton, remembering those days. No doubt that was a great moment for her, performing before five thousand screaming sailors, but it was an even greater moment for them, a moment they would remember and cherish every day of their lives, each and every man jack of them. Of course, bombing North Vietnam twelve hours a day, some of them didn't have very many days left. The loss rate then was almost a plane a day. No doubt Ann-Margret had known that.

"Mine too," said Jake Grafton, and together with the admiral walked into the corridor where he said goodbye. The admiral went back toward his office as Jake set off alone for the subway.

At six o'clock, as Jake Grafton was boarding the subway at the Pentagon station, Luis Camacho closed the last of the files piled up on his desk. It was hopeless: 218 files, 218 political appointees in the Department of Defense, including the service secretaries and unders and assistants. He had selected just eighteen files: the Under

Secretary of Defense for Acquisition, his political aides, and the assistants and under secretaries in SECDEF's office. And SECDEF. All these men had held their positions for at least three years. But it was still hopeless.

If one of these men was the Minotaur, no hint of it came from the FBI background investigations that had been completed for the Senate confirmation process. The common thread was that they were pillars of the establishment, the kind of men generations of mothers prayed their daughters would marry. All eighteen were white, well educated, leaders in their local communities, respected by all those similarly situated. Several had previously held elected or appointed office. Most were family men or divorced family men. Thirteen of them had graduated from an Ivy League school. Tennis was the most popular sport and golf a close second. Several were yachtsmen. Every single one of them could be labeled independently wealthy, most from old family money, a few from small fortunes they had made themselves.

It was sickening. Wealth, privilege, power, spelled out in these files in black and white. Oh, they had a few little peccadillos. One man had flunked out of three colleges before he had completed his education in a fourth. Three drunken-driving convictions. One illegitimate child. One man had been known to frequent prostitutes in his younger days, and one had been accused of being a closet homosexual by a disgruntled soon-to-be-ex during a messy divorce. Luis Camacho, career cop, thought it pretty tame stuff.

For several seconds he sat and stared at the piles of folders spread over the table. No cop, he told himself, ever looked seriously at a more unlikely group of suspects. There wasn't even one man with a family or background that might be vulnerable to intense scrutiny. Not here. These men had had every advantage that birth, wealth, and social position could confer. Sadly he shook his head.

If the key to the Minotaur's behavior was in his past, it was going to remain buried unless a small army of agents with a lot of time were told to dig deep. The agents Camacho could get. What frustrated Camacho was his suspicion that he was running out of time. What infuriated him was his conviction that no matter how deep they dug, the investigators could come up dry. And without something . . . some artifact . . . something tangible, how could he sell a man to Albright as the Minotaur? Albright would want a man he could understand, with a motivation that could be reduced to writing and passed from the Aquarium to the Kremlin and would explain. The committee should have thought this problem through two years ago.

He went back to his office and found a photo of Terry Franklin in the file. Actually there were four of them. The one he selected was a full-figure shot taken with a hidden camera. Franklin was looking just to the right of the camera, perhaps waiting for a car to pass the parked van the photographer had used. This picture he placed in an inside pocket of his sports coat. He glanced at his watch. If he went to the Pentagon, he could probably still catch Vice Admiral Henry, who rarely left before 7 P.M.

Terry Franklin stopped at a neighborhood bar after he got off the bus from work. On the Friday evening of the longest week of his life, he deserved a few drinks. Waiting for the ax to fall was squeezing the juice right out of him. He had been a bumbling fool all week, botching one job after another, having to ask the chief for help with several problems that were so minor he had been embarrassed. The chief was solicitous, asking if he was having problems at home.

The problem was he couldn't think about anything else. He could no longer concentrate on his job, his wife, the kids, anything. He *had* to get his mind off it and he just couldn't! Sitting here at the bar, he glanced warily at the other customers, then bit his lip. A panic-stricken scream was just beneath the surface. He was losing it. It was like one of those nightmares he had as a kid—he was fleeing from a hideous monster and his legs went slower and slower and the monster was reaching out, within inches of catching him—and he woke up screaming with pee soaking his pajamas.

He was going to have to get all this crap stuffed into one sock, going to have to wire himself together so he could get from one end of the day to the other. He had all of tonight, all day Saturday, all day Sunday—three nights and two whole days—before he had to face his demons on Monday.

He ordered another CC on the rocks. Sure, he could do it. No one knew. No one was going to arrest him. No one was going to toss him into prison with a bunch of homo thieves and killers. After all, this is *America,* land of the gullible, home of the foolish.

He would deliver and collect on another dozen floppies or so. Then he would empty his safe-deposit box and be on his way to a new life. Perhaps Rio. He would lie on the beach all day and fuck beach bunnies at night.

He sipped on his drink and thought about how it would be. The life he had always wanted was right there within his grasp, so close, within inches. But he was going to have to be realistic about the monsters, going to have to keep trotting. No urine-soaked pajamas. No screaming fits. Amen.

He paid the tab and left two quarters on the bar. Outside he forced himself to pause and examine the headlines on the newspaper in the vending stand. Same old crap. The world was still turning, things were burning down, trains were still crashing . . .

He walked the two blocks home with his head up, breathing the spring air. It seemed just yesterday that it was so cold and miserable. *Spring is here. And I've got a fortune in the bank and no one knows but me.*

His neighbor was washing his car in the driveway. "Hey, Terry, how's it going?"

"Pretty good. And you?"

"Just fine. Say, I've been meaning to ask you. How's the spy business?"

Terry Franklin froze.

The asshole tossed his sponge into a bucket and wiped his hands on his jeans. He grinned as he reached for his cigarettes. "Lucy has been telling Melanie that you're a spy. I laughed myself sick. So . . ."

Terry didn't hear any more. He lurched for the front door.

"Lucy!" He slammed the door behind him and charged for the kitchen. *"Lucy,"* he bellowed, "you *stupid—*"

Lucy was sitting with her mother drinking coffee at the counter. Both women stared, openmouthed.

"What—what does Jared mean—about Melanie? *What* did you tell Melanie?" He thought he was doing pretty well under the circumstances, staying calm and keeping the legs going. But it came out as a roar.

"Now listen here, Terry—" Lucy's mom began.

"Lucy, I need to talk to you." He grabbed her arm and half lifted her from the stool. "Now, Lucy."

"Let go of her, Terry!"

"Mom Southworth, *please!* I need to talk to—"

"No!" The old lady had a voice like a drill instructor.

"Lucy, what did you tell that moron Melanie?"

"I told her that—"

"Get your hands off her, Terry. I know all about you. You stupid, greedy—" The older woman was fat, with two chins. Just now Terry Franklin thought her the ugliest woman he had ever laid eyes on.

"Shut up, you nosy old bitch! What the hell are you doing here anyway? Lucy, I want to talk to you." He grabbed her arm and dragged her from the stool toward the downstairs half-bath. He pulled her inside and slammed the door. "What in the name of God have you been saying to Melanie?"

Lucy was scared witless. "Noth—"

"Did you tell her I was a spy?"

Terry didn't need an answer; it was written all over her face. The mother-in-law was pounding on the door and shouting. Something about calling the police.

"You—you—" he whimpered as his legs turned to wood and the monster's fetid breath engulfed him.

Lucy opened the door and slid out as he sagged down onto the floor and covered his face with his hands. His whole life was shattered, smashed to bits by that silly, simple twat!

It was 8:30 P.M. when Luis Camacho parked in front of Mrs. Jackson's house and locked his car. It was a delightful spring evening, still a nip in the air, but almost no wind. The foliage was budding. Summer was coming and the earth was ready.

As he walked down the street Camacho glanced at the crack house. Someone was peering though a curtain on the second floor; he saw it move. No one on the sidewalk. Mrs. Jackson's gate was ajar, but not a light showed through the curtains.

He mounted the stoop and rapped on the door. As he waited he glanced around. Street still empty. Such a beautiful evening. He knocked some more. Perhaps she had gone to the store, or to a neighbor's?

Suddenly he knew. He tried the knob. It turned. He pushed the door open several inches and called into the darkness, "Mrs. Jackson? Mrs. Jackson, are you here?" He gingerly pushed the door open wider and reached under his jacket for the butt of the .357 magnum on his right hip.

All the lights were off. Camacho closed the door behind him and stood in the darkness listening with the revolver in his hand.

Nothing. Not a sound. Not a squeak, not a creak, nothing.

He waited, flexing his fingers on the butt of the gun. All he could hear was the thud of his own heart.

Slowly, carefully, he groped for the light switch on the wall.

She was lying near the kitchen door with her right leg twisted under her, staring fixedly at the ceiling. In the center of her forehead was a small red circle. No blood. She had died instantly.

With the revolver ready he went from room to room, turning on lights and glancing into closets. Everything was neat, clean, tidy. Satisfied that the killer was gone, he came back to the living room and stood looking at Mrs. Jackson. He stooped and touched her cheek. She had been dead for hours. Around the bullet hole in her forehead was a black substance. A powder burn.

The phone was in the kitchen. Her purse sat beside it, the catch still latched. Camacho wrapped his handkerchief loosely around the telephone receiver before he picked it up. He dialed with a pen from his shirt pocket. As he waited for the duty officer to answer, he idly noticed that the fire under the coffeepot had been turned off. A professional hit. With any luck the body would not have been discovered for days and the time of death would have been problematic.

"This is Special Agent Camacho." He gave them the address. "I've discovered a corpse. Better send the forensic team and the D.C. police liaison officer. And call Dreyfus at home and ask him to come over."

Back in the living room he tried to avoid looking at Mrs. Jackson. Something shiny in a candy dish on the sideboard caught his eye. He stepped carefully over the body and bent to look. A spent .22 caliber Long Rifle cartridge. The killer hadn't bothered to retrieve the spent casing! And why should he? Twenty-two caliber rimfire ammunition was sold everywhere and was virtually untraceable. But how had this shell got here?

He went back to the corpse and stood near it. Then he stooped down and felt her head carefully. Another bullet hole in the back of her head. Okay, where is the second shell?

The FBI agent got down on his hands and knees and looked under everything. He found it in a corner, half hidden by the edge of the carpet, bearing the Remington "U." Camacho didn't touch it.

So Mrs. Jackson had opened the door and admitted her killer. Locks not forced or scratched up. She had started back toward the kitchen, the killer behind, and he had shot her in the back of the head. She had died on her feet and collapsed where she stood. He had walked over to her and fired a second shot into her brain with the pistol held inches from her face. That shell casing was ejected by the pistol into the candy dish. The killer had then proceeded on through the house, checking for other people, turning off lights, turning off the stove, making sure nothing would cause a fire or call attention to the house. Then he had left and closed the door carefully behind him. He hadn't bothered to lock it.

Even that was smart. No doubt the assassin had worn gloves, so he left no fingerprints. If the local punks tried the knob and came in to see what they could steal, they would probably not be so sophisticated, and they would automatically become the prime suspects in Mrs. Jackson's murder. All very slick.

The bastard!

Camacho was standing by the front window looking at the crack house when the lab van pulled up, followed immediately by a sedan with city plates and two sedans with U.S. government tags. Two hours later the forensic team and the other people departed with the body. Dreyfus and a lieutenant from the D.C. force remained with Luis Camacho.

"When are you going to raid that crack house, shut it down?" Camacho asked the question of the plainclothes lieutenant as he jerked his head at the building across the street.

"Who says it's a crack house?"

"What're you afraid of? Think the mayor might be in there?"

"Listen, asshole! If you've got any evidence that dwelling is being used for illegal purposes, I'd like to see it. We'll do some affidavits, find a judge and get a warrant. Then we'll raid the place. Now are you all hot air or do you have some *evidence*?"

"We have a statement from a woman now dead. We sent a copy over to you guys three days ago."

"I saw that statement, then routed it to the narcs. All it said was that there was suspicious activity over there. A little old woman thought something nasty was going on in her neighborhood. Big fucking deal! No judge in this country would have called that probable cause and issued a warrant, even if that statement had been sworn, which it wasn't. Now where's the goddamn *evidence*?"

"Whatever happened to 'usually reliable sources'?"

The lieutenant didn't reply.

"All you guys must belong to the ACLU." Camacho stood looking at the house, the peeling paint, the mortar missing from the brick joints, the trash in front of the place, the light leaking around drawn blinds. Just then a large old Cadillac hardtop came around the corner and drifted slowly to a stop at the curb. Four young black men got out. One went up the steps toward the door of the house, which opened before he reached it and closed behind him.

"Just follow me," Camacho said. "I'll get you some evidence." Even before he finished speaking he was out the door and going down the stairs to the sidewalk two at a time.

He went across the street toward the Cad at a brisk walk. The three men were staring.

"Hi." He reached into his jacket pocket with his left hand and pulled out his credentials. "FBI—"

One of the men was moving, going sideways and reaching under his shirt. Camacho rammed his left shoulder into the nearest man and fell on top of him as he drew his revolver. He heard a shot, then two more in quick succession. The man who had gone for his gun fell backward against the car, then slid to the sidewalk as Camacho jammed his revolver against the teeth of the struggling man under him.

"Don't!" The man opened his mouth and Camacho jammed the gun in up to the trigger guard. "Freeze, shithead!"

On the other side of the car someone was pleading, "Don't shoot, don't shoot."

"You even hiccup, I'm gonna blow your brains out." Camacho felt the man for a weapon as he stared into his wide eyes. There was an automatic in his waistband. The agent extracted it and turned the man so he could look over his shoulder at the house.

Dreyfus was checking the man on the sidewalk and the police lieutenant was cuffing the third one.

Camacho pulled the barrel of the revolver clear of his man's lips. "Is there a back way outta there?"

The lips contorted. Camacho cocked the revolver and placed the barrel right between his eyes. "Answer me, or so help me God . . ."

"Yeah. The alley."

Camacho pulled the man from the sidewalk and shoved him behind the Cad. "Quick, on your belly, hands behind your back. Assume the position, fucker, right *now*." As the man obeyed, Camacho tossed his cuffs to the lieutenant, then began to run for the corner.

He rounded the corner at a run just as a car was coming out of the alley in the middle of the block, its engine howling. He dived onto his face. An automatic weapon roared as the rear of the car slewed and smoke poured from the tires. Scrambling behind a parked car, Camacho managed to fire one shot at the fleeing car, although he knew that the hollow-point +P .38 slug had no chance of penetrating the body of the car. Someone leaning out a rear passenger window hosed another burst in his general direction as the car ran the stop sign at the next corner. The bullets slapped the concrete and parked cars. Luis Camacho huddled behind a car and listened to the engine noise fade away.

When he walked back to the Cadillac, Dreyfus was watching the cuffed men lying in the street and lighting his pipe while the police lieutenant used his car radio. Camacho looked at the man who had been shot. He was dead, with two holes in his chest about four inches apart. A cocked nine-millimeter Beretta automatic lay on the street near him.

"Was it you that got this guy?" Camacho asked Dreyfus.

"Yeah. After he took a shot at you."

"No shit."

"You are a goddamn hopeless romantic, Luis."

The lieutenant came over at a trot. His face was livid. "You fucking *idiot*! Are you tired of living? You almost got one of us *killed*! We're the *good* guys, or haven't you keyhole peepers heard?"

"I'm sorry. I just didn't think it through."

"The FBI, the fearless band of idiots." The lieutenant said the words softly, a benediction, a sublime pronouncement of irrefutable truth. He looked up and down the street, breathing deeply. The red tinge in his cheeks subsided slowly. Finally he said, "Okay, Rambo. How do you want this to read?"

"Hell, just tell it straight. This car came along and parked in front of a crime scene. I approached them and identified myself and one of them pulled a weapon." He shrugged.

The police officer nudged one of the prone men with his foot. "A real smart bunch of punks. Drive right up and park across the street from two cars with government plates. You shitheads deserve to be in jail. Just in case you haven't figured it out, you're under arrest."

The wail of an approaching siren caromed from the fronts of the dilapidated houses.

"See you around, Lieutenant," Camacho said.

"Leaving? Some congressman fucking his secretary tonight?"

"You city guys can handle this. Mrs. Jackson's my problem."

"The old lady can cool off without you, Rambo. I'm gonna go get a search warrant for this house, and you're gonna have to sign an affidavit. A couple of them. You and your sidekick here, J. Edgar Earp, are gonna be working with me for the next eighteen hours. Now get your cute little ass over here and start searching this car. Let's see what these hot shooters were driving around."

The lieutenant was right. It did take eighteen hours.

Terry Franklin never knew how long he stayed in the bathroom. The flowers on the wallpaper formed a curious pattern. Each had a petal that joined to an offset flower, all of them; it was very curious how they did that. He thought about how the flowers joined and about nothing at all for a long, long time.

When he came out of the bathroom the house was dark and silent. He flipped on the kitchen light and drank milk from the carton in the refrigerator. He was very tired. He climbed the stairs and lay down on the bed.

The sun was shining in the windows when he awoke. He was still dressed. He used the toilet, then went downstairs and found something to eat in the refrigerator. Cold pizza. He ate it cold. It was left over from a week or more ago when he had taken the whole family to Pizza Hut. He thought about that for a while, trying to recall just when it had been, remembering the crowd and the kids with the cheese strings dangling from their mouths and hands. The memory was fresh, as if it had happened just a short while ago, yet it was all wrong. The memory was from the wrong perspective, like when you remember a scene from your childhood. You remember it as you saw it as a child, with everything large and the adults tall and the other children just your size. That's the way he remembered Pizza Hut.

He sat the empty plate in the sink and ran some water into it, then went into the living room and lay down on the couch. He was tired again. He slept most of the day.

12

At four o'clock Saturday afternoon an exhausted Luis Camacho arrived home with a raging headache and went straight to bed. When he awoke the house was quiet and dark and his wife was asleep beside him. He checked the luminous display on the clock-radio on the bedside stand: 12:47. Slipping on his robe, he padded downstairs to the kitchen, where he raided the refrigerator. He got a plate from the dishwasher and helped himself to some leftover meat loaf and a couple of big spoonfuls of tuna casserole. He nuked it for a minute in the microwave while he poured a glass of milk.

From the kitchen table he could see Albright's bedroom window across the waist-high cedar fence, just twenty feet or so away. The window was dark. Good ol' Harlan Albright. Peter Aleksandrovich Chistyakov. Yuri.

Matilda Jackson had unlocked her front door and opened it for her killer, then turned her back on him. So it was someone she thought she had no reason to fear. A small-caliber automatic with a good silencer, the point-blank coup de grace, the methodical search of the house for possible witnesses and the turning off of the lights and appliances; certainly he was no thief or teenage drug guard-turned-gunman. No, Mrs. Jackson had been the victim of a trained, experienced assassin who convinced her it was safe to admit him into her house. Perhaps he told her he was with the FBI? Then he put two bullets into her brain.

Not to protect Pochinkov, who had diplomatic immunity and could not be arrested or prosecuted. The Americans needed no testimony from Mrs. Jackson or anyone else should they decide to declare Pochinkov persona non grata. Camacho thought about the picture of Terry Franklin in his jacket pocket, which he had hoped Mrs. Jackson might recognize. He had discussed the possibility of Mrs. Jackson identifying Franklin with Harlan Albright.

And Albright had lost no time. Why take a chance? Why risk endangering a valuable agent? He probably had not pulled the trigger himself. Just a quick call from a pay phone and Mrs. Jackson was on her way to the graveyard.

The ability to kill people with a telephone call—that's the ultimate manifestation of power, isn't it? And those ignorant charlatans in the Caribbean are still sticking pins into dolls. If only they could comprehend how far mankind had progressed with the wondrous aid of modern technology, developed from the triumphant findings of rigorous, unbiased science. Two thousand years *anno domini* murder is no longer uncertain, affected by mysterious forces and mystic symbols and the position of the moon and planets. We civilized moderns just let our fingers do the walking . . .

Camacho rinsed the dirty dish, glass and fork and placed them in the dishwasher. Somewhere here in the kitchen his wife had cigarettes hidden. They had both quit smoking six months ago, but she still liked to savor a cigarette in the afternoon over a cup of coffee while a soap blared on the television. And she thought he didn't know. A cop is supposed to know things, lots of things, and occasionally he finds he knows too much.

The pack was on the top shelf in the pantry, behind a box of instant rice. After a couple of puffs, he poured himself a finger of bourbon and added water and ice. He sat at the kitchen table and opened the sliding glass door to the backyard a few inches to exhaust the smoke.

Beyond the back fence the houses facing the next street over were silhouetted against the glare of the streetlights. The shapes cast weird shadows in his backyard. He smoked two cigarettes before he finished the whiskey and put both butts in the garbage under the sink. In the family room he lay down on the couch and pulled the throw blanket over him.

As he tried to relax the faces and images ran through his mind in a disjointed, unconnected way: Albright, Franklin, Matilda Jackson with her obscene third eye, Admiral Henry, Dreyfus with his pipe and files, Harold Strong blunt and profane, all the letters with their penciled block words that said nothing at all and yet whispered of something, something just beyond his understanding . . . It was a long time before Luis Camacho drifted off to sleep.

He awoke to the smell of coffee and bacon. Breakfast was strained, as usual. In a crisis of identity last fall, their sixteen-year-old son had transformed himself into a punk all in the course of one sunny Saturday at the mall. The boy sat sullenly at the table this morning with his remaining hair hanging over his forehead and obscuring his eyes. The shaved place above his left ear, clear up to where his part used to be back in those old, "normal" days, looked extraordinarily white and obscenely naked, his father thought, rather like a swatch of an old maid's thigh. Luis Camacho sipped coffee and studied the tense, quivering lips visible below the cascading hair.

When the boy had left the table and ascended the stairs, Luis remarked, "What *is* his problem?"

"He's sixteen years old," Sally said crossly. "He's not popular, he's not a good student, he's not an athlete, and the girls don't know he's alive. The only thing he does have is acne."

"Sounds like an epitaph."

"It's his whole life."

Camacho was just starting on the Sunday paper when the phone rang. His wife answered. "It's for you," she called.

It was Dreyfus, calling from a car phone. "Luis, it's Smoke Judy. He's out driving this morning. Left his house in Morningside ten minutes ago. Maybe a meet."

"Where is he now?"

"Going north on the beltway. We just passed the Capital Centre arena."

"You guys got the van in standby?"

"Nope. It's back at the shop." The shop was headquarters, the J. Edgar Hoover Building. "Nobody thought we'd need it today."

"Get it. I want a record this time. Any idea where he's going?"

"Not a glimmer."

"I've got to get dressed and shaved. I'll be in the car in fifteen minutes. Call me on the car phone then."

"Sure."

Sally came into the bathroom while he was shaving. "You're in the paper today." She showed him the story and the photo. "You didn't tell me there was a shooting."

"Friday night. Dreyfus shot a guy."

"It says here the dead man had already shot at you."

He eyed her in the mirror, then attacked his upper lip.

"Luis, you could have been killed."

"Then Gerald could shave his head as bare as his ass and run around in a loincloth."

She closed her eyes and shook her hair. "Weren't you scared?"

He hugged her. "Yeah. I seem to be spending more and more time in that condition."

Camacho was driving south on New Hampshire Avenue past the old Naval Ordnance Lab, now the navy's Surface Weapons Center, when the car phone buzzed. It was only 9:30 on Sunday morning, but already a good volume of traffic was flowing along the avenue. It seemed as if all the Silver Spring suburbanites had big plans for this spring day, which was partly overcast. He wondered if it would rain as he picked up the phone. "Camacho."

"He turned off the beltway and is headed north on I-95 toward Baltimore."

"How many cars do you have?"

"Seven."

"Stay loose. He'll be looking." A car would be in front of the suspect vehicle and another well behind, but in sight. The additional cars would be at least a mile back. Every four or five minutes the car behind would pass Judy as the lead car accelerated away and got off at the next exit, where it would watch the cavalcade pass and join as the last car. The third car would assume the position immediately behind Judy. If this was done properly, Judy would never notice he was being followed. Had the agents had a helicopter or light plane this morning, none of the cars would have even been in sight of the suspect.

Camacho drove onto the beltway eastbound and went down two miles to the I-95 exit, where he merged with a string of cars and trucks headed north. He eased the car up to five miles per hour over the speed limit and stayed in the right-hand lane.

In the two weeks that Camacho's men had had Commmander Smoke Judy under surveillance, he had gone driving on only one occasion. That time he had gone to a mall and spent forty-five minutes in an electronics store watching college basketball on television, eaten two slices of pepperoni pizza and swizzled a medium-sized Sprite, and gawked for five minutes in a store that specialized in racy lingerie. Just another debonair bon vivant out on the town.

As he passed the Fort Meade exit rain began to fall. Dreyfus called once. The subject was still headed north. Dreyfus had had the lead car take the Route 32 exit in case Judy was on his way to Baltimore-Washington International Airport, but Judy passed it by. After a U-turn the FBI car was back on I-95 chasing the caval-cade. Camacho hung up the telephone and listened to the wipers. Since this was his personal car, he didn't have a radio to monitor the surveillance.

In a few minutes the rain ceased. The clouds still looked threat-ening with patches of blue here and there. The car ahead flung up a spray from the wet road that kept Camacho fiddling with his wiper control and wishing he had taken the intermittent wiper option.

Following the ribbon of interstate highways, Smoke Judy circled Baltimore and headed north toward York. Just short of the Penn-sylvania line he began to slow in the left lane. Dreyfus was in the car immediately behind and used the radio to call the trailing car, which was three miles back. When Judy swung through an emer-gency vehicle turnaround and accelerated south, the trailing car was already southbound at fifty miles per hour, waiting for Judy to catch up. Dreyfus and the drivers of the other car waited until Judy was completely out of sight before they gunned across the median throwing mud and turf and resumed the pursuit. One of the cars almost got stuck.

"He thinks he's being cute," Dreyfus told Camacho, who took the first exit he came to and crossed over the highway, then sat at the head of the on-ramp to wait.

"Think he's spotted you?"

"I don't—we'll see. He'll go straight home if he has."

Smoke Judy didn't go home. He went to the inner harbor of Baltimore and parked in an outlying lot, then walked unhurriedly past the aquarium and the head of the pier where the three-masted frigate *Constellation* was berthed and sat in front of the giant in-door food mall, near the water. He sat for almost twenty minutes watching the gulls and people as a gentle wind blew in from the bay.

Camacho and Dreyfus watched him through one-way glass mounted in the side of a Potomac Power van parked on a yellow line near the frigate pier. From the outside of the van the glass appeared to be a sign unless one inspected it from close range. A man wearing jeans and a tool belt had rigged yellow ropes around the vehicle as soon as it came to a stop to ensure that no one got that close.

The distance from the van to where Judy sat was a little over a hundred yards. Camacho aimed a small television camera mounted on a pedestal while Dreyfus snapped photos with a 35mm camera with a telephoto lens. Beside them an agent wearing earphones huddled over a cassette recorder. A parabolic microphone on top of the van was slaved to the video camera, but right now the audio was a background murmur, like the background noise of a baseball radio broadcast.

"He isn't saying anything," Camacho muttered to reassure the audio technician.

"I'll bet he goes inside," Dreyfus said.

"More than likely. Too chilly to sit outside for long."

"He's looked at his watch twice."

Camacho turned the pedestal camera over to the second technician and helped himself to coffee from a thermos. "Appreciate you guys coming out this morning."

"Sure."

As he sipped his coffee, Camacho glanced at his watch. 11:47. The meet was probably scheduled for twelve o'clock. Albright? If not, then who?

"Have we got the camera and audio units inside?"

"Yes, sir. The guys are already in the food court."

Camacho took another large swig of coffee, then tapped the man at the camera on the shoulder. He moved aside. The camera had a powerful zoom. Camacho could see the expression on Judy's face. He looked like a tourist until you studied his face—alert, ready, in absolute control.

The agent backed off a tad on the zoom and scanned the camera. The crowd was large, lots of families and young couples. With the earpiece in his left ear he picked up snatches of conversation as the camera moved along. Feeling a bit like a voyeur, he aimed the camera at a stream of people coming from the dark interior of the huge, green-glass building into the light. A stringy youth in a black Harley shirt held hands with a vacant-eyed girl with large, unrestrained breasts and a slack jaw. Adenoids? ". . . that AIDS is bad shit. Had a hell of a time shaking it last time."

A tight-faced gray-haired woman spoke to her male companion in a polished whine: ". . . too far to walk. My feet hurt and it's been just a terrible . . ." Camacho moved on, sampling the faces and polyglot sounds.

"I'm not hooked, I tell you. I just like the rush . . ." In her mid-thirties, she wore a one-piece designer outfit and a wind-blown coiffure and was speaking to a man in gray slacks and camel-colored cardigan who was chewing on his lower lip. Not wishing to hear more, Luis Camacho swung the camera away.

"He's moving," Dreyfus said. "Toward the door. He's looking at someone. Do you see him?"

Camacho searched for the door to the mall and saw only backs. He waited. The light was fading noticeably now as a dark cloud choked off the sunlight. In a few seconds Smoke Judy entered his range of vision from the left and joined the crowd streaming into the interior gloom. Camacho released the camera and rubbed his eyes.

Dreyfus was on the radio, talking to the watchers inside. "Here he comes," one of them said, and launched into a running commentary on Judy's direction of travel for the benefit of his comrades stationed throughout the building.

"I'm going inside," Camacho said. Judy had never met him, so that wasn't a concern. Depending on who it was, Judy's contact might recognize him, but even so he wanted to see—see now, with his own eyes—the person Smoke Judy did not want to be seen with. He would try to stay out of sight. Just in case.

A spatter of drops came in at an angle, driven by the strong breeze, as Luis Camacho walked across the head of the quay. A solid curtain of rain over the water moved rapidly this way. The crowd around two jugglers on unicycles dissolved as people began to run. The FBI agent reached the double doors and hurried through just as the deluge struck. A crowd was gathering by the exit, looking out and chattering nervously, but audible above the babble was the drumming of the rain on the glass windows of the building.

Camacho put the earpiece on his radio in place and rearranged his cap. The radio itself was in an interior jacket pocket. The microphone was pinned inside his lapel: he merely had to key the transmit switch and talk.

A voice on the radio reported that Judy was upstairs, on the second floor, wandering from booth to booth. That meant the person he had come to meet was still unknown, still moving through the crowd looking for watchers. Camacho stood near the door and looked at faces, an ocean of faces of all ages and colors and sizes. Could one of them be the Minotaur? No chance. The Minotaur was too careful, too circumspect. This wasn't his kind of risk. He didn't need men like Smoke Judy for his treason. Or did he?

"He's in line at the taco joint."

Camacho was tempted to move. Not yet! Not yet!

"There's a man behind the subject, Caucasian male about fifty-five, five feet nine or so, about a hundred ninety pounds, wearing dark slacks, Hush Puppies and a faded blue windbreaker. No hat. Balding."

Camacho shifted his weight and examined the people on the stairs. Families. Youngsters. Five black teenage boys with red ball caps and scarves. No one was looking at him.

"Guy in the windbreaker said something to the subject."

"Get pictures." That was Dreyfus in the van.

"Camera's rolling." The lawyers at Justice loved these portable video cameras with automatic focus and light-level adjustment. Jurors raised in the television age thought prosecutors should have a movie of every ten-dollar back-alley deal. At last technology had delivered. The government's shysters could show each greedy, grubby, loving little moment in living color on the courtroom Zenith—and play it over and over again until even the stupidest juror was firmly convinced—while the defendants writhed and the defense shysters planned their appeals.

"Subject paying for his grub."

Camacho swiveled his eyes again, looking at no one in particular, seeing everyone.

"Windbreaker paying, just dropped a coin. Kid retrieving it for him. He's nervous, looking around . . . Now he's following subject . . . They're gonna share a table. That's our man. That's him!"

He moved for the stairs, climbing slowly, listening to the running commentary from the observer. Pausing with his eyes just at the level of the second-story floor, Camacho scanned to his left, toward the taco stand. The observer said they were near there at a two-person table. He climbed carefully, watching, peering through moving legs and around bodies. He glimpsed Judy's face. Another step. He was at the top of the stairs. He moved left, keeping a fat woman between himself and Judy. Against the far wall he saw a man from the power company up on a step ladder, bending over a toolbox on the ladder's little platform. The video camera was in the toolbox. Judy's face was panning again, examining the crowd.

Camacho turned his back. A pretzel stand was right in front of him. He pointed one out to the girl and asked for a soft drink. As she thumbed the dispenser he checked the mirror on the back wall. There was Judy again. And *there* was the man across from him.

Luis Camacho studied the face in the mirror. Fleshy, clean-shaven, pale.

He paid the girl and turned to his right, back toward the stairs, as he sipped the drink through a straw. Descending the stairs he kept his eyes glued on the back of the teenager in front of him in a conscious effort to avoid any possibility of eye contact with a nervous Smoke Judy. He threw the pretzel and nearly full cup in a trash hamper by the main door and pushed on through, out into the rain.

The wind threatened to blow his cap off. He held it with his hand as the wind whipped his trouser legs.

"So?" said Dreyfus as Camacho wiped the water off his face with a handkerchief when he had gained the shelter of the van.

Luis Camacho shrugged. "They'll probably bus their own table. Put their trash in a receptacle. Have one of the guys take the whole bag."

"Fingerprints?"

"Uh-huh."

"Think it's the Minotaur?"

"What in hell would the Minotaur have to say to Smoke Judy?"

"How're they hanging down in your shop? How'd you like to ski Moscow? Quit fucking my wife. The possibilities—" The radio speaker squawked to life with another report from the food court and Dreyfus closed his eyes to listen.

Camacho took off the radio he was wearing and handed it to one of the technicians. "See you tomorrow at the office," he said to Dreyfus during a silent moment, then let himself out of the van and walked through the drizzling rain toward his car.

Harlan Albright came over to Camacho's house after supper. He accepted a cup of coffee and the two of them went to the basement. The boy was there, and he got up with a wounded look on his face and took the stairs two at a time. His father watched him go, then settled onto the couch and picked up the television remote control and began flipping channels.

"I see in the paper that Matilda Jackson is dead."

Camacho grunted. Two of the channels had those damned game shows, people answering trivial questions to win flashy, useless consumer goods.

"Who killed her?"

"Someone who knew exactly what he was about." Camacho stared at the sex goddess flipping answer cards on Channel 4.

"Too bad. Had you had a chance to show her Franklin's picture?"

"No."

"Well, she was an old woman, had lived a long life. It would have come soon anyhow."

Camacho jabbed the remote savagely. The television settled on the educational channel. Some Englishman was talking about cathedrals. "Listen, asshole. I'm not in the mood for that shit tonight. It's been a long goddamn weekend."

"Sorry. I read about that shooting incident in front of Jackson's house. That must have been touch and go."

He examined the Russian's face. "I know you probably dropped a dime on her, so don't waste the hot air on me. You don't give a damn about that old woman or anybody else."

"Sometime—"

"Shut up!"

The Englishman was explaining about flying buttresses. He used a computer model to graphically depict the forces transferred through the stone.

Albright stood up. "I'll drop over some night this week when you're in a better mood."

"Ummm."

Camacho listened to the footsteps climbing the stairs and the noises of Sally letting him out the front door. He stared at the television without seeing it, lost in thought.

When Luis Camacho returned to his office from his usual Monday-morning conference with his boss, he was in a foul mood. The boss had made several candid remarks about Camacho's conduct Friday night.

"Look at this shit," he roared, waving a section of the Sunday *Washington Post*, "the special agent in charge of counterespionage standing on a street corner with two punk dopers, in front of a fucking crack house, for Christ's sake! What in hell has busting dopers got to do with catching spies?"

Camacho remarked that he had asked the newspaper photographer not to take his picture.

"Ha! Apparently you haven't read the Constitution lately, mister."

"That's what he said."

"And I'm saying it too. I don't ever want to see your sweet little puss in the public press again, mister, or you're going to wind up in Pocatello chasing Nazis through cow shit up to your armpits. Those crackpots are probably the only nut cases around who never read the goddamned paper!" The boss had been irked for months by press coverage of the FBI investigation of the Aryan Nations white supremacy fanatics, and ridiculed it and them every chance he got. Sometimes he made up chances. "If you wanta be famous, get a lobotomy and become a rock star."

After he'd calmed down, he wanted a complete oral report on Matilda Jackson and Smoke Judy. That had taken an hour. Then the boss had asked questions for a half hour and discussed tactics and strategy for another thirty minutes. When he signaled the discussion was over, Luis Camacho was tired and needed to go to the rest room.

Now Camacho slumped in his office chair and shuffled through the paper in his in basket. He was rereading a new administrative procedure for the third time when Dreyfus tapped on his door, then stuck his head in. Pipe smoke swirled into the room. "Wanta watch the tape of Smoke Judy we made yesterday?"

"Sure."

"Got it on the VCR."

The two men went to the little conference room next door and Dreyfus pushed buttons. "The plates and glasses they used are at the lab. Should have some good prints."

"Terrific."

"The lab wizards synched up the sound from one of the mikes with the video." Judy and the beefy man in the windbreaker appeared on the television screen. Dreyfus twiddled the color knob and adjusted the volume.

". . . not happy with all the media on procurement problems down there." The beefy man had a well-spoken baritone voice, but his nervousness was evident.

Judy replied, but his back must have been to the parabolic mike that picked up this sound track, because his words were indistinct. Dreyfus punched the pause button and said, "We have two other audio tracks and think we got it all, but it'll take a few hours to come up with a complete transcript."

Camacho nodded and the tape rolled on.

". . . big risks. Some people will be going to prison," Judy's companion said, "after they've been drawn and quartered in a public trial that will take six months."

Judy leaned forward and spoke earnestly. Snatches of his remarks came through. ". . . you people . . . a lifetime building the company . . . literally millions at stake. You guys really need this because . . . You'll make tens of millions in the next twenty years and I'll get a little stock and a paycheck and a pension . . . not much . . ." The rest was too garbled to follow.

"That's enough," Camacho said after another five minutes. "Let me see the transcript when it's finished."

Dreyfus stopped the tape and pushed the rewind button. "I think that guy's gonna buy what Judy's selling."

"When you get that rewound, come on back to my office."

In his office Luis Camacho took a sheet of scratch paper and printed one word: "Fallacy." He handed it to Dreyfus when he came in. "See if this is in any of the Minotaur's letters."

Dreyfus dropped into a chair and began to fiddle with his pipe. He put the paper in his shirt pocket after a glance. "Where'd you get it?" he asked when he had his pipe going again.

"Ask me no questions and I'll tell you no lies."

"Vice Admiral Henry, huh?"

"I found it in the john."

"Why can't we get a list of all the code words from NSA?"

"We've been all through this before."

"So I'm not too bright. Tell me again."

"NSA won't give us the code words without the approval of the committee. The committee has not approved." The committee was slang for the ultrasecret group that formulated intelligence community policy and coordinated the intelligence activities of all U.S. agencies. Some of its members included the directors of the FBI and CIA, the Secretary of Defense, the Secretary of State, the National Security Agency chief, and speaking directly for the President, the National Security Adviser.

"So what does that tell you?" Dreyfus asked, his voice sharper than usual.

Camacho rubbed his eyes, then his face. "You tell me."

"If it walks like a duck, quacks like a duck, and leaves duck shit all over, it probably is a duck."

"Umm."

"I think those assholes already know what the Minotaur has given away. So they're in no rush for us to put a list together." Dreyfus flicked his lighter and puffed several times. "Somebody in Moscow has gotta be telling them."

"Maybe," said Luis Camacho, weighing it. "Or maybe they're hoping this whole thing will crawl into a corner and die quietly without becoming a major embarrassment. Budgetary blood feuds in Congress, some big-ticket military programs on the chopping block, Gramm-Rudman—hell, they'd be less than human if they didn't try to play ostrich for a while."

"So what are we gonna do about Smoke Judy?"

"What would you suggest?"

"That shithead is shopping secrets to defense contractors. He wants more than a military pension. What'd the boss say when you told him this morning?" His voice had a belligerent, bitter edge.

"Hang loose. Keep an eye on him."

"Fuck us! The same old story. No matter what we turn up, we get the same answer from ol' brass ass. Be cool, guys!"

"Calm down, Dreyfus. You've been around long enough—"

"How much shit you gonna eat, Luis, before you decide you don't like it? Right now the Minotaur is busy figuring what secrets to give away next and scribbling another little love letter to the Russian ambassador. Terry Franklin is still running around loose, you're sneaking code words from friends in the Pentagon—we're doing some dynamic drifting but our investigation is going nowhere. You know that! And the sickening thing is the committee is quite comfortable with that state of affairs." His voice had risen to almost a shout. "I'll tell you what *I* think—*I* think the guys on that committee are laughing themselves silly. *I* think they're tickled pink that the fucking Russians are seeing this stuff. That's what the hell *I* think."

"*I* think you're an idiot, Dreyfus, with a big mouth and a piss ant's view of the world. I've heard enough. Now get back to work."

Dreyfus bounced to his feet and rammed his right hand out in a Nazi salute. *"Ja wohl—"*

"You son of a—"

"Don't bullshit yourself, Luis. I know you're doing the best you can. But, goddamn, I'm sick of this fucking around!"

Camacho jerked his head at the door and Dreyfus went.

13

The Naval Weapons Center, China Lake, lies in the desert of southern California east of the range of mountains that form the eastern wall of the San Joaquin Valley. The air at China Lake is clean, hot, and dry. Tuesday afternoon Jake Grafton dragged in lungfuls of it as he walked across the baking concrete toward the air terminal with Helmut Fritsche and Samuel Dodgers. Behind them, still trading quips with the female crew of the T-39 that had flown them here from Andrews AFB in Washington, via NAS Moffett Field where they had collected Dodgers, Toad Tarkington and Rita Moravia supervised the loading of the luggage into a navy station wagon.

An hour later Dr. Dodgers lifted his ball cap and scratched his head. He was standing with Grafton and Fritsche in a hangar that was empty except for an A-6E Intruder. Sentries were posted on the outside of the doors with orders to admit no one.

The men were examining grease-pencil marks placed on the plane by Fritsche. These were the locations he recommended for the special antennas of Dodgers' Athena system. And Sam Dodgers was scratching his head as he surveyed Fritsche's artwork. "Well," he said unenthusiastically, "I guess these spots will work okay, after we tweak the output of each antenna. But . . ." His voice trailed off. Jake glanced at him without curiosity. He had already discovered that Dodgers' enthusiasm came in uneven dribbles.

"It's the left side of the airplane only," Fritsche said firmly. "Fourteen antennas. Side of the tail, fuselage, left outboard pylon, under the cockpit rail, forward on the nose . . . and one on the left wingtip in place of the position light."

"You really need one in front of the left intake, where that flat plate is. That plate is probably the biggest single contributor to the plane's RCS when viewed from this side—makes up maybe half of it."

"Can't put one there. Might get broken off by the airflow and go down the intake. It'd destroy the engine."

"How about in front of that plate?"

They discussed it. Yes.

"This jury rig is just for test purposes," Fritsche told Jake. "An operational Athena system for an aircraft will have to have conformal antennas, 'smart skin' in the jargon of the trade. Literally, the antennas will be part of the aircraft's skin so they won't contribute to drag or ever be broken off."

"How much is that going to cost?"

"Won't be cheap. Conformal antennae are under development, but they'll be new technology and aren't here yet."

"Forget I asked."

Jake wandered over to where Tarkington and Moravia stood with Commander L. D. Bonnet, the commanding officer of the A-6 Weapons System Support Activity, which owned the airplane. All three saluted Jake as he approached and he returned the gesture with a grin. "So, L.D., are you going to let these children fly your plane?"

"Yes, sir. They appear sober and reasonably competent."

"I appreciate your letting us borrow the plane and hangar for a few days."

"Admiral Dunedin's very persuasive."

Jake flashed a grin. L.D. must have hesitated a few seconds before he agreed to the Old Man's requests. "Here's what I'd like to do. Fritsche and Dodgers are going to take a day or two to install some little antennas on the left side of the plane. They'll use glue and drill a few holes, then install a tiny fairing in front of each antenna. They're going to need the help of a couple of good, capable airframe technicians who can keep their mouths shut."

Bonnet nodded.

"Then Rita and Toad will fly the plane up to the Electronic Warfare range at Fallon since the EW range here at China Lake is out of service this week. Fritsche and I will fly up there ahead of them. Dodgers will stay here to work on the gear in the plane. Rita, I want you to keep the plane under three hundred knots indicated to minimize the airflow stress on these antennas. They're going to be jury-rigged on there with a little bubble gum and Elmer's glue."

"Aye aye, sir," she said.

"L.D., I need you to loan me a couple of young officers with at least ten pounds of tact each. They'll alternate duty, so that one of them will be with Dodgers day and night. They're to escort him to work, stay with him all day, escort him to the head, take him back to the BOQ, eat with him, see that he talks to no one but them. And I mean no one."

After discussing the details, Commander Bonnet departed. Jake Grafton explained to Rita and Toad exactly what he expected of his flight crew. He finished with a caution. "This device, the project name, everything, is classified to the hilt. Admiral Dunedin tells me he has cells reserved at Leavenworth for anyone who violates the security regs. I don't want you to even whisper about this in your sleep."

"I love secrets," Toad said.

"I know. Just my luck, I get one of the world's great secret lovers. Keep it zipped, Toad."

Jake went back to watch the installation process, so Toad and Rita set out on foot for base ops to plan their flights to and from Fallon, Nevada. As they walked along, Rita asked, "What was it that Captain Grafton wanted you to keep zipped, Toad? Your mouth or—"

"Never ask a question if you think you might not like the answer. That's Tarkington's Golden Rule for survival in Uncle Sam's navy."

They grinned at each other. Her hand slipped into his for a fleeting squeeze. Instinctively they both knew to play it cool. No hand-holding or huggy-squeezy or deep eye contact during duty hours. No winks or sighs or casual touching. If Captain Grafton saw any of that, the roof would fall in.

As Toad walked his shoulders were back and his head up. He was acutely conscious of how good he felt, how pungently vigorous and healthy. Takes a woman to do that for you, he told himself, and began whistling a lively little tune that seemed appropriate. Life *is* good.

Toad's feeling of euphoric bonhomie lasted precisely one hour and thirty-seven minutes, just the length of time it took to plan the flights to and from the Electronic Warfare Range near Fallon, Nevada, fill out the flight plans, visit casually with the weather briefer about the long-range forecast for the next three or four days and make a pit stop in the head. On the walk back to the hangar where Grafton and the wizards labored, Rita was quieter, more subdued than she had been the last few days.

"Do you like me?" she asked finally, wearing a gentle semiserious look that Toad Tarkington, man of the world, recognized as trouble.

His jovial mood returned to earth with an unpleasant splat. Commitment time! It's their hormones, biology maybe, something to do with genes. "Sure. You're a very nice lady who's fun to be with."

"Oh."

"You know what I mean. You're not one of those girls who write poetry until two in the morning and read Albert Camus in the cafeteria."

"Uh-huh."

"You're"—and here Toad grinned broadly and arranged his features in what he always thought was his most sincere, let's-fuck-tonight look—"you're the kind of girl a guy likes to be around."

"I understand," Rita said, nodding. "You like girls who open zippers with their teeth and wear crotchless panties."

He didn't like the way she said that, with lips parted but almost immobile, her eyes narrowing ever so slightly.

"Rita, I try to avoid discussing serious relationships at midafternoon in parking lots."

"Maybe if I shave my pussy and put four or five earrings in my left ear?"

Oh, so she wanted a little blood, huh! "Right ear. Left ear is for lesbi—"

"You *asshole!*" She stalked away, her head down, braced against the hurricane.

"Hey, Ginger . . ." Ginger was her nickname, what the other aviators called her. She even had it on the name tag of her flight suit.

She spun around to face him, her hands clenched at her sides. "Don't you *ever* call me that, Tarkington. Not *ever*. Not *you.*"

"Hey—" he said, but he was talking to her back. He raised his voice and shouted, "I'd like to get to know you. But I'm not getting engaged in a parking lot, not even if you're the Queen of Sheba."

When she was fifty feet away, she turned to face him. "I wasn't asking you to get engaged," she shouted back.

"Oh yes you were! Crotchless panties, shaved pussies, what the hell is wrong with you?"

She was walking away again. Toad turned back toward base ops. Ten feet away a lieutenant commander stood looking at him, shaking his head.

"You know, Lieutenant, when I discuss intimate apparel or personal hygiene with a lady friend, I usually try to find a slightly more private place."

Toad turned beet red. "Yessir," he mumbled through clenched teeth and stalked by with his head down.

Samuel Dodgers forked his food without wasting an erg of precious energy. The utensil bit into the mashed potatoes and peas in one swift, brutal motion, then soared aloft by the most direct route to the waiting depository, where it was wiped clean in the blink of an eye and dispatched down for another load. A man working this hard should devote his attention to the job at hand, and Dodgers wisely did so. If he heard the conversation around him, he gave no sign.

Toad Tarkington gave Rita a hopeful wink when her eyes shifted to him from Dodgers and his rapidly emptying plate. Her eyes snapped down to her food. She pressed her lips firmly together and inhaled deeply through her nose, which strained the cloth and buttons on her khaki shirt. Toad sourly noted that the younger Dodgers shared his interest in the physics of Rita's bust expansion. It wasn't that she was extraordinarily endowed, but rather that she was so perfectly proportioned. Her gorgeous breasts formed symmetrical mounds that seemed . . . just so exactly, perfectly right, with the gentle swelling just visible in the deep V formed by the neckline of her shirt. Toad gave those twin masterpieces yet another glance as he sliced more meat from his pork chop and pondered the vicissitudes of love.

"Well, Toad," he heard Jake Grafton say, "are you satisfied with this tour of duty?"

"Yessir. You bet." The captain was looking at him with an amused expression on his face. "Just challenging as hell, sir."

This remark drew a grunt from the gourmet at the other end of the table, who appeared to be finished anyway. Dodgers laid down his fork and used his napkin on his mouth. As far as Toad could see, he hadn't missed with a single gram. "The road to hell may be challenging, sir, but the road to heaven is more so."

"Uh-huh," Toad Tarkington said, and attacked the remnants of his chop.

"The pathway of the righteous is narrow and difficult, and many there are who find the way too treacherous, too steep, too rigorous." Dodgers was rolling, his phrases sonorous and heartfelt. "The pathway of the righteous is strewn with the temptations of the flesh, of the spirit and of the heart, all exits from the difficult, righteous way, all exits to that short, smooth road that leads down straight to *hell.*"

"A soul freeway for the pink Cadillac. Amen," Toad muttered, and didn't even glance at Rita when she kicked him in the shin.

"The pathway of the wicked is that straight, steep ro—"

"I'm sure," Jake Grafton interrupted firmly. Looking at Rita, he asked, "Have you got the flight to Fallon planned?"

"Yes, sir." She described the route, mentioning navigation aids, time en route and her estimate of what her fuel state would be when she arrived over the Electronic Warfare range. Jake asked everyone present if they had been to NAS Fallon, and proceeded to tell anecdotes of his many visits there throughout his career. Toad Tarkington knew Grafton was going to monopolize the conversation through dessert just so he wouldn't have to listen to Dodgers' preaching. Apparently no one had ever told the physicist that three things were never discussed at a wardroom table—women, politics and religion.

Grafton was going easily from anecdote to anecdote when Rita finished eating and excused herself. Toad lingered, engrossed in the captain's tales. The younger Dodgers ordered dessert and asked several questions: even his old man seemed somewhat amused by Grafton's tales of ten-cent craps in Mom's saloon and midnight motorcycle rides through the desert by half-drunk fliers trying to sober up so they could fly at 5 A.M.

Dr. Fritsche lit a cigar and sighed contentedly. He too seemed to find Grafton's tales of his younger days very pleasant this warm evening in a navy wardroom a hundred miles from the sea.

Like Jake Grafton, I love this life, Toad found himself thinking. As he listened he recalled his first two-week weapons deployment with his squadron to Fallon, before his first cruise. It was in Fallon that the ties to wives and girlfriends were temporarily broken and the twenty-four-hour-a-day camaraderie began to weld friendships among the junior officers that would last a lifetime. The challenge was to fly the planes as weapons, two or three flights a day, and on liberty to play as hard as they flew. As Jake Grafton described it and Toad remembered it, it was a gay, carefree, exciting life, the perfect existence for a youngster growing into manhood.

When Jake wound down, Toad smiled at everyone and excused himself. Walking toward the BOQ he found himself whistling again. I'm doing a lot of that lately, he thought, and laughed aloud. He was spending his life wisely and well. He liked the thought so much he roared heartily, and then chuckled contentedly at his own foolishness, his animosity toward Rita this afternoon forgotten.

There was no answer when he tapped on Rita's door. Perhaps she was in the head or down in the laundry room. Oh well, he would try to call her later.

When he opened the door to his room the lights were on and Rita was sitting in the chair by the small desk. Her hair was down over her shoulders and she was wearing only a teddy, a filmy little thing that . . . Toad gawked.

"Well, close the door before everyone in the building stops by to visit."

"How'd you get in?" Toad asked, still staring.

"Just asked for a key at the desk."

He got the door closed and latched and sat down on the end of the bed, close to her. The furniture was early Conrad Hilton, and there wasn't much of it.

He cleared his throat as she stared straight into his eyes.

"I was writing a letter," she said, her eyes never wavering from his. "To you."

"Uh-huh."

"I can finish it later."

"What's it going to be about?"

"I'm sorry about the scene today in the parking lot. I just wanted—oh, I—let's forget it, shall we?"

"Sure," he said. "It was only a little pothole on the hard, righteous road." His gaze was drifting lower and lower. "Not enough to get us sidetracked onto that short, steep road that leads down . . . down straight . . ." Her nipples were visible through the lace of the teddy, ripe, red . . .

Rita stood in one smooth, fluid motion. "I want to make love to you," she murmured as she peeled off the teddy, "but I don't want to be too forward."

He pursed his lips and nodded. "Uh-huh." He reached out and she slid into his arms, her skin all silky and smooth.

"Should we turn off the lights?" she suggested as he caressed her breasts with his lips.

"You're pretty enough for lights," he said, and pulled her down on the bed beside him.

"I don't want you to get the idea that I just want you for sex," she said tentatively.

His mouth was full of breast, so the best he could manage was a reassuring noise.

"The sex is great, of course, but I want us to have something else." She ran her fingers through his hair, then smoothed the stray locks. "You're a pretty terrific guy, and it's more than sex. That's what I was trying to get at this afternoon in the parking lot."

Toad reluctantly took a last lick at that swollen nipple, then shifted his body until his eyes were inches from hers. "Are you trying to tell me you're in love with me?"

She frowned. "I suppose. It hasn't happened quite the way I always dreamed it would. Girls have their fantasies." She took a tiny little nip on her lower lip. "I hope I'm saying this right. You don't mind, do you?"

"I'm delighted. I'm falling in love with you and I'm glad you feel the same way."

"I love you," Rita Moravia said softly, savoring it, then gently pulled his mouth onto hers.

When she was asleep, Toad eased out of bed and peered through the curtain. He was restless. Why had he said that—that falling-in-love stuff? Only a cretin tells a woman that just before he beds her. He sat in a chair and worried a fingernail. He was getting in over his head again and he had his doubts. Was he just scared? Nah, a little frightened maybe, nervous, but not scared. Why is it all women want to fall in love? He wondered what Samuel Dodgers would say on that subject.

Dreyfus laid it on Camacho's desk and sat down to light his pipe. Camacho knew what it was: his boss had called him. It was a copy of a letter. The original was at the lab.

He opened the folder that the lab technicians used for copies and glanced at it. There was no date. The envelope was postmarked Bakersfield, California, three days ago. The message was in florid longhand, yet quite legible.

Dear Sir,

I think it's my duty to inform you that my daughter's husband, Petty Officer First Class Terry Franklin USN, is a spy. He works at the Pentagon. Computers, or something like that. I don't know how long he has been a spy, but he is. My daughter Lucy is sure he is and so am I. He got a funny phone call once that Lucy overheard and he got really really mad when he found out Lucy mentioned her suspicions to a neighbor. Lucy is afraid of him and so am I. He is crazy. He is a spy like that Walker fellow.

We are good citizens and pay our taxes and know you will do what has to be done. We are sorry for him but he did this himself. Lucy had absolutely nothing to do with this spy thing, and that's why I am writing this letter. I wanted her to write it but she said she just couldn't, even though she knows it has to be this way. Please arrest him and keep Lucy and the kids out of it. Please don't tell the newspapers he is married. His name is Terry Franklin and he works at the Pentagon and he is a spy. And PLEASE, whatever you do, don't tell Terry we told on him. He is crazy.

Sincerely,
Flora May Southworth

"Can you get a divorce in California if your spouse is a spy?"

Dreyfus snorted. "You can get a divorce in California if your spouse farts in bed."

"Progressive as hell."

"Right out front."

"Better call out there and have an agent go interview them. Tell him to stay all afternoon and take lots of notes."

"You don't want them going to the press?"

"Do you know what the committee is going to want to do about this?"

"Well, they sure are gonna have to do something. Now we got the mother-in-law writing us letters. They probably talked to their minister and a lawyer and every neighbor in a five-block radius."

"Not letters. A letter. One letter with no hard facts and a variety of unsubstantiated allegations. We get two dozen letters like this every month from people out to get even with someone in a sensitive job. I repeat, do you know what the committee—"

"No." He spit it out.

"So we had better do our best to convince Mrs. Southworth we are going like gangbusters on this hot tip. Pledge confidentiality. Better send two agents. Tell them to be thorough. Then two days later go back for a follow-up interview with more questions. New questions, not repeats."

"A major break like this, maybe you want to send me out there to see that they do it right? I could go by bus, get there in a week or so."

Camacho ignored him. He picked up the letter and read it again. Then he pulled a legal pad around and began making notes. Dreyfus got the message and left in a swirl of smoke, closing the door behind him.

Camacho threw the legal pad at the door.

14

With its twin engines bellowing a
roar that could be heard for several miles, the Intruder departed
the earth with a delicate wiggle, a perceptible rocking of the wings
that Rita Moravia automatically smoothed with the faintest side
pressure on the control stick. She had let the takeoff trim setting
rotate the plane's nose to eight degrees nose-up and had stopped it
there with a nudge of forward stick in that delicious moment when
the weight of twenty-five tons of machine and fuel was transferred
from the main landing gear to the wings. This was the transition to
flight, a shimmering, imprecise hesitation as the machine gathered
its strength and the wings took a firm bite into the warm morning
air.

Now safely airborne, Rita slapped the gear handle up with her
left hand. Her right thumb flicked at the coolie-hat button on the
top of the stick, trimming the stick pressure to neutral as the twin-
engined warplane accelerated.

She checked to make sure the landing gear were up and locked.
They were. Temps, RPMs, fuel flow normal. Oil and hydraulic
pressure okay. Using her left hand again, she raised the flap handle
as she caressed the stick with her right to hold the nose steady
through the configuration change. Accelerating nicely. Flaps and
slats up and in and the stabilizer shifted, she isolated the flight
hydraulic system and continued to trim. At 290 knots indicated

she pulled the nose higher into the sky in order to comply with Jake Grafton's directive not to exceed 300 knots.

Toad had activated the IFF and was talking to Departure. Now he switched to Los Angeles Center. The controller asked him to push the identification button on the IFF—"squawk ident"—and he complied. "Xray Echo 22, radar contact. Come left to a heading of 020. Passing Flight Level 180, proceed on course."

Rita Moravia dipped the left wing as Toad rogered.

When she leveled the wings on course, still climbing, he was humming and singing over the ICS as he tuned the radar presentation and checked that he had properly entered the computer waypoints. "Hi-ho, hi-ho, it's off to work we go, with a hi-hi-hee and a fiddly-dee, hi-hi, ho-ho . . ."

Rita grinned behind her oxygen mask. Flying with the Toadman was an experience. No wonder Captain Grafton's face softened every time he saw Tarkington.

She leveled the plane at Flight Level 310—31,000 feet—and engaged the autopilot. Just above them a thin, wispy layer slid across the top of the canopy, so close it seemed they could almost reach up and let the gauzy tendrils slip around their fingers. Rita looked ahead and tried to find that point where the motion of the ropy filaments seemed to originate as they came racing toward the cockpit, accelerating as the distance closed. It was like flying just under an infinite, flat ceiling—some Steven Spielberg effect to give the audience a rush of speed and wonder as the woofers oomphed and the seats throbbed, before the credits came on the screen.

After a moment she disengaged the autopilot and let the nose creep up a smidgen. Almost imperceptibly the plane rose a hundred feet, where the cloud layer literally sliced around the cockpit. Toad picked that moment to withdraw his head from the radar scope and look slowly around. After a moment he glanced at her and caught her eye. She saw him wink, then readjust the hood and devote his attention to the computer and radar.

A lifetime of work, all for this.

She had been an outstanding student at an excellent suburban high school, one of those bright youngsters who applied themselves in a frenzy of self-discipline and diligence that separated her from her classmates, who were more interested in boys, music and peer acceptance than school. She had shocked everyone, including her parents, by her announcement that she wanted to attend a military academy. In due course an appointment to the Naval Academy came from a congressman who knew better than to echo her mother's surprise or horror in an era when socially correct posturing was more important than his voting record.

So she set forth bravely that summer after high school, at the age of eighteen, set off into the unknown world of plebes at the Naval Academy, this girl who had never set foot on a military installation, this girl who knew only that she wanted to make her own way in life and that way would be much different from those of her mother or the friends of her youth.

It had been worse than different. It had been horrid, humiliating nightmare beyond anything she had imagined in her worst moments of trepidation. All the sly taunts of her friends, bound for sororities and, they hoped, excellent marriages, hadn't even hinted at the emotional trauma she experienced those first weeks. During the day she braced and marched and ran and endured the hazing and shouting to the point of exhaustion, and at night she sobbed herself to sleep wondering if she had made the right choice. Finally one day she realized that she hadn't cried in a week. Her second, more important revelation occurred one morning at breakfast when an upperclassman had demanded to know the name of the Soviets' chief arms negotiator. She had answered the question correctly, and as he turned his attention to a gawky boy from Georgia seated beside her, she realized that these people were demanding nothing from her she could not accomplish. From then on she had cheerfully endured, and finally excelled.

She thought of those times this morning as the Intruder flew out from under the thin cloud layer into a crystal-clear desert sky and Toad Tarkington, the professional who had been there and back, caressed the system with a loving touch. She had made the right choice.

Sixty miles out she once again disengaged the autopilot and lowered the nose slightly, then slowly pulled the throttles aft as her speed crept up toward 300 knots indicated. She always liked the feel of the plane as it descended in these long, shallow, power-on glides, gravity helping the engines drive the plane down into the thicker, denser air near the earth. She could feel every knot of the airspeed the engines didn't generate—free airspeed it seemed, though of course it wasn't. Because she was the airplane and it was her, the energy was hers: the speed and the life and the power, she absorbed and possessed and became all of it.

Wingtip speed brakes cracked, but not enough. She flicked them out some more and felt the buffeting of the disturbed air, a gentle shaking that imparted itself to her through the stick and throttles and the seat in which she sat. Satisfied, she slid the speed-brake switch forward with her left thumb. The boards closed obediently and the buffeting ceased.

The desert below was baked brown and red and grayish black unleavened by the green of life. As she came down she could see sand and dirt in valleys and washes and rock the color of new iron in jagged cliffs and ridges.

Toad was chatting with Jake Grafton on the radio. "Never fear, the pros are here."

"Amen," Grafton replied. It's a good thing Dodgers is back in China Lake, Rita thought.

"Okay, Misty, I have you in sight. Drop to about 8,000 on the pressure altimeter"—the land here was 4,000 feet above sea level—"and come north up the valley until you see the van. It's red and has a yellow cross on the top."

"What kind of a cross," she asked curiously.

"Dodgers' son painted it. Three guesses."

"I see it." At this height it was just a speck amid the dirt and boulders.

"Okay, circle the van at a distance of three miles or so and I'll tell you when to turn on your gadget."

"Roger that," Toad said, and Rita flew away from the van, then turned to establish herself on the circle with her left wingtip pointed at the van.

Toad again examined the little box that had been taped to the top of the glare shield in front of him. The box wasn't much. It had a three-position power switch which he had had in the middle, or standby, position for the last five minutes. While in standby the coolant was circulating around the Athena computer. Beside the power switch was a little green light that would come on to verify that the computer was receiving electrical power, and another light, yellow, to show when the system was detecting signals from an outside source. When that yellow light was on, the Athena system was doing its thing. There was a red light too, but that would illuminate only when the temperature of the super-cooled computer exceeded a level that endangered it. If that light came on, Toad was to turn off the system.

Down on the ground Jake watched Harold Dodgers and Helmut Fritsche at the radar control panel. "Got em," Fritsche said after a bit, speaking loudly over the steady snoring of the engine of the generator mounted on the trailer behind the van. The engine noise muffled the moan of the Intruder's engines except when it had passed almost overhead. Jake looked at the green display. "Tell 'em to turn it on."

Jake did so. In less than two seconds the blip faded from the scope. Magic! Involuntarily he looked toward that spot in the sky where the plane had to be. Yes, there it was, just now a flash as the sun glinted from the canopy, then fading to a dull yet visible white spot in the washed-out blue. He looked again at the scope. Nothing.

"Maybe if they tightened the circle, flew closer," Fritsche suggested.

The plane was still invisible. However, at five miles from the radar the strength of the emissions from Athena was too much: it beaconed and a false blip appeared at two miles and another at five.

"Dad's gonna have to tweak it," Harold Dodgers said, his voice confident and cheerful. "But by gum, it works."

"Sure enough does," Jake Grafton said, and wiped the perspiration from his forehead. Hard to believe, but that crackpot and his genius son had invented a device that would revolutionize warfare. Just as Admiral Henry had known it would.

After another twenty minutes, during which the Intruder flew back and forth in straight lines tangent to the five-mile circle so that Fritsche could chart the Athena's protection envelope, Jake told Rita and Toad to go on back to China Lake, where Dr. Dodgers would tweak the computer. Then Rita and Toad would bring the plane back here for another session. Jake would have preferred to stage the plane from NAS Fallon, just a few miles west, but Admiral Dunedin had vetoed that on the grounds that base security there would be inadequate.

"Helmut, you better drive over to the range office and call Dodgers on the scrambler and tell him how it went. Then call Admiral Dunedin in Washington."

"Sure." Fritsche trotted over to the gray navy sedan parked near the van and left in a cloud of dust. Harold Dodgers killed the generator, which backfired once and fell silent. Now the Intruder's engines were plainly audible, the moan echoing from the rocky ridges and outcrops.

"CAG," said a male voice on the radio. "Are we sweet or what?"

"You're sweet, Misty. See you this afternoon back here."

Jake watched the white dot shrink to nothing in the blue sky as Rita climbed away to the south. When even the engine noise was gone and all he could hear was the wind whispering across the sand, he walked over to the shade by the side of the van and sat down.

Any way you looked at it, Athena was mind-boggling. A religious crackpot working in a shop that looks as if it should be full of broken-down cars comes up with an invention that will instantly obsolesce all conventional radar technology. But perhaps it wasn't as wild as it appeared. After all, without the benefit of budgets, bureaucrats, and MBA supervisors worried about short-term profitability, Thomas Edison had single-handedly electrified the world and along the way fathered the recording and motion-picture industry. With the same advantages Samuel Dodgers had made junk of all existing military radar systems and the tactics and strategy built around those systems. And if you're keeping score, he also just blew the B-2 program out of the sky. Why buy stealth bombers for $516 million each when you can make an existing plane invisible with a $250,000 device and some superglue?

A lot of people were going to be seriously unhappy when they heard. Powerful people, the kind that had both their senators' unlisted Washington numbers on their Rolodex.

Jake Grafton picked up a handful of dirt and let it trickle through his fingers. Tyler Henry, Ludlow, Royce Caplinger—they were sitting on a bomb. No doubt they'll let Jake Grafton go it alone for a while, stand out there by himself in front of the crowd as the duty expert. After he had run the bloomers up the flagpole and they had precisely measured the direction and velocity of the wind, then and only then would they decide what to do.

They must have been ecstatic when they realized that Jake Grafton was just the man they needed: a genuine, decorated live hero whom they could stand with shoulder to shoulder or disavow as a crazed maverick, whichever way the cookie crumbled. They would throw him to the sharks without a second thought if they concluded that course looked best. *Too bad, but he always was an officer who couldn't take orders, not a team player. And after that El Hakim thing, a bad concussion, psychiatrists; he was never right in the head. Too bad.*

These powerful people whose boats would start leaking when the

Athena secret came out, what would they do? Fight. How? What would be their weapons?

The dirt escaping his fingers made a sculpted pile. The wind swirled away a portion of each handful. The slower the dirt trickled from his fingers, the more of it the wind claimed.

The most probable argument, Jake decided, was that Athena would destabilize the existing East-West military balance. This argument had finesse. Athena was too cheap to argue the dollars. So argue the consequences. Argue that Athena pushes Russia closer to a first strike. Argue nuclear war and radioactive ashes and the Four Horsemen. If you can't dazzle them with logic or baffle them with bullshit, then scare the bejesus out of them.

Jake stood and stirred the pile of dust with his toe. The wind carried it away grain by grain.

It was late afternoon, on the third flight of the day, and Rita was flying straight legs north and south, each leg one mile farther west of the radar site. Toad was bored. He was using the navigation system to ensure she stayed precisely where Captain Grafton wanted her to be. That was the hard part. After he had turned on the Athena system there was nothing to do but monitor its "operating" light. He did keep an eye on the Athena temp light, so if it came on he could turn off the system in a smart, military manner. For this the U.S. Navy was using its best Naval Flight Officer, a professional aerial warrior. Peace is hell.

Off to the west, down on the desert, was a long shadow cast by the two-story black windowless building that constituted the only structure in the town known as Deegon's Well. That building was a whorehouse. Presumably it also contained the office of the mayor and the rest of the municipal employees. From this distance it appeared to be just a tiny box on the desert. He knew it was painted black and had two stories and no windows because he had once inspected it from the parking lot in front. Just a tourist, of course.

He keyed his ICS mike to call Rita's attention to this famous landmark, but thought better of it.

Rita was checking the fuel remaining in the various tanks. He pressed his head against the radar hood and examined the cursor position.

He heard a whump, a loud, loose whump, and instantaneously the air pressure and noise level rose dramatically. Something struck him. He jerked his head back from the hood and looked around wildly.

The wind howled, shrieked, screamed, even through his helmet. Rita was back against her seat, slumped down, covered with gore, her right hand groping wildly for her face.

A bird! They had hit a bird.

He keyed the ICS without conscious thought and said her name. He couldn't hear the sound of his own voice.

The plane was rolling off on one wing, the nose dipping. He used his left hand to grab the stick between Rita's knees and center it.

Slow down. They had to slow down, had to lessen the velocity of the wind funneling through that smashed-out left quarter panel. The bird must have come through there and crashed against Rita as she bent over the fuel management panel on the left console.

He pulled back on the stick to bring the nose up into a climb and concentrated on keeping the wings level. Higher. Higher. Twenty degrees nose-up. Airspeed dropping: 250 indicated, 240, 230—he should drop the gear and flaps, get this flying pig slowed way down —210 knots.

The gear handle was on the left side of the instrument panel, right under the hole where the plexiglas quarter panel used to be, right under that river of air that was pressurizing the cockpit.

He tried to reach it. Just beyond his fingertips. Harness release unlocked. No go. Juggling the stick with his left hand, he used his right to release the two Koch fittings on the top of his torso harness. If the seat fired now he wouldn't have a parachute. He reached again. Nope. He was going to have to unfasten the Koch fittings that held his bottom to the ejection seat. With fingers that were all thumbs he released the two catches, then attacked the bayonet fittings on his oxygen mask. Might as well get it off too. He jerked loose the cord that went to the earphones in his helmet.

Damn—he was stalling. He could feel the buffet and the nose pitched forward. He let it go down and got some airspeed, then eased it back.

He was having difficulty holding the wings level. Power at about 86 percent on both engines. That was okay. But the smell—Jesus God!

The overpowering odor made his eyes water. He tried to breathe only through his mouth.

No longer restrained by the inertia reel in the ejection seat, he grasped the stick with his right hand and stretched across with his left to the gear handle and slapped it down.

Now for the flaps. He was lying across the center console, trying to keep his head out of the wind blast as he felt for the flap lever beside the throttle quadrant. Leave the throttles alone. Get the flaps down to thirty degrees. Fumbling, he pulled the lever aft.

Toad was overcorrecting with the stick as he fought to keep the wings level, first too much one way, then too much the other. Goddamn, those peckerhead pilots do this without even thinking about it.

There! Gear down and locked. Flaps and slats out, stabilator shifted. Hallelujah.

He glanced up at Rita. She had shit and blood and gore all over her face and shoulders. Feathers. They were everywhere!

Her helmet—it was twisted sideways. Using glances, he tried to wipe off the worst of the crap with his left hand as he concentrated on holding the plane straight and level: 140 knots now, 8,300 feet on the altimeter. Conditions in the cockpit were a lot better.

Were there any mountains this high around here? He couldn't remember, and he couldn't see over the top of the instrument panel, bent over the way he was.

First things first. He twisted her helmet back straight. The face shield was shattered, broken, but it had protected her face and eyes from the worst of the impact.

She was dazed. She damn well better come out of it quick, because he sure couldn't land this plane.

Her right eye was covered with goo, whether hers or the bird's he couldn't tell. He wiped at it with his gloved fingers. The bird's.

Her left eye was clear but unfocused, blinking like crazy. "C'mon, Rita baby. I can't keep flying this thing!" In his frustration he shouted. She couldn't hear him.

Back to the panel: 135 knots. Maybe he could engage the autopilot.

Yeah, the autopilot. If it would work. He jabbed at the switches and released the stick experimentally. Yeah! Hot damn! It engaged.

He devoted his attention to her. Cuffed her gently, rubbed her cheeks. She shook her head and raised her right hand to her face.

He got himself rearranged in his seat and held his mask to his face. "Rita?" Nothing. No sound in his ears. Now what? He had forgotten to plug the cord to his helmet back in. He did so. *"Goddamnit, Rita,"* he roared. "Snap out of it."

Someone was talking on the radio. He listened. He could hear the words now. It was Grafton. Toad keyed the radio mike. "We took a bird hit. Rita's a little dazed. We're going to land at Fallon when she comes around."

"Understand you took a bird. Where?"

"Right in the cockpit, CAG. Hit Rita in the head. We're going to Fallon when she comes around. Now I'm leaving this freq and calling Fallon on Guard." Without waiting for a reply, he jabbed the channelization switches and called Fallon tower. "Fallon tower, this is Misty 22 on Guard. Mayday. We're fifteen or twenty miles out. Roll the crash truck."

Which way are we heading? 120 degrees. He tugged the stick to the right and settled into a ten-degree turn, which the autopilot held. Fallon was off to the west here somewhere. He craned to see over the instrument panel in that direction.

"Misty 22, Fallon tower on Guard. Roger your Mayday. Come up . . ." and the controller gave them a discrete frequency.

Hey, stupid, look at the radar. He examined it. Be patient, Toad, be patient. You're doing okay, if only Rita comes around. And if she doesn't, well, screw it. You can figure out some way to eject her right over the runway, then you can hop out. Too bad those penny-pinchers in the puzzle palace never spent the bucks for a command ejection system for the A-6. But you can get her out somehow. It's been done before. There—that must be the base there, just coming onto the screen from the right. He waited until it was dead ahead, then pushed the stick left until the wings were level. Now he dialed in the Fallon tower freq and gave them a call.

Rita was using her right arm to get her left up to the throttle quadrant. "Toad?"

"Yeah. You okay?"

"What—"

"Bird strike. All that goo on you is bird shit and gore. Relax, it ain't you. Can you see?"

"I think—right eye's blurred. This wind. Left is red—blood—can't see . . ."

"Okay. I got the gear and flaps down and we're on autopilot motoring toward Fallon. After a while or two you're gonna land this thing. Just sit back right now and get yourself going again."

She rubbed at her face with her right hand.

The autopilot dropped off the line. Automatically she grasped the stick and began flying.

"See," exclaimed Toad Tarkington triumphantly, "you *can* do it! All fucking right! We're almost home. Raise your left wing." She did so and he resumed his monologue, only to pause occasionally to answer a question over the radio.

Rita Moravia flew by instinct, her vision restricted to one eye, and that giving her only a blurred impression of the attitude instruments on the panel before her. It was enough. She could feel the plane respond to her touch, and confirmation of that response was all she needed from her vision. Needed now. She would need to see a lot better to land. The wind—it was part of the problem. The wind wasn't coming into the plane through the shattered quarter panel at 140 knots—the closed cockpit prevented that—but it was coming in at an uncomfortable velocity and temperature.

Cold. She was cold. She should slow some more.

She tugged at the throttles with her left hand. Her arm was numb: her fingers felt like they were frozen. The power levers came back, though the engine-RPM and fuel-flow tapes were too blurred to read. Still she turned her head and squinted with her good eye. She could make out the angle-of-attack stoplight indexer on the glare shield and trimmed to an on-speed condition.

For the first time she looked outside, trying to see the ground. Just a blurred brown backdrop. But Toad could get her lined up.

She tried to make her left thumb depress the ICS button, and after a few seconds succeeded. "Where are we?"

"Come left about twenty degrees and start a descent to . . . oh, say, six thousand. Can you see?"

"I can see to fly. Can't see outside very well. Get me lined up and all and I think I can do it."

Toad got back on the radio.

She made the heading change and only then retarded the throttles slightly and let the nose slip down a degree or so. One thing at a time. She had once had an instructor who liked to chant that to his students, who were often in over their heads. When it's all going to hell, he used to say, just do one thing at a time.

The plane sank slowly, the altimeter needle swinging counterclockwise with about the speed of an elevator indicator. So they had all day. Go down slow and you have an easy transition at the bottom. Go down too fast and . . . As she sat there she continued to blink and flex her left arm. Doesn't feel like anything's broken, just numb. Maybe the world's most colorful bruise on my shoulder, some orange-and-purple splotch that will be the envy of every tattooed motorcyclist north of Juárez.

She was hurting now. As the numbness wore off she was hurting. Her face felt like someone had used a steak hammer on it. Like she had slid down the sidewalk on her cheekbone for a couple hundred yards.

"Come right about fifteen degrees or so and you'll be lined up," Toad said. "You got fourteen thousand feet of concrete here, Rita, but I think we should try for a wire." He reached up with his left hand and pulled the handle to drop the tailhook. "Just keep it lined up and descending wings level and we'll be in fat city."

"Fuel? How's our fuel?"

"About ten grand or so. Just a little heavy. Let's dump the fuel in the wings."

Rita reached with her left hand, up there under that blown-out quarter panel, for the dump switch on the fuel management panel. "I can't get it," she said finally.

"I'll get it." Toad leaned across and hunted until he had the proper switch.

"Landing checklist."

"Okay, you got three down and locked, flaps and slats out, stab shifted, boards?" She put them out and added some power. It took a while to get the plane stabilized on speed again.

"Pop-up?" Toad murmured when she once again had everything under control. "Can you check the flaperon pop-up?" The switch was on her left console. She had to lower her head and look as she fumbled with numb fingers. "Watch your wings," Toad warned.

She brought the wings back to level.

"Screw the pop-up," Toad announced, figuring that she just couldn't ascertain the switch position. "It's probably still on. Check the brakes."

This also took some doing. She had to lift both feet free of the deck where her heels rested and place the balls of her feet on top of the rudder pedals, then push. She had never before realized what a strain that put on her stomach muscles. She was weak as a kitten. She struggled and got her feet arranged and pushed hard. They met resistance. "Brakes okay." She would have to do this again on the runway if the hook skipped over the short-field arresting gear or she landed long. For now she let her feet slide down the pedals until her heels were once again on the deck.

"My mask." She gagged. "Get my mask off!"

Toad got her right fitting released just in time. She retched and the vomit poured down over her chest.

Seeing Rita vomit and smelling that smell, Toad felt his own stomach turn over. He choked it back and helped her hold the plane level until she stopped heaving.

"Okay," she said when she finally got her mask back on, "check your harness lock and we're ready to do it." She took her hand off the stick and locked the harness lever on the forward right corner of the ejection seat.

"Oh, poo," Toad said. She glanced his way. He was reconnecting his Koch fittings. "Sort of forgot to strap myself back in," he explained.

She ran her seat up as far as she could and yet still reach the rudder pedals. This put her a face a little higher out of the wind, and in seconds she could see better, but only out of her right eye. Her left was still clogged with blood.

"You're coming down nicely, passing six thousand MSL, eighteen hundred above the ground. Let's keep this sink rate and we'll do okay. Come left a couple degrees, though."

She complied.

"A little more. And gimme just a smidgen more power."

When she squinted and blinked a few more times, she could make out the runway. There was a little crosswind and Toad had her aimed off to the left slightly to compensate.

The approach seemed to take forever, perhaps because she was hurting and perhaps because she was unsure if she could handle it at the bottom. She would just have to wait and see, but it was difficult waiting when she was so cold, and growing colder.

She let the plane descend without throttle corrections, without wiggling the stick or trying to sweeten her lineup. With three hundred feet still to go on the radar altimeter, she made a heading correction. She was going to have trouble judging the altitude with only one eye, and she thought about that. She could do it, she decided. There was the meatball on the Optical Landing System. She began to fly it, working mightily to move the throttles. Still coming down, on speed, lined up, across the threshold. Now! Throttles back a little and nose just so, right rudder and left stick to straighten her out . . . oh yes!

The mainmounts kissed the concrete.

The pilot used the stick to hold the nose wheel off as she smoothly closed the throttles. She had no more than got the engines to idle when she felt the rapid deceleration as the tailhook engaged the short-field arresting gear. The nose slammed down. As the plane was jerked to a rapid stop, she applied the brakes.

She got the flap handle forward with her left hand, but knew she wouldn't be able to tug hard enough to pull the parking brake handle out. Toggling the harness lock release by her right thigh, she got enough freedom to reach it with her right.

Toad opened the canopy. As it whined its way aft a fire truck came roaring up and screeched to a halt with firemen tumbling off.

Canopy open, Rita checked that the flaps and slats were in. Her left shoulder was aching badly now and it was difficult to make her fingers do as she wished. One of the firemen ran out from the wheel well and made a cutting motion across his throat. He had inserted the safety pins in the landing gear.

Both throttles around the horn to cutoff, engine-fuel master switches off as the RPMs dropped. Then the generators dropped off the line with an audible click and everything in the cockpit went dead. Exhausted, she fumbled with the generator switches until they too were secured.

It was very quiet. She got the mask loose and, using only her right hand, pried the helmet off. The compressor blades tinkled steadily, gently, as the wind kept them turning, like a mobile on the porch of your grandmother's house when you returned after a long absence.

A man was standing on the pilot's boarding ladder. He looked at her and drew back in horror.

"A bird," she croaked.

She heard Toad give a disgusted exclamation. "Wipe it off her, man! It's just bird guts. It ain't her brains!"

They were loading Rita into an ambulance and the crash crew was filling out paperwork when a gray navy sedan screeched to a halt near the fire truck. Jake Grafton jumped out and strode toward Toad as white smoke wafted from the auto's engine compartment.

"Looks like you were in a hurry," Toad said, and managed a grin. He was sitting, leaning back against the nose wheel, too drained to even stand. He felt as if he had just finished a ten-mile run. The crash chief tossed the captain a salute and he returned it even though he wasn't wearing a hat. He obviously had other things on his mind.

"How's Rita?"

"Gonna be okay, I think. When they looked at her they thought she had brains and eyeballs oozing out everywhere, but they got most of it cleaned off. Never saw so much shit. Must have been a damn big bird. They're taking her over to the hospital for X rays and all."

Jake Grafton deflated visibly. He wiped his forehead with a hand, and then wiped his hand on his trousers, leaving a wet stain.

"How come you didn't answer me on the damned radio? I about had heart failure when you started doing whifferdills."

"I'm sorry, sir. I disconnected my plugs and got a little unstrapped so I could reach over and fly the plane. Rita was sorta out of it there for a little while."

Jake climbed the pilot's ladder and surveyed the cockpit. He examined the hole left in the plexiglas quarter panel by the late buzzard or eagle or hawk. "She come around okay?"

"Came to and landed this thing like it was on rails. Real damn sweet, CAG. Never saw a better landing."

A sailor drove up aboard a yellow flight-line tractor. He swung in front of the plane and backed a tow bar toward the nose wheel. "Well," said Jake Grafton as he made a quick inspection of the Athena antennas, all of which seemed to be firmly in place, "you better zip over to the hospital and let them check you over too. I gotta get this plane put someplace private."

"Uh, CAG, you're still gonna let us fly the prototypes, aren't you? I mean, it wasn't like we tried to hit that bird or anything."

Jake looked at Toad, slightly surprised. "Oh," he said, "you two are my crew. If the doctors say you can fly. Now get over to the hospital and find out. Better get cleaned up too. You look like you've been cleaning chickens and the chickens won."

"Yessir. You bet. But, uh, I don't have a ride. Can I take your car?"

"Aw, Toad, you're gonna get that bird goo all over the seat." He glanced at the car. Smoke was still leaking out. It was junk. "Keys are in it. But be careful—it's government property."

Amazingly enough, the car engine actually started after Toad ground on it awhile. Jake had driven about forty miles at full throttle, about a hundred miles per hour, so he shook his head in wonder when the transmission engaged with a thunk and Toad drove away trailing smoke.

15

The base dispensary contained an emergency room, but no other hospital facilities. After Rita Moravia was cut out of her flight gear, cleaned up and examined by a doctor, she was taken to a hospital in Reno, seventy miles away. Toad Tarkington arrived at the dispensary as the ambulance was driving away.

"Oh, Doctor," the corpsman called when he saw Toad coming through the door, "here comes the other one."

The doctor was only a year or two out of med school, but he had already acquired the nuances of military practice. "In here." He gestured to an examining room. A corpsman followed them in and closed the door. "Strip to the skin," the doctor said. "How do you feel?" He grasped Toad's wrist and glanced at his watch.

"Okay, Doc. The pilot took the bird hit. I just got splattered."

"Did you become hypoxic, pass out, inhale any feathers or anything like that?"

"No, sir. I just peed my pants."

The doctor checked his watch again, then looked at Toad with raised eyebrows.

"Not really," Toad said, suddenly aware that he was no longer in the company of his peers. "Sorry. How's Moravia?"

The doctor was still all business. "Blurred vision in her left eye, some bruises and cuts, nothing serious. But she's an excellent candidate for a major-league infection. I gave her a large dose of penicillin and sent her to the hospital in Reno for X rays and observation. She can stay there until we're sure she's okay."

"And her eye?"

"I think it'll be okay. They'll look at that in Reno."

The doctor spent the next five minutes examining Toad. He peed in a bottle and gave a blood sample. The corpsman gathered up his flight gear. Toad insisted it all be put in a duffel bag. He stood holding his flight suit, which already had a hen-house smell. "What am I going to do for clothes?"

"Got any money?"

He dug his wallet from the chest pocket. "Fifty-three dollars."

The doctor added fifty dollars of his own money to Toad's fortune and sent the corpsman to the exchange for underwear, trousers, shirt, and tennis shoes. "Should be open until nineteen hundred hours. You can make it if you hurry." Toad gave the enlisted man his sizes and expressed a few opinions about color and style. The corpsman flashed Toad a wicked grin as he headed for the door.

An hour later Tarkington had talked the doctor into loaning him one of the navy sedans belonging to the dispensary. He was on his way to the parking lot in his new duds when he met Jake Grafton coming in.

"You okay?" the captain said.

"Yessir. Just fine. Thought I'd grab a little liberty." Toad gave Jake back the keys to the sedan he had used to get to the dispensary, and displayed the keys to his borrowed vehicle. "I think your car's had it. Want to come with me?"

"Where you going?"

"Reno. That's where they took Rita." He told Jake what the doctor had said.

Jake begged off. He still had security arrangements and phone calls to make. "Call me from the hospital and tell me how she is. I'll be at the BOQ. Leave a message at the desk if I'm not there."

Jake watched Toad drive away toward the main gate, then went into the dispensary to see what the doctor really thought about Rita's left eye. She needed two great eyes to fly. Better than the doctor or even Toad, Jake Grafton knew what flying meant to Lieutenant Rita Moravia, U.S. Naval Aviator.

They had her in a semi-private room with a beautiful white-haired lady who was fast asleep. Toad spent ten minutes talking to the floor nurse and the internist before he went in. "They say you're gonna be okay," he told Rita with a grin. She had a patch over her left eye. Scratches and small cuts were visible on her cheek.

She raised a finger to her lips. "Mrs. Douglas went to sleep a few minutes ago," she whispered. Toad stood at the end of the bed glancing uneasily at the shiny, stark hospital equipment. Just being in a hospital made his leg ache.

"Here," she said, still whispering, "pull this chair over and sit down. Have you had any dinner?" It was almost 10 P.M.

"Uh-uh. How you doin'?" He sat gingerly on the forward portion of the seat.

She shrugged. "Thanks for saving my bacon."

He waved it away. "What's wrong with her?" he asked, glancing at the sleeping Mrs. Douglas.

"Broken hip. She fell in her kitchen this morning. They're going to pin it tomorrow evening. She's been in a lot of pain today."

Toad nodded vaguely and examined the sheets that covered Rita. Hospital sheets always looked so perfect, even with a body between them. Her hair was a mess. They had cleaned it and made no attempt to pretty it up. That's what's wrong with hospitals—your dignity is left at the front door on the way in.

"That shirt you're wearing is the most *horrid* garment I have— What are those colors? Chartreuse and mauve?"

"Beats me," Toad muttered, glancing at his torso with distaste. "One of the corpsmen picked it out at the exchange. He thought I would cut a dashing figure in it, I guess."

"Dashing is not the word I would use."

They sat for a while, each trying to think of something to say. "Guess your helmet visor saved your eyes," he said at last. "Cushioned the impact."

"It's amazing, when you stop to think about it. I thought about it all the way over here in the ambulance. The ambulance only goes ten miles over the speed limit, so everything on the road passes it. Lights flashing, and everyone whizzing by. So I had plenty of time to think about the odds. It's amazing."

"What is?"

"How with the whole wide sky to fly in, all those thousands of cubic miles, that bird and I tried to fly in exactly the same little piece of it. A foot further left, that bird would have missed the cockpit, a foot to the right and it would have hit the nose, a foot higher—"

"Life's like that. No guarantees. You never know."

"Is that what combat is like?"

"I wouldn't know."

"Weren't you and Captain Grafton—over the Med?"

Toad shrugged and slid further back into the chair. He crossed his leg with the pin in it over the good one and massaged it gently. "One flight. A couple minutes of being scared stiff and too busy to even sweat it. That wasn't combat. Combat is day in and day out knowing they're going to be shooting and being scared before you go and going anyway. I've never done that. Hope I never have to." He grinned wryly and cocked his head to better match the angle of hers against the pillow. "I'm a peacetime drugstore cowboy. Didn't you know? Make love not war."

"The Silver Star fooled me."

"Medals don't mean shit. Over the Med CAG had the guts and determination, enough for him and me both with a lot left over. He's a balls-out fighter. Those Arab fighter jocks were hopelessly outclassed—at least that's what I kept telling myself then. Still tell myself that on nights when I wake up thinking about it. I'm even beginning to believe it."

She smoothed the sheets with her right hand.

"How's your left shoulder?"

"Just bruised. Hurts now. If this eye clears up . . ."

"It will."

"Got some cuts on the eyeball. Lots of bird flesh and even the stem of a little feather."

"It'll be okay."

"I suppose."

"You'll fly again. Just wait and see. You're too good to stay on the ground. A person with your talent belongs in a cockpit."

"Ummm."

He put his feet on the floor, leaned forward and captured a hand. "Listen, Rita—Ginger—I know how you feel. The fickle finger of fate just reached out and zinged you a little one and reminded you that you're mortal clay. We all are. But—you know all this— you've got to live every day the best you can, put the throttles against the stops and fly. Flying is what it's all about. And when that final flight comes, that last day, as come it will, then look the Man straight in the eye and tell Him it's been a hell of a great ride. And thank Him. *That's* the way you have to live it. That's the only way it can be done."

She took her hand from his and touched his cheek.

"Get a good night's sleep. Get well. You got a lot of flying left to do." He stood. "I'll look in on you tomorrow afternoon. Hang tough."

"Thanks for coming by."

He paused at the door and winked. "We fly together. Remember?"

"Kiss me, lover."

He glanced at Mrs. Douglas. Her eyes were closed and she seemed to be asleep. He bent over Rita and gave her his best effort.

It was 1 P.M. the next day when Luis Camacho pulled into his driveway in Silver Spring and let himself into his house. His wife was at work and his son was in school. The house felt strange on a weekday with both of them gone. He walked slowly through the downstairs, looking it over, listening to the refrigerator hum, looking out the windows.

He found his leather driving gloves in the hall closet, the pigskin ones his parents had given him two Christmases ago that he never wore because they were too nice. The batteries in the flashlight stowed in the catchall drawer in the kitchen still had some juice, amazingly enough. He tucked the light into his hip pocket and let himself out the kitchen door into the backyard. The wooden fence between his house and Albright's had a gate with a rusty latch, no lock. The Labrador wanted to come with him, but he shooed it back and latched the gate behind him.

He opened his packet of lock picks on Harlan Albright's picnic table. He stared at them a moment, trying to decide. It had been a while. Let's see, the lock is a Yale.

Opening it took ten minutes. The Lab finally quit whining next door. Probably he went back to his favorite spot in the sun and lay down. Camacho was beginning to think he wasn't going to get this lock when it clicked.

Albright had no fancy alarms, or none that Camacho had ever seen. Service manager at a local garage, he couldn't afford the visibility that a Fort Knox security system would give him. But no doubt he had some little doodads here and there to let him know if he had any unwanted visitors.

Luis Camacho stood in the door and carefully examined the interior. It looked precisely as he remembered it, exactly the way he had seen it for years. He stepped inside, eased the door shut and listened.

Albright's house was similar to his, one of four variations on the same basic floor plan the tract builder had used in half the houses in this subdivision. Other than minor interior adjustments, most of the differences were in the front façades.

As he stood there the faint hum of the refrigerator shut off. Albright's fridge was quieter than his. Probably newer too. He closed his eyes and concentrated, trying to shut out the faint sound of a car passing on the side street. Only a few creaks and groans as the house continued to warm in the early afternoon sun.

He moved slowly through the kitchen and into the family room. A bachelor, Albright spent his evenings here, watching TV or reading. Camacho moved slowly, checking the walls and looking behind pictures—O'Keeffe prints—and tugging at the carpet edges. He inspected the books in the built-in bookcase, then randomly removed a few and checked the integrity of the wall behind by rapping with a knuckle. He didn't know what he hoped to find, but he would recognize it when he saw it. If there was anything to find, which was doubtful.

The garage was next, then the basement. It was still unfinished, no ceiling or drywall to cover the unpainted cinder blocks. Damp. Only two naked bulbs overhead, plus the one on the stairs. He glanced at the accumulated junk and the layers of dust and grime, and decided Albright cleaned his basement on the same schedule used by every other bachelor who owned one—never. There were some tools piled carelessly in one corner: a drill, a saber saw, a hammer, a box of hand tools. They were covered with the same thickness of dirt that covered everything else. Some cans of paint that looked like they had never been opened. Perhaps he had had a fit of enthusiasm which had waned on the way home from the hardware store. Camacho went back upstairs, consciously reminding himself to flip off the light switch at the head of the stairs.

He stopped dead in the kitchen. He turned and went back to the basement door. He opened it. Light switch on. What was that? Was it a noise? Lights off. Yes, there was a noise, some kind of faint grinding, just for a half second or so. He repeated the procedure. He wasn't imagining things. He could hear *something*.

In the slanted ceiling of the stairway, down about three feet from the bulb, was a dusty screen. Several of the strands had been pushed aside, perhaps by a careless jab from a broom handle, leaving a hole. He flipped the light several more times. He could just barely hear it, the most minute of noises, hard to recognize.

The screen was held on with four screws. Bare metal could be seen on the screw slots. When he got them out and lowered the screen he could see the camera lens. Rubber padding held on with rubber bands covered the camera body. A wire led to it. He stood on the stairs and examined it with his flashlight, then reached up and removed the camera, excess wire following along.

The wire was connected to a gadget on top with a small alligator clip. With the stairwell light off, he unclipped it and carried the camera to the kitchen table. Unwrapping the rubber padding with gloves on was difficult, so he took them off.

The gadget on top was some kind of an electromagnetic doohickey with a lever. When the current was turned on by flipping the light switch, the magnet was energized and caused this steel pin to push the camera shutter button, tripping the shutter. When the current ceased, a spring reset the lever, which released the shutter button and allowed the film to be automatically advanced by the camera.

It was a nice camera, a Canon. The little window said that it was on its ninth exposure. How many times had he turned that light on and off. He tried to count them. Six. No, five. So the film counter should be on four.

He opened the camera and removed the film, then pulled the celluloid completely from its cartridge and held it up to the window. Rewinding the film back onto the cartridge was a chore, but he managed, and after wiping the cartridge carefully, he reinstalled it in the camera. He used a dry dishcloth on the camera and wrapped it carefully. Working by feel with the overhead stair light off, he returned the device to its hole and screwed the screen back on. He flipped the light switch three times and was rewarded each time with that faint noise.

There were three bedrooms upstairs, exactly the same floor plan here as in his house next door, but only two of them were furnished. The largest was obviously lived in, but the middle-sized room was ready for a guest. Luis Camacho tried to remember if Harlan Albright had ever had an overnight guest that he knew about. No.

He checked the carpet. Albright might have some kind of pressure device under there, or perhaps heat-sensitive paper. Nope. Another camera? Apparently not.

There was a little trapdoor in the hall ceiling that led to the unfinished attic. An upholstered chair sat just inside the guest bedroom. He put his nose almost to the seat and scrutinized it carefully. Yes, a few smudges of dirt were visible.

Luis Camacho pulled the chair under the trapdoor, took his shoes off and stood on it. He eased the door up. It was dark up there. A few flakes of dust drifted down. He stood on tiptoe and used the flash. He felt between the joists.

Several items. One was a soft leather baglike thing, a zippered pistol rug. The other was a large, heavy metal toolbox that just fit through the trapdoor. He almost dropped the toolbox getting it down.

The pistol rug contained a Ruger .22 autopistol with black plastic grips and a partially full box of Remington ammunition. Bluing was worn off the pistol in places. The front sight and its sleeve were amputated, and threads were machined into the outside of the barrel to take the silencer, which was also in the rug. This was strictly a close-range weapon: with no front sight, it would be useless at any distance.

He sniffed the barrel of the pistol. Cleaned since last use. He pushed the catch and the magazine dropped out of the grip into his hand. It was full. He shoved it back in until it clicked. No doubt the cleaning rod and patches and gun oil were up there in the joists somewhere. He replaced the items in the rug and zipped it closed.

The toolbox wasn't locked. Neatly packed in and padded to prevent damage were fuses, a roll of wire and a two-channel Futaba radio transmitter for radio-controlled models. Lots of servos, ten of them. A little bag containing crystals to change the frequency of the transmitter. Four miniature radio receivers, also made by Futaba. A bunch of nickel-cadmium batteries and a charging unit. Four six-cell batteries wrapped with black plastic. There was even a manual alarm clock.

But the pièce de résistance, the item that impressed Luis Camacho, was a radio receiver with a frequency-adjustment knob, volume knob, earpiece and spike meter. This device would allow the careful craftsman to check for possible radio interference in the area in which he intended to do his bit to improve the human species, before he armed his own device. Better safe than sorry.

All in all, it was an impressive kit. Everything recommended by *Gentleman's Quarterly* for the well-heeled professional bomber was in there, including a case containing a set of jeweler's screwdrivers and wrenches.

Camacho repacked the items carefully, trying to put everything back exactly as he found it. After much straining he got the tool-box back through the trapdoor into the attic.

He checked carefully in the joists as far as he could reach and see, then replaced the pistol rug. He was meticulous in restoring everything to its proper place, wiping a few flecks of dust from the chair arms and retrieving a larger piece from the carpet. When he had given everything a last look, he went down to the kitchen and seated himself at the table.

Where was the plastique? It had to be here someplace. Using his flashlight, he descended again to the basement and examined the paint cans. He hefted them, shook them gently. They contained something, but it probably wasn't paint. Oh well.

He locked the kitchen door behind him and crossed through the back gate to his own yard.

Standing in his own kitchen with a pot of coffee dripping through the filter, he thought about Albright's treasure as he maneuvered a cup under the black coffee basket to fill it. With the Pyrex pot back in place, he sipped on the hot liquid as he dialed the phone.

After talking to three people, he was connected with the man he wanted, an explosives expert. "Well, the material's ability to resist the effects of heat and cold and humidity depends on just what kind of stuff it is. Semtex is a brand real popular right now, made in Czechoslovakia. Heat won't do it any good, but if the heat is not too severe or prolonged, it shouldn't take much of its punch away."

"How about storage in an uninsulated attic?"

"Here, in this climate?"

"Yes."

"Not recommended. Best would be a place slightly below room temperature, a place where the temp stays pretty constant."

"Thanks."

"I keep mine in the wine cellar."

"Sure."

Camacho finished the cup of coffee, dumped the rest of the pot down the sink and turned off the coffee maker. He wiped the area with a dishrag and threw the wet grounds into the garbage. He didn't want his wife noticing he had been there.

It was three o'clock when he locked the front door and drove away.

At about the same instant that Luis Camacho was starting his car to return to his office, Toad Tarkington was parking at the Reno hospital. When he arrived in the room, Rita was sitting in a chair talking with Mrs. Douglas, her roommate. After the introductions Toad pulled up the other chair, a molded plastic job made for a smaller bottom than his.

"When are they going to let you go?" he asked as he tried to arrange himself comfortably.

"Probably tomorrow. The doctor will be around in an hour or so."

"Did you get a good night's sleep?"

"Not really." She smiled at Mrs. Douglas. "We had a series of little naps, didn't we?"

"We did." Mrs. Douglas had a delicate voice. "I don't sleep much anymore anyway." She bit on her lower lip.

"Perhaps we should go for a little walk," Rita suggested. She rose and made sure her robe belt was firmly tied. "We'll be back in a little bit, Mrs. Douglas."

"Okay, dear."

Out in the hall Toad said, "I see you fixed your hair."

"Wasn't it a fright? A hospital volunteer helped me this morning. She said it would help how I felt, and she was right." She walked slowly in her slippers, her hands in her pockets. "Poor Mrs. Douglas. Here I've been so concerned about my little half-acre and her two daughters came in this morning and told her she has to go to a nursing home. She's very upset. Oh, Toad, it was terrible, for all of them. They're afraid she'll fall again with no one there, and the daughters work, with families of their own."

Toad made a sympathetic noise. He had never given the problems of elderly people much thought. He really didn't want to do so now either.

Rita paused for a drink from a water fountain, then turned back toward her room. "I just wanted you to know the situation. Now we'll go back and cheer her up."

Toad put his hand on her arm. "Whoa, lady. Let's run that one by again. Just *how* are we going to do that?"

"You cheered me up last night. You make me feel good just being around you. You can do the same with her."

Toad looked up and down the hall for help, someone or something to rescue him. No such luck. He looked again at Rita, who was absorbing every twitch of his facial muscles. "Women my own age I don't understand. Now it's true I've picked up a smattering of experience here and there with the gentle sex, but eighty-year-old ladies with busted hips are completely out of—"

"You can do it," Rita said with simple, matter-of-fact faith, and grasping his hand, she led him back along the hallway.

In the room she nudged him toward the chair near Mrs. Douglas. He started to give Rita a glare, but when he realized Mrs. Douglas was watching him, he changed it to a smile. It came out as a silly, nervous smile.

Women! If they didn't screw there'd be a bounty on 'em.

"Rita says you're facing some very significant changes in your life."

The elderly woman nodded. She was still chewing on her lip. At that moment Toad forgot Rita and saw before him his own mother as she would be in a few years. "Pretty damned tough," he said, meaning it.

"My life now is my garden, the roses and bulbs and the annuals that I plant every spring. I do my housework and spend my time watching the cycle of life in my garden. I wasn't ready to give that up."

"I see."

"I have most of my things planted now. The bulbs have been up for a month or so. They were so pretty this spring."

"I don't suppose any of us are ever ready to give up something we love."

"I suppose not. But I had hoped that I wouldn't have to. My husband—he died fifteen years ago with a heart attack while he was playing golf. He so loved golf. I was hoping that someday in my garden I . . ." She closed her eyes.

When she opened them again Toad asked about her garden. It was not large, he was told. Very small, in fact. But it was enough. That was one of life's most important lessons, learning what was enough and what was too much. Understanding what was *sufficient*. "But," Mrs. Douglas sighed, "what is sufficient changes as you get older. It's one thing for a child, another for an adult, another thing still when you reach my age. I think as you age life gets simpler, more basic."

"I'm curious," said Toad Tarkington, feeling more than a little embarrassed. He shot a hot glance at Rita. "Do you pray much?"

"No. It's too much like begging. The professional pray-ers always want things they will never get, things they just can't have. Like peace on earth and conversion of the sinners and cures for all the sick. And to prove they really want all these things that can never be, they grovel and beg."

"At least they're sincere," Rita said.

"Beggars always are," Mrs. Douglas shot back. "That's their one virtue."

Toad grinned. Mrs. Douglas appeared to be a fellow cynic, which he found quite agreeable. Perhaps the age difference doesn't matter that much after all. A few minutes later he asked one more question. "What will heaven be like, do you think?"

"A garden. With roses and flowers of all kinds. My heaven will be that anyway. What yours will be, I don't know." Mrs. Douglas waggled a finger at him without lifting her hand from the bed. "You are two very nice young people, to spend time with an old woman to cheer her up. When are you going to marry?"

Toad laughed and stood. "You tell her, Mrs. Douglas. She absolutely refuses to become an honest woman." He said his goodbyes and Rita followed him into the hall.

"Thanks. That wasn't so hard, was it?" She had her arms folded across her chest.

"Hang tough, Rita. If they let you take a hike tonight or tomorrow, give me a call at the BOQ. Captain Grafton or I will come get you and bring you some clothes."

She nodded. "You come if you can."

"Sure." He paused. "What do you want from life, Rita? What will be sufficient?"

She shook her head. He winked and walked away.

16

In an era when the average American male stood almost six feet tall, Secretary of Defense Royce Caplinger towered just five feet six inches in his custom-made shoes with two-inch heels. Perhaps understandably, his hero and role model was Douglas MacArthur, of whom he had written a biography ten years before. The critics had savaged it and the post-Vietnam public had ignored it. Caplinger, said one wag, would have won MacArthur sainthood had the book been even half true.

How deeply this experience hurt Caplinger only his family might have known. The world was allowed to see only the merciless efficiency and detached intellect that had made him a millionaire by the time he was thirty and president and CEO of one of the twenty largest industrial companies in the nation when he was forty-two. Now worth in excess of a hundred million dollars, he was a man who believed in himself with a maniacal faith; in the world of titanic egos in which he moved he saw himself as a giant and, to his credit, others saw him the same way.

Rude and abrasive, Caplinger never forgot or forgave. He had never been accused of possessing a sense of humor. He won many more battles than he lost because he was *right*, often terrifically right, as his many enemies freely acknowledged. He often won when he was wrong too, because he could play major-league hard-ball with the best of them. Years ago his subordinates had labeled him "the cannibal," whispering that he liked the taste of raw flesh.

Caplinger had the brain of Caesar and the soul of a lizard, all housed in the body of a chimpanzee, or so one of his more daring victims had groused to *Time* magazine. This quote crossed Jake Grafton's mind just now as he watched the secretary's gaze dart back and forth across the faces of the men at the luncheon table as they were served pear halves in china dishes bearing the seal of the Navy Department by a steward in a white jacket.

Jake was back in Washington for a week while the China Lake crowd fixed their A-6, Rita Moravia recovered, and Samuel Dodgers tinkered with the Athena device. This was Jake's first meal in the Secretary of the Navy's dining/conference room, so today he was playing tourist and taking it all in.

The room was spacious and paneled with dark wood, perhaps mahogany. Deep blue drapes dressed up the windows. A half dozen oil paintings of sailing ships and battles, with little spotlights to show them to advantage, were arranged strategically between the windows and doors. Gleaming brass bric-a-brac provided the accents. Sort of early New York Yacht Club, Jake decided, a nineteenth-century vision of a great place for railroad pirates and coal barons to socialize over whiskey with nautical small talk about spankers and jibs and their latest weekend sail to Newport. He would describe the room for Callie this evening. He sipped his sugarless iced tea and turned his attention to the conversation.

In keeping with his temperament, Caplinger was doing the talking: ". . . the Congress has ceased to exist as a viable legislative body since Watergate. They can't even manage to give senior leaders or the judiciary a pay raise without making a hash of it. Without strong, capable leaders, Congress is a collection of mediocrities drifting . . ."

Jake used his knife to slice the fruit in his dish, two whole halves, to make it go further. Already he suspected this wasn't going to be much of a meal.

At the opposite end of the table from the Secretary of Defense sat today's host, Secretary of the Navy George Ludlow. He was nibbling at pieces of pear he nicked off with his fork and listening to Caplinger. No doubt he was used to these monologues; he had married Caplinger's second daughter, a modestly pretty young woman with a smile that looked vacuous in news photos. Jake Grafton had never met her and probably never would.

". . . five hundred thirty-five ants on a soapbox drifting down the Potomac, each of them thinking he's steering." Caplinger chuckled and everyone else smiled politely. Jake had heard that old saw before.

Across the long table from Jake sat Tyler Henry, Under Secretary of Defense for Acquisition Russell Queen, and the Chief of Naval Operations, Admiral Jerome Nathan Lanham.

Lanham was a submariner, a nuke, with all the baggage that term implies: team player, risk minimizer, technocrat par excellence in the service of the nuclear genie. His patron saint was Hyman Rickover, the father of the nuclear navy, whose portrait hung in Lanham's office. Like Rickover, Jerome Nathan Lanham was reputed to have little use for nonengineers. Just now he sat regarding Jake Grafton, A.B. in history, with raised eyebrows.

Jake nodded politely and speared another tiny hunk of pear. The dish was half full of juice. He wondered if he should go after it with a spoon and surveyed the table to see if anyone else was. Nope. Well, hell. He used the spoon anyway, trying to be discreet, as Caplinger ruminated upon the current political situation in Japan and the steward began serving a tiny garden salad. ". . . wanted to hang Hirohito after the war, but MacArthur said no, which was genius. The Japanese would never have forgiven us."

"If we conquered Iran today, what would you do with Khomeini?" Helmet Fritsche, seated to Jake's right, asked the question of Caplinger, who grinned broadly.

"Such a tiny hypothetical—he should have been a lawyer," Ludlow muttered sotto voce as the others laughed.

"Make Khomeini a martyr? No. I'd ensure he didn't get any older, but the autopsy—and there would be one—would read 'old age.' "

After the salad came small bowls of navy bean soup accompanied by some tasteless crackers. Even Caplinger thought they were insipid. "George, these crackers taste worse than some of my old predictions."

When the soup was gone, the steward filled coffee cups and whisked away the dishes, then retired. Jake watched incredulously. Apparently they had just had the entire meal. At least Ludlow wasn't blowing the whole navy budget this year on grub.

"Well, Grafton," Caplinger said, "will Athena work?"

"Yessir. It's the biggest technical advance in naval aviation since I've been in the navy."

"If it works"—the Secretary of Defense eyed Jake across the rim of his coffee cup—"it'll be the biggest leap forward for the military since the invention of radar. The air force is going to want this technology yesterday. It'll save their strategic bomber program." Jake understood. The air force would be able to use much cheaper bombers than the B-2, which they would never get any significant number of at a half billion dollars each.

"I want it right now," Admiral Lanham said. "These devices will make surface ships invisible to radar satellites and cruise missiles. The entire Soviet naval air arm will be obsolete. I want a crash program that puts Athena in the fleet *right now,* and *damn* the cost."

Caplinger shifted his gaze to Helmut Fritsche, on Jake's right. "Will it work? Can it be made to work?"

"Anything's possible given enough time and money."

"How much?" demanded Under SECDEF Russell Queen. In civilian life he had been president of a large accounting firm. White skin, banker's hands, bald, Queen had long ago lost the battle of the bulge. He was a humorless man with thick glasses. Jake decided it would require prodigious faith to believe Russell Queen had once been young or ever loved a woman. "How much do you think will be enough?"

Fritsche's shoulders rose a quarter inch and fell. "Depends on how you go about it—how you structure the contract, how many units you buy annually, how big a risk you're willing to take on unproven technology. We didn't test a full-up system. All we did was prove the concept, and we have some more work to do on that next week. We're a long way from an operational system that will protect just one tactical airplane."

"How long?"

Helmut Fritsche took out a cigar and rolled it thoughtfully between his hands. He didn't reach for a match. "Two or three years —if you can make all the paper pushers keep hands off. Four or five if it's business as usual." Every head at the table bobbed its owner's concurrence.

"Humph," snorted Caplinger, who sucked in a bushel of air and sent it down as far as it would go, then exhaled slowly. "I can try to put—maybe slip it under the stealth stuff—but . . ." His enthusiasm wouldn't fill a thimble. Even the Secretary of Defense couldn't control the legions of bureaucrats with rice bowls to protect. They were too well armed with statutes and regulations and pet congressmen. "Russell, you'll have to make this work, find some dollars in one of your little hidey-holes, keep it too small for anyone to get curious about. And no fucking memos."

Queen nodded slowly, his smooth round face revealing his discomfort. He looked, Jake thought, like a man staring into a dark abyss that he has been told to lower himself into.

"I don't think that's the way to do it," Ludlow said. "Admiral Lanham wants it now and the air force will too. We're going to have to fund Athena as one of our highest-priority items. We're going to have to throw money at it and hope the technology works."

"Do you agree, Admiral?"

"Yes, sir. I'd rather have Athena than a whole lot of projects I can name, including the A-12."

"We need them both," Caplinger said. "So we'll keep Athena in with the ATA and request funding for them both."

"What about Congress?" Ludlow murmured. When no one replied, he expanded the question. "How will Athena be seen by the liberals dying to chop the defense budget? Will they think it gives us such a large qualitative technical advantage over the Soviets that they can chop our capital budget? Shrink the navy?" To maintain a navy, worn-out, obsolete ships must be constantly replaced with new ones. New ships are expensive and require years to construct. A decision not to build as many as necessary to maintain current force levels was a decision to shrink the navy. Insufficient ships to fulfill continuing worldwide commitments forced planners to delay ship overhauls and keep sailors at sea for grotesquely long periods, which wore out ships prematurely and devastated enlisted retention rates. It was a cruel downward spiral. This was the post-Vietnam nightmare from which the navy was just recovering.

"No democracy will ever buy enough ships," Jake Grafton said. "Not over the long haul."

"You're saying we can't maintain a six-hundred-ship navy," Lanham said, frowning.

"We don't have six hundred ships now, sir, and we're not likely to ever get them," Jake shot back, suddenly sure he didn't want Lanham to think he could be cowed.

"Lessen the primary threat and we won't need as many ships. That's the argument," said Ludlow.

"Politicians never understand commitments," Royce Caplinger said dryly, "perhaps because they make so many of them. The federal deficit is totally out of control due to mandated increases in social program expenditures. They borrowed money and never asked if they could afford the interest. They approved treaties and never weighed the cost in defense expenditures."

The CNO made a gesture of frustration. "We have more practical concerns. The air force is facing institutional death. They gave up the close air support mission to the army a generation ago. The strategic bomber mission is on the ropes. All they have left are ICBMs—which the army could run—and tactical air and airlift. Their bases are fixed, vulnerable to ICBMs and political upheavals. The world is passing them by. They're panicking. And they have a *lot* of friends. If they don't get Athena and get it now . . ."

"It'll get ugly," Ludlow agreed.

"*I* am the Secretary of Defense," Caplinger said, his voice hard. "*I* will take care of the air force. You people take care of the navy."

The heavy silence that followed was broken by Tyler Henry. "No one has mentioned the Minotaur." All eyes turned to the vice admiral. An uncomfortable look crossed his face, as if he had just farted in church.

"What about him?" Caplinger asked.

"He hasn't gotten Athena yet, but the minute we start bringing defense contractors into the loop, he will."

Caplinger leaned forward. "Where will we be if he gives Athena to the Russians?"

Henry had recovered his composure. "We'll have lost our advantage," he said with a trace of irritation in his voice. "They outgun us two to one. We need the technological edge to stay in the game."

Caplinger got to his feet and reached for the jacket draped over the back of his chair. "Thanks for lunch, George. Russell, you talk to these people and get this Athena business on track. I want it in production as soon as possible. We'll include it with the ATA in the budget. Black all the way." He paused and surveyed the faces at the table. "The navy can develop this. Keep it under wraps. Security as tight as a miser's money belt. Develop it for planes *and* ships. But the air force must be brought into this as soon as we have to start talking to Congress. This may kill the B-2, but it'll save the B-1."

"But what about the billions we're pouring into stealth planes now?" Russell Queen the bean counter asked his boss.

"Heck, Russell, this Athena gizmo may not work. Probably won't. Sorry, Tyler, but after all! A religious crackpot in a backyard workshop? It's too good to be true. Sounds like something Tom Clancy dreamed up after he had a bad pizza."

An hour later as Tyler Henry and Jake Grafton walked along the E-Ring back toward the admiral's office, Jake remarked, "At lunch, Admiral, you said we need a technological edge to stay in the game. What if the game has changed?"

"You mean Gorbachev reforming the Kremlin, converting the commies? Bull fucking shit."

"The Soviets packed up and pulled out of Afghanistan. They helped get the Cubans out of Angola. They're relaxing their hold on Eastern Europe. They're even talking to the Chinese. *Something's* going on."

"So the sons of Uncle Joe Stalin have given up their goal of world domination? The fucking thugs who murdered twenty million of their *own* people? My aching ass. That's all big-lie propaganda that liberal half-wits *want* to believe. Twenty *million* men, women and children! They make Adolf Hitler look like a weenie waver. We'd better have the edge when the shit splatters, because we'll never get a second chance."

"So you're maintaining an open mind on the question."

"You've been hanging around with that loose-screw Tarkington too long, Grafton. You're beginning to sound like him." Dunedin must have mentioned Tarkington to Henry, Jake surmised. He was sure Henry had never met the lieutenant.

"But what if Royce Caplinger and the politicos in Congress *think* the game has changed?"

"Caplinger isn't a fool." Two paces later Henry added, " 'Thinking politician' is an oxymoron."

After Jake parted from the admiral he walked to the cafeteria, where he bought a packet of Nabs and washed them down with a half-pint of milk. Humans are unique animals, he reflected. What other species has man's ability to see the world as he wants it to be, rather than as it actually is? He couldn't think of any. The worst of it is that this human trait deprives you of the ability to recognize reality when you see it. On this gloomy note his thoughts turned to Callie.

"What d'ya think's wrong with it?" Camacho asked nervously as he and Harlan Albright stood listening to Luis' car. It had a ragged, sick sound, most likely because Camacho had taken out one of the spark plugs and pounded the little arm against the core until there was no gap at all, then reinstalled it.

"Sounds to me like you got a cylinder missing, but I'm no mechanic," Albright said, and made notations on the service form. "We'll have a guy look at it this afternoon and give you a call. I can't give you an estimate or tell you how long it'll take to fix until we find out what's wrong."

"What neighborhood of finance are we talking here? Checking, savings, or second mortgage?"

Albright grinned and slid the form across the counter for Camacho to sign. "We'll call you."

"Well, poo. How about running me back downtown?"

The service manager glanced at the wall clock. "I get off for lunch in about thirty minutes. You wait and I'll take you. Go browse in the showroom or get some coffee."

Albright was driving a new car with dealer plates. Camacho settled into the passenger seat and fastened the seat belt as Albright pulled out into traffic. "Thought I oughta drop by and fill you in. Sally and I have to go to a church dinner tonight. The only thing wrong with my car is a bad spark plug. Don't let your mechanical wizards screw me."

"So what's happening?"

"We've got a letter from Terry Franklin's mother-in-law. She says he's a spy and wants us to bust him."

Albright glanced at the FBI agent. "You must get letters like that all the time."

"We do. And we check them out. Which is precisely what we're going to do with this one. Sometime toward the end of next week we'll have to interview Franklin. Thought you ought to know."

"I appreciate that. And the search for the Minotaur?"

"We need a letter from *his* mother-in-law."

"Maybe you already got it. Maybe Franklin is the Minotaur."

"Yeah. And I'm Donald Trump. I just live like this because I think money is vulgar. Jesus, you know damn well that little shit doesn't have the balls or the brains."

"I've been thinking about it." He coasted the car up to a stoplight and waited until it turned green. "It's possible he could be hacking the codes from the computer, mailing them to the embassy, then waiting for us to pay him to copy the files. Maybe he's slicker than anyone suspected. Maybe being a schlep is his idea of secondary cover."

"Seriously, I thought of that some time back. But I can't find a shred of evidence. And this stuff you're getting—I thought you said it was good."

"Excellent."

"So the Minotaur knows quality. It's not Franklin or any other computer clerk. It's somebody so high they know what you need."

Albright acknowledged this logic. In the world of espionage, need determines value. He spotted a Burger King and turned in. With the engine off, he leaned back in his seat and adjusted his testicles to a more comfortable position. "You're stringing me along, Luis."

Camacho already had his door open, but he pulled it closed. "Say that again."

"I think you're a lot closer to the Minotaur than you're telling me. You may even know who he is. That leads me to some interesting speculations."

Camacho had been expecting this, but now that it was here he still didn't know how to play it. "So I'm a double agent. Is that it?"

Harlan Albright raised an eyebrow, then looked away.

"Start the fucking car. Take me to the office. I don't have time to sit around and shoot the shit with you over a greaseburger."

Albright turned the key. The engine caught. Two blocks later he said, "You going to deny it?"

"Why bother? You have never given me a list of the stuff you got from the Minotaur. Now today you give me this crap about Franklin being the Minotaur and I'm supposed to go charging off like Inspector Clouseau. Why don't you go back to Moscow and tell Gorby you screwed the pooch? Mail me a postcard when you get to Siberia. I hear it's lovely in the snow."

"I don't know the file names. Even if I did, I don't have the authority to give them to you."

"Go tell it to somebody who gives a shit. I don't."

"What about Smoke Judy?"

"What about him?"

"What's he up to?"

"He's trying to peddle inside knowledge of defense contracts. So far without much success, as far as I can tell. Apparently he doesn't think money is vulgar."

"Are the fraud people onto him? IG or NIS?" IG was the Inspector General. NIS meant Naval Investigative Service.

"If somebody's opened a file on him, I don't know about it."

"Don't turn him over to them."

"Why not?"

"Because I'm asking you not to."

"Well, kiss my ass. You're taking a big chance, asking a double agent for a favor. Stop up here at the corner." They were going west on Constitution Avenue. "This is close enough. I need some air."

Albright pulled over to the curb and braked to a stop. "Don't turn him over."

"Up yours."

"I was just trying to motivate you. You know I don't doubt your loyalty."

"If I was a double agent we would have pulled in Terry Franklin a long time ago and squeezed him for the name of every file that you don't want me to know. He'd sing like a canary."

"I know," Albright replied as Camacho opened the car door and stepped out.

"You don't know shit. You don't know how many anonymous fraud, waste and abuse hot lines there are over at the Pentagon. The damn numbers are posted everywhere. Don't like your boss? Nail him to the cross on your coffee break. Busybodies and prissy fat ladies are burning up the wires. Somebody could drop a dime on Judy any minute. Then I'll be your fall guy, the double agent."

"Find the Minotaur."

"That mechanic screws me, I'll break your nose." Luis Camacho shut the door firmly and walked away.

As he trudged through the tourists and secretaries on lunch break he tried to decide if he had handled it well or poorly. The lies were plausible, he concluded, but he was suspect. Peter Aleksandrovich was nobody's fool. And "schlep"—what an interesting word for a commie to use. Underestimating this man could be fatal.

The new Amy Carol Grafton frowned at the peas on her plate. She glowered at the carrots. She carved herself a tiny chunk of meat loaf and put it in her mouth, where she held it without chewing as she stared at the offending vegetables.

"What's the matter, Amy?" Callie asked.

Amy Carol sat erect in her chair and tossed her black pageboy hair. "I don't like vegetables."

"They're good for you. You need to eat some of them." Amy's

brand-new mom was the soul of reason. Jake Grafton took another sip of coffee and the last bite of his meat loaf.

"I don't like green food."

"Then eat your carrots, dear." Callie smiled distractedly. If the child didn't eat her peas, what would be her vitamin count for vegetables today? Callie had spent the past week researching diets for diabetics. Right now she was swamped with strange facts.

"I don't like orange stuff either."

"Amy," said the new father with a glint in his eye, "I don't care what you like or don't like. Your mom put this stuff on the table, so you're going to eat it. Now start."

"She isn't my mom. And you're not my dad. My parents are dead. You're Callie and Jake. And I don't like you, Jake, not one little bit."

"Fine. But you're going to sit there until you finish those vegetables and I say you can get up."

"Why?" Her lower lip began to quiver and her brows knitted. Callie thought Amy looked so cute and helpless when she clouded up. Jake thought Callie had a lot to learn.

"Because I said so." Jake picked up the newspaper, opened it ostentatiously and hid behind it.

Callie got up and went to the sink, rinsing dishes. Jake reached around the paper every so often for a sip of coffee. Their second meal with their new daughter. Another disaster.

The youngster was trying to establish who's in charge, Jake told his wife. He thought Callie was making the same mistake Neville Chamberlain did. He used precisely those words to the new mother last night, after the first, opening-day debacle at the dinner table, when the youngster was finally in bed, and had been told in no uncertain terms that he was a lout.

Lout or not, "I am wearing the trousers," he said with his right trigger finger pointed straight up, "and we are going to establish very early that I have the last say on junior-senior relations around here. Somebody has to be in charge and it's not going to be an eleven-year-old."

"Just because you wear trousers, huh?"

"No. Because when I was growing up my father was the head of his family, and I intend to be the head of mine. It's a tried and true system with ancient tradition to commend it. We're going to stick with it."

"You can't issue orders around here, Captain Grafton. Amy and I don't wear uniforms." She raised a finger, mimicking his gesture.

This evening was also off to a rocky start.

Jake put down his newspaper and examined the vegetable situation. The child apparently hadn't touched a pea or a carrot. She was staring fixedly at her plate with a sullen, defiant look.

"How was school today?" Jake asked.

No answer.

"I asked you a question, Amy."

"Okay."

"Tell me about your teachers."

"What do you want to know?"

"Their names, what subjects they teach, what they look like, whether you like them. That kind of stuff."

"Wellll," Amy said, her gaze flicking across Jake's face, "some of them are nice and some aren't." And away she went on a five-minute exposition that covered the school day from opening to closing bell. Jake tossed in an occasional question when she paused for air.

When she had exhausted the teacher subject, Jake asked, "What subjects do you think you're going to like best?"

Away she went again, debating the merits of math versus English, social studies versus science. This time when she ran down, Jake asked if she had any homework.

"Some math problems."

"Need any help with them?"

"The division ones," she said tentatively.

"Eat some of those peas and carrots and we'll clear the table and work on the problems."

"How many do I have to eat?"

"Two spoonfuls of each."

She made a face and did as she was bid. As he carried the dishes to the sink, Jake asked, "Just what vegetables *do* you like?"

"Not any of them."

"Well, do you have some that you don't hate as much as others?"

"Corn. Corn is okay. But not the creamed kind." She squirmed. "And I like lima beans."

"No kidding? So do I. Maybe we can have some tomorrow night. How about it, Callie?"

His wife was standing by the little desk that served as a paper catchall, looking once again at the diet book. She turned to Jake and nodded. She had tears in her eyes. He winked at her.

"Amy, better get your school books. And, Callie, don't we have some sugarless dessert around here for little girls who eat their dinner?"

17

A woman from the garage called at 10 A.M. and said his car was ready: $119.26. Camacho told her he would stop by after work. She hung up before he could even ask what the problem had been.

Dreyfus gave him a ride and dropped him in front of the showroom.

The new cars gleamed shamelessly and flashed their chrome with wanton abandon as he walked by. Light, easy-listening music sounded everywhere. Two salesmen asked if he needed help.

He paid for the repairs at a window where a harried young woman juggled two phones as she pounded numbers into a computer. He surrendered his driver's license for her scrutiny before she asked. Without even glancing to see if his puss matched the photo, she copied the number onto the check and slid it back at him.

His six-year-old car sat amid twenty or so others of its vintage on a gravel lot out back. Dingy and coated with road grime, it hadn't seen wax since . . . not since he gave his son twenty dollars that Saturday two years ago and the kid let the wax dry like paint all over the car before he tried to wipe it off.

Camacho unlocked the door, rolled down the windows and tossed the yellow card dangling from the rearview-mirror bracket onto the floor. The car started readily enough and ran sweetly. He examined the invoice. Diagnostic test. Defective spark plug. Defective lead cable? Ouch—they got him there! Labor. How is it a garage can charge $55 per hour for a mechanic's time?

About two miles from the garage was a shopping center with a large parking lot, most of which was empty except for light poles and a couple of cars that looked as if they had sat in those spots all winter. One even had two flat tires.

He parked near it and got his jack from the trunk. The rear end went up first. He had an old army blanket in the trunk and spread it under the car so he wouldn't get too filthy.

With coat and tie on the back seat, flashlight in hand, Luis Camacho slid gingerly under the car. He knew exactly what he was looking for, but it might be hard to spot.

Five minutes later he stood beside the car and scratched his head. If Albright had put a bomb in this thing, where was it?

After a thorough scrutiny of the engine compartment and the trunk cavity, he attacked the door panels and rockers with a Phillips-head screwdriver. How many possible places were there? The backseats? Could he get them loose and look under them? The odds of a bomb being there were small, of course, but there was a chance. Just how big a chance, Camacho didn't know. Peter Aleksandrovich Chistyakov was not a man to take unnecessary risks. That double-agent discussion yesterday had frightened Camacho, coming as it did from a man who owned an assassin's pistol and had enough gadgets in his attic to blow up half the cops in Washington.

To assess just how likely it was that good ol' Harlan Albright had decided to eliminate a possible threat, one would need to know just what it was that was being threatened. How many other agents was he running? What kind of information were they getting?

Of course, Albright could slip a bomb under the car any night while Camacho snored in his own bed. Risky, but feasible. But perhaps he had planted a bomb with a radio-actuated device as insurance, hoping he wouldn't have to use it, but with it already in place should the need arise. A careful man might do something like that, right?

Apparently Albright was a careful man. The bomb was in the driver's door, behind the panel, below the window glass when it was rolled completely down. It had been carefully taped in place so it wouldn't rattle.

At a glance it appeared to contain a couple pounds of plastique. One fuse stuck out of the oblong mass. A wire ran from the fuse to a servo and from the servo to a six-volt battery. A little receiver was wired to the servo and four AA batteries were hooked up to power it. A tiny wire attached to the receiver was routed all along the inside of the door. It was a simple, radio-actuated bomb. Simple and effective.

Luis Camacho pulled the fuse from the bomb and used a penknife to cut the wire. The plastique and the rest of it he left in place.

Sweating in spite of the fifty-five-degree weather and fifteen-mile-per-hour wind, he replaced the jack in the trunk. The door panel he put in the backseat.

Had he figured it right? Was this merely insurance? Or had Albright-Chistyakov already decided to push the button?

Standing there beside the car, he looked around slowly, checking. A lot of good that will do you, Luis. Cursing under his breath, he got behind the wheel and started the car.

There was a little hardware store in the shopping center, right between a gourmet food store and a factory fabric outlet. Inside Camacho bought a small flashlight, a coil of insulated wire, and some black electrician's tape.

Out in the parking lot he used the knife and screwdriver to disassemble the flashlight. The bulb he mounted with tape on a hole he carved in the door panel. Fifteen minutes later he had the last screw back in place and the crank for the window reinstalled.

There! Now if Albright pushes the button, instead of a big bang, this flashlight bulb will illuminate and burn continuously until that six-volt ni-cad battery in the door is completely discharged. Assuming he sees the illuminated bulb—and the unsoldered wire connections don't vibrate loose—our saintly hero Luis Camacho, FBI ace spy catcher, will then have time to bend over and kiss his ass goodbye before the bullets from the silenced Ruger .22 send him to a kinder, more gentle world.

What more could any man ask?

He sat behind the wheel staring at the storefronts. After a moment he got out of the car and walked back across the parking lot to the gourmet store, the Bon Vivant. The place smelled of herb and flower leaf sachets. The clerk, a woman in her forties with long, ironed hair, was too engrossed in a book to even nod at him. He wandered through the aisles, looking at cans and jars of stuff imported from all over the world. Nothing from Iowa here. If it's green or purple and packed in a jar from Europe or the Orient, with an outrageous price, you know it's got to be good.

He selected a jar of blue French jam, "Bilberry" the label said, paid $4.32 plus tax to the refugee from Berkeley, and walked back across the empty, gray parking lot to his car.

The flight surgeon at the China Lake dispensary pronounced Rita fit to fly on Friday afternoon. Jake Grafton spent Saturday in the hangar with Samuel Dodgers and Helmut Fritsche going over the computer program and modifications to Athena that were needed.

As he worked Jake became even more impressed with Dodgers' technological achievement and even more disenchanted with Dodgers the human being. Like every fanatic, Dodgers thought in absolutes which left no room for tolerance or dissent. On technical matters his mind was open, inquiring, incisive, leaping to new insights regardless of where the leap took him or the hoary precedents shattered by the jump. On everything else, however, every aspect of the human condition, Dodgers was bigoted, voluble, and usually wrong. It was as if his maker had increased his scientific talents at the expense of all the others, thus creating a mean little genius who viewed the world as a collection of wicked conspiracies hatched by evil, godless agents of the devil. His opinion of most of his less gifted fellow men was equally bleak. And he *did* believe in the devil. He waxed long and loud on Satan and his works whenever he had a half minute that was not devoted to the task at hand.

How Fritsche tolerated these diatribes Jake couldn't fathom. He found himself increasingly irritated, and retreated to the head or the outside of the building when he had had all he could stomach.

"How can you listen to that asshole without choking him?" Jake asked during a brief interlude when nature called Dodgers to the head.

"Whatszat?" Fritsche asked, raising his eyebrows curiously.

"These endless scatterbrained rantings," Jake explained patiently. "In the last hour he's slandered every racial and ethnic group on the planet and denounced everyone in government as thieves and liars and worse. How can you listen to this?"

"Oh. That. I never listen. I'm too busy thinking about Athena. I shut out all that other stuff."

"Wish I could."

"Hmmm," said Fritsche, obviously not paying much attention to Jake either.

"If he doesn't cool it some, I'll probably strangle him by dinner-time. Better learn all you can this afternoon."

"Uh-huh," said Fritsche, who was bending and reexamining the cooling unit that kept the computer temperature down. It was certainly a marvel of miniaturization and engineering. "How this man made this in a backyard workshop just boggles the mind. Look here, the craftsmanship of these welds, the way he polished this forging with acid to minimize heat loss. Look here! See how he built this to maximize cooling and shorten the wire runs. And he didn't even use a computer to design this!"

"Instinct. The troll's a genius," Jake Grafton admitted reluctantly.

The other shoe fell on Sunday morning, when Jake received a telephone call from Washington. George Ludlow was on the other end of the wire. "Royce Caplinger's flying out to see you this afternoon. He's bringing Senator Hiram Duquesne with him. Each of them will have an aide along. Get them rooms in the BOQ."

"Jesus, Mr. Secretary. This project's got a security lid tight as a virgin's twat. We don't need any godda—any senator—"

"Duquesne *had* to be told, *Captain*. He's the *chairman* of the Senate Armed Services Committee. I'm not asking your opinion. I'm *informing* you. Got it?"

"Yessir. I got it. Have you also informed Admiral Dunedin?"

"Yes." The connection broke. Jake cradled the phone. He soon learned there were but two empty rooms in the BOQ, so he sent the two junior members of his party to a motel off base. Those two were Toad and Rita, neither of whom looked very distressed when they tossed their bags into the back of a navy station wagon and drove away.

He wore his only clean white uniform and was standing in the sun in front of the terminal when the T-39 taxied up and Royce Caplinger stepped out. The CO of the base was standing beside Jake. Both officers saluted smartly. They also snapped a salute to Senator Duquesne, who was dressed in slacks and pullover shirt and looked like he had had a couple snorts on the trip. As Duquesne blinked mightily at the bright light, a woman descended the little stair from the plane.

Jake recognized her even as Caplinger said her name. "Ms. DeCrescentis. She's a guest of Senator Duquesne."

"Consolidated Technologies. She's a vice president, isn't she?"

"Yep," said Duquesne. "Good to see you again, Captain," he said in a tone that implied just the opposite.

"Hitchhiking today, Ms. DeCrescentis?"

"She's here to take the tour with us," Caplinger said.

"Could I talk to you privately for a moment," Jake said, not a question, and walked away from the group.

Twenty paces or so away Jake turned around. Caplinger was right behind. Jake let him have it: "Ludlow said you were coming for a briefing with a senator, even though this project is classified to the hilt. But I'm not about to let a vice president of a defense contractor that is going to be bidding on the ATA have a look at Athena or be a party to any conversation on the subject. She has no bona fide need to know at this stage of the game. She doesn't have access. Not only no, but hell no. Sir."

"My responsibility," Caplinger said, then clamped his lips into a thin line.

"No, sir. Ludlow didn't mention any defense contractors, and even if he had, I'd have to clear this with Admiral Dunedin. I take orders from him. He'd probably have to talk to CNO. Her presence would violate a couple dozen reg—"

"Call him."

"Now?"

"Yes, goddamnit, right fucking now. We'll wait in the lounge." Caplinger stalked for the blue carpet that led inside, followed by Jake Grafton. The base CO led the others inside.

Jake used the phone in the operations officer's office on the second deck.

He reached Dunedin at his office in Crystal City on the first try and outlined the situation. "Fuck!" said the admiral.

"Yessir."

"I'll call Ludlow. If that goes sour I'll call CNO."

"Okay." Jake gave him the phone number where he could be reached.

"You're really sticking your neck out, Jake."

"So fire me."

"I'll call you back."

Thirty minutes went by. Jake stared out the window at the little passenger jet and watched the men with the gas truck refuel it as heat waves rose off the tarmac. Blue mountains lay on the horizon. Not a single airplane stirring this Sunday morning. After a while he examined the photos and mementos the ops boss had arranged on his walls. He recognized some of the names and faces in the group pictures.

He was sitting behind the desk with his feet propped on it and doodling on a scratch pad when the phone rang. "Captain Grafton."

"George Ludlow. Admiral Dunedin tells me there's a problem."

"Yessir. Caplinger and Duquesne arrived here a while ago with a vice president of Consolidated Technologies tagging along. They want her to see Athena. It's classified special access, above top secret, and she's getting an unfair advantage over the other contractors. I said no."

"What did Caplinger say?"

"He wasn't happy."

"Do you understand that Hiram Duquesne is chairman of the Senate Armed Services Committee? We have to have his support if we're going to get a replacement aircraft for the A-6. Without it we're pissing up a rope."

"I understand that. And I understand that you chose me for this job because I can wear a Medal of Honor on my shirt and because I'm expendable. You're going to have me make a recommendation on which plane to buy based on a short operational evaluation fly-off, and if you like it, I'll have to go over to Congress and defend it. You can disavow me anytime. I understand all of that. I took the job anyway. Now I'm telling you, I can't go over to the Hill and make a recommendation if five or six senators and congressmen are out to cut my balls off with a scalping knife because I let Consolidated in on the ground floor in violation of the law and DOD regulations. I won't be able to hide behind Royce Caplinger over there. That little shit is too goddamn small to hide behind."

Ludlow chuckled, a dry sound that lasted three or four seconds. "Go get Caplinger. I'll talk to him."

Jake left the phone lying on the desk and went downstairs to the VIP lounge. "Mr. Secretary, you have a phone call upstairs."

Duquesne's face was still red and mottled. DeCrescentis looked like she could chew up all of them and spit hamburger. The base CO was nowhere in sight. He had probably attacked in another direction, maybe toward the golf course.

Jake followed the Defense Secretary back up the stairs.

As soon as Caplinger recognized his son-in-law's voice, he shooed Jake from the office. Jake could hear his voice booming through the door. It wasn't just the Advanced Tactical Aircraft he was concerned about—it was the entire defense budget. As he roared at Ludlow: ". . . you and I both know that Grafton will probably recommend the TRX plane. With Athena, it's the obvious choice. But that leaves Duquesne in political trouble at home and we *need* his support. Jesus fucking Christ, George, you people have an aircraft carrier up for funding, three Aegis cruisers, two boomer boats, the air force wants more F-117s and some B-2s, the army wants more tanks. SDI is desperate for money. And Congress is trying to cut the deficit! Don't tell *me* to tell Duquesne to *fuck off*!"

He was silent for a moment, and when he spoke again his voice was low and Grafton couldn't hear the words. He knew Ludlow well enough to know how it was going, however. Let Grafton take the heat, the Secretary of the Navy was probably saying. Make Grafton the villain.

And that was how it went. When Caplinger came out of the office he buttonholed Jake. "You're going downstairs and explain to the senator that *you* personally must put DeCrescentis back on that plane. You will brief me and the senator this afternoon on Athena and we'll see it in operation tomorrow. But *you* are going to insist that woman goes home *now,* and *you* are going to make Duquesne like it. Got it?"

"Aye aye, sir."

The senator didn't like it, of course, and DeCrescentis liked it even less, but when Grafton made it clear that the law was going to be obeyed regardless and he was the man insisting, both of them gave ground with what grace they could muster. Duquesne had more of it than the corporate vice president did, perhaps because he knew that even Caesar had to retreat occasionally.

After an hour with Samuel Dodgers in the hangar, it appeared Hiram Duquesne wished he had joined DeCrescentis on the plane.

Dodgers gave Athena no more than half his air and used the rest to blast away at Congress, corporations and the communist-Jew-nigger conspiracy. Finally Jake told him to shut up. It didn't take. Jake told him again in terms and tones that would have stopped a rock band in full screech. Dodgers stormed off, leaving Caplinger and Duquesne gaping foolishly at each other.

Jake Grafton took a deep breath, made his excuses to the two politicians, and left them in the care of a stunned Helmut Fritsche.

In the parking lot, he caught up with Dodgers, trembling with outrage. "You owe me an apology," the scientist spluttered, holding himself rigid, his fists clenched.

"No, sir," Grafton said in a normal voice. "You owe me one. And you owe apologies to all three of those men in there."

Dodgers was speechless.

"You have inflicted yourself on everyone within earshot since the day I met you. Now there's not going to be any more of that while I'm around. Do you understand?"

"How *dare* you talk to *me* like this!" When Dodgers got it out, it came out loud.

Jake lowered his voice still more. "I'm the officer responsible. That's *it* as far as you're concerned. You do your work and keep your personal opinions to yourself, and you and I will get along."

The scientist spluttered. "I don't want to get along with you, *you* . . ." He couldn't find the word.

"You'd better reconcile yourself to it if you want this project to go anywhere."

". . . sinner. Agent of Satan."

"You want money for your church, right? *I'm the man.*" With that Jake turned his back on Samuel Dodgers.

The little neighborhood bar was fairly well lit and not very fancy, with cheap furniture and oilcloth table covers. A television high in one corner was tuned to a ball game, one of the NCAA tournament semifinals. Smoke Judy slid into an empty booth and ordered a draft. The waitress flirted for a moment when she brought it, then skipped away.

Smoke sipped his beer and watched the body posture of the men leaning against the bar and sitting on the stools. Some were absorbed in the game, some were talking to a buddy. Most of them were doing a little of both.

This was Smoke Judy's favorite weekend beer spot, only a mile from his place. He knew the bartender casually and they often exchanged pleasantries on slow days. There were a lot worse ways to make a living, Smoke decided, than running a neighborhood bar where the guys could stop in after work or take a break from lawn mowing and garage cleaning. The crowd was nice and the work pleasant, although the money wouldn't be great.

Maybe he would get a place like this when he retired next year. He had dropped a hint to the bartender—who also owned the place

—a few weeks back, trying to find out if he had ever thought of selling, but the man didn't get his drift, or pretended he didn't.

He was going to retire next year, with twenty-two years in. By law, as a commander he could stay in the navy until he had completed twenty-six years of service, but he wasn't going to endure the hassle of staff job after staff job with no chance of promotion.

The end of the line had been a tour in command of a training squadron in Texas. Four of those damn kids had crashed, three fatally. Hard to believe. He had worked hard and flown hard and done it by the book, and still those goddamned kids just kept smashing themselves into the ground like suicidal rats. The accident investigators had never said or even implied he was at fault. Yet every crash had felt like God whacking him on the head, compressing another two vertebrae. He had gotten punchy toward the end, a screamer in the cockpit, afraid to certify any student safe for anything. He left that for the lieutenants.

The admiral had been sympathetic, of course, but he had no choice. He said. He had to rate Judy the lowest of all his squadron commanders. After all, four accidents? Nine million dollars' worth of airplanes and three lives? That had been God's final whack. Judy would never be promoted or given another command. All that remained was a decision on when to retire.

He had seen it coming, like something from a Greek tragedy, after that second kid augered in on a night instrument solo. A fucking Canoe U. grad no less! Then the third one, that kid punched out of a perfectly good airplane on a solo acro hop after he flew into the only cloud for fifty miles in any direction for ten whole seconds and got the plane into a high-speed spiral and panicked. But he stood there in the CO's office afterwards and said he was sorry! The fourth one, that shithead—Judy had personally given him a down once already—one clear, cloudless day that spastic bastard failed to get the nose up to the horizon on a pullout from a simulated strafing run and pancaked in, smearing himself and his airplane across a half mile of cow pasture. The commanding officer is always responsible. And so it had been, like a judgment from the Doomsday book.

Next year. With twenty-two in. That would give him 55 percent of his base pay, and if one or two of these little deals he was working with hungry contractors came through, he would do all right. Not rich, but okay.

He paid for the beer and left two quarters for a tip. His car was parked just fifty feet down the street, but as he walked toward it, the car in front backed right into it!

"Awww . . ."

The driver got out and walked back to examine the damage.

"Awww, shit!" Smoke Judy exclaimed when he saw the broken grille, the smashed headlight and the bowed-out fender. "Get your goddamn driver's license yesterday?"

"Jesus, mister, I am sorry! My foot just slipped off the brake. Don't know how it happened."

"Awww, damn. The second time this year somebody has smacked it when it was parked. Look at this fender, willya? Those Japs must make these things out of recycled beer cans. Look how this thing's sprung! And this headlight socket!"

The other driver turned from examining his own bent fender and smashed taillight and surveyed Judy's damage. He was chunky, fifty or so, flecks of gray in his hair. "Don't worry. I got insurance. They'll fix it good as new. But honest, I am really sorry."

"I suppose." Smoke Judy shook his head.

"Maybe we'd better exchange information."

"Yeah." Judy unlocked his car and fished the registration and insurance certificate from the glove box while the other driver rooted in his.

"Maybe we should go inside and do this," the chunky man suggested. "Can I buy you a beer?"

"Why not." Smoke turned and led the way back into the bar he had just come out of. "My name's Judy. Smoke Judy."

"Sorry we had to meet like this. I'm Harlan Albright."

Dodgers kept his opinions to himself at dinner Sunday evening, partially because he was too busy with his food to waste effort on small talk, and partially because he could not have gotten a word in edgewise against Caplinger's verbal flow. There were just the four of them around a table in an empty dining room—empty because the officers' club was usually closed on Sunday evening and Secretary Caplinger declined to go off-base to eat—Dodgers, Caplinger, Senator Duquesne, and Jake Grafton. Caplinger discussed the budget deficit, Third World debt, global pollution, and the illegal drug industry with a depth of knowledge and insight that amazed Jake and even quieted the senator, who was the only person at the table who tried to participate in the conversation. It was obvious that Royce Caplinger not only had read widely but had thought deeply about all these issues. Less obvious but equally impressive was the way he wove the strands of these mega-issues into one whole cloth.

After the steward placed a coffeepot in the center of the table and departed, closing the door behind him, Caplinger eyed Jake speculatively. "Well, Captain, it seems to me that now would be a good time to sound you out."

"I'm just an O-6, Mr. Secretary. All I see are the elephant's feet."

Caplinger poured himself a cup of coffee and used a spoon to stir in cream. He surveyed Samuel Dodgers as if seeing him this evening for the first time. "Good of you to share your Sabbath with us, Doctor. We're looking forward to seeing your handiwork tomorrow."

Dodgers wiped his mouth and tossed his napkin beside his plate. "Tomorrow." He nodded at everyone except Grafton and departed.

When the door had firmly closed behind the inventor, Caplinger remarked, "Senator, what will happen on the Hill if it becomes common gossip that the father of Athena is a fascist churl?"

"You'll be in trouble. That man couldn't sell water in Death Valley on the Fourth of July."

"My thought exactly. We'll have to make sure he stays out of sight and sound. Little difficult to do in America, but not impossible." He grinned. When he did his face twisted. It didn't look like he made the effort very often. "So how do the elephant's feet look, Captain?"

Jake Grafton reached for the coffeepot. "I confess, sir, that I'm baffled. Seems to me that these new weapons systems under development, with the sole exception of Athena, are going to be too expensive for the nation ever to afford enough of them to do any good."

All traces of the smile disappeared from Caplinger's face. "Go on."

"As the cost goes up, the quantity goes down. And every technical breakthrough seems to double or triple the cost. If anything, Athena will be the exception that proves the rule. Athena should be a fairly cheap system, all things considered, but it'll be the only one."

"And . . ." prompted the Secretary of Defense.

"Well, if our goal is to maintain forces which deny the Soviets any confidence in a favorable outcome in any probable nuclear war scenario, we seem to have reached the treadmill. We can't maintain forces if we can't afford them."

"You made a rather large assumption."

"So what is our goal?"

"The general public regards nuclear war as unwinnable. That's the universal popular wisdom, and like anything that almost everyone believes, it's wrong. The Soviets have invested heavily in hardened bunkers for the top leadership. They've built underground cities for the communist elite. *Somebody* over there thinks they can win! Now their idea of victory and ours are two very different things, but as long as they think they can win, the likelihood of a nuclear war increases. Nuclear war becomes *more likely* to happen."

Caplinger glanced at the senator, then turned his attention back to Jake. He seemed to be weighing his words. "Our goal," he finally said, "is to prevent nuclear war. To do that we must make them *think* they can't win."

"So you are saying that any method of denying the Russians confidence in a favorable outcome—however they define favorable —is acceptable?"

Caplinger tugged at his lower lip. His eyes were unfocused. Jake thought he seemed to be turning it over in his mind yet again, examining it for flaws, looking . . . Slowly the chin dipped, then rose again. "We need . . ." His gaze rose to the ceiling and went slowly around it. "We need . . . we need forces that can survive the initial strike and respond in a flexible manner, forces that are controllable, programmable, selective. It can't be all or nothing, Captain. It can't be just one exchange of broadsides. If all we have is that one broadside, we just *lost.*"

"Explain," prompted Senator Duquesne.

"We'll never shoot our broadside. That's the dirty little secret that they know and we know and we will *never* admit. No man elected President of the United States in the nuclear age would order every ICBM fired, every Trident missile launched, every nuclear weapon in our arsenal detonated on the Soviets. Not even if the Soviets make a massive first strike at us. To massively retaliate would mean the end of life on the planet Earth. No rational man would do it." Caplinger shrugged. "That's the flaw in Mutual Assured Destruction. No sane man would ever push the button."

Royce Caplinger sipped his coffee, now cold, and made a face.

"We must deny the communists the ability to *ever* come out of those bunkers. We need the ability to hit pinpoint, mobile targets on a selective, as-needed basis. That's the mission of the F-117 and the B-2. If we can achieve that, there will never be a first strike. There will never be a nuclear war."

Caplinger pushed his chair back away from the table. "Life will continue on this planet until pollution ruins the atmosphere and sewage makes the seas a barren, watery desert. Then life on this fragile little pebble orbiting this modest star will come to the end that the Creator must have intended when he made man. Watching our Japanese televisions, listening to our compact laser disks, wearing our designer clothes, we'll all starve."

He rose abruptly and made for the door. Jake Grafton also got to his feet. When the door closed behind Caplinger, Jake shook the senator's hand and wished him good night.

"He's a great man," the senator said, trying to read Jake's thoughts.

"Yes."

"But he is not sanguine. The political give-and-take—it depresses him."

"Yes," Jake Grafton said, and nodded his farewell. Suddenly he too needed to be alone.

On Monday morning Jake put Secretary Caplinger, Senator Duquesne, and their aides on a plane to Fallon with Helmut Fritsche and Harold Dodgers. He had decided to stay at China Lake and supervise the good doctor.

Sam Dodgers was in a foul mood, muttering darkly about money and conspiracies. Jake managed to keep his mouth shut. When the Athena device was ready and installed in the A-6, he helped strap Rita Moravia and Toad Tarkington into the cockpit. Toad was whistling some tune Jake didn't recognize.

"No birds today. Okay?"

"Whatever you say, boss." Toad was in high spirits. Higher than usual. He must be screwing Moravia, Jake decided, trying to catch some hint between them. The pilot was all business.

"Work the long distances today. Start at thirty miles and let Fritsche call you closer when he has the info he wants. Just keep the radar he's using on your left side."

"Sure, CAG. We understand." He resumed his whistling as Jake helped him latch his Koch fittings.

"You know who whistles in the navy, Toad?"

"No, sir."

"Bosun's mates and damn fools."

Toad grinned. "I'm in that second category, sir. Enjoy your day with Dr. Dodgers."

Jake punched him on the shoulder and climbed down the boarding ladder.

As the Intruder taxied out, Jake climbed into the yellow ramp truck that the base ops people had loaned him. He had no desire to return to the hangar and watch Dodgers tinker with a computer.

He drove down a taxiway and parked near the duty runway. He got out and sat on the hood. Already the morning was warm, growing hotter by the minute as the sun climbed higher and higher into the deep blue sky. Singing birds were audible here, away from the hustle and bustle of the ramp. A large jackrabbit watched him from the safety of a clump of brush.

He could hear the faint murmur of engines in the distance, and assumed that was Rita and Toad. The minutes passed as he sat there in the sun with the breeze in his hair. He had joined the navy those many years ago to fly, and now he was reduced to sitting beside a runway waiting for younger people to take off. Yet this was the world he knew. The world Royce Caplinger had spoken of last night—nuclear deterrence, global strategy—that was an alien environment, as foreign to him as the concerns of headhunters in the jungles of the Amazon.

He saw the tiny tail of the warplane moving above the swell in the runway. It turned and became a knife edge. Still at least a mile away, the visible tail came to a stop and remained motionless for several minutes.

Caplinger's pessimism troubled him. Sure, the world had its problems, but every generation had faced problems: problems were the stuff life was made of. A man as brilliant as Caplinger, he shouldn't be so . . . so *bitter*.

He heard the engines snarl, yet the tiny white speck of tail did not move. No doubt Rita was standing on the brakes, letting the engines wind up to full power and the temps stabilize before she let it roll. Now . . . now the tail began to move, slowly at first, then faster and faster.

The Intruder came over the swell in the runway accelerating quickly. A river of hot, shimmering air poured down and away behind the bird.

He pressed his fingers in his ears as the sound swelled in volume and intensity. The nose wheel rose a foot or so above the concrete. With a delicate wiggle the bird of prey lifted itself free of the earth and continued toward him in a gentle climb as the wheels retracted into the body of the beast. The howl of the engines grew until it was intolerable.

Now the machine was passing just overhead, roaring a thunderous song that enveloped him with an intensity beyond imagination. He glimpsed the helmeted figure of Rita Moravia in the cockpit with her left hand on the throttles, looking forward, toward the open sky.

He buried his face in his shoulder as the plane swept past and waves of hot jet exhaust and disturbed air cascaded over him.

When the gale subsided the noise was fading too, so he looked again for the Intruder. It was climbing steeply into the blue ocean above, its engine noise now a deep, resonant, subsiding roar.

He got down from the truck hood and seated himself behind the wheel. The birds in the scrub were still singing and the jackrabbit was still watching suspiciously.

Grinning to himself, Jake Grafton started the engine of the pickup and drove away.

18

The day Terry Franklin died was a beautiful day, "the finest day this year" according to a TV weatherman on one of Washington's local breakfast shows. The sun crept over the edge of the earth into a cloudless sky as a warm, gentle zephyr from the west stirred the new foliage. The weather reader promised a high temperature of seventy-four. Humidity was low. This was the day everyone had dreamed of while they endured the cold, humid winter and the wet, miserable spring. Now, at last, it was here. And on this day sent from heaven Terry Franklin died.

He certainly didn't expect to die today, of course, or any other day in the foreseeable future. For him this was just another day to be endured, another day to live through on his way to the life of gleeful indolence he was earning with his treason.

He awoke when his alarm went off. If he heard the birds singing outside his window he showed no sign. He used his electric razor on his face and gave his teeth a very quick pass with the cordless toothbrush he received for Christmas from his kids, whom he hadn't seen or heard from for three weeks and, truthfully, hoped he wouldn't hear from. If he heard from the kids he would also hear from Lucy, and she would want money. He assumed that she was back in California with her mother, the wicked witch of the west. If so, Lucy didn't need any money: her father the tooth mechanic could pay the grocery bill and buy the kids new shoes.

He put on his uniform while the coffee brewed. The coffee he drank black, just the way he had learned to like it on his first cruise, which he had made to the Med aboard a guided-missile frigate.

He paused automatically on the front stoop and looked around for the morning newspaper, then remembered that there wouldn't be one and pulled the door closed and tried it to ensure it was locked. He had canceled the paper a week after Lucy left. He never read it and Lucy only scanned the front page and read the funnies. She always wanted it for the crossword puzzle, which she worked every morning while watching Oprah. Twenty-five cents a day for a fucking crossword puzzle. He had relished that call to the circulation office.

The Datsun started on the first crank. He backed out of the drive and rolled down his window as he drove toward the stop sign at the corner. He fastened his seat belt, punched up the Top 40 station on the stereo and rolled. He only had three miles to go to the Park'N'Ride, but still he enjoyed the private little world of his car. These few minutes in the car, with the music he liked adjusted to the volume he liked, he cherished as the best part of the day.

He hadn't heard from the Russians since his talk with that Yuri fellow, and he had mixed emotions about that. In a way it was quite pleasant not sweating drop trips or clandestine computer time or the slim chance of being searched leaving the Pentagon. Yet every day that went by without a call was another day he had to waste on his dreary, humdrum job, on this humdrum bus ride, on this humdrum colorless suburb. Every day he spent here was a day he wasn't *there*, lying in the sun, fucking the beach bunnies, drinking Cuba Libres and enjoying life.

His fantasy was *there*, waiting, and he was firmly and hopelessly planted *here*. What made the waiting so frustrating was the money he already had in the bank. That he had committed a variety of serious crimes to obtain the money troubled him not a whit. He had never given it a moment's thought. In fact, he felt exactly like all the other people who see a large sum of unearned money come their way—lottery winners, traffic accident victims, legatees, swindlers, personal injury lawyers and so on—the money was his by divine right. Somehow, some way, the rulers of the universe had decreed that he deserved the good things and good times that big money will buy because he wasn't like all those schmucks who flog it eight to five. He was different. Special. The money *made* him special. The unique and wonderful emissions given off by large quantities of money made him tingle.

Perhaps because he felt so good about himself, Terry Franklin took the time this morning, the last morning of his life, to smile at the bus driver as he boarded and to nod at a woman he recognized as he went down the aisle.

As the bus threaded its way through rush hour traffic, he watched the scenery roll by without seeing a thing. He rode lost in reverie, already enjoying his fantasy.

The morning was spent cleaning and repairing a computer keyboard on which a secretary had spilled coffee. She also had a taste for doughnuts and potato chips, he noted with a sneer as he worked with a toothbrush to rid the mechanism of soggy crumbs. He could just picture her: still young but already overweight, always dieting or talking to her fellow airheads about dieting as she munches yet another doughnut and swills yet another cup of coffee loaded with sugar. She must have had at least three lumps in this stuff she spilled. Lucy's clone.

He almost decided to tell the chief to trash this keyboard, then changed his mind. The chief had cut him a lot of slack these past three weeks: he should try to prove to the chief that he could still carry his share of the load. He put more WD-40 on the keyboard and reattacked the sticky mess with the toothbrush.

Terry Franklin's last meal was a hot dog with mustard, catsup and relish, a small order of fries and a medium Sprite. He ate it with another sailor from his section in the main cafeteria. They discussed the new secretary in the division office—was she really a blonde, would she or wouldn't she, was it worth trying to find out, and so on.

The afternoon went quickly. The chief sent him with one other man to work on a balky tape drive in the enlisted manpower section, and the afternoon flew by. They had found the problem but had not yet repaired it when quitting time rolled around.

So he carried his tools back to the shop and exchanged guffaws with his shipmates, then walked to the bus stop outside and found a place in the usual line.

Had he known what was coming, one wonders what he would have done differently. No doubt a larger man who knew the end was nigh might have lived his last day pretty much as he had all his others, but Terry Franklin was not a big man in any sense of the word, and he had come to realize that in the last three weeks, since the fiasco of the bungled drop. He knew he was a coward, a weakling without backbone or character, but, he thought, only he knew, and so what? Superman lives in Metropolis and Batman lives in Gotham. The rest of us just try to get along.

Yet, given who he was and what he was, should he have known he might be approaching the end of his string? The signs were certainly there if he had thought it through dispassionately, with some detachment. He didn't, of course.

He used most of his last hour on earth to stare out the bus window and think about the feel of the sun on his back and sand between his bare toes, and to daydream of a hard young female body under him mingling her sweat with his. She didn't have a face, this girl in his dreams, but she had firm brown tits and a flat stomach and long brown legs with taut thighs.

When he turned the key in the car ignition the radio boomed to life as the engine caught. ". . . like a bat outta *hell,* ba-dupe, ba-dupey . . ."

He rolled the window down and fastened his seat belt and patted the steering wheel with his hands in time to the music.

The car in front of him turned right after four blocks, and the one behind turned left a block later. Terry Franklin paid no attention. He drove out onto an old boulevard now lined with small strip businesses and proceeded about a mile before he swung the car onto a side street. He liked to drive through these quiet residential streets because they had so little traffic and he thought he made better time, though he had never clocked it.

At the first stop sign he came to, a little girl was crossing the street pushing a miniature baby carriage containing her doll. That she had chosen to cross the street at just this time and place probably gave Terry Franklin another minute of life.

One minute was just about the time it took for him to wait until the little girl was clear, depress the accelerator and cruise down to the next cross street. He glanced both ways, no traffic, and took his foot off the brake to roll on through. ". . . like a bat outta *hell* . . ."

That's when the bomb underneath the vehicle, directly under the driver's seat, exploded.

Terry Franklin felt a concussive impact as his knees came up to smash into his chin, but that was the only sensation that he was conscious of in the thousandth of a second he had left to live. The floor of the car came apart and the seat springs and fabric and padding were all forced explosively upward. His skull popped like a ripe melon when this rising, accelerating column on which he sat smashed into the roof of the car and bowed it upward. The windows exploded outward as the fireball continued to expand, showering the area with glass. Fragments of springs and plastic and fabric were forced deep into Terry Franklin's now lifeless corpse, which began to sear from the intense heat.

The car, still in gear and torn almost in two, moved like a wounded crab diagonally across the intersection and lightly impacted a parked vehicle. Then the engine quit from fuel starvation. The severed fuel line dumped its liquid into the molten mess in the center of the vehicle and the smoldering wreckage became an inferno. In ten seconds the fire was so hot the fuel tank exploded.

Coming around the corner four blocks away, FBI agent Clarence Brown saw the rising fireball from the exploding gas tank. He grabbed the dash-mounted mike. "Holy shit, his car blew up. It blew up! The subject's car blew up!"

The voice on the telephone had a hollow, metallic sound, like it was coming through a long pipe. "Little development I thought you would want to know about, Luis. Probably nothing important. Terry Franklin just went out with a bang. His car blew up."

"Anybody else hurt, Dreyfus?"

"Not another soul. We had an agent following him, keeping tabs per your instructions, and he saw the gas tank go poof. The lab guys are on the way. The agent at the scene, Brown, says it looks like a bomb."

"What time, exactly?"

"Sixteen fifty-seven."

Camacho looked at his watch. Seventeen minutes ago. "Get a search warrant for his house."

"Already doing the affidavit."

"Send a man over to the house to watch it. And you'd better alert somebody out in California that they'll have to do a next-of-kin notification when we get a positive ID from the medical examiner."

"The ID's gonna take a while. The corpse is still in the car, roasted like a Christmas turkey."

"Have the people in California quietly check to see that his wife and in-laws are physically there."

"You *knew* this was going to happen, didn't you?"

"I just follow orders, asshole," Camacho snarled. "Why don't you do the same?" He slammed the phone onto its cradle.

Two minutes later it rang again. "Yes."

"Dreyfus again. Already we're getting calls from TV stations. There's a chopper overhead now. It's real visual with the smoke column and all. Evening news for sure, distraught housewives and sobbing kids, the whole bit. What's the official hot screaming poop?"

"We're investigating, cooperating with the local police. Off the record, hint at drugs."

"Roger hint."

"Is local law on the scene?"

"Yeah. Couple cruisers and a big red fire truck."

"Don't let 'em touch anything."

"Roger Wilco, over and out."

Luis Camacho pulled into his driveway at five minutes after midnight and checked the jury-rigged bulb in the hole in the door panel. Still off. Amen.

The night air retained some of the heat from the day. The FBI agent stood in his shirt sleeves beside his car and breathed the deep, rich scent of the earth.

The neighborhood was quiet. He could hear crickets.

All the lights were off in Harlan Albright's house. Only a gleam of the hall light was visible through the window of his own door. Camacho picked up the package on his front seat and locked his car, then used his key on the front door. He shot the bolt behind him.

There was a note by the phone. Albright had called.

Camacho poured himself a bourbon and added three ice cubes from the tray in the freezer. He opened the kitchen door and stood there sipping his drink and looking at the shadows in the backyard. The dog whined and wagged its tail.

Taking his time, Camacho strolled the length of the yard and seated himself in the tire swing hanging from the old oak. He absently petted the dog and made comforting noises as he sipped the liquor and let the alcohol take effect.

It would be interesting to see how many of those servos were still in Albright's mad bomber kit. And the batteries and fuses.

You sure had to take your hat off to Peter Aleksandrovich, a.k.a. good ol' Harlan. Terry Franklin's sudden end had been a nice tidy job. No loose ends. No secondary casualties that might fester into an eventual murder indictment that would make a spy swap impossible, should the worst happen and he get arrested by the FBI. Terry Franklin had been very neatly and permanently silenced. Scratch one asset-turned-debit. Clean up that balance sheet. Wipe off the red ink, and, *voilà!* we have a profitable enterprise, as anyone can plainly see.

Good ol' Harlan's house was as dark as a tomb. The big maples in front shielded it from the streetlights and the oaks and beeches here in back performed a similar service with that little alley light. So the house was just a looming black shape.

Camacho thought about the stairs up to the bedroom, pictured himself once again slipping up there, careful as a mouse, looking for booby traps, prying open the trapdoor to the attic—he shivered as he thought about it. Good ol' Harlan would probably rig some more unpleasant surprises, like plastique that goes boom when the someone coming into a room steps in the wrong place, or forgets to turn the light on and off three times in three seconds. Good ol' Harlan would be just the man for a little rig like that.

Wonder if Harlan's found the blank film in the camera? Had Camacho been careful enough with the operation? Had he tripped a camera he didn't find? If so, that bulb in the door would come on very soon.

His fatigue hit him all at once. It was all he could do to walk back to the house, lock the door, and ascend the stairs. He stripped off his clothes and fell into bed.

"I don't want to ever get married," Rita said.

"Me neither," Toad Tarkington agreed fervently. "Half the marriages fail, kids in single-parent households, everybody broke—who needs it?" It was a pretty Saturday morning and they were on their way to a restaurant for breakfast, with Toad at the wheel.

"People should be free to have a relationship without being *bound*," she said.

"When two people break up they shouldn't have to hire lawyers to fight over the dog."

"Marriage is an obsolete institution."

"It's doomed," Toad pronounced, sounding a good bit like Samuel Dodgers denouncing sin, which was probably unintentional. But to prove he wasn't a bigot he added, "Of course, my parents are happily married. Thirty-five years this July. It's a lot tougher nowadays, though. My sister was only married three years, one kid —the divorce was real messy. My dad had to help her with the legal fees."

"Did she get custody?" Rita asked.

Toad told her about it. Both of them shook their heads sadly. Truly, modern marriage was a misery.

"Two people who love each other don't need all that," Rita sniffed. "I want a man who loves me and wants to be with me, not because he has to, but because he wants to."

"It's the has-to part that turns me off," Toad explained. "You know, I think it's terrific that you and I think so much alike."

"Well, we're very similar. We both have middle-class backgrounds, good educations, we're naval officers, we fly. You're only a year older than I am. It's no wonder."

"I guess."

Toad wheeled her Mazda into the restaurant parking lot and found a space. He opened the door for Rita and she smiled her thanks, a gorgeous little grin that he returned. She rested her fingers lightly on his arm as they walked across the macadam. He held the door for her and she preceded him through. He had never felt better in his life—so alive, so *into* all of it. They loved each other without strings. And the best part, he told himself, was that they could be so forthright, so frank with each other. Wouldn't the world be a better place if everyone's relationships were so open and honest?

They were married that afternoon in Oakland, Maryland.

The glider wheeled and soared six feet above the dune, the sun flashing on its wings. Jake Grafton sat in the sand with the wind at his back. David and Amy sat beside him, hugging their knees. He manipulated the levers on the radio control box without taking his eyes from the free-flying bird.

"Remember to keep the nose up in the turns," David reminded him as the glider reached the tuft of sea grass a hundred feet north along the dune where Jake had been turning. He had the technique now, he hoped. He hadn't crashed in ten minutes. He thought he could stay aloft as long as the wind remained steady.

Back the glider came, crossing silently above their heads. "Totally awesome," David murmured.

"Awesome" seemed to be *the* word this year in the sixth grade.

What had it been when Jake had been twelve years old? He tried to remember and drew a blank.

Amy Carol stretched out in the sand on her stomach, her chin on her forearms. Her figure was still a collection of straight lines. Callie said she would start to fill out soon. David matched her position, his big feet incongruous beside Amy's petite ones. No doubt his growth would also spurt in the next year or so; he already had the feet of a good-sized man, though the rest of him had a lot further to go.

"Your dad's gonna be a pretty good pilot," David told her.

"He isn't my dad. He's Jake."

"He's gonna be good," David insisted.

"That's not so tough to do," she said, sitting up.

"Oh no? Why don't you try it."

"Can I, Jake?"

"Yeah. Come over here and watch me for a minute." He explained the controls and demonstrated how they worked. After two passes up and down the beach with Amy watching intently, he turned the box over to her. She overbanked and nosed the plane in on the very next turn.

David smacked his hands together in exasperation. " 'Nothing to it.' Girls!" He pronounced the last word as if it were spelled "gurls."

The left wing had torn skin and a broken spar. The three aviators collected their gear and trudged for the house. "Don't worry, Cap'n," the boy said with a disgusted glance at Amy, "I can fix it good as new."

"I'm sure you can," Jake told him, grinning.

"Girls don't know nothin' about flyin'."

"Don't bet on it, Dave. There's a woman pilot working for me, and she's real darn good."

Amy squared her shoulders, threw her head back and marched proudly before them, at long last assuming her rightful place among the exalted sisters.

"You're *what?*" exclaimed Harriet, Rita's horrified roommate. It was Sunday evening and they were in the bedroom. Out in the living room Toad had settled in to watch a Knicks game.

Rita held up her left hand and waggled it proudly. "Here's the ring. I'm married."

"My *God!* How long have you known him? A month? How long were you engaged?"

"A little over an hour. We were driving to Deep Creek Lake for the weekend and around Frostburg we decided to get married. So Toad drove off the next exit and into Oakland. We found the most delightful minister. He knew a lady in the county clerk's office—she was a member of his church—and she drove downtown and opened up the courthouse just to issue us a license. Wasn't that sweet?"

Harriet lowered herself onto the bed and covered her face with her hands.

"The minister's wife gave me some flowers from her garden. Some paper-white narcissus and tulips and multicolored butterfly daffodils, all accented by bridalwreath in a beautiful bouquet. I cradled them in my right arm when we said our vows." She sighed, remembering. "I have the best ones down in the car. I thought you and I could press them."

"A *one-hour* engagement! Rita, Rita, Rita, you poor poor child. What do you know about this man? What?" Harriet opened the bedroom door a crack and looked with loathing at the groom sagged out in front of the TV with a beer in his hand. No wonder they called him Toad.

"My God, Rita, how could you?" she hissed. "What do you *know* about him? He could be AC-DC or a closet pervert, or even a Republican! What *will* your mother say?" Harriet spun like a lioness ready to pounce. "Have you told her yet?"

"Wellll—"

"I *knew* it! When are you going to tell her? After all, Rita, she is your *mother.* She once told me that after buying a thousand wedding presents for all of your friends, she was so looking forward to inviting every one of them to your wedding. You're her *only* daughter!" Harriet threw herself backward onto her bed and bounced once. "How *could* you?" she moaned.

"It was easy," Rita Moravia Tarkington said lightly. She dearly enjoyed Harriet's tantrums. "It was so romantic. Just like I always wanted it to be. He's so handsome, so . . . We're going to be so very happy all our lives. He's . . . he's . . ." She sighed again and smiled.

"One thing's for sure," Harriet said acidly, "he's all yours now."

* * *

On Monday morning Lieutenant Toad Tarkington and Lieutenant Rita Moravia entered Jake's office together, side by side. They stopped in front of his desk and waited at parade rest until he looked up from the report he was working on.

"Yeah."

"We have some news for you, Captain," Rita said.

Jake carefully surveyed their expectant faces. He scowled. "Why have I got the feeling I'm not going to enjoy this?"

Rita and Toad both grinned broadly and glanced at each other. "We're married," Toad said.

Jake Grafton clapped his hands over his ears. "I didn't hear that. Whatever it was, I didn't hear it. And I don't want to hear it." He stood and leaned slightly toward them, his voice low: "I have enough problems around here without people sniping at me about the romantic status of my test crew. What you two do on your own time is your business. But until we get the prototype testing completed and I submit the report, you two puppies are going to walk the line for me. All business. No kissy-facey or kootchy-koo or groping or any of that other goofy hooey. No glorious announcements. Strictly business."

"Yes, sir," Rita said.

"I warned you about this, Tarkington. No romances, I said. And look at you! It's disgusting, that's what it is."

"Yessir," Toad said.

"I can't let you out of my sight for a minute."

"I just couldn't control myself, sir."

"You two are going to be very happy someday. But not today or tomorrow. Right now you're serious, committed, dedicated professionals. Pretend. Try real hard."

"Yessir," they both said.

"Congratulations. Get back to work."

"Aye aye, sir." They came to attention like plebes at the Naval Academy, did a smart about-face and marched out, Rita leading. Jake Grafton bit his lip and resumed work on his report.

19

Somebody explain how this airplane is going to be used." Jake Grafton looked from face to face. He had his staff gathered around while he stood at the office blackboard with marker in hand. "Who wants the floor?"

"Captain, there's been two or three studies on that written during the last three or four years," said Smoke Judy.

"I know. Somebody dug them out for me and I read them. I want to hear your ideas."

"Seems to me," said Toad Tarkington, "that the first thing it has to do is land and take off from a carrier. Must be carrier-compatible."

Jake wrote that down. Obvious, but often overlooked. Any navy attack plane must have a tailhook, nose tow, strong keel, routinely tolerate a six-hundred foot-per-minute sink rate collision with the deck on landing, fit into allotted deck space and accept electrical power and inertial alignment information from the ship's systems. It had to be capable of being launched from existing catapults and arrested with existing machinery. In addition, it would have to be able to fly down a 3.5-degree glide slope carrying enough power to make a wave-off feasible, and with a low enough nose attitude so that the pilot could see the carrier's optical landing system. Amazingly enough, in the late 1960s the navy was almost forced to buy a plane that wasn't carrier-compatible—the TFX, which the air force called the F-111 and immediately began using as an all-weather tactical bomber with a system identical to the A-6's.

"Corrosion-resistant," Tarkington added as Jake made furious notes. "Has to be able to withstand long exposure to salty environment without a lot of expensive maintenance."

"Maintenance," muttered Les Richards. "Got to have easy maintainability designed in. Easy access to engines, black boxes and so forth, without a lot of special equipment."

The requirements came thick and fast now, as quick as Jake could write. Range, speed, payload and a lot of other parameters. After ten minutes he had filled up most of the board and his staff paused for air.

"How're we going to use this thing?" he asked again. "What I'm getting at is this: these stealth designs appear to be optimized for high-altitude ingress over heavily defended territory. Presumably at night. Are all our missions going to be at night?"

"We can't afford to give away the day," someone said.

"What's that mean in the way of aircraft capability? Daytime means enemy fighters and optically aimed surface-to-air missiles. They'll see our plane. Do we have to be able to engage the fighters and dodge the missiles? How much G capability do we need? Sustained turning ability? Dash speed? Climb speed? Will we go in low in the daytime? If so, how about ability to withstand bird strikes and turbulence?"

The staff spent an hour on these questions. There was no consensus, nor did Jake expect one. No plane in the world could do everything, but any design must meet most of the major requirements for its intended employment. Shortcomings due to design trade-offs would have to be overcome or endured.

"Weapons." The ideal plane would carry and deliver every weapon in the U.S. and NATO inventory, and a lot of them. Was that a realistic goal with the stealth designs under consideration?

After four hours of brainstorming, the staff reexamined the proposed test program for the prototypes. In the five flights of each airplane that SECDEF had budgeted money and time for, they needed to acquire as much information as possible to answer real questions. Company test pilots had already flown both planes. These five flights of each plane by the navy would have to produce data that verified or refuted the manufacturers' claims. More importantly, the flights would determine which plane was best suited to fill the navy's mission requirements, or which could be made so by cost-effective modifications.

"We really need more than five flights per plane, Captain," Les Richards said.

"Five flights are enough for what we want to find out, if we do it right. This little evolution is just a new car test drive with us doing the driving. Five flights are enough for what we want to find out if we do it right, which is precisely what we're going to do. Henry and Ludlow and Caplinger want a fast recommendation and a fast decision."

"Don't they always? Then the paper pushers in SECDEF's office will spend a couple years mulling it over, sending it from in basket to in basket."

"Ours is not to reason why . . ."

The pace accelerated relentlessly in the office. Working days lasted twelve hours now, and Jake ran everyone out and turned off the lights himself at 7 P.M. He insisted that no one work on Saturday and Sunday, believing that the break would make people more productive during the week.

The weeks slid by, one by one.

Jake spent less than half his time in the office and the rest in an endless series of meetings with people from everywhere in government: SECNAV, SECDEF, OPNAV, NAVAIR, NAVSEA, the FAA, the EPA, the air force, the marines, and a host of others. Most of the time he attended these conferences with Admiral Dunedin or Commander Rob Knight.

The meetings went on and on, the paper piled higher and higher. The same subjects kept cropping up in different meetings, where they had to be rehashed again and again. Government by committee is government by consensus, and key players from every office high and low had to be listened to and pacified.

Jake felt like the sorcerer's apprentice as he tried to pin people down and arrive at final resolutions of issues. Meetings bred more meetings: the final item on every agenda was to set the times and places for follow-up meetings.

He discovered to his horror that no one person had a complete grasp of the tens of thousands of regulations and directives that covered every aspect of procurement. At every meeting, it seemed, someone had another requirement that needed to be at least given lip service. He finally found where all this stuff was stored, a library that at last measurement contained over 1,152 linear feet of statutes, regulations, directives, and case law concerning defense procurement. Jake Grafton looked at this collection in awe and disgust, and never visited the place again.

The silent army of faceless gnomes who spent their working lives writing, interpreting, clarifying, and applying these millions of paragraphs of "thou shalts" and "thou shalt nots" took on flesh and substance. They came in all sexes, shapes, and colors, each with his or her own coffee cup and a tiny circle of responsibility, which, no matter how small, of course overlapped with that of three or four others.

The key players were all known to Jake's staff: "Watch out for the Arachnid," someone would say before a meeting. Or "Beware of the Sewer Rat. He'll be there this morning." "The Gatekeeper will grill you on this." The staff named these key players in the procurement process because of their resemblance to the characters in the game Dungeons and Dragons. When he returned from battle Jake had to contribute to the office lore by recounting the latest exploits of the evil ones.

"It's a miracle that the navy even owns a rowboat," Grafton remarked one day to Admiral Dunedin.

"True, but the Russians are more screwed up than we are. They manage every single sector of their economy like this, not just the military. You can't even buy toilet paper in a store over there."

"The bureaucrat factor is a multiplier," Jake decided. "The more people there are to do paperwork, the more paper there is to be worked and the slower everything goes, until finally the wheels stop dead and only the paper moves."

"The crat factor: it's a law of physics," Dunedin agreed.

Jake took a briefcase full of unclassified material home every night, and after Callie and Amy were in bed he stayed awake until midnight scribbling notes, answering queries, and reading replies and reports prepared by his staff.

He spent countless hours on the budget, trying to justify every dollar he needed for the next fiscal year. He had to make assumptions about where the ATA program would be then, and then he had to justify the assumptions. Athena was still buried deep, outside the normal budgetary process. Still he would need staff and travel money and all the rest of it. He involved everyone he could lay hands on and cajoled Admiral Dunedin into finding him two more officers and another yeoman. He didn't have desks for them. They had to share.

But things were being accomplished. A Request for Proposal (RFP) on the Athena project was drafted, chopped by everyone up and down the line, committeed and lawyered and redrafted twice and finally approved. Numbered copies went by courier to a half dozen major defense contractors who were believed to have the technical facilities and staff to handle development of a small superconducting computer for aviation use. The office staff had to be informed, and this had been done by the admiral.

Inevitably the number of people who knew about Athena and what it could do was expanding exponentially. Access was still strictly need-to-know, but the system ensured that a great many people had the need, or could claim they did, citing chapter and verse of some regulation or directive no one else had ever read or even seen.

Callie was understanding about the time demands Jake faced. She had spent enough years as a navy wife to know how the service worked. Amy was less so. She and Callie were still going round and round, and she found Jake a pleasant change. He made rules and he enforced them, and he tucked her into bed every night. She wanted more of his time and he had precious little to give. The weekends became their special time together.

"Why do you spend so much time at work, Jake?"

"It's my job. I have to."

"I'm not going to have a job like yours. I'm going to get a job that gives me plenty of time to spend with my little girl."

"Are you my little girl?"

"No. I'm Amy. I'm not anybody's little girl. But I'm going to have a little girl of my own someday."

"Do you ever think much about those somedays? What they'll be like?"

"Sure. I'll have lots of money and lots of time and a very nice little girl to buy stuff for and spend time with."

"How are you going to get lots of money if you don't spend much time earning it?"

"I'm going to inherit it. From you and Callie."

"Guess we'd better work hard then."

One day in early May, Special Agent Lloyd Dreyfus made an appointment to see Luis Camacho's boss, P. R. Bigelow, without telling Camacho. He had thought about it for a week before he made the appointment with the secretary, and then he had two more days to wait. Jumping the chain of command was as grievous a sin in the FBI as it was in the military, yet he had decided to do it anyway and to hell with what Camacho or anyone else thought. As the day and hour approached, however, the enormity of his transgression increased with each passing hour. Surely Bigelow would understand. Even if he didn't, he must realize Dreyfus had a right and duty to voice his concerns.

Dreyfus rehearsed his speech carefully. It wasn't technically a speech: perhaps a better description would be "short, panicky monologue." He had to justify himself as soon as he opened his mouth, get Bigelow's sympathetic attention before he had a chance to start quoting the regulations, before he lost his cool and went ballistic. Was Bigelow a ballistic kind of guy? Dreyfus couldn't recall Camacho ever saying.

He tried to recall everything he had ever heard about P. R. Bigelow, and that wasn't much. Strange, when you stopped to think about it. Camacho *never* mentioned his superior officer, never said, "Bigelow wants this," or "Bigelow is pleased," or "Bigelow says blah-blah." Come to think of it, Camacho *never* talked about *anyone.* If the Director himself told Luis Camacho to do thus and so, Camacho would just tell Dreyfus, "Do this" or "Do that." He sometimes said what he hoped to find or achieve, but he *never* even hinted who had told him to cause something to happen, or why it was to happen. He *never* expressed a personal opinion. Curious as hell. Camacho was one weird duck, beyond a reasonable doubt.

Sitting in Bigelow's reception area with the secretary checking him out surreptitiously as she did her nails, Dreyfus went over his list one more time. He wanted everything right on the tip of his tongue. It would be worse than disastrous to think of the clincher on the way to the surgery in the dungeon. Once again he assured himself he was doing the right thing. *The* right thing. Doing the *right* thing. He fondled his pipe in his pocket as if it were a set of worry beads.

The ten-button phone on the nail polisher's desk buzzed to attract its owner's attention. After listening a moment and grunting into the instrument in a pleasant, respectful way, she hung up and said to Dreyfus, "He'll see you now." Her painted eyebrows arched knowingly, condescendingly.

P. R. Bigelow was eating a large jelly doughnut at his desk. He mumbled his greeting with his mouth full, a glob of red goo in the corner of his mouth.

Dreyfus took a chair and launched into his prepared remarks. "I've asked for this time, sir, to ensure you know what is going on with the Minotaur investigation. The answer is almost nothing. For months now we've been spinning our wheels, begging computer time to try and crack the Minotaur's letters to the Soviet ambassador, following a few people hither and yon all over Washington, monitoring some phone lines, wasting an army of manpower and bushels of money, and we are going essentially nowhere. I thought you should know that."

Bigelow wiped the jam from his lips with a napkin, sipped coffee from a white mug labeled "World's Best Dad" and took another bite of doughnut.

His attitude rattled Dreyfus, who got out his pipe and rubbed the bowl carefully. "Our best lead was a navy enlisted computer technician in the Pentagon, a guy we thought was tapping the computer for some of this stuff. Name of Terry Franklin. Yet Camacho never let us pick the guy up. So we sat and watched him do his little thing, and we were diligently following him, right on his tail, in March when his car blew up with him in it."

Bigelow finished the doughnut and used a moist finger to capture and convey the last few crumbs to his mouth. Then he dabbed his lips a final time and used two napkins to scrub the powdered sugar and flecks of jelly from his oak desk. He put this trash in the wastebasket and, sighing contentedly, rearranged his bottom in his chair.

"And . . . ?" said P. R. Bigelow.

"A hit man wiped a walk-in witness to a drop with Franklin. Camacho talked to her a couple times, but she got eliminated before we could get her to look at any photos. A professional hit. Two twenty-two caliber slugs in the skull. We've got the autopsy and lab reports and we've talked to neighbors up and down the street. We've got nothing at all. We're absolutely dry on this one."

"Anything else?"

"Yes," said Lloyd Dreyfus with an edge in his voice. He was beginning to lose his temper and didn't care if it showed a little. "One of the staff officers in the navy's ATA project—a Commander Judy—is trying to peddle classified inside info to interested defense contractors. We got interested in this officer when the project manager was murdered over in West Virginia one Friday evening in early February. That murder is unsolved—no one is doing anything on it—and Camacho doesn't appear to be doing any follow-up on Judy's contacts. He hasn't even turned the file over to the fraud investigators or NIS. We know some of the people Judy's talked to and . . ." Dreyfus threw up his hands in frustration.

"Finished yet?"

"Yes, I think that about covers it."

"So you asked for this appointment on the off chance that Camacho has been lying to me about the activities of his office, purposely bungling the search for this mole, wasting millions of dollars and thousands of man-hours on wild-goose chases." Dreyfus opened his mouth to interrupt, but Bigelow held up a hand. "I grant that you can probably phrase it more tactfully. You notice I did not suggest that you came up here to tattle and gain some personal advantage. You are a better man than that." He sighed heavily, almost a belch. "Of course there is another possibility. Perhaps you just wanted to see if I was so stupid as to be satisfied with the progress of the investigation to date."

"I—" The upraised palm stopped him again.

"I *am* satisfied. Camacho has kept me fully informed of the activities of his subordinates, of which you are one, by the way. His lines of inquiry have been initiated with my knowledge and, where necessary, my approval. He has discussed his concerns with me and I have informed him of mine. He has followed orders to the letter. I am completely satisfied with his performance. He is one of the most talented senior officers in the bureau."

Dreyfus just stared.

"Before you go back to work, do you wish for me to arrange a meeting for you with the Director?" Bigelow managed to make his face look interested and mildly amused at the same time. Yes, Lloyd, you miserable, disloyal, alarmist peckerhead, you jumped from the top of the cliff, but you seem to have had the luck to strike a bush a few feet below the edge, which arrested your downward progress. Do you wish my help in completing your suicidal plunge?

Dreyfus shook his head no.

"I suggest that you not mention this little conversation to any of your colleagues."

"Yessir."

"I don't want to see you in this office ever again, Dreyfus, unless you have your supervisor with you, or unless I send for you."

"Yessir."

"Let's both get back to work." P. R. Bigelow nodded toward the closed office door and Dreyfus took the hint.

By mid-May the dance of the dwarves at the Pentagon had reached a critical frenzy. A thousand details were beginning to come together for a trip into the desert with the prototypes in June. The airplanes had been moved weeks earlier to the Tonopah Test Range in Nevada, the same secret field where the air force had tested its stealth prototypes. Also known as Area 58, or Groom Lake, the field lay about a hundred miles northwest of Las Vegas on a huge government reservation with excellent physical security. Here the contractors' field teams readied the planes in separate hangars and installed telemetry devices.

Toad and Rita would leave for Nevada two weeks before Jake and the rest of the staff. They had intensive sessions planned with company test pilots and engineers to learn everything they could about the planes and how they flew. The Saturday night before they left, Jake and Callie had them to dinner at the house in Rehoboth Beach.

"How do you like being married?" Callie asked Rita in the kitchen.

"I should have had a brother," Rita confided. "Men are such sloppy creatures. They don't think like we do."

On the screened-in porch, Jake and Toad sipped on bourbon and Amy slurped a Coke. "So how's married life, Toad?"

"Oh, so-so, I guess. Isn't exactly like I thought it would be, but nothing ever is. Ol' Rita can think up stuff for me to do faster than I can do it, and we only live in an apartment. If we had a town house or something with a basement and a lawn, she'd have worked me to death by now."

Amy Carol thought this remark deliriously funny and giggled hugely.

"Why don't you go visit with Mom and Rita?"

She stood regally and tossed her hair. "I do believe I will join the ladies, but she isn't my mom. I wish you'd stop calling her that." She flounced off toward the kitchen.

"The day she"—Jake pointed after the departing youngster—"gets married, I am going to get down on my knees and give thanks."

"That bad, huh?"

"She's about driven Callie over the edge. That poor woman had no idea what she was getting into. No matter how much love she pours on Amy, the kid still does exactly as she chooses. She intentionally disobeys and cuts up just to get her goat. And Callie never gets mad, never pops off, never gives her anything but love. She's gonna go nuts."

"Maybe she should get angry."

"That's what I think. And Callie insists she doesn't want my help or advice."

"They're all alike," Toad said, now vastly experienced.

Amy was back in five minutes, hopping from foot to foot, so excited she bounced. "Can we fly the glider now, so I can show Rita? She's a *pilot.*"

Toad gasped. "She is?"

"You're teasing me," Amy said, stamping her foot.

"The wind's wrong," Jake pointed out. "It isn't coming in from the sea. This evening it's a land breeze."

"David said we might be able to fly the glider above the house in a land breeze. He said the wind just goes right up and over our house."

"I never thought of that. Well, run down the street and see if he can spend a half hour consulting with us." As Amy scampered off, Jake told Toad, "There's an aviation expert right down the street who is kind enough to offer advice from time to time."

The aviation expert was apparently unoccupied at the moment. He showed up wearing a monster-truck T-shirt bearing the legend "Eat Street." His shoelaces were untied, his cowlicks fully aroused, and his grin as impish as ever. He listened carefully to Jake's plan. "Sounds to me like it might work, Cap'n," he said with a sidelong glance at Toad. "Might ding up your plane a little, though."

"I'll risk it if you'll fix the damage."

"Callie! Rita!" Amy called excitedly. "We're going to fly."

Jake readied the plane for flight in the front yard under David's supervision. Eight rubber bands were stretched to hold the six-foot wing to the fuselage. Batteries were tested and inserted, the cover closed, switch on, controls waggled to the full extent of their travel using the radio control box: Amy checked each item after Jake performed it while David briefed Toad on proper launch procedure. In five minutes they were ready for the sky.

Toad climbed the ladder from the garage and scaled the sloping roof until he sat perched on the ridgepole with the plane in hand.

"Pretty good breeze up here," he informed the crowd below, which now included Callie and Rita.

"Don't you jump off there, Darius Green," Rita called as Toad sucked on a finger and held it aloft.

"As you can plainly see, dear wife, I'm not wearing my wings tonight," Tarkington replied lightly. He flapped his elbows experimentally. " 'I'll astonish the nation and all creation, by flyin' over the celebration! I'll dance on the chimneys, I'll stand on the steeple, I'll flop up to winders and scare all the people,' " quoteth he, striking a precarious pose, or trying to, up there on the ridge of the roof with an airplane grasped carefully in his right hand.

"Maybe I'd better alert the emergency room at the hospital," Callie said, laughing.

"Oh, Callie," Amy groaned. "He's not going to jump! Really!"

Toad finished his recitation with a flourish: " 'And I'll say to the gawpin' fools below, What world's this here that I've come near?' "

Jake Grafton handed the radio control box to David. "You're up first. Whenever you're ready."

The youngster centered the control levers and shouted to Toad, "Let 'er go!"

With the gentlest of tosses, Toad laid the glider into the rising air currents. The boy immediately banked left and raised the nose until the aircraft was barely moving in relation to the ground. As it reached the end of the house, he reversed the controls and flew it back the other way. The ship soared upward on the rising current of air. It floated above Toad's head, back and forth along the peak of the roof, banking gently to maintain position and rising and falling as the air currents dictated.

"All right!" Toad shouted and began to clap. On the ground the spectators all did likewise.

"There's just enough wind," Jake told David, grinning broadly. "Now, by God, that's *flying*!"

"Awesome," David agreed, his pixie grin spreading uncontrollably.

After a few minutes, David handed the control box to Jake. He overbanked and the plane lost altitude precipitously, threatening to strike Toad straddling the roof's ridge. "Keep your nose up," David advised hurriedly. "You can fly slower than that." As the glider responded, he continued. "That's it! She's got plenty of camber in those wings and good washout. She'll fly real, real slow, just riding those updrafts. That's it! Let 'er fly. Just sorta urge 'er along."

He was right. The plane soared like a living thing, banking and diving and climbing, seeking the rising air and responding willingly. The evening sun flashed on the wings and fuselage and made the little craft brightly lustrous against the darkening blue of the sky above.

"Let Rita try it," Amy urged.

"Don't you want to?"

"No. Let Rita."

"Come over here, Rita Moravia." The pilot did as she was bid. She watched the captain manipulate the controls as he explained what each was. "The thing you gotta watch is that the controls work backwards as you look at the plane head-on. Turn around and fly it by looking over your shoulder. Then left will be left and right will be right."

Rita obediently faced away from the house and looked back over her shoulder. Toad waved. Jake handed her the radio control box. As David and Amy tried to offer simultaneous advice, Rita clumsily swung the plane back and forth and worked the nose hesitantly. She overcontrolled as David groaned, "Not too much, no no no."

But the wind was dying. She got the nose too high trying to maintain altitude: the plane stalled and the nose fell through. The plane shot forward away from the house, toward the street. David scrambled, but Rita stalled it again and the left wing and nose dug into the sandy lawn before the running boy could reach it. The rubber bands let loose and the wing popped free of the fuselage, minimizing the damage.

"Nasty," David declared.

"My dinner!" Callie exclaimed, and charged for the door.

"You did great for a first solo," Amy assured Rita. The pilot pulled the girl to her and gave her a mighty hug and a kiss on the cheek. She got a big hug in return.

"She ain't banged up too bad, Cap'n," David called.

Up on the roof Toad was laughing. He blew Rita a kiss.

After dinner Callie shooed Jake and Toad off to the screened-in porch while she cleaned up the dishes. Rita and Amy helped.

"So what did your parents think of Toad when they met him, or have they yet?" Callie asked Rita.

"We went to visit them two weekends ago. Mother invited a few of their closest friends over to meet the newlyweds. Then she cornered Toad, and making sure I was in earshot, she asked him, 'Now that you're married, when is Rita going to give up flying?' " Rita laughed ruefully, remembering. "How well do you know Toad?" she asked Callie.

"Not very well. I met him for the first time last year in the Mediterranean."

"Well, he looked at Mother with that slightly baffled, Lord of the Turnip Truck expression of his, and said, 'Why would she do that? Flying is what she does.' I could have kissed him right there in front of everyone." Rita chuckled again.

"Doesn't your mom want you to fly," Amy piped, her chin resting on a hand, her eyes fixed on her new heroine.

"My mother is one of these new moderns who have elevated the elimination of risk to a religious status. She serves only food certified safe for laboratory rats. She writes weekly letters to congressmen urging a national fifty-five-mile-per-hour speed limit, helmets for motorcyclists, gun control—she has never been on a motorcycle in her life and to the best of my knowledge has never even seen a real firearm. Her latest cause is a ban on mountain climbing since she read an article about how many people per year fall off cliffs or die of hypothermia. This from a woman who regards a walk across a large parking lot as a survival trek."

"I'm not afraid of things," Amy assured Rita.

"It's not fear that motivates Mother. She thinks of government as Super-Mom, and who better to advise the politicians than the superest mom of them all?"

"Flying is risky, inherently dangerous. I can understand your mother's concern," Callie said as she rinsed a pot. "Flying is something I've had to live with. It's a part of Jake and his life, a big part. But I've had very mixed emotions about his being grounded." As she dried the pot she turned to Rita. "You or Toad may be killed or crippled for life in an accident. After it happens, if it happens, it won't matter whose fault it is or how good you are in a cockpit. I know. I've seen it too many times."

"*Life* is risky," Rita replied. "Life isn't some bland puree with all the caffeine and cholesterol removed. It doesn't just go on for ever and ever without end, amen. For every living thing there is a beginning, a middle, and an end. And life is chance. Chance is the means whereby God rules the universe."

The flier thought a moment, then continued, choosing her words carefully. "I have the courage to *try* to live with my fate, whatever it may be."

"Do you have enough?" Amy asked, dead serious.

"I don't know," said Rita. She smiled at the youngster. "I hope so. I haven't needed much courage so far. I'm healthy, reasonably intelligent, and I've been lucky. But still, I gather courage where I find it and save it for the storms to come."

20

Through the years Jake Grafton had become a connoisseur of air force bases. Visiting one was like driving through Newport or Beverly Hills. With manicured lawns, trimmed trees, well-kept substantial buildings and nifty painted signs, air force bases made him feel like a poor farm boy visiting the estate of a rich uncle. In contrast, the money the admirals wheedled from a parsimonious Congress went into ships and airplanes. The dedication of a new cinder-block enlisted quarters at some cramped navy base in the industrial district of a major port city was such a rare event that it would draw a half dozen admirals and maybe the CNO.

The Tonopah facility, however, didn't look like any air force base Jake had ever seen. It looked like some shacky, jerry-built temporary facility the navy had stuck out in the middle of nowhere during World War II and had only now decided to improve. Perhaps this base was just too new. Bulldozers and earthmovers sat scattered around on large, open wounds of raw earth. No trees or grass yet, though two trenchers appeared to be excavating for a sprinkler system. When the wind blew, great clouds of dust embedded with tumbleweeds swept across the flat, featureless desert and through the stark frames of buildings under construction, and the wind blew most of the time.

Security was as tight as Jake had ever seen it in the military. Air policemen in natty uniforms with white dickeys at their throats manned the gates and patrolled chain link fences topped with barbed wire while they fought to keep their spiffy blue berets in place against the wind. The fences were woven with metal strips to form opaque barriers. Signs every few yards forbade stopping or photography. You needed a pass to enter any area, and prominent signs vibrating in the wind advised you of that fact.

The place reeked with that peculiar aroma of government intrigue: *Important, stupendous things are happening here. You don't want to know! We who do also know that you couldn't handle it. Trust us.* In other words, the overall effect was precisely the same gray ambience of don't-bother-us superiority that oozes from large post offices and the mausoleums that house the departments of motor vehicles, social services, and similar enterprises throughout the land.

Even the sergeant at the desk of the Visiting Officers' Quarters wanted to see Jake Grafton's security documents. He made cryptic notations in a battered green logbook and passed them back without comment as he frowned at Helmut Fritsche's facial hair. After all, didn't Lenin wear a beard?

As he escorted Jake and Fritsche down the hall toward their rooms, Toad Tarkington said, "This place is really dead, Captain. The nearest whorehouse is fifty miles away."

Fritsche groaned.

"Tonopah makes China Lake look like Paris after dark," Tarkington told the physicist with relish. "This is as far as you can get away from civilization without starting out the other side." He lowered his voice. "There's spies everywhere. The place is crawling with 'em. Watch your mouth. Remember, loose lips sink—"

"Loose lips sink lieutenants," Jake Grafton rumbled.

"Yessir, them too," Toad chirped.

That evening Jake inspected the Consolidated Technologies airplane. Under the bright lights of the cavernous hangar, it was being tended by a small army of engineers and technicians who were busy checking every system, every wire, every screw and bolt and rivet. Adele DeCrescentis watched a man fill in a checklist. Each item was carefully marked when completed. Rita Moravia walked back and forth around the aircraft, looking, probing, asking more questions of the company test pilot who stood beside her. Toad Tarkington was in the aft cockpit, going over the radar and computer one more time as a nearby yellow cart supplied electrical power and cooling air.

At 9 P.M. they gathered in a large ready room on the second deck of the hangar's office pod. The room was devoid of furnishings except for one portable blackboard and thirty or so folding chairs.

The meeting lasted until midnight. Every aspect of tomorrow's flight was gone over in detail. Consolidated's people approved the test profile and agreed on the performance envelope Rita would have to stay within on the first flight. The route of the flight was laid out on a large map which was posted on one wall and briefed by Commander Les Richards. He pointed out the places where ground cameras would be posted. Real-time telemetry from the airplane would be supervised by Commander Dalton Harris. Smoke Judy would fly the chase plane, an F-14 borrowed from NAS Miramar, and a carefully briefed RIO would film the Consolidated prototype in flight from the F-14's backseat.

After the meeting broke up, Jake Grafton spent another thirty minutes with his staff, then went down to the hangar deck. Only a dozen or so technicians were still on the job.

The overhead floods made little gleaming pinpoints where they reflected on the black surface of the Consolidated stealth plane. As he walked, the tiny pinpoints moved along the complex curved surfaces in an unpredictable way. With his face only a foot or so from the skin of the plane, he studied it. The dark material seemed to have an infinite depth, or perhaps it was only his imagination.

The outer skin, he knew, was made of a composite that was virtually transparent to radar waves. Underneath, carrying the stresses, was a honeycomb radar-absorbent structure made of synthetic material formed into small hexagonal chambers. The honeycomb was bonded to inner skins of graphite and other strong composites. He touched the airplane's skin. Smooth and cool.

From this angle the curves and smooth junctions of the skin became art. No wonder the Consolidated people were so proud of their creation.

But how would it hold up aboard a ship? Could it stand the rough handling and salt air and the poundings of cat shots and traps? Thousands of them? Would it be easy to fly, within the capabilities of the average pilot—not just a superbly trained, gifted professional like Rita Moravia, but the average bright lad from

Moline or Miami with only three hundred hours of flight time who would have to learn to use this Art Deco sculpture as a weapon?

Five flights. He needed a lot of answers in just a short time. Rita and Toad would have to get them.

He walked away musing about Rita's lack of test experience and wondering if he had made a mistake giving her this ride.

Tomorrow. He would know then.

But the following day problems with the telemetry equipment kept the prototype firmly on the ground. The engineers were still laboring in the sun on a concrete mat where the temperature exceeded a hundred and ten when Jake glanced at his watch and ordered the plane towed back into the hangar. The Soviet satellite would soon be overhead. The hangar's interior was shady and cool. And since the air force owned it, it was air-conditioned.

The next morning, Wednesday, the F-14 took off with a cracking roar that seemed to split the desert apart. Smoke Judy pulled the power off when he was safely airborne and made a dirty turn to the downwind leg. He came drifting down toward the earth paralleling the runway and stabilized at one hundred feet just as Rita began to roll.

The prototype was noticeably quieter, so quiet that its noise was barely audible above the howl of the Tomcat's engines as Smoke used his throttles to hang the heavy fighter just above the runway as the stealth bird accelerated. When Rita lifted off and retracted her gear, Smoke added power to stay with her and the sound of the stealth plane was entirely muffled.

"Damn quiet," George Wilson remarked. "About like a Boeing 767, maybe less." The low noise level was a direct by-product of burying the exhaust nozzles and tailpipes in the fuselage, shielded from the underside, to reduce the plane's infrared signature.

In the cockpit Rita concentrated on maintaining the selected test profile and getting the feel of the controls. She had spent hours sitting in the cockpit the last few weeks memorizing the position of every switch, knob, and gauge, learning which buttons she needed to press to place information where she wanted it on the MFDs, and so even now, minutes into her first flight in the plane, it was familiar.

In the backseat Toad was busy with the system. He checked the inertial; it seemed okay. With ring laser gyros, it had not a single moving part and was more accurate than any conventional inertial using electromechanical gyros. It would need to be. To keep the stealth plane hidden, it would be necessary to fly with the radar off most of the time, and the ring laser inertial would have to keep a very accurate running tally of the plane's position.

The computer was also functioning perfectly. He had encoded the waypoint and checkpoint information onto optical-electronic—optronic—cards on the ground and loaded them into the computer after engine start. The two-million-dollar pocket calculator, he called it. It hummed right along, belching readouts of airspeed, groundspeed, altitude, wind direction and velocity, true course, magnetic course, drift angle, time to go to checkpoint, etc., over fifteen readouts simultaneously. He had this information on the right-hand MFD, roughly the location on the panel where it would be in an A-6E.

Some of the displays were not yet hooked up since development work was not yet complete. Consequently the three-dimensional information presentations on the pilot's holographic Heads-Up Display could not be tested.

The phased-array radar in the nose received Toad's attention next. The antenna was flat and fixed, it did not rotate or move. Actually it was made up of several hundred miniature antennas, individually varying their pulse frequencies to steer or focus the main beam. A conventional radar dish would have acted as a reflector to send the enemy's radar signals back to him. Toad tuned the radar to optimize the presentation and dictated his switch and dial positions on the ICS, which, like the radar presentation, was being recorded on tape for later study.

The next major pieces of gear he turned on and integrated into the system were, for him, the most interesting. Two new infrared search and tracking systems that were able to distinguish major targets as far away as a hundred miles, depending upon the aircraft's altitude and the relative heat value of the target. One could be used for searching for enemy fighters while the other was used to navigate or locate a target on the ground. The range of these sensors was a tenfold improvement over the relatively primitive IR gear in the A-6E. Since a stealthy attack plane would fly most of its mission with its radar off, these new gizmos would literally be the eyes of the bombardier-navigator.

Toad took a second to glance to his left. Smoke had the F-14 about a hundred feet away in perfect formation. The backseater's helmet was hidden behind his camera, which was pointed this way.

That videotape would show every twitch of the flight control surfaces. Toad turned back to the task at hand.

He felt the plane yawing as Rita experimented with the controls and advanced and retarded each throttle independently. She was talking on the radio, telling Smoke what she was doing, reading the engine performance data to the people on the ground so it could be coordinated with the telemetry data, giving her impressions of the feel of the plane.

"Seems responsive and sensitive in all axes," she said. "Engine response is good, automatic systems functioning as advertised. Got a hundred feet a minute more climb than I expected. Fuel flow fifty pounds per hour high. Oil pressure in the green, exhaust gas temps are a hundred high. I like it. A nice plane."

She leveled the plane at Flight Level 240 at .72 Mach, 420 knots true. Toad checked the range and depression angles of the radar and IR sensors, and ran checks on the inertial and computer.

Thirty minutes later, after hitting three navigation checkpoints, Rita dropped the nose two degrees and began a power-on descent back toward Tonopah. She leveled at 5,000 feet at 550 knots and raced toward the field. Smoke Judy was a hundred feet away on the right side, immobile in relation to the stealth bird.

In the backseat Toad ran an attack. His target was the hangar that had housed the plane. The system gave Rita steering and time and distance to go to a laser-guided bomb release. Everything functioned as advertised. No weapon was released because the plane carried none, but a tone sounded on the radio and was captured on all the tapes, and it ceased abruptly at the weapons-release point, interrupted by the electronic pulse to the empty bomb rack cunningly faired into the airplane's belly.

After three attacks at different altitudes, Rita slowed the plane with speed brakes and dropped the gear and flaps. She entered the landing pattern.

Two fleet Landing Signal Officers that Jake had borrowed from Miramar—they had flown the F-14 to Tonopah—stood on the end of the runway in a portable radio-equipped trailer that a truck had delivered. They had spent the last three days painting the outline of a carrier deck on the air force's main runway and rigging a portable Optical Landing System—OLS—which the truck had also delivered. Now they watched Rita make simulated carrier approaches flying the ball, the "meatball," on the OLS. Jake Grafton stood beside them.

"Paddles has you," the senior man told Rita as she passed the ninety-degree position. One other LSO wrote while the first watched the approach with the radiotelephone transceiver held to his ear and dictated his comments.

"On speed, little lined up left, little too much power . . ." The plane swept past and its wheels whacked into the runway, right on the line that marked the target touchdown point. The nose wheel smacked down and the engines roared and Rita flew it off the runway. The LSO shouted to his writer, "Fair pass."

Jake Grafton stared at the plane in the pattern. It just looks weird, he told himself. The lifting fuselage and invisible intakes and the canards and the black color, it didn't look like a real airplane. Then he knew. It looked like a *model*. It looked like one of those plastic planes he had glued together and held at arm's length and marveled at.

"You're carrying too much power in the groove," the LSO told Rita after the second pass.

"I'm just floating down with the power way back," she replied. "And we're hearing a little rumble. Maybe incipient compressor stall. I'll use the boards next time around."

The Consolidated engineers had thought the speed brakes would be unnecessary in the pattern. Yet with the intakes on top of the plane, behind the cockpit, maybe the air reaching them was too turbulent when the plane was all cocked up in the landing configuration. Jake Grafton began to chew on his lower lip. The air force doesn't land planes like this, he reminded himself. They wouldn't have tried these maneuvers when they flew the plane.

With the boards out the plane approached at a slightly higher nose attitude, its engine noise louder. The speed brakes allowed—required—Rita to come in with a higher power setting. "This feels better," she commented. "But I'm still hearing that rumble. Little more pronounced now, if anything."

"Looks better," the junior LSO told Jake. "I think the boards give her more control."

"Six-hundred-feet-a-minute sink rate," Rita reported. Once again the main mounts smacked in with puffs of fried rubber from each tire as it rotated up to speed. The main oleos compressed and the nose slapped down, then she was adding power and pulling the nose right back up into the sky.

After the sixth pass she pulled the throttles back to idle and the plane stayed on the deck. The engine noise was really subdued.

"Quiet bugger, ain't it?" one LSO said, grinning. "We'll have to call this one the Burglar. First we had the Intruder, now the Burglar."

"I think it ought to be called the Penetrator," the senior man said. " 'Yeah, baby, I'm a Penetrator pilot.' " He cackled at his own wit.

When Rita cleared the runway, Smoke Judy called the LSOs. "Since you guys are all set up, how about giving me a couple?"

"If you got the gas, you get the pass," the LSO radioed.

The debriefing took until 9 P.M. with an hour break for dinner. The telemetry data and the videotapes were played and studied. Rita and Toad were each carefully debriefed as a dozen engineers gathered around and the naval officers hovered in the background.

The plane was then thoroughly inspected by a team of structural engineers. The simulated carrier landings had placed stresses on the structure that the air force had never anticipated when it developed the specifications for this prototype. No one expected visible damage, and there was none, but if the plane were to be put into production, strengthening would inevitably be needed. Just where and how much was the concern, and the telemetry data would pinpoint these locations.

And some minor equipment problems had surfaced. The Consolidated technicians would work all night to fix those as navy maintenance specialists watched and took notes. The intake rumble in the landing pattern was the most serious problem, and Adele DeCrescentis discussed it on the phone with the people at the Consolidated factory in Burbank for over an hour.

All in all, it had been a fine day. Rita and Toad were still going a mile a minute when Jake loaded them all into the vans at 9 P.M. for the two-mile trip to the VOQ, the Visiting Officers' Quarters.

Jake and his department heads gathered in his room that evening. Someone produced a cold six-pack of beer and they each took a bottle.

"The day after tomorrow. It'll all be decided then," Les Richards, the A-6 bombardier, told the assembled group. "Day after tomorrow we pull some Gs, and I don't think we can live with a five-G limitation. I don't think the navy needs an attack plane for a low-level mission that is that G-limited. It'll get bounced around too much down low, and if a fighter ever spots it or someone pops an IR or optically guided missile, this thing is dead meat."

"What if they beef it up?" someone asked. "Strengthen the spars and so on?"

"Cut performance too much. More weight. We don't have a whole lot of performance to begin with. And what if the compressors stall?"

"Could they enlarge the automatic flaps on the intakes that raise up and scoop more air in when the engines need it?"

"It'd be turbulent air. We learned today that those two engines like a diet of smooth, undisturbed air."

"Oh no we didn't."

So it went. Jake ran them all out at midnight and collapsed into bed.

The following day was spent in further intensive review of the videotapes and telemetry data, and planning the second flight.

Glitches developed. Under the usual ground rules for op-eval fly-offs, the manufacturer cleared various areas of the flight performance envelope for the navy test pilots to explore. Rita wanted to examine the slow-flight characteristics of the aircraft before she proceeded to high-angle-of-attack/high-G maneuvers. Consolidated's chief engineer did not want her below 200 knots clean and 120 knots dirty.

When Jake joined the conversation, Rita was saying, "I flew the plane at 124 knots yesterday, three o'clock angle of attack. Now, is that 1.3 times the stall speed or isn't it? How are we supposed to verify the stall speed if we can't stall it?"

Jake merely stood and listened.

"We've told you what the stall speed is," the engineer explained patiently, "at every weight and every altitude and every configuration. Those speeds were established by *experimental* test pilots."

"Well, I'm an engineering test pilot—all navy test pilots are trained to that standard—but I can't see how we can do a proper operational evaluation of your airplane if we don't explore the left side of the envelope."

The civilian appealed to Jake. "Listen, Captain. This is the only prototype we have. If she drills a deep hole with it, we have big problems. It'll be goddamn hard to sell an airplane when all we have is the wreckage."

"What makes you think," Jake asked, "that she can't safely recover from a stall?"

"I didn't say that. You're putting words into my mouth."

"Get DeCrescentis over here." The chief engineer went off to find her.

"We have to stall that plane, Captain," Rita told him. "If those rumbles in the landing pattern yesterday were incipient compressor stalls, we'll get some real ones if we get her slowed down enough. I think that's what Consolidated doesn't want us into."

Adele DeCrescentis backed her engineer. Jake heard her out, then said, "I don't think you people really want to sell this plane to the navy."

The vice president set her jaw. "We sure as hell want it in one piece to sell to somebody."

"Well, I'll tell you this. We're going to fly that plane the way *I* want it flown or we'll stop this show right now. The navy isn't spending ten million bucks for a fly-off if all we can do is cruise the damn thing down the interstate at fifty-five. We're trying to find out if that plane can be used to fight with, Ms. DeCrescentis, not profile around the Paris Air Show."

She opened her mouth, but Jake didn't give her a chance. "I mean it! We'll fly it my way or we won't fly it. Your choice."

She looked about her, opened her mouth, then closed it again. Finally she said, "I'll have to think about it for a bit." She wheeled and made a beeline for the Consolidated offices and the phones, the chief engineer trailing after her.

"Maybe you had better make a phone call too," Rita suggested.

"Nope." He looked at Rita and grinned. "Captains have to obey orders, of course, but George Ludlow and Royce Caplinger shoved me out in front on this one. They want me to make a recommendation and take the heat, so they sort of have to let me do it my way." He shrugged. "Generally speaking, doing it your way is not very good for your career, but I've been to the mat once too often anyway. That's *why* I got this job. Ludlow's a pretty good SECNAV. He understands the navy and the people in it. He wouldn't send a guy with a shot at flag over to Capitol Hill to get his balls cut off, not if he had any other choice."

Rita looked dubious.

"Are you right about this, Miss Moravia?"

"Yes, sir. I am."

"I think so too. So that's the way we'll do it. As long as I'm in charge."

When Adele DeCrescentis returned, she agreed with Jake. Apparently the president of the company could also read tea leaves.

"Go find that Consolidated test pilot," Jake told Rita when they were alone. "Take him over to the club and buy him a drink. Find out everything he knows about stalling this invisible airplane, off the record."

"Aye aye, sir," Rita said, and marched off.

Cumulus clouds and rain squalls moving through the area from the west delayed the second flight another day, but when she finally got the plane to altitude, Rita attacked the performance envelope with vigor while Smoke Judy in the F-14 hung like glue on first one wing, then the other.

Stalls were first.

They were almost last. With the nose at ten degrees above the horizon and the power at 70 percent, she let the plane coast into the first one, but didn't get there because the pitty-pat thumping began in the intakes and increased in intensity to a drumming rat-a-tat-tat played by a drunk. The EGT rose dramatically and RPMs dropped on both engines. She could feel vibrations reaching her through the seat and throttles and rudder pedals.

Compressor stalls! Well, that mousy little test pilot for Consolidated hadn't been lying. She pushed the nose over, which incidentally worsened the thumping from behind the cockpit, and held it there while her speed increased and the noise finally abated, all the while reading the numbers from the engine instruments over the radio.

With the engines back to normal, she had another thought. If a pilot got slow and lost power in the landing pattern, on final, this thing could pancake into the ground short of the runway. Aboard ship the technical phrase for that turn of events was "ramp strike."

She smoothly pulled the nose to twenty degrees above the horizon and as her speed dropped began feeding in power until she had the throttles forward against the stops. The airspeed continued to decay. This was "the back side of the power curve," that flight regime where drag increased so dramatically as the airspeed bled off that the engines lacked sufficient power to accelerate the plane.

The onset of compressor stall was instantaneous and dramatic, a violent hammering from the intakes behind the cockpit that caused the whole plane to quiver. Before she could recover, the plane stalled. It broke crisply and fell straight forward until the nose was fifteen degrees below the horizon, then the canard authority returned. Still the engine compressors were stalled, with EGT going to the red lines and RPM dropping below 85 percent.

Rita smartly retarded the throttles to keep the engines from overtemping. The pounding continued.

Throttles to idle. EGT above red line.

She chopped the throttles to cutoff, securing the flow of fuel to the engines.

The pounding ceased. The cockpit was very quiet.

Toad remarked later that all he could hear as Rita worked to restart the engines "was God laughing."

This time as Rita approached touchdown, she flared the plane and pulled the throttles aft. Sure enough, the pounding of turbulent air in the intakes began just before the main wheels kissed the runway. She held the nose off and watched the EGT tapes twitch as the plane decelerated. When she was losing stabilator authority, she lowered the nose to the runway and smoothly applied the brakes.

"Another day, another dollar," Toad told her on the ICS.

Removing the engines from the airplane, inspecting them, inspecting the intakes and reinstalling the engines took three days, mainly because Jake Grafton demanded that a factory rep look at the compressor and turbine blades with a borescope, which had to be flown in.

Consolidated's chief engineer was livid. He was so furious that he didn't trust himself to speak, and turned away when anyone in uniform approached him. Adele DeCrescentis was equally outraged, but she hid it better. She listened to Rita and reviewed the telemetry and videotapes and grunted when Jake Grafton spoke to her.

The navy personnel left the Consolidated employees to their misery.

"We're wasting our time flying that bird again," Les Richards and George Wilson told Jake. "It's unsat and there is no possible fix that would cure the problem. The whole design sucks."

"How do you know they can't fix it?"

"Well, look at it. At high angles of attack the intakes are blanked off by the cockpit and the shape of the fuselage, that aerodynamic shape. How *could* they fix it?"

"Goddamn, I'm not an aeronautical engineer! How the hell would I know?"

"Well, I am," Wilson said, "and they *can't.*"

"Never say never. Regardless, we're going to fly this bird five times. I don't want anyone to say that we didn't give Consolidated a fair chance."

"We're wasting our time and the navy's money."

"What's a few million?" Jake asked rhetorically. The real objective was to get money for an acceptable airplane from Congress. So he was philosophical.

Toad Tarkington slipped down the hall to his wife's room when he thought everyone else was in bed. They had been running a low-profile romance since they arrived in Tonopah.

"Tell me again," Toad said, "just what that Consolidated test pilot said about stalls when you pumped him. What's his name?"

"Stu Vinich. He just said they had had some compressor-stall problems at high angles of attack."

"Nothing else? Nothing about how serious they were?"

"He couldn't, Toad. The company was downplaying the whole subject. People who talk out of school draw unemployment checks."

"We were damned lucky that thing didn't spin. And we were lucky the engines relit."

"Luck is a part of the job," Rita told him.

"Yeah. If we had punched and our chutes hadn't opened, Vinich would have just stood at our graves and shook his head."

"He said enough. I knew what to expect."

Toad turned out the light and snuggled down beside her.

Jake Grafton was poking and prodding the plane, trying to stay out of the technicians' way, when he noticed Adele DeCrescentis watching him. He walked over. "You know," he said, "this thing reminds me of a twelve-ton Swiss watch."

"A quartz watch," the vice president said.

"Yeah. Anyway, I was wondering. Just how hard would it be for your folks to put a twenty-millimeter cannon on this plane?"

"A gun?" She appeared dumbfounded, as if the idea had never occurred to her.

"Uh-huh. A gun. A little Gatling, snuggled inside the fuselage with five hundred rounds or so. What do you think?"

"When we were designing this plane, not a single, solitary air force officer ever even breathed the word 'gun.' "

"Somehow that doesn't surprise me. But would it be feasible?"

"With some fairly major design changes, which will cost a good deal of money, I suppose it might be. It would take a full-blown engineering study to determine that for sure. But why? A machine like this? You want it down in the weeds dueling with antiaircraft guns? Shooting at tanks?"

"When tanks are the threat, Ms. DeCrescentis, we won't be able to shoot million-dollar missiles at all of 'em. The Warsaw Pact has over fifty *thousand* tanks. A nice little twenty-millimeter with armor-piercing shells would be just the right prescription."

Senator Hiram Duquesne was not philosophical when he telephoned George Ludlow. "You keeping up on what's going on out in Tonopah?" he thundered.

"Well, I get reports from Vice Admiral Dunedin. Captain Grafton reports to him several times a day."

"I want to know why the officer in charge out there insisted on performing maneuvers that the manufacturer did not feel the plane was ready for, or safe to perform."

"He's doing an op eval. He knows what he's doing."

"Oh does he? He's got a twenty-five-year-old woman with no previous test experience flying that plane, a *four-hundred-million-dollar prototype!*"

"She's not twenty-five. She's twenty-seven."

"Have you seen her?"

"What do you mean?"

"I mean what the hell is going on over there, George? A lot of people have a lot riding on the outcome of this fly-off. And you got Bo Derek's little sister out there flying the planes! Is she the best test pilot you people have? My God, we've been spending millions for that Test Pilot School in Pax River—is she the best you've got?"

"If you have any information that implies she's incompetent, I'd like to hear it."

"I hear she intentionally shut down both engines while she was up in the sky. Now Consolidated is spending a ton checking them for damage. I'll bet Chuck Yeager never shut down both engines on a test flight at the same time!"

"I wouldn't know. You'd have to ask the air force."

"Don't get cute. I'm serious. Dead serious. Don't let that hero fly-boy Grafton and his bimbo test pilot screw this up, George. I'm warning you."

"Thanks."

"By the way, the authorization for reactors for that new carrier you guys want to start? My committee voted this morning to delete it. Maybe next year, huh?"

The senator hung up before Ludlow could respond.

Jake Grafton changed Rita's test profile for the last three flights. He had her avoid all high-angle-of-attack maneuvers, though he did let her ease toward the advertised five-G limit, where the airflow to the engines once again became turbulent and began to rumble.

The three flights took another ten days. When they were finished the navy crowd spent three more days correlating their data and talking to Consolidated engineers, then packed up for the return to Washington. It would be three weeks before they came back to fly the TRX prototype.

On their last night in Tonopah the navy contingent threw a party in the officers' club for a very subdued group from Consolidated. Adele DeCrescentis didn't attend, which was perhaps just as well. Along toward midnight, after Toad Tarkington had enjoyed the entire salubrious effect of alcohol and had begun the downhill slide, he spotted Stu Vinich in a corner putting the moves on some woman from Consolidated's avionics division. He strolled over, tapped Vinich on the shoulder, and as the test pilot turned, flattened him with one roundhouse punch.

21

Jake Grafton was amazed when he saw Amy at the passenger terminal at Andrews Air Force Base. In the three weeks he had been gone the child had visibly grown. "Hi, Jake," she warbled, and ran to throw her arms around him.

"Miss me?" he asked.

"Not as much as Callie did," was the sophisticated reply.

As he and Callie waited for the luggage to be off-loaded from the airplane, Callie visited with the other officers who had ridden the DC-9 from Tonopah. Jake made a fuss over Amy and teased her a little, causing her cheeks to redden. But she stayed right there beside him, saying hello to everyone and smiling broadly when spoken to.

"So how'd it go?" Callie asked him as they walked to the car.

Jake shrugged. Everything was classified. "Okay, I guess. And you?"

"I stopped going to Dr. Arnold. Last Friday was my last appointment."

Jake set his luggage on the pavement and gave her a tight squeeze as Amy skipped on ahead, her black hair bobbing with every bound. Callie looked happier than Jake had seen her in a long, long time.

* * *

The next morning, a Tuesday, he spent closeted with Admiral Dunedin going over the test results. They watched videotapes and looked at numbers, and began writing down tentative conclusions.

"So how did Moravia do?" the admiral asked at one point.

"Fine. Good stick, keeps her wits about her, knows more aeronautical engineering than I even knew existed."

"So you want to keep her for the TRX bird?"

"No reason not to."

The admiral told him about the conversation Senator Duquesne had had with George Ludlow. "The secretary didn't tell me to fire her, or keep her, or anything else," Dunedin concluded. "He just relayed the conversation."

"Let me see if I understand this, Admiral. Duquesne's committee deleted the appropriation for reactors for the new carrier from this year's budget. Is he implying that if we get another test pilot he'll put it back in?"

"No. I think the message is that unless the navy buys the Consolidated plane, he's not going to be—he'll be less enthusiastic about navy budget requests."

"Sir, I don't think Consolidated's plane can be modified enough to meet the mission requirements for a new attack plane. And you have to factor Athena into the equation. With Athena we won't need to buy all that expensive stealth stuff on every airplane."

"Fly the TRX plane. Then we'll see."

"Do you want me to get another test pilot?"

"I just wanted you to understand what's going on. The temperature is rising. Ludlow and all the politicos in SECDEF's office are playing politics right along with everyone else in this town. The admirals and generals are parading over to the hill for hearings. It's that merry time of year."

"I think we have to keep Moravia. After she's flown both planes she can make point-by-point comparisons that can't be questioned for extraneous reasons. Consolidated will beat us to death with Rita's corpse if we use another test pilot to fly the TRX plane, and then recommend it instead of theirs. They'll claim they got shafted by an incompetent, inexperienced pilot. You and I will look like blundering idiots, or worse."

"I agree," the admiral said.

Proposals from contractors were arriving based on the navy's Request for Proposal (RFP) on the Athena project. The afternoon was devoted to examining these documents, which were as thick as metropolitan telephone directories. "How come these guys can't just say what they want to say and leave it at that?"

"Lawyers wrote these."

"I can't make head or tail of some of this stuff. They've used every acronym in the book and made up a bunch more. These things look like dispatches from Babel."

One morning several days later Dreyfus stuck his head in Luis Camacho's office door. "The Minotaur mailed the Russians another letter."

Dreyfus handed Camacho a copy and sank into a chair while his boss perused it. Addressed to the Soviet ambassador, the letter was a commentary on Gorbachev's recent visit to Cuba. The last paragraph contained some advice on how the Soviets should handle Castro.

"On generic copy paper, as usual. Just like all the others."

"Has the original been through the lab yet?"

"Nope. I just took it down."

"Go get it. I want to see it."

"What for? That's an accurate copy."

"Please. Now."

With a shake of his head, Dreyfus complied.

Camacho opened his desk drawer and pulled out a pair of rubber gloves, which he worked onto his hands without the benefit of baby powder. Then he extracted a jar from the lower left drawer. He opened it and used a letter opener to smear a little of the blue jelly on his desk. Oops, too much. He used a piece of paper from a legal pad to blot the mess, then stared at the stain on the back of the paper. After firmly closing the jar, he stowed it back in his desk.

When Dreyfus returned with the letter, Camacho was at the window idly watching the pedestrians on E Street. He gingerly opened the plastic bag and extracted the letter while Dreyfus watched openmouthed. He laid the fully opened letter on the desk and pressed. Then he turned it over and examined the blue smear on the back. Satisfactory. Not too much, yet enough for the lab to get a sample. He refolded the letter and replaced it in the see-through plastic bag.

"Take it back to the lab."

"Did I see that?"

"No. You are as ignorant as you look."

"You're the boss."

"Indeed. And while you're at it, see if this word is encoded in the text." Camacho seized a piece of scratch paper and carefully printed a word. "Kilderkin." He passed the paper to Dreyfus.

"Anything else?" Dreyfus asked hopefully.

"Like what?"

"Oh, I dunno. I've got the feeling that neat and wonderful wheels are turning like crazy, though I haven't the foggiest idea why. Or where the wheels will take us."

"What do you want? A Tuesday-morning miracle?"

"It doesn't have to be a miracle. A tiny little sleight of hand would be welcome. Or a very brief explanation."

Camacho shot his cuffs. "See. Nothing up my sleeves. No hat, so no rabbit."

Dreyfus stood and ambled toward the door. "Kilderkin, huh? You know, I get the impression that—"

"Never trust your impressions. Wait for evidence."

"So what do we do with the original letter when the lab's through with it?" The agent fluttered the plastic bag gently.

"The usual. Stick it back in its envelope and let the post office deliver it. I'm sure the ambassador will convey the writer's advice to the members of the Politburo at his earliest opportunity. This may be the great watershed in U.S.-Soviet re—" He stopped because Dreyfus was already out the door and had closed it behind him.

At ten o'clock Dreyfus was back. He waited patiently until Camacho was off the phone, then said, "Okay, how'd you know?"

"Know what?"

"That that antique word from merry ol' England would crack it?"

"Kilderkin?"

"Yeah."

"Elementary, my dear Watson. A kilderkin is a barrel or cask. It contains something, as that letter did."

"Shit."

Camacho extended his hand. Dreyfus passed him a small piece of white paper containing the three words from the message and waited while he examined it. The second word was "kilderkin."

"That's all," Camacho said, looking up as he folded the small page and stuck it into his shirt pocket. "Thanks."

"Always a pleasure, Holmes."

When he was again alone, Camacho dialed a telephone number from memory and identified himself to the woman who answered. In a moment the person he wanted was on the line and he said, "Let's have lunch."

"Can't today. Pretty busy."

"Appointments?"

"Yep."

"Cancel them."

"Where and when?"

"On the mall, in front of the Air and Space Museum. Twelve or so."

The line went dead in Camacho's ear. He cradled the instrument. He leaned back in his chair and looked out his little window at the buildings on the other side of E Street. He pursed his lips and, breathing deeply in and out, gently massaged his head with one hand.

An hour later he was out on the sidewalk in his shirt sleeves, striding along. He had left his pistol locked in his desk drawer, his jacket and tie over the back of his chair. He was violating FBI policy but so be it. The summer heat was palpable, a living, breathing monster no doubt goaded by the sheer numbers of humans who were defying it this midday. Where did all these people come from? The streets were packed with cars, taxis, snorting buses and trucks, the sidewalks covered with swarming humanity.

Overhead the summer haze made the sky appear a gauzy, indistinct white, but it failed to soften the sun's fierce glare. Camacho's shirt wilted swiftly and glued itself to the small of his back. He could feel the perspiration soaking into his socks. Little beads of sweat congealed around the hairs on the back of his hands, and he automatically wiped the palms on his trousers as he walked.

Every shady circle under the mall trees was home to office workers and tourists who could no longer stay on their feet. Children sprawled and played on the hard-packed dirt. The grass that had grown under the trees so profusely this spring had succumbed weeks ago under the impact of infinite feet. An endless stream of joggers and serious runners pounded up and down the gravel paths of the mall, little dust spurts rising from the thud of each foot. The combined effect was a thin brown curtain of dust that rose into the air and tilted away toward the monolithic art museums that lined the northern side of the open expanse.

The street in front of the Air and Space Museum was bumper to bumper with tour buses. As he came closer, Luis Camacho threaded his way through the hordes of teenagers and middle-aged pink people in shorts and cutesy T-shirts.

The great American sightseeing excursion was in full swing. Herds of Japanese tourists clad in the requisite button-down short-sleeved shirts clustered near some of the buses and busily snapped their cameras at each other, the huge windowless museums to the north, the distant Washington Monument and the dome of the Capitol rising in the east like a corpulent moon. In spite of the oppressive heat, the mood was cheerful, gay.

Camacho found a spot in the shade near a tree and sat down gratefully. Cigarette butts and candy-bar wrappers littered the ground. He didn't care. To his left a souvenir stand was doing a land-office business in film, soft drinks and ice-cream bars. Squall-ing youngsters and frisky youths queued like soldiers in the sun as they waited for their turn to surrender their money to the happy merchant.

Derelicts shuffled slowly through the human forest. They were blithely ignored as they mined the trash bins for pop cans. A cou-ple of alkies snoozed further away from the street in the shade cast by the treetops, out where the grass still survived: their day had apparently ended some hours ago when the critical intoxication level had been reached and surpassed.

He had been there no more than five minutes when he spotted the man he had come to meet feeling his way through the crowd, looking about him. Camacho stood and walked toward him.

"Morning, Admiral."

"Let's get the hell out of this crowd," Tyler Henry growled. "Next time pick a quieter spot." Henry was clad in beige slacks and a yellow pullover with a little fox on the right breast. His eyes were hidden behind the naval aviator's de rigueur sunglasses.

"Aye aye, sir."

The two men walked east, toward the duck pond at the base of Capitol Hill. When they were out of earshot of the tourists and drunks, Henry said, "Okay. I haven't got much time today. What d'ya want?"

"We intercepted another letter from the Minotaur this morning. Thought you'd be interested. Here's the coded message it con-tained." The FBI agent passed him the little square of words with the three words penciled on it.

Admiral Henry stopped dead and stared at the words on the

paper. "Kilderkin. Holy fuck! The damned Minotaur is giving away *Athena*!"

"Yes."

"Awww, *goddamn*! Awww . . ."

Camacho gingerly removed the paper from the admiral's fingers, refolded it and put it in his pocket.

"And I suppose you assholes with badges just stuffed the fucking letter back in the envelope and gave it to the postman?" When he saw Camacho's silent nod, Henry scuffed angrily at the dirt. He indulged himself in some heavy cussing.

"Do you know what Athena is? Do you silly half-wit peepers have *any* idea what the hell Athena is all about?"

"Well, you said—"

"I *know* what I told you! I'm asking if any of your superiors have even the slightest glimmer how valuable Athena is."

"I don't know."

The admiral gestured hugely in exasperation. "Just what in the name of God is going on, Luis?"

They had reached the edge of the duck pond. Camacho stood with folded arms and gazed across the placid surface, past the statue of U.S. Grant on horseback, at the imposing edifice of the Capitol building. "I can only guess," he said softly.

"But do they have any idea what Athena is—just what the hell they are giving away?"

"I don't know what they know."

"This isn't fiber optics, or ring laser gyros, or any of that other magic shit they've been letting the Minotaur cart out of the vault. Athena is the Hope Diamond, the mother lode, the most precious, priceless treasure in the vault. Do those stupid, ignorant, incompetent, half-wit political pimps have even the faintest glimmer what it is the Minotaur just laid his filthy hands on?

"I don't know!"

"Athena will make radar obsolete. Inevitably it will become cheaper and we'll be able to miniaturize it, get it so small and cheap we can use it to hide tanks and jeeps, not just ships and airplanes. We can hide satellites with it. In ten years or so we can probably hide submarines with it. Athena will revolutionize strategy, tactics, weaponry. And *we've* got it! The Russians don't! Yet! If we can keep them from getting it for just a couple years—just a couple years—I tell you, Luis, Athena will give America such a

huge technological edge that war will become a political and military impossibility. *War will be impossible!"*

"I believe you."

"Then *why?* Tell me that! *Why?"*

Camacho shrugged.

"What could be so goddamn valuable that they would bet the ranch, the nation, the future of mankind?"

"I don't know for sure, and I couldn't tell you if I did."

The admiral exploded. Thirty-some years in the navy had really taught him how to swear. Camacho didn't think he had ever heard such a virtuoso performance.

Finally Henry stopped spluttering. Bitterness had replaced his exasperation. "I think there's some treason going on over in your shop, Camacho. That's all it could be."

"Better go easy with that word."

"Treason." Henry spit it out. "Don't like it, huh? By God, if Congress gets hold of this, that may be the kindest word those slimy spook bastards ever hear. People will go to prison over this. You wait and see."

Camacho lost his temper. "I showed you that piece of paper so you could take some reasonable steps to protect Athena, you swabbie," he snarled. "Like change the code or empty the file. Not so you could shoot your mouth off about things you know nothing about, things that will ruin you and *me.* Now I've heard all the crap from you that I'm gonna listen to. I've heard *enough.* One more crack out of line and I'll come get you with a national security warrant and you can sit in a padded cell at St. Elizabeth's until I think it's safe to let you out. That may be when you're a corpse. Is *that* what you want?"

"No," said Tyler Henry contritely, aware that he had gone too far.

"Just one word, Admiral, just one little slip by you, and I'll come after you with that goddamn warrant. You'd better believe it! You and John Hinckley can spend your declining years together."

Camacho wheeled and walked away, leaving Henry standing there staring at his retreating back.

22

Tyler Henry accompanied the ATA project crew when they returned to Tonopah in July. The admiral shook hands with the TRX engineers and spent three hours inspecting the plane, which occupied the hangar where the Consolidated bird had rested, and asking questions. At his request Rita Moravia and Toad Tarkington remained beside him. Many of his questions were directed at Rita, but when he wanted to know something about the navigation/attack system, he asked Toad.

"Is that right, Franks?" the admiral growled at the TRX program manager after he had listened carefully to one of Toad's answers.

Harry Frank nodded his assent. It looked to Jake as if Franks had lost ten pounds or so, but the cotton of his colorful sport shirt still seemed loaded near its tensile strength where it stretched over his middle. Franks rolled the stump of a dead cigar from one corner of his mouth to the other and winked at Jake.

With his shoulders thrown back and his genial air of self-assurance and command, Franks reminded Jake of the salty chief petty officers he had grown to respect and admire when he was a junior officer. Franks certainly was no modern naval officer or chief in mufti, not with that gut. In today's navy even the chief petty officers were slimmed down or retired, victims of rigid weight standards enforced with awesome zeal. The senior admirals liked to think of their service as a lean, mean fighting machine, which of course it was not. More accurately, the navy was a host of skinny technocrats. Not only were most sailors technicians, most of the officers spent the vast majority of their professional lives as administrators, experts on instructions, notices, regulations, and budgets. The bureaucracy was mean but certainly not lean.

Confusing, Jake mused, glancing once again at Franks's portico, very confusing.

Unlike the trendy and not so trendy humans who stood admiring it, TRX's prototype was exquisite functionality. The mission was all-weather attack. The plane would be launched from the deck of an aircraft carrier, in any weather day or night, to penetrate the enemy's defenses, find and destroy the target without outside aid, and return to the tiny ship in the vast ocean from whence it came, there to be refueled and rearmed and launched again. Every form and feature had been carefully crafted for the rigid demands of this mission, and no other.

As he stood listening to the engineers describe their creation, Jake Grafton's eye fell on Rita Moravia and Toad Tarkington, two intelligent young people in perfect health with good educations. They and others like them would have to use this machine as a weapon, when and if. The technocrats would build it and take it to sea. Yet the plane would never be anything but a cunning collection of glue, diodes, and weird alloys. The attack must come from the hearts of those who rode it down the catapult into the sky.

The important things in war never change. As always, victory would go to those who prepared wisely, planned well, and drove home their thrusts with a grim, fierce determination.

When the F-14 chase plane was safely airborne, Rita Moravia smoothly advanced the throttles to the stops and let the two improved F404 engines wind up to full power as she checked the trim setting one more time. The cockpit noise level was higher than in the Consolidated plane, and no doubt the roar of the engines outside was also louder. The exhausts had not been as deeply inset above the wing and cooled as extensively with bypass air from the compressors; consequently more of the engine's rated power was available to propel the plane through the atmosphere. And the noise was not the only clue: she could feel slightly more vibration and a perceptibly greater dip of the nose as the thrust of the screaming engines compressed the nose-gear oleo.

"Anytime you're ready," Toad announced.

After dictating all the engine data onto the audio recorder wired into the ICS, Rita released the brakes. The nose oleo rebounded and the plane rolled smartly, picking up speed.

The little thumps and bumps as the wheels crossed the expansion joints in the concrete runway came quicker and quicker. The needle on the airspeed indicator came off the peg. On the holographic Heads-Up Display—the HUD—functioning in this prototype, the symbology came alive. The sound of the engines dropped in volume and pitch as the machine accelerated.

Now the weight came off the nose wheel as the stabilator and living wing controls took effect and began to exert aerodynamic force on the nose, trying to lift it from the runway. Oh yes. With the joystick held ever so lightly in her fingers, she felt the nose wheel bobble, skip lightly, then rise from the concrete as the wings gripped the air.

The master warning light illuminated—bright yellow—and beside the HUD the right engine fire warning light—brilliant blood red.

She smoothly pulled both throttles to idle, then secured the right one. Nose held off until the main mounts were firmly planted, decelerating nicely, speed brakes and flaperon pop-up deployed, five thousand feet of concrete remaining, slowing . . .

"Ginger aborting," she broadcast on the radio. "Fire light, right engine, roll the truck."

Nose wheel firmly on the concrete, Rita applied the brakes with a firm, steady pressure. She rolled to a stop and killed the remaining engine as she opened the canopy. The fire truck charged toward them.

Rita pulled her helmet off. "Any fire?" she shouted at the man on the truck as the engine noise died. Without conscious effort, her fingers danced across the panels turning off everything.

"Not that we can see."

"Let's get out anyway," Rita told Toad, who had already toggled his quick-release fittings and was craning out of the rear cockpit, looking for smoke.

Standing beside the runway, perspiring profusely as the summer desert sun cooked them, Rita and Toad heard the news five minutes later from Harry Franks. A swarm of technicians already had the engine bay doors open. "Electrical problem, I'm sure. We'll tow it into the hangar and check it out. Nice abort," he added with a nod at Rita. "You two want to ride back in the van? It's air-conditioned."

"Yep," said Tarkington. "Nothing like air force hospitality."

They flew the plane for the first time the following day. Rita came back from the flight with a large smile on her face. "Captain," she told Jake Grafton as she brushed sweat-soaked hair from her forehead and eyes, "that's one sweet machine. Power, handling, plenty of G available, sweet and honest. A *very* nice airplane."

Before Harry Franks' grin could get too wide, she started detailing problems: "Controls are oversensitive. Twitchy. Flying the ball is a real challenge. The left generator dropped off the line twice, which was maybe a good thing, because we found the power relay works as advertised; the inertial stayed up and humming. Toad got the computer running again without any problem each time. And the rudder trim . . ."

When Rita paused for air, Toad chimed in. "I'd like to go over how those fiber optic data buses work with someone, one more time. I'm still trying to figure out how . . ."

The routine was exactly like it had been a month before. Telemetry, videotapes and the Flight Data Recorder info were carefully reviewed and the data compiled for a later in-depth analysis. Those problems that could be fixed were, and major problems were carefully delineated for factory study.

Jake Grafton demanded all his people quit work at 9 P.M. He wanted them rested and back at the hangar at six each morning. Harry Franks worked his technicians around the clock in shifts, although he himself put in eighteen-hour days and was on call at night.

Toad tried to get out of the hangar as often as possible. The air force was using this field for stealth fighters—F-117s—and several other low-observable prototypes, including the B-2. Every so often if he was outside he would hear a rumble and there, before his very eyes, would be some exotic shape that seemed to defy the laws of gravity and common sense as it cleaved the hot blue desert air. He felt vaguely guilty, and slightly naughty. To satisfy his idle curiosity he was seeing something that the Powers That Be—Those Who Knew—the Appointed, Anointed Keepers of the Secret—didn't think his little mind should be burdened with. So he stood and gawked, curious and mystified, a little boy at the knothole watching the love rites of the groping teenagers. He would go back to work shaking his head and trot outside again, hopefully, several hours later.

He bumped into Jake Grafton on one of these excursions. The captain stood with his hands in his pockets watching a pair of F-117s come into the break.

"Amazing, huh?" Jake said.

"Yes, sir."

"I've been flying for twenty-five years," Grafton said, "and reading everything I could about planes for ten more. And all this time I never even *dreamed* . . ."

"I know what you mean. It's like science and technology have gone crazy in some kind of souped-up hothouse. The technology is breeding, and we don't recognize the offspring."

"And it's not just one technical field. It's airframes and engines, composites and glues, fabricating techniques, Computer-Assisted Design, avionics and computers and lasers and radars. It's everything! In five years everything I learned in a lifetime will be obsolete."

Or less than five years, Jake told himself glumly as the bat-winged B-2 drifted quietly overhead. Maybe everything I know is obsolete *now*!

When Toad Tarkington thought about it afterwards, he remembered the sun. It was one of those little details you notice at the time and don't think about, yet remember later.

He had seen the sun many times before in the cockpit, bright and warm and bathing everything in a brilliant, clean light, its beams darting and dancing across the cockpit as the plane turned and climbed and dived. A clean light, bright, oh so bright, warming bodies encased in Nomex and sweating inside helmets and gloves and flying boots. This was part of flying, and after a while you didn't notice it anymore. Yet for a few seconds that morning he did notice it. The memory of it stayed with him, and somehow, looking back, it seemed important.

He was deep into the mysteries of the radar and computer and how they talked to each other, acutely aware of how little time aloft he had. The radar's picture was automatically recorded on videotape, but he muttered into the ICS—the audio track of the tape—like a voodoo priest so he would know later just what the gain and brightness had been for each particular presentation. He worked fast. These flights were grotesquely short.

Rita concentrated on flying the plane, on keeping it precisely on speed and on altitude, exactly where the test profile required. She was extraordinarily good at this type of flying, Toad had discovered. She had the knack. It required skill, patience and self-discipline as one concentrated on the task at hand to the exclusion of everything else, all qualities Rita Moravia possessed in abundance. The airspeed needle stayed glued on the proper number and all the other needles did precisely what they were supposed to, almost as if they were slaves to Rita's iron will.

Toad also kept track of their position over the earth, and every now and then wasted three seconds on a glance over at the chase plane. Still there, precisely where it should be. Smoke Judy was a no-nonsense, Sierra Hotel pilot who had almost nothing to say on the radio; he knew how busy Rita and Toad were.

Periodically Toad reminded Rita of which task was next on the list. He could just see the top of her helmet, partially masked by the top of her ejection seat, if he looked straight ahead. He could also see the upside-down reflection of her lap and arms in the canopy, weirdly distorted by the curvature. Her hand on the stick —he could see that because in this plane the control stick was where it should be, between the pilot's legs.

And the sun. He saw the brilliance of the sun's gaze as the sublime light played across the kneeboard on his right thigh and back and forth across the instruments on the panel before him.

"How's control response?" he asked.

"Better." In a moment she added, "Still not right, though."

He would never have known it from the sensations reaching him through the plane. The ride was smooth as glass. "I told Orville and Wilbur they were wasting their time. They wouldn't listen."

"What's next?"

She already knew, of course. She had prepared the flight profile. To humor her, Toad consulted his copy. "High-G chandelles."

"Okay."

He felt the surge as the power increased. Rita wasted no time. He saw her glance at Smoke Judy, assuring herself the F-14 was clear, then the left wing sagged gently as the nose began to rise and the G increased. The G came on in a steadily rising grunt as the horizon tilted crazily. Rita was flying the G line on the holographic HUD. Toad temporarily abandoned his radar research and strained every muscle in the classic M-1 maneuver, trying to retain blood in his head and upper body as he forced air in and out past his lips. The inflatable pads in his G suit had become giant sausages, squeezing his legs to keep the blood from pooling there.

This maneuver was designed to allow Rita to explore the limits of G and maneuverability at ever-changing airspeeds. Toad felt the nibble of the stall buffet, and for the first time felt the wings rock sloppily, almost as if Rita were fighting to control their position.

"I'm having some troub—" she said, but before she could complete the thought the plane departed.

The down wing quit flying and the upper wing flopped them over inverted. The plane began to gyrate wildly. Positive Gs mashed them for half a second, then negative Gs threw them up against their harness straps, but since the airplane was inverted, it was upward toward the earth. The airplane spun like a lopsided Frisbee, bucking up and down madly as the Gs slammed them, positive, negative, positive, negative. The ride was so violent Toad couldn't read the MFDs on the panel before him.

"Inverted spin," he gasped over the ICS.

"The controls—it won't—" Rita sounded exasperated.

"You're in an inverted spin," Toad heard a hard, calm male voice say. Smoke Judy on the radio.

"I'm—the controls—"

"Twenty-nine thousand . . . twenty-eight . . ." By a supreme effort of will Toad made himself concentrate on the altimeter and read the spinning needles.

"Spin assist," he reminded her. This switch would allow the horizontal stabilator its full travel, not restricted by its high-speed limited throw. The danger was if the pilot pulled too hard at high speed without the mechanical limit, the tail might be ripped away. Right now Rita needed all the help she could get to pull the nose down.

"It's on."

"Twenty-five thousand." He was having trouble staying conscious. The ride was vicious, violent beyond description. His vision closed in until he was looking through a pipe. He knew the signs. He was passing out. "Twenty-two," he croaked.

Miraculously the violent pitching action of the nose decreased and he felt as if he were being thrown sideways. As the G decreased, his vision came back. Rita had them out of the spin and diving. She had the power back, about 80 percent or so. She rolled the plane upright and the G came on steadily as she pulled to get them out of their rocketing dive. "Okay," she whispered, "okay, baby, come to Mama."

The wings started rocking again as the G increased, and Toad opened his mouth to shout a warning. Too late. The right wing slammed down and the plane rolled inverted again. "Spin," was all he could get out.

He fought the slamming up and down. "Seventeen thousand . . ."

"Rita, you'd better eject." The hard, fast voice of Smoke Judy.

"I've got it," Rita shouted on the radio. "Stay with me." That was for Toad. She had the nose coming steadily down now, that yawning sensation again as she fed in full rudder.

"Fifteen grand," Toad advised.

They were running out of sky.

"It's the controls! I've—"

"Thirteen!"

She was out of the spin now, upright, but the nose was still way low, seventy degrees below the horizon. Power at idle, she deployed the speed brakes and began to cautiously lift the nose.

"Eleven thousand."

"Come on, baby."

"Ten."

The ground was horribly close. Their speed was rapidly building, even with the boards out and engines at idle. The ground elevation here was at least four thousand feet above sea level, so they were within six thousand feet of the ground, now five, still forty degrees nose down. They would make it. Rita added another pound of back pressure to the stick.

The left wing snapped down.

Toad pulled the ejection handle.

The windblast hit him like the fist of God. He was tumbling, then he wasn't, now hurling toward the earth—an earth so close he could plainly see every rock and bush—and cursing himself for the fool that he was for waiting so long. Lazily, slowly, as if time didn't matter, the seat kicked him loose with a thump.

The ground was *right there,* racing up at him. He closed his eyes. He was going to die now. So this is how it feels . . .

A tremendous shock snapped through him, almost ripping his boots off. The opening shock of the parachute canopy.

The ground was right there! He swung for another few seconds, then smashed into a thicket of brush. Too late he remembered he should have protected his head. He came to rest in the middle of an opaque dust cloud.

He was conscious through it all. He wiggled his limbs experimentally. Still in one piece, thank the Lord!

Rita! Where was Rita?

He was standing before the dust had cleared, ripping his helmet off and trying to see. He tore at his Koch fittings. There! Rid of the chute.

Striding out of the brush, almost falling, looking.

Another dust cloud. Several hundred yards away and down the hill slightly. Something had impacted there. Rita? But there was no chute visible.

Mother of God!

He began to run.

23

You still here?" the doctor asked when he saw Toad leaning against the counter at the nurses' station. The doctor was about forty and clad in a loose green hospital garment with tennis shoes on his feet.

"How is she?"

"Unconscious." The doctor swabbed the perspiration from his forehead with his sleeve. "I don't know when she'll come around. I don't know if she ever will."

"What's wrong with her?" Toad demanded, grasping the doctor by the arm.

"Everything." He patiently pried Toad's hand loose. "Her spleen exploded. Fractured skull with severe concussion. Blood in her urine—kidney damage. Broken ribs, busted collarbone, two fractured vertebrae. That's just the stuff we know about. We're still looking."

"She hit the ground before her parachute opened," Toad explained. "The drag chute was out and the main chute must have been partially deployed. She just needed another hundred feet or so."

"Her status is extremely unstable." The doctor took out a pack of cigarettes and lit one. "I don't know how she's made it this long." He flipped the ash on the floor, right in front of the No Smoking sign. "The average person wouldn't have made it to the hospital. But she's young and she's in great shape, good strong heart. Perhaps, just perhaps . . ." He took a deep drag and exhaled the smoke through his nose, savoring it.

"Is she gonna be able to fly again?" Toad wanted to know.

The doctor took a small portable ashtray from his pocket and stubbed out the cigarette in it after a couple more deep drags. He looked Toad over carefully before he spoke. "I don't think you heard what I said. She'll be lucky if she lives. Walking out of this hospital will be a miracle. There's nothing you can do for her. Now why don't you go back to the Q and take one of those sleeping pills the nurse gave you. You need to get some rest."

The doctor turned away from Toad and leaned his elbows on the counter of the nurses' station. "When you get Lieutenant Moravia's emergency data sheet from the navy, let me know. We'll have to notify her next of kin. They may want to fly out here to be with her."

Toad smacked the waist-high counter with his hand. "I am her next of kin. She's my *wife.*"

"Oh," he said, looking Toad over again, then rubbing the back of his neck. "Sorry. I didn't know that."

"I want to be in the room with her. I'll sit in the chair."

The doctor opened his mouth, closed it and glanced at the nurses, then shrugged. "Sure, Lieutenant. Okay. Why not?"

Thirty minutes later Jake Grafton stuck his head into the room. He looked at Rita, the two nurses, the doctor, the IV drips and the heart monitor, then motioned to Toad, who followed him out into the hall.

"How is she?"

"She's in a deep coma. She may die." Tarkington repeated what the doctor had told him.

Jake Grafton listened carefully, his face expressionless. When Toad finally ran down, he said, "C'mon. Let's go find a place to sit." They ended up in the staff lounge in plastic chairs at the only table, between a microwave oven and a pop machine. "What happened out there today?"

Toad's recapitulation of the flight took thirty minutes. After he had heard it all, from takeoff to loading Rita into the meat wagon, Jake had questions, lots of them.

They had been talking for over an hour when a young enlisted man opened the door and stuck his head in. "Captain Grafton? There's an Admiral Dunedin on the phone for you."

"Tell him I'll be right there."

On the way down the hall he told Toad, "You go check on Rita. I'll see you in a bit."

The phone was in the duty officer's office. Jake held it to his ear as the air force officer, a woman, closed the door on her way out. "This is Captain Grafton, sir."

"Admiral Dunedin, Jake. We got your message about the crash. How's Moravia?"

"In a coma. It's an open question whether she'll pull through. She ejected too low and her chute didn't fully open before she hit the ground. She's got a fractured skull, damaged spleen and a variety of other problems. Five or six bones broken."

"And Tarkington?"

"Not a scratch."

"So what happened?"

"Well, sir, the way it looks right now, the fly-by-wire system is suspect. We were having troubles with the control inputs—they were too much at low speeds—so we went with new E-PROMs. Now, all those parameters are supposed to be trouble-shot and double-checked on the bench test equipment and all that, but something went wrong somewhere. The plane got away from Rita in a high-G maneuver and went into an inverted spin. She recovered, then it departed again when she pulled G on the pullout. Coming out of the second spin, she just ran out of sky. It flipped on the pullout and Toad punched.

"Hindsight and all, they should have ejected on the second departure, but . . . They were trying to save the plane. Now it looks like Toad may have punched too late for Rita."

"How's Tarkington taking it?"

"Blaming himself. I might as well tell you, if you didn't know, they're married."

There was a pregnant silence. "I didn't know."

"Yeah."

"Did that have any bearing on this accident?"

"Not that I can see. They stayed with the plane because it was a prototype and they were trying to save it. Rita thought she could save it all the way down. The last departure at five thousand feet above the ground made it a lost cause, so Toad punched them both out while they still had a little room left in the seat performance envelope. Apparently they were closer to the edge of the envelope than he thought."

"TRX doesn't have another prototype."

"I know. We're going to have to go with the data we have. I'll get started on the report as soon as I get back to Washington. But I would appreciate it if you would get a team of experts from the company that made that fly-by-wire system out here, like tomorrow. Have them bring their test equipment. We need some instant answers."

"You have the box?"

"One of them, anyway. It's a little mashed up, but all the circuitry and boards appear intact. I'm hoping they can test it."

"Why not just put it on a plane to the factory?"

"I want to be there when they check it out. And just now I can't leave here."

"I understand."

They talked for several more minutes, then hung up. Both men had a lot to do.

Toad wandered the corridors, looking in on Rita from time to time. A nurse was with her every minute. The evening nurse was a woman in her thirties, and she never gave him more than a glance. Rita was in good hands, he told himself. But she didn't move. She just lay there in the ICU cubicle with her eyes closed, her chest slowly rising and falling in time with the mechanical hissing and clicking of the respirator. The IVs dripped and the heart monitor made its little green lines on the cathode-ray tube. What he could see of her face was swollen, mottled.

So after looking yet again at Rita and her bandages and all the equipment, he would wander off down the hall, lost in his own thoughts.

Hospitals in the evening are dismal places, especially when there aren't many visitors. The staffers rush on unknown errands along the waxed linoleum of the corridors. In the rooms lay the sick people with their maladjusted televisions blaring out the networks' mixture of violence and comedy and ads for the consumer trash of a too wealthy society. The canned laughter and incomprehensible dialogue float through open doors and down the clean, sterile corridors, sounding exactly like the insane cackling of a band of whacked-out dopers. No one in the captive audience laughs or even chuckles at the drivel of the screens. It's just noise to help survive a miserable experience. Or background noise while you die.

Toad hated hospitals. He hated all of it—the pathetic potted plants and cut flowers, the carts loaded with dirty dinner trays, the

waiting bedpans and urine bottles, the gleaming aluminum IV
frames, the distant buzzer of someone trying to summon a nurse,
the moans of some poor devil out of his head, the smell of disinfectant, the whispering—he loathed it all.

He relived the final minutes of the flight yet again. It didn't
matter that he was in a hospital corridor with the TV noise and the
nurses talking in the background: he was back in the plane with the
negative Gs and the spinning and Rita's voice in his ears. In his
private world the events of seconds expanded into minutes, and
every sensation and emotion racked him more powerfully than
before.

He found himself in the staff lounge. He hadn't eaten since
breakfast, but he wasn't hungry. He got a pop from the machine
and sipped it while he inspected the bulletin board. Apparently
management was having the usual trouble keeping the staff lounge
clean. And the bowling league still needed more people. Come on,
people! Sign up and roll a few lines on Thursday nights and forget
all these bastards here in the hospital for a little while. They'll still
be here on Friday.

He thought about calling Rita's parents, and finally decided to
do it. He tried for three minutes to persuade the long-distance
operator to bill the call to his number in Virginia, and when she
refused, called collect. No one answered.

Back down the corridor to check on Rita. No change. Another
glance from the nurse.

He walked and walked and flew again, spinning wildly, out of
control, the altimeter winding down, down, down, out there on the
very edge of life itself.

"So what are the possibilities?" Jake addressed the question to
George Wilson, the aerodynamics expert. The group had watched
the videotape made by the chase plane flown by Smoke Judy.

"It's an inverted spin, no question," Wilson said.

"Why?"

"The plane has negative stability. All these low-observable designs do. The fly-by-wire system is supposed to keep it from stalling and spinning, and obviously it didn't." Everyone there knew
what the term "negative stability" meant. If the pilot released the
controls, a plane with positive stability would tend to return to a
wings-level, stable condition. Neutral stability meant that the airplane would stay in the flight attitude it was in when the controls

were released. Negative stability, on the other hand, meant that once the plane was displaced from wings-level, it would tend to increase the rate of displacement if the controls were released.

"So the fly-by-wire system is the first place to look," Jake Grafton said. "Smoke, you saw this whole thing up close and personal. Do you have anything you want to add?"

"No, sir. I think the movie captured it, got even more of it than I remember seeing at the time. We could sit and niggle over her decision to recover from the second spin instead of ejecting, but I doubt that would be fair. It was a prototype and she's a test pilot."

Jake nodded. He agreed with Smoke, as he usually did. He had tried keeping Smoke Judy at arm's length after that night he saw him in West Virginia, yet except for that unexplained sighting, he had nothing else against the man. Judy was proving to be a fine officer and an excellent pilot, a man whose opinions and judgment could be trusted. Which was precisely why Jake had assigned him to fly the chase plane.

They discussed the test results they had and decided how to proceed. As Jake had told the admiral, his report was going to be written with the data the group had gathered. The reason for the crash would have to be included, if it could be established by the time he was ready to submit the document. So this evening he assigned the bulk of his staff to compiling test results and the rest to investigate, or monitor the contractor's investigation of, the crash.

"Except for the people who are working with TRX, the rest of you need to get back to Washington and dig in. Admiral Dunedin and SECNAV will want the report ASAP."

Jake Grafton came back to the hospital about ten that night to look in on Rita and talk to the doctor on duty. When he was finished, he dragged Toad off to the VOQ. "If you're blaming yourself about this, you'd better stop," he said when they were in the car.

Tarkington was glum. "She fought it all the way down. The controls were just too sensitive. The plane was out there on the edge of the envelope—high G, high angle of attack—and every time she thought she had it under control she lost it again. She kept saying, 'I've got it this time.' "

"She's not a quitter."

"Not by a long shot." Toad looked out the passenger's side window. "A hundred and twenty pounds of pure guts."

"So now you're telling yourself you should have ejected on the second departure."

"Only a thousand times today."

"Why didn't you?"

"I should have."

"Why didn't you? Because she is your wife?"

"Naw," said Toad Tarkington, swallowing hard. "That wasn't it. For just a few seconds there I was flying with you again, over the Med, and you were telling me to hang in there, Toad-man, hang tough. So I hung tough. I wanted to give Rita that chance. She was asking for it. So I sat there and watched the altimeter unwind and waited for her to perform her miracle, and look—I may have killed her, or crippled her for life."

"It's all your fault, is that it?"

"Aw, Christ, CAG."

"Well, if you'd been in the front seat and she'd been in the back, what would you have done?"

"About what Rita did. If I were as good a pilot as Rita."

"I've been around these planes for a few years, Toad, and let me tell you, there are no *right* answers. Some answers are better than others, but every option has unforeseen twists. If you had jumped when the plane departed the second time, with fifteen or sixteen thousand feet of altitude, you and Rita would have spent the rest of your lives thinking you jumped too soon, that you might have saved it if you had hung in there just a little longer. My father always called that being between a rock and a hard place."

Toad shook his head.

"Years ago, in Vietnam, I learned that you can't second-guess yourself. You have to do the best you can all the time, make the best decision you can in the time you have to make it—which is always precious little—and live with the consequences regardless. That's the way flying is. And occasionally you're going to make a mistake, fuck it up. That's inevitable. The trick is to not make a fatal mistake."

Jake Grafton's voice hardened. "Flying isn't chess or football or checkers! Flying isn't some *game*! Flying is life distilled down to the essence—it's the straight, two hundred-proof stuff. And Rita *knows*; she's a U.S. Naval Aviator. She chose this line of work and worked like a slave to earn that ride today. She *knows*."

"Yes," Toad admitted. "She knows."

At 3 A.M. Rita's mother answered her phone in Connecticut. She had obviously just awoke. "This is Toad Tarkington, Mrs. Moravia." You know, the guy who married your daughter? "Sorry to bother you this time of night. I tried to call earlier—"

"We were at a party. Is everything okay?" She was wide awake now and becoming apprehensive.

"Well, not really. That's sorta why I'm calling. I thought you should know."

She went to battle stations while Toad tried to collect his thoughts.

He interrupted her torrent of words. "What it is—Rita and I jumped out of an airplane today, Mrs. Moravia. Rita's over in the hospital now."

He could hear her talking to Mr. Moravia. The pitch in her voice was rising.

"Anyway, Rita's banged up pretty good and I thought you should know."

"How bad is it?"

"She's in a coma, Mrs. Moravia. She hit the ground before her parachute had time to open." Silence. Dead silence. Toad continued, "Anyway, I'm with her and she's getting the best medical treatment there is and I'll call and let you know when anything changes."

Mr. Moravia spoke now. Perhaps his wife had handed him the phone. "What's the prognosis, son?"

"She could die, Mr. Moravia. She's in bad shape."

"Should we come out there?" He didn't even know where Toad was calling from.

"Not now. When she comes out of the coma, that might be a good idea. But not now. I'll keep you advised."

"Are you okay?"

"Fine, sir. No injuries." Nice that he should ask, Toad thought.

"We'll pray for her."

"Yes. Do that. I'm doing some of that myself."

Harry Franks, the program manager for TRX, stood in the middle of the hangar issuing orders. A small army of workmen were placing wreckage in piles as he directed. They had been working since dawn.

He greeted Jake Grafton without enthusiasm. "Give me five more minutes and we'll go upstairs," he said, then pointed to a pile for a forklift operator with a piece of what looked like outboard wingtip.

Jake and the commanders wandered toward the door, trying to get out of the way. The plane had exploded and burned when it hit, so the pieces that were left were blackened and charred.

In an office on the second floor, the engineers from the company that had manufactured the fly-by-wire system, AeroTech, were completing the setup of their equipment. An AeroTech vice president sat on one of the few chairs, sipping coffee and watching the final installation of the network of wires that powered and connected the test boxes. He didn't look very vice presidential. He and the engineers had flown in early this morning and had had only a few hours' sleep. He stood up to shake hands with Jake.

After the introductions, they got right to it. The only surviving processor from the crashed prototype was carefully removed from its bent, damaged box and its innards exposed. It was physically examined by the assembled experts with all the curiosity of a group of med students examining a man with a new disease.

Jake backed off to let the experts have room. He found himself beside Harry Franks. "Tell me again how the fly-by-wire system works."

"The aircraft had negative stability," Franks said, hooking his thumbs behind his belt and warming to the subject. "Most high-tech tactical aircraft today have negative stability." Jake nodded.

Franks continued. "A human cannot fly a negatively stable machine. It would be like trying to keep a barn door balanced on top of a flagpole. So computers actually do the flying. In that way we could build a highly maneuverable aircraft and optimize its low-observable—stealth—features without worrying that we were compromising or negating the ability of the pilot to control it. Now, the way it works is pretty neat."

Jake allowed himself a small smile. All engineers think elegant solutions to technical problems are neat.

"There are three computers," Harry Franks continued. "They each sample the aircraft's attitude and all the other raw data—like air density, temperature, airspeed and so on—forty times a second. Then they see what control input the pilot has made. The pilot's control input merely tells the three computers what the pilot wants the plane to do. The computers then figure out what control throws are necessary to comply with the pilot's order, and they compare their answers. They take a vote. Any two computers can overrule the third. After the vote, the agreed electrical signal is sent to the hydraulic actuators, which move the controls. This little sequence takes place forty times a second. You understand?"

"Yep. I think so. But how does the computer know how much to move the controls? That's what the pilot does in a conventional airplane."

"Well, obviously, the computer has to be told. So the data that it uses is placed in a Programmable Read-Only Memory, a PROM. Since it's electrical, we call it an E-PROM. There are other types, like UV-PROMS and—"

Jake halted him with his hand. "So what you guys did when Rita complained of control sensitivity was to change the E-PROMs?"

"Yeah. Exactly. They come on chips. The data is just fried into the little beggars. We called AeroTech and they cooked us some more and flew 'em down. That's all there was to it."

"But the plane crashed."

"Yeah," said Harry Franks defensively, "but we don't know yet—"

"Something went very wrong. We know that much," Jake Grafton said. "The plane went into three inverted spins. Rita was trying to get it out and succeeded twice."

"Maybe she—"

"Uh-uh. Nope. She knew exactly what she was doing. She recovered from more inverted spins at Test Pilot School than you've even seen."

The vice president of AeroTech had a cherubic, round face. The face looked like it had spent two days in the tropical sun when he faced Jake an hour later and said, "I don't know how it happened, but the data is wrong on this chip."

"How's that?"

He gestured futilely. "I mean we've run the data three times, and I don't know how the heck it happened, but the E-PROM data on this chip is just flat wrong. Look here." He flipped open a thick computer printout. "See this line here?" He read off the number, which was all it was, a number. "Now look here. This is the data on this chip." His finger moved to another computer printout, one

Jake had just watched running though the printer. Jake looked. It was a different number.

"How could this happen? I thought you people checked these things."

"We *do* check the data. After the chip is cooked, we check every damn number. I don't know what—I'm at a loss what to tell you."

"This is only one box," Harry Franks said. "There were three of them. Maybe this is the only one that was defective."

"We'll never know," Jake Grafton said slowly, surveying the faces around him and trying to catalogue their reactions. "The other boxes got smashed and burned. This is the only one left in one piece."

"I don't know what to say," the AeroTech executive said.

Jake Grafton walked out of the room, looking for a phone.

Luis Camacho listened to Admiral Henry's voice on the telephone and doodled on a legal pad. Today he was drawing houses, all with the proper perspective of course. He had the roofline and baseline right, he decided.

"Okay, so AeroTech sold you a defective E-PROM chip. Or two or three of them. Sue the bastards. What do you need the FBI for?"

"I had the aircraft's control data base printed out from our computer. It's wrong. Now, I don't know if the AeroTech chip has this data on it or not, but the stuff in the Pentagon computer is *wrong.* So I got on the phone to that National Security Agency computer doctor who tends our stuff, Kleinberg. Fred Kleinberg. He played with his top secret programs that I'm not supposed to know jack about, and tells me the last guy who made a change on that data base was Harold Strong."

Camacho extended the lines of the roof, eaves, and base of the house until they met at the perspective convergence point. Of course, Albright's house had more shrubs around it, and with the fence and all you would never see it looking just like this.

"You still there, Luis?"

"Yeah. I'm still here."

"I want you and your guys to look into it."

"You called NIS?" NIS was the Naval Investigative Service.

"Nope. Since you are apparently the only guy inside the beltway who knows what the fuck is going on, I want you to investigate this."

"Investigate what?"

"This computer screw-up, you spook asshole. A four-hundred-million-dollar prototype airplane that's *supposed* to be black as the ace of spades just made a smoking hole in the ground and the pilot is at death's door. The data on the computer chips that fly the plane is wrong. The last guy who messed with the data is dead, murdered. Somebody, someplace is bound to have committed a federal crime. Now get off your fat ass and figure out if the Minotaur or some other bastard is screwing with my program! Goddamn, what have I got to do? Call the Director? Go see the President? Maybe I should put an ad in the *Post*?"

"I'll be over in a little while."

The admiral slammed the phone in Camacho's ear. The agent cradled his instrument and went to the door. "Dreyfus? Come in here."

At three o'clock Eastern Daylight Time that afternoon Lloyd Dreyfus and two other FBI agents boarded a plane at National Airport for a flight to Detroit, where a man from the local field office would meet them. They planned to drive straight to Aero-Tech's headquarters in the suburbs.

The agents were airborne somewhere over Pennsylvania when Toad Tarkington arrived at the hospital at the air force's Tonopah facility. He stopped at the nurses' station. "How is she?"

The nurse on duty had been there yesterday when they brought Rita in. She was an air force captain. She looked at Toad with sympathy. "No change, Lieutenant. I'm sorry."

"The doctor around?"

"He's eating a late lunch. He'll be back in a half hour or so."

"Can I see her?"

"Sure."

The ICU nurse nodded and Toad pulled a chair over near Rita's bed. Her chest was still rising and falling rhythmically, the IVs were dripping, the green line on the heart monitor was spiking—she lay exactly as he had seen her yesterday and this morning when he looked in.

The IV needles were in her left arm, so he picked up her right hand and massaged it gently. In a moment he wrapped her fingers around two of his. "Rita, this is Toad. If you can hear me, squeeze my hand a little."

The hand stayed limp.

"Try real hard, Rita."

Nothing.

"Harder."

He gave up finally and continued to lightly knead her fingers.

There was a window there by her bed. When he pulled the curtains back he could see the distant blue mountains. Clouds were building over the peaks.

Life is not fair. Good things happen to bad people and vice versa, almost as if the goodness or badness of those who bear the load was not factored into the equations for that great computer in the sky. Toad stood facing out the window and ruminated upon it. Somehow he had survived this last ejection all in one piece and Rita hadn't. It wasn't because he was a good person, or because of his pious rectitude or exemplary morals or conspicuous faith. He was physically okay because he had been lucky, sort of. And Rita was smashed up because her luck deserted her. Yet perhaps the ejection had cost him something more valuable than his life.

Your luck won't last forever, Tarkington. The day will come, Toad-man, the day will come. Regardless of how you live or the promises you keep, on that day to come your luck will desert you. You won't recognize the morning, you won't recognize the noon, but that *will* be the day. And on that day you'll lose her forever.

He slumped into the chair. Looking at Rita in her bandages was hard, looking at the IV racks, respirator, and heart monitor was harder. He twisted, trying to get comfortable.

Somehow, someway, the E-PROMs in the fly-by-wire computers were screwed up. He had heard them talking this afternoon. How could it happen? How could TRX and AeroTech's checks and double checks and Quality Assurance programs all go south at precisely the same time?

Someday hell! She might die today, or tomorrow. Or the day after. You could lose her any day.

He picked up her hand again and massaged it slowly and gently. Finally he placed it carefully back on the covers. He leaned over Rita and kissed the two square inches on her forehead not covered with a bandage. "Hang tough, Rita. Hang tough."

24

The corporate offices and manufacturing facilities of AeroTech sat in a manicured industrial subdivision of a Detroit suburb in a low, sprawling, windowless building among a dozen similar buildings carefully arranged amid the lawns and pruned trees. A gardener was laboring in a flower bed as the FBI car swung into the parking lot.

Agent Lloyd Dreyfus decided that the goddess of the post-industrial revolution had come, conquered, and already departed this corner of Michigan. Smokestacks now belonged only to the inter-city poor and wretched Third World peasants. Not a single one of the antique structures blighted the skyline in any direction.

After a display of credentials to the wide-eyed receptionist, the agents were ushered in to see the president of the company, who had trouble understanding just why the FBI were here at the Aero-Tech facilities. No, Dreyfus did not have a search warrant. He had not thought one necessary since AeroTech was a defense contractor with annual billings in the millions and the agents were here to investigate, not to search. But he could, of course, get such a warrant if the official thought it necessary. Did he? No. Company employees examined security clearance documents with care and led the government men to an empty conference room.

The investigation took time. At 9 P.M. the FBI team had established that the data contained on the E-PROM chip from the TRX prototype that crashed in Nevada did not correspond to the data that AeroTech had used to manufacture its chips. Yes, a call had been received last week from a TRX engineer in Tonopah, and yes, he had updated the data base via computer modem. The company had manufactured new E-PROM chips based on the revised data. The new chips had been taken to the mail room for overnight shipment. Yes, the records in the mailroom showed three chips sent by a bonded commercial overnight courier.

So at 9 P.M. Dreyfus sat in the conference room and scratched his head. He had been making notes all evening on a yellow pad, and now he went over them again, placing a tick mark by each item after he considered it carefully. One of the agents had gone out for burgers, and now Dreyfus munched a cold cheeseburger and sipped a Coke in which all the ice had melted.

He decided he had two problems, and he decided to tackle the one that he thought would be the simpler first. He asked to see the company president, who was shown into the conference room and motioned into a chair beside Dreyfus.

"Sorry we're taking so long," Dreyfus said as he wadded up the cheeseburger wrapper and tossed it at a waste can.

"Quite all right," the president said cheerfully enough. His name was Homer T. Wiggins. The company prospectus, which Dreyfus had thumbed through earlier in the evening at a slow moment, said he was the largest shareholder of AeroTech and one of its four founders.

"It appears we have a little problem that necessitates a search. Now, when we got here this afternoon I told you we were here to investigate, not search. Now we want to search. We can do so with your permission, or we can go get a warrant. It's your choice." Dreyfus got out his pipe and tobacco and began the charging ritual.

"Why do you want to search?" Wiggins asked.

Dreyfus shrugged. "I can't tell you. I should tell you, though, that I believe I have enough information to persuade a judge to find probable cause and issue a search warrant."

"On what grounds? Just what is it you're investigating?"

Dreyfus took his time lighting his pipe. He puffed experimentally to ensure it was lit and drawing properly. Finally satisfied, he tucked his lighter into a pocket and took a deep drag on the pipe. "I can't tell you."

Homer T. Wiggins had the look of a very sick man. "Just what is it you want to search for?"

"Oh! Didn't I tell you? E-PROM chips."

Bewilderment replaced the pain on Wiggins' face. "Go right ahead. Search to your heart's content."

After escorting the president out of the conference room and posting an agent to guard the paper spread out on the table, Dreyfus led the other two down the hall and around the corner to the mail room. "Okay," he said. "I want computer chips. Start looking."

It took an hour. One agent found three chips in a package without an address within fifteen minutes, but it was an hour before Dreyfus decided those were the only chips in the room. Back he went to see the president with the chips in hand. The president's eyes expanded dramatically.

"Okay. Now I want one of your engineers to put these on your testing machine and let me know what these chips are."

With a glance at the clock, Wiggins picked up his phone. A half hour later a rumpled, unhappy engineer with long hair and the faint odor of bourbon about him appeared in the door. "Sorry, Tom, but these men want some tests run this evening. Apparently it can't wait until tomorrow." He held out the bag with the chips in it.

"Go with him, Frank, and explain what we want," Dreyfus told one of the agents, then resumed his exploration of an industry magazine that resided on a side table.

The agent appeared in the door at five minutes before midnight and motioned to Dreyfus, who joined him in the hall. "Okay, Dreyfus. Those were the chips that they manufactured last week with the new data from TRX. The engineer is printing out the data now, but it's exactly the same."

"Good. The guy in the mail room just sent the wrong chips to Tonopah."

"But when the chips reached Tonopah, wouldn't TRX test them before installation?"

"No doubt they should have, but I suspect someone will admit that there was a mistake, human error, and somehow or other the chips that did get installed didn't get checked." After all, Dreyfus knew, mistakes made the world the happy place it is today. What should have happened and what did happen were usually vastly different things.

"Then where the hell did the bad chips come from?"

"From here. Right here." The question was, how did AeroTech

get the erroneous data that was burned into the bad chips? That data was the stuff Admiral Henry said was in the Pentagon computer, stuff that Harold Strong had been the last man to revise. A phone call from Camacho earlier in the afternoon had given Dreyfus that fact. And the bad data had been cooked onto chips at AeroTech.

"Well, Frank, it looks like it's going to be a long night. I want you to go back to the local office and wake up someone in the U.S. Attorney's office. Have him get cracking. I want a search-and-seizure warrant for all AeroTech's travel, long-distance-telephone and expense-account records and all the data-base files. Until we have the warrant, we'll lock this place up and post a guard. Someone around here has a nasty little secret. If we can find the smoking gun, we'll know who and when and can save ourselves the trouble of listening to a lot of lies."

"You'll need to come down to the office and write the affidavit."

"Yeah." He was going to have to call Camacho at home. No doubt Luis Camacho could think of a plausible story for the judge.

The phone call came at 2 A.M. and woke Camacho from a sound sleep. He listened to Dreyfus' recitation of the events of the evening as he tried to move noiselessly around the bedroom and put on his robe and slippers. When Dreyfus had completed his summary, Camacho told him to call back in five minutes. He was down in the kitchen sipping a glass of milk when the phone rang again.

"Dreyfus again, boss. What do I put on the affidavit?"

"The truth. Suspected illegal sale of classified defense information. Don't name any names."

"I don't have any names to name yet."

"Don't give me that, you pilgrim!"

"Oh, you don't want me to use Smoke Judy's name? Oh! Okay, John Doe strikes again. Anything else?"

"Bye."

"Night, Luis."

The lights were off over at Albright's house. Camacho checked from the backyard as he walked out to the swing. It was a hot, still, muggy night. He didn't stay on the swing long. The gnats and mosquitoes were still hunting for rich, red blood. Cursing, Camacho swatted furiously until he regained the safety of his kitchen and got the sliding glass door closed behind him.

Wide awake now, he flipped on the radio and twiddled the dial.

They were still playing a ball game out on the Coast. Baltimore versus Oakland. Eleventh inning, three runs apiece.

José Canseco was coming to the plate. The A's announcer was all atwitter. Camacho searched through the cupboard for something to eat. Didn't she have some crackers in here? Cookies? Or did the teenage food monster eat every crumb?

He heard a rapping and turned. The sliding glass door was opening.

"Hi, Harlan. Come on in."

"Saw your light. Couldn't sleep. The air conditioning crapped out today and that place is too stuffy to sleep in."

"It'd be better if there was a breeze."

"What a climate!"

Canseco took the first pitch. Strike one. "Want some milk?"

"Yeah. That'd be good. Got any cookies?"

"I'm looking." Up here, behind the flour. Half a package of Fig Newtons. He carried them over to the counter where Albright sat and took one from the package and bit into it. "Little stale, but edible."

The radio audience sighed. Foul tip up toward the press box. Strike two. Harlan Albright helped himself to a cookie while Camacho poured him a glass of milk.

Another foul tip. The sound of the bat on the ball was plainly audible.

Both men nibbled a cookie and sipped milk as they listened. The announcer was hyping the moment for all it was worth. Men on first and second, one out. Two strikes on José Canseco.

Another foul tip.

"Guy ought to quit fouling the ball," Albright said. "Sometimes you want them to either hit it or strike out, it doesn't matter, as long as the game goes on."

"Yeah," Camacho mumbled with his mouth full. He swallowed. "But the guy keeps swinging to stay alive."

The Baltimore pitcher swung around and threw to second. Too late.

"Now the pitcher's doing it." Albright helped himself to another Fig Newton.

Camacho finished his milk and set the glass in the sink.

"Here's the pitch," the radio blared. The crack of the bat started the crowd roaring. "Through the hole, looks like it's going to the wall. Man rounding third is trotting home. And that's it, folks. The

A's win it in the eleventh inning on an RBI double by José Canseco." Camacho flipped the radio off.

"A good player," Albright told him.

"Good kid," Luis agreed.

"Gonna be a superstar."

"If he lasts."

"Yeah. They all gotta last. Everyone has high expectations, then for some reason, sometimes the kid sorta fizzles. Know what I mean?"

Camacho nodded and put Albright's glass in the sink.

"We had high hopes for you—"

"Why don't you go home and swelter at your house, Harlan. It's two-thirty in the morning and I have to work tomorrow."

"I don't. Got the air conditioner guys coming in the morning. I'll call in sick. Tomorrow night my place is going to be like Moscow in winter."

"Terrific."

Albright heaved himself off the stool and reached for the sliding glass door. As his hand closed on it, he paused and looked at Camacho. "Anything new?"

"Yeah. One or two little things, since you mentioned it. The Soviet ambassador got a letter several weeks ago. For some reason there was a stain on it, a jelly stain. We analyzed it. Looks like a French brand of blueberry. Imported. We have a dozen agents on it."

"Amazing." Albright shook his head like a great bear. He brightened. "That might lead to something, eh?"

"It might. You never know."

"Amazing. All those letters, over three and a half years! The Minotaur has never made a mistake, not even one tiny slip. And now he sends a letter with a jelly stain on it? It's too good to be real."

"You take your breaks where you find them. If it is a break. We'll find out if I can keep enough people working on it. Another development just cropped up."

"Like what? Peanut butter on the envelope?"

"Nothing to do with the Minotaur."

"What?" Albright was no longer amused.

"Crash of the navy's ATA prototype. Augered in yesterday out in Nevada." He glanced at the wall clock. "Day before yesterday, actually. Seems somebody has been peddling erroneous information to a defense contractor. AeroTech. So the smelly stuff has hit the fan, so to speak."

"Keep your people on the Minotaur." His tone was flat.

"What am I supposed to do now? Salute?"

Albright slid the door open. "I'm not kidding, Luis. We need some progress." He stepped through the door and pulled it shut behind him. Then he disappeared into the darkness.

A minute or so later, Luis Camacho locked the door and pulled the drapes.

After Jake Grafton and the rest of the staff left for Washington, the atmosphere at the base at Tonopah took on the ethereal silence of a graveyard, or so it seemed to Toad Tarkington. He divided his time between the hangar, where a TRX crew was mocking up the remnants of the airplane he and Rita had abandoned, and the hospital, where Rita remained in a coma.

Toad drove the two miles back and forth between the two locations in an air force sedan that one of the commanders had assumed he would return to the motor pool. He would, eventually, but he was in no hurry. After all, the commander had signed for the car and hadn't really *ordered* him to return it.

The lounge in the VOQ was empty. The other guests apparently were too busy to hang around the pool table and bet dimes and swap lies while the TV hummed in the background, as the naval aviators had. The camaraderie was an essential part of naval aviation. Those who flew the planes gave and demanded this friendship of each other.

That first evening alone Toad tossed the cue ball down the table and watched it carom off the rails. He looked at the empty seats and the blank TV screen and the racks of cue sticks, and trudged off to his room to call Rita's parents yet again. He was talking to them twice a day now.

He was also calling his own folks out in Santa Barbara once a day, keeping them updated on Rita and talking just to hear their voices. Likely as not his parents were slightly baffled and secretly pleased by this attention from the son who usually phoned once a month and never wrote because he had said everything in the phone call.

It's funny, he mused, that now, *now*, with Rita in such bad shape, the sound of his mother's voice was so comforting.

After the second day alone, it finally occurred to him that the problem was that he had almost nothing to do. He was standing in the hangar watching, listening, but he had no people to supervise or reports to write or memos due, so he merely observed with his mind in neutral. At the hospital he sat beside Rita, who was moved to a private room, and did a monologue for her or stared at the wall. And thought. He pondered and thought and mused some more.

That evening on the way to the hospital he stopped by the exchange and bought a spiral notebook. In Rita's room he began to write. "Dear Rita," he began, then sucked on the pen and looked out the window. He dated the page. Dear, dear Rita: "Someday you will wake, and when you do, I will give you this letter."

He wrote, sometimes for several hours at a sitting. He started out writing about Toad Tarkington: growing up in southern California with the beach and surf just down the road, baseball and football in the endless summer, the hard-bodied bimbettes chased and wooed and sometimes conquered. He described how he felt about his first true love, and his second and third and fourth. He devoted page after page to college and grades and all-night parties.

Finally he decided he had squeezed the sponge pretty dry on his youth, so he turned to the navy. Without his even realizing it, his style changed. Instead of the light, witty, listen-to-this style he had adopted for tales of his youth, he wrote seriously now, with no attempt at humor. Facts, impressions, opinions, ambitions, they came pouring from his pen.

In four days the TRX crew finished their work and mysteriously vanished. Several days later a group of officers and civilians from Washington arrived unannounced. They poked and prodded the dismembered, blackened carcass and photographed everything, then climbed back into the waiting planes parked on the baking ramp in front of base ops. Toad was left with his solitude and his writing.

So the days passed, one by one, as Rita slept.

In Washington, Jake Grafton was also writing, though he went about it in a vastly different manner than Tarkington. He dictated general ideas into a recording machine and gave the tapes to his subordinates, who expanded the ideas into smooth, detailed drafts which Jake then worked on with a pencil. Flight test data and observations were marshaled, correlated and compiled. Graphs were drawn and projections made about performance, maintenance manhours, mean time between failures and, of course, costs. Money dripped from every page. Every officer in the group had an input, and conclusions and recommendations were argued and re-argued around Jake's desk, with him listening and jotting notes and occasionally indicating he had heard enough on one subject or another. All of it went into a mushrooming document with the words "top secret" smeared all over.

Vice Admiral Tyler Henry spent some unhappy hours with Luis Camacho. It had been quickly established that the data contained on the E-PROM chip from the crashed prototype was identical to the erroneous data contained in the Pentagon computer file that had last been changed by the deceased Captain Harold Strong. TRX's latest, correct batch of E-PROM data was also in the computer, but under another file number.

Three days and a dozen phone calls after he had sent Lloyd Dreyfus to Detroit, Camacho went himself. On Thursday at noon he rode the Metro out to National Airport and was sitting in the president of AeroTech's office in Detroit at 3:50.

Homer T. Wiggins had gotten himself a lawyer, a manicured, fiftyish aristocrat in a Brooks Brothers suit and dark maroon tie. His stylish tan and his gray temples and sideburns made him look like something sent over from central casting. "Martin Prescott Nash," he pronounced with a tiny nod at Camacho, then pointedly ignored the proffered hand. Camacho retracted his spurned appendage and used a handkerchief to wipe it carefully as he sized up Wiggins, who was apparently trying his best to look like a pillar of outraged rectitude.

"My client is one of the most respected leading citizens of this state," Nash began in a tone that might come naturally to a feminist activist lecturing a group of convicted rapists. He had it just right—the slight voice quaver, the distinct pronunciation of each word, the subtle trace of outrage. "He is active in over a dozen civic organizations, gives over half a million dollars a year to charity and provides employment to six hundred people, every one of whom pays the taxes that provide salaries for you gentlemen." He had just the slightest little bit of difficulty pronouncing the word "gentlemen."

Nash continued, listing the contributions Homer T. Wiggins had made to the arts, the people of the great state of Michigan and the human race. Camacho settled into his chair and let him go, occasionally glancing at his watch.

Dreyfus waited until he had Camacho's eye, then winked broadly. Wiggins saw the gesture and winced.

Finally, as Nash paused for breath, Camacho asked, "Are you a criminal lawyer?"

"Well, no," admitted the pleader. "I specialize in corporate law. My firm has advised Homer for ten years now. We handled his last stock offering, over ten million shares on the American Exchange, and the subordinated debenture—"

"He needs a criminal lawyer."

Deflated, Nash looked to his left, right at the pasty, perspiring face of leading citizen Homer T. Wiggins, who was staring at Camacho and licking his lips.

"Read him his rights, Dreyfus."

Both agents knew this had been done on one prior occasion, yesterday, and Wiggins had declined to answer questions unless his lawyer was present. Dreyfus removed the Miranda card from his credentials folder and read it yet again, slowly, with feeling. The warning usually had a profound effect on men who had never in their lives thought of themselves as criminals. All the color drained from Wiggins' face and he began to breathe in short, rapid breaths. It was as if he could hear the pillars crumbling and see the plaster falling from the ceiling of that magnificent edifice of position, responsibility and respect that had housed him so well all these years.

As Dreyfus put the card away, Wiggins squeaked, "You going to arrest me?"

"That depends."

"On what?" said Martin Prescott Nash, who was looking a little pale himself.

"On whether or not I get some truthful answers to the questions I came here to ask."

"Are you offering immunity?"

"No. I have no such authority. I am here to question Mr. Wiggins as a principal about bribery of a government employee and illegally obtaining classified defense information. Both charges are felonies. If you want to talk to us, Mr. Wiggins, we'll listen. We may or may not arrest you today. I haven't decided. Anything you say will be included in our reports and will be conveyed to the Justice Department. The attorneys there may or may not use it as evidence against you. They may take it into account when they are trying to decide if prosecution is warranted, or they may not. They may consider your cooperation when they make a sentencing recommendation after your conviction—if there is one—or again, they may not. I have nothing to offer. You have the right to remain silent, but you've heard your rights and your attorney is here with you. Or you can decide to cooperate with the government that you and your six hundred employees support with your tax dollars by telling us the truth. It's up to you."

Nash wanted to talk to his client in private. The agents went out into the hall and walked toward the cafeteria.

"Have you really got it?" Camacho asked Dreyfus.

"Chapter and verse. He turned in expense-account reports for every trip to Washington, including credit-card receipts for dinners with the name Thomas H. Judy on the back as a business guest in his own handwriting. Apparently he didn't want any more trouble with those IRS troglodytes about his expense account."

"Can you tie him personally to the data?"

"Yep. An engineer here got the computer printout about seven months ago—Wiggins himself handed it to him. Told him to make up some experimental chips to see if they could validate the method and their computer stuff, and to develop a cost projection. All of which he did. Other people swear to that. I've got a sworn statement in writing from this engineer burning Wiggins and a cassette recording of him telling it to me originally. And the NSA computer records show Judy as one of the officers who had routine access to the E-PROM data. We've got Homer T. cold as a frozen steak."

"Is this the right time?" Camacho muttered, thinking aloud.

"Well, shit!" Dreyfus hissed. *"I don't know!* I just dig this stuff up. You—"

Camacho silenced him with a glance. Dreyfus lit his pipe and walked along with smoke billowing.

"So why the big screw-up with the chips?" Camacho asked when they reached the cafeteria, which housed three microwaves and a wall full of vending machines.

"Oh, AeroTech got in four or five different data dumps from TRX and even one from the Pentagon, all in the last three months. The first three chips just sat there on the engineer's desk. No one is sure how or when they went to the mail room. No one knows how they got mixed up with an outgoing shipment. The mail-room guy is from Haiti, with a heavy accent. He denies everything. Rumor has it he used to be a medical doctor in his former life." Dreyfus

shrugged. "Looks like human error, that plus the usual careless-
ness and a tiny pinch of rotten luck. *Voilà!* Anything that can go
wrong, will. Isn't that the fourth or fifth law of thermodynamics or
Murphy or the Georgia state legislature?"

"Something like that." Camacho removed a plastic cup full of
decaffeinated coffee from the vending machine and sat on a plastic
chair at a plastic table beneath a fluorescent light with a faulty
igniter—the light hummed and flickered.

"I think the doctor in the mail room is an illegal."

"You asked to see his green card?"

"Nope."

"Going to?"

"Not unless you tell me to."

"Let's go see if Wiggins wants to talk."

Dreyfus stoked his pipe again on the stroll down the hall. Wiggins' secretary glared at them. Dreyfus gave her a sympathetic
grin, which she ignored.

They sat silently and flipped through the magazines on the
stand. It was five more minutes before the buzzer sounded and they
were waved into the inner sanctum.

"My client," said the counselor, "wishes to cooperate. With the
understanding, of course, that he can cease answering questions at
any time."

Wiggins had met Smoke Judy on five different occasions. Judy
knew that AeroTech needed contracts and offered to help in return
for a small cash payment and some stock. On two occasions he
talked about a job after he retired. Wiggins had been noncommittal
about the job, but had agreed to the money and the stock. Five
thousand dollars cash and a bearer certificate for a thousand shares
of AeroTech—currently worth $12.75 each—had bought the com-
pany an advance peek at the flight control data for the TRX prototype. The navy was just floating a Request for Proposal (RFP) for
the fly-by-wire system. AeroTech bid for the chip business and won
the contract.

All this Wiggins admitted, but he stoutly denied any wrongdo-
ing. "This company, it needs the business. And we underbid every
other contractor for those chips. We *saved* the government *a lot of
money.* We didn't do *anything* that other defense contractors don't
routinely do. It's a cutthroat business."

The FBI agents seemed unimpressed.

"Listen, if I hadn't agreed to Judy's offer, he would have peddled that information to my competitors. Then where would I have been? No contract. I have a duty to this company." Color returned to Homer Wiggins' cheeks.

"Of course," Dreyfus said, "you could have called us when Judy first approached you."

"I've spent fifteen years building this business. I did it with my bare hands, with no money, with a ton of sweat, taking risks that would scare the wits out of a Vegas gambler. *I built it!*" Camacho found himself staring at Wiggins' gold wedding ring and gold class ring. Was that Yale?

"Now the navy wants me to make E-PROMs cheaper than anyone else. So I do. And *this* is the gratitude, *this* is the reward! *I am treated like a criminal!*" He sprayed saliva across the desk, and for the first time Camacho saw the drive and determination that had built a successful corporation.

"I am treated like a criminal for doing what everyone else does and for making E-PROM chips cheaper than anyone else can."

Camacho looked at his watch: 5:30. Maybe he was still in the office. "Do you want to go to jail tonight?"

Wiggins gaped. The blood drained from his face, and for a moment Camacho thought he had stopped breathing.

"No," he whispered.

"Now see here—" the lawyer began, but Camacho cut him off with a jab of his hand.

"Have you talked to Judy this week?"

"No. No!"

"I want you to call him for me. I'll tell you what to say. I'll listen on an extension. You will say precisely what I tell you and nothing else. Will you do it?"

"What choice do I have?" Wiggins was recovering. This man's recuperative powers were excellent. He could handle it.

"You don't go to jail this evening. I make my report to the Justice Department and they take it from there. If they indict you, that's their business. My report will show that you cooperated."

"I'll make the call."

"Homer," said Nash, "maybe—"

"I'll make the call. And you go on home, Prescott. Thanks for being here this afternoon. I'll call you."

"Are you sure you—?"

Wiggins was examining his hands. Martin Prescott Nash rose from his chair and went out the door. It swung shut behind him.

        * * *

"Smoke, this is Homer Wiggins."

"I told you never to call me—"

"Something's come up. The FBI are here, in Detroit. They're checking out the chips. I'm just letting you know."

Smoke Judy was silent for several seconds. "Have they talked to you?"

"Yes."

"What—?" His voice fell. "Do they know?"

"About you? I don't know. I think—they might. Definitely."

"Did you—?"

"I've got to go now, Smoke. I just wanted you to know." Wiggins held the instrument away from his ear, and at a nod from Camacho, Dreyfus simultaneously depressed the buttons on both telephones, severing the connection.

When they were alone in the car on the way back to the airport, Camacho said, "I got a little job for you tomorrow, Dreyfus. We're going to need all our people, and you'll probably have to borrow a bunch."

Dreyfus fished out his pipe and tobacco and merely glanced at his boss.

"I want to keep track of a man. We'll need discreet surveillance teams, couple of choppers and the electronics boys."

"Anyone I know."

"Nope. It's my next-door neighbor, guy named Harlan Albright."

"You know, in my fifteen years in the FBI I have never felt more like a mushroom than I have working for you. You've kept me in the dark and shoveled shit at me for eighteen months now. If you got croaked tomorrow, I couldn't even tell the old man what the hell you were working on. I don't know."

Camacho, behind the wheel, kept his eyes on the road. "The electronics guys already put listening devices in his house, three days ago when his air conditioning went out. It was too good an opportunity to pass up."

Dreyfus got his pipe going strongly and rolled down his window. The car's air conditioning was going full blast. "Think he's screwing your wife?"

"Read the security regulations lately, Dreyfus?"

"Listen, boss. And listen good. You want good solid work from me but you don't want me to know anything. Now I am just about one day away from submitting my resignation. I don't need this shit and I'm not gonna keep taking it! Not for you, not for the old man, not for the Director, not for any of you spook dingdongs. And you can put that in my final evaluation!"

Camacho braked the car to a stop at a light. He just sat there behind the wheel, watching the light, waiting for it to change. When it did, he glanced left and hesitated. An old junker car was going to run the red. As it hurled by, Dreyfus leaned out his window with his middle finger jabbed prominently aloft.

Camacho took his foot off the brake and fed gas.

"Okay," Luis Camacho said. "You want to know what's going on. I'll tell you." And he did.

25

On Saturday the sun rose into a clean, bright sky, a pleasant change from the haze that had been stalled over the Potomac River basin for a week. The morning weatherman credited a cold front that had swept through during the night and blessed the metropolitan Washington area with some much-needed showers.

Commander Smoke Judy absorbed the weather information while he scraped at his chin. He had acquired the habit of listening to the morning forecasts during his twenty years in naval aviation, and it was hard to break. Yet he wasn't paying much attention. His mind was on other things.

After finishing at the sink and dressing, he poured himself a glass of orange juice and opened the sliding glass door to his apartment balcony. The view was excellent, considering he was only six floors up. From out here he could see the gleam of the Potomac and, on the horizon, the jutting spire of the Washington Monument. As usual, the jets were droning into and out of National Airport. Even with that cold front last night today would be hot. Already the sun had a bite to it.

He sat on the little folding chair in the sun and thought once again about Harold Strong and the flight control data and Homer T. Wiggins of AeroTech. Nothing in life ever works out just the way you think it will, he told himself bitterly. They should put that over the door of every public building in Washington.

Strong had gotten suspicious. Judy had spent one too many evenings in the office, asked one too many questions about that TRX fly-by-wire system. So Strong had doctored the data, rendering it worthless unless one knew exactly how and where it had been changed.

When Smoke found out, it was too late. He had already given the data to AeroTech, to Homer T. Wiggins. Oh, even defective it was good for what Homer wanted it for, to check the AeroTech manufacturing capability and cost out the manufacturing process. Heck, he could have written Homer a purely fictitious report that would have allowed AeroTech to accomplish the same thing. So it wasn't like he had stiffed Homer. And both he and Homer *knew* that the preliminary data would be changed, probably many times, during the course of development. There was no possibility that the erroneous stuff would end up in an airplane that someone was going to try to fly.

And still, it happened! It happened. All the checks that were supposed to be done, the fail-safe, zero-defects program, all of it went down the crapper in an unbelievable series of coincidences. *Now* TRX was going to fire a couple of clowns who each thought the other guy had done the checks. So neither did them.

He tossed off the last gulp of orange juice and wiped his mouth with his fingers. He sat the empty glass on the concrete beside his chair and sat looking at the city.

Nothing he had ever attempted in his whole life had worked out right. What was it the hippies called it? Karma?

Funny, killing Harold Strong had been easier than he thought it would be. Probably too easy. No doubt someway, somehow, he had fucked that up too.

Looking back, it had been a bad decision. Strong probably had nothing but a few baseless suspicions that he couldn't prove.

Ah well, what was done was done. You signed for the plane and flew it as best you could and if today was your day to die, you died. That was life.

He had wanted something besides a pension, and now he had his savings—about $56,000—and the cash from five little deals— $30,000—and some stock he probably couldn't sell. Plus his pension, a lousy 55 percent of his base pay if he lasted twenty-two years. Yet if he cut and ran, his pension would evaporate like a gob of spit on a hot steel deck. If he didn't run, well . . . he would have to give his savings and the cash to a lawyer to try to stay out of prison.

FBI agents were probably watching him this very minute. Sitting somewhere in one of these apartments or in a vehicle down in the lot, watching him. If Wiggins had been telling the truth . . . But there was really no reason for him to lie. What did Wiggins have to gain by lying?

Judy had gone to work yesterday, though he had been sorely tempted to call in sick. That little conversation Thursday evening with Wiggins, just before he walked out of the office, that had shaken him. He had locked up his papers, bid everyone a pleasant good evening and walked out sweating.

That evening he had convinced himself there really wasn't any hurry. It might be six months or a year before they got around to arresting him, if they ever did, and he could get out on bail. And where could he run? What with?

He pushed himself up, out of the chair, and went inside. He drew the curtains. Rummaging through the bottom drawer of his dresser, he found the .38 he always wore in his flight gear. He flipped out the cylinder. Empty. Did he have any cartridges? He sat on the bed and tried to remember. There should be six in the left, radio pocket of his survival vest, which was piled in a corner of the closet. He had put them there when he emptied the pistol after his last flight in that F-14 at Tonopah.

He found the brass cartridges and dropped them into the cylinder holes.

The pistol was old, with the bluing completely gone in places. Nowadays they issued the kids nine-millimeters, but he had always liked the old .38. Amazingly enough, this was the one they issued him twenty years ago when he checked into his first fleet squadron.

The money was in a gym bag on the other side of the closet floor. He spread it on the bed and examined the miserable pile. Fifteen bundles of a hundred twenties each. Three weeks' take for a twelve year-old crack salesman. For this he had wagered his pension and risked years in prison?

He went into the kitchen and poured himself the last of the bourbon, added some ice and water and went back out onto the balcony.

"Here's to you, Smoke Judy, you stupid, unlucky bastard."

He sipped the liquor and watched the shadows shorten as the

sun rose higher into the sky. Already it was hot. It was going to be a scorcher.

Twenty miles north of where Smoke Judy sat, Luis Camacho was trying to get his lawn mower started. He diddled with the choke and jerked the starter rope repeatedly. The plug fired a few times, then gave up. He decided he had flooded it. He could take out the plug and pull it through a few times, but no.

He sat in the shade on the concrete of his driveway, with his back against the wall, and waited for the recalcitrant device to purify itself. He was trying to work up the energy to stand and again assault the machine when Harlan Albright came out of his house, saw him, and crossed the grass toward him.

"Hey," Albright said.

"Hey yourself. Know anything about lawn mowers?"

"Cars are my bag. I pay a kid to cut mine."

"Why didn't you hire my kid?"

"You must be kidding! He doesn't even cut *your* grass."

"He needs a better offer than I can make." Camacho stood, flexed his arms a few times experimentally, then grasped the rope. Choke off. He yanked. The engine spluttered.

Albright bent and adjusted the needle valve. "Now try it."

It started on the next jerk of the lanyard. Albright played with the needle valve until the engine ran smoothly.

When Luis finished the front and back yards and put the machine back in the garage, Albright had a beer waiting. Ten o'clock. "What the heck, it's Saturday."

They sat on Albright's front steps, in the shade of the big maple.

"What's new in the glamorous, dazzling world of counterespionage?"

"Our people visiting the gourmet food stores had a nibble. A store over in Reston. Not much of anything, but it was all we got. One of the clerks got to talking about how many famous people buy their stuff at that store. She had a name, but she couldn't remember if he had ever bought any jam. She said he or his secretary come in there once a month or so."

"Who?"

"It isn't evidence. The clerk was a dingbat. The agent said she looked like she had terminal anorexia. Didn't look like she weighed ninety pounds. Obviously been eating her own stuff."

"Who?"

"Royce Caplinger."

Albright's eyebrows rose once, then fell back into place. "She sure?"

"I told you, she was bragging. She also said she had three senators, five congressmen, two ex-congressmen, a dozen flag officers from all services, and three high-class hookers that buy stuff from her on a regular basis."

"Hookers, huh? What's the name of the store?"

"The Gourmet Market."

"You going to follow up?"

"Yeah. Sure. I've got a SWAT team sitting on the place twenty-four hours a day. A cockroach couldn't get in or out without us knowing it. If Caplinger ever shows up again and buys French blueberry jam, we'll bust him on the spot." He drained the beer can and stood. "Still, it's a lead. Someplace to look."

"How's the ATA crash investigation going?"

"So-so. The usual. Dazzle. Glamour."

"Why are you in that investigation anyway?"

"The admiral in charge is scared to death of the Minotaur. And he knows I'm the best; he won't talk to anybody else. No shit." He tossed the empty can at Albright. "I gotta go. Taking Sally to the mall. Thanks for the beer."

When he held the door open for Sally, Camacho automatically glanced across the car at the little bulb he had inset in the driver's door. It was dark.

He got into the car and started the engine and backed out onto the street.

"I want to run by the Richards house and pick up Gerald." The boy had spent the night with a friend.

"Why? He can walk home this afternoon and he has a key to the house."

"I'm taking you two to the airport. I want you to go visit your mother for a week or two."

"But I'm not packed! The PTA has a benefit on Thurs—"

"I want you both out of town for a while. Don't argue. I mean it."

"What about our clothes?" his wife protested. "We can't—"

"Oh yes you can! Buy some more clothes. You have your checkbook."

"Luis, what is this all about?"

He pulled over to the side of the street and put the car in neutral. He turned in the seat to face his wife. "I'm working a case. The people we're after know where I live. I'd just feel a whole lot better if you and Gerald weren't home until I wrap this up. Now there's no danger, but why take a chance?"

"You're really serious, aren't you?"

"Yes. I am."

"Mother—how will I explain dropping in on her and Dad like this?"

"Tell them we had a fight and you want some time alone."

"Mom won't believe that! She knows you too well to—"

"*You* think of something. Tell them we're redoing the downstairs and you've developed an allergy to paint. I don't care. Just don't tell the truth. Your mother'll spill it to every one of her friends, and it's a very small world." He put the car in gear and rolled.

Sally chewed on her lip and twisted the strap of her purse. "I don't like this, Luis."

"I don't either, but this is the way it has to be."

Smoke Judy was sipping beer in a booth at his favorite bar when he saw Harlan Albright come in and ask for change for the parking meter. Judy waited several minutes, paid his tab and left.

Albright was behind the wheel of his car. Judy opened the passenger door and sat down. "Hi."

"Want to take a little ride?"

"Sure. Why not?" Smoke took his sunglasses from the neck of his shirt, where they hung suspended by an earpiece, cleaned them on a shirttail, then put them on. He tossed his gym bag onto the backseat.

After several blocks, Albright glanced at Judy and asked, "How's things at the office? Hear you guys had a crash."

"Where'd you hear that?"

"Oh, people talk."

Judy shrugged.

"Got anything on today?"

"Not really."

"Want to go over on the Eastern Shore and get some dinner? I know a great little place that serves the best crab in Maryland."

"They'll serve us like this?" Both men were in jeans. Albright was wearing a pullover shirt that sported a Redskins logo.

"I think so."

"Why not?"

Albright drove to the beltway and got on it headed east. Traffic was heavy, as usual. He took the exit toward Annapolis and engaged the cruise control. Judy turned on the radio and found a ball game. The Orioles, only the second inning.

Judy noticed that Albright kept checking the rearview mirrors, but he quit after a while and drove with his left elbow out the window. "Can't stand air conditioning," he muttered, and Judy nodded.

Luis Camacho sat in his backyard with a beer in his hand. He had carried out the portable TV that Sally normally watched in the kitchen, and rigged up the extension cord. He had the Orioles game on.

When he returned from the airport, Albright's car was missing. He had called the office and got Dreyfus. "Where is he?"

"On the beltway heading east. Picked up a guy at a bar in Alexandria, but we don't know who. Couldn't get close enough."

"Okay. Any idea where they're going?"

"He made no phone calls before he left the house. Didn't say anything. About thirty minutes after you left for the airport, he got in his car and drove off. He went over to Reston and stopped by the Gourmet Market."

"Heard from Susan yet?" Susan was the wife of an FBI agent. She and her husband owned the market, and Camacho had enlisted their help. Susan was the skinniest woman Camacho had ever met, but to the best of his knowledge she was not suffering from anorexia.

"Yeah. Said he came in and bought some things, stood and chatted, said he was new in the neighborhood. Spent about fifteen minutes in the store. She says he never asked about Caplinger or anyone else, and she didn't volunteer. She wants to know if you think he'll be back."

"Tell her probably not. I think Albright just wanted some tangible verification of my little tale."

"Okay. I'll call you back when he gets to wherever he's going and let you know."

"Dreyfus, I meant what I said yesterday. Under *no* circumstances, *none,* do I want him to burn the tail. Lose him if you have to, but *don't* give him a chance to figure out we're watching."

"Gotcha, boss."

Now Camacho sat in his backyard with the TV going. He nursed the beer and paid no attention to the game.

Everything that could be done had been done. Nothing had been rushed. The situation had been allowed to ripen naturally, and now all was in readiness. Including Dreyfus, he had sixty-five agents on this case. They were in the main telephone exchange in case Albright used a pay phone, Albright's house was wired and continuously monitored, a fleet of unmarked cars was at this very minute preceding and following Albright as he drove the highways, two vans full of cameras and parabolic listening devices trailed the caravan, two helicopters were airborne, Dreyfus had a stack of signed John Doe warrants in the desk. What else? Oh yes, all the top lab technicians were on call.

He sipped his beer and tried to think of something else that should be done, some contingency that he had not foreseen. He could think of nothing. Well, that wasn't really true. This whole operation could fizzle, any operation could, but it wouldn't be because he hadn't prepared as well as possible. His worst handicap was the requirement to stay loose on Albright, to remain completely hidden. Well, that was the only way it could be, so no use worrying.

But he was worried. When he could sit still no longer, he got the lawn rake from the garage and set to work on the grass clippings as the ball-park announcer chanted the summer myth yet again and the afternoon heat continued to build.

Smoke Judy was impressed. The building wasn't much, but the prices on the menu were reasonable and the seafood heaped on the plates of the early diners looked scrumptious and smelled the same. Didn't they call this decor "rustic"? Unfinished boards on the interior walls, with fishing nets and crab pots hanging from the ceiling. Subdued lighting. "The food's great," Albright assured him. "Deviled crab is the house specialty."

They had ordered their dinner and were sipping the foam off frosty glasses of beer when Albright said, "Got a little proposition for you, if you're interested."

Judy wiped off his foam mustache with a finger. "Depends."

"Did you ever hear the term 'kilderkin'?"

Smoke set the beer mug down and straightened in his chair. He looked around at the other guests with interest. Two or three looked like they could be the right age and level of fitness. His eyes swung back to Albright. "Let's go to the john."

He rose and led the way.

It was a one-seater with a urinal and a sink. Not the cleanest rest room he was ever in, but better than most. And it was empty. Judy turned and set his feet, the right slightly behind the left. He got his weight up on the balls of his feet and bent his knees slightly. "Hands on the door, feet back and spread. The position, man."

Albright stood with his hands on his hips a moment, then did as he was told.

"I'm not wearing a wire."

"Uh-huh." He felt Albright all over, including his crotch. He inspected his belt and his shoes and his pen. He examined his sunglasses. He looked at the patch on his jeans. Then he removed Albright's wallet and moved back against the sink. "You can turn around now."

Albright watched him go through it. He looked at the driver's license carefully, the library card, the automobile registration and insurance cards, the receipts from the food store and the laundry, the credit cards. He counted the cash. It was in hundreds, twenty of them. "Gonna play poker tonight?"

"I like to pay in cash."

"Why the credit cards then?"

"You never know."

Judy passed the wallet back. "You want to talk to me, then you walk out there and cancel our dinner orders and pay the tab. Leave a tip. We'll go to a place I pick. You drive, but I don't want you to say one word in the car. Not a word. Got it?"

"Okay."

In the car Judy pointed in the direction he wanted Albright to go. Meanwhile he watched the other cars. They weren't being followed. He had Albright make a series of random turns, then take the road leading east. Fifteen miles later they came to a big roadhouse at a crossroads. Judy gestured and Albright drove into the lot and killed the engine.

They went to a booth in the back and Judy seated himself so that he could watch the door.

"You were saying?"

"Kilderkin."

"What about it?"

"Kilderkin is the access word for a file in the computer at the

Pentagon. It's a file held in the office where you work. The Athena file. I can supply you with the code words to get to it. I want you to copy the Athena file onto a floppy disk and give it to me."

"All of it? All the documents?"

"Yes. It might take more than one disk."

"Might. What do I get out of it?"

"A hundred grand."

Commander Smoke Judy stared at him a while, then looked around the room thoughtfully. In a moment the waiter came over. They asked for beers and menus.

"What do you know about that file?" Judy asked.

"I'm not going to tell you. Let's just say I want it."

"Why?"

"All you need to know is I want it a hundred thousand dollars' worth."

"You don't want it bad enough."

"How badly do I have to want it?"

"If you ever decide you want it for a quarter million reasons, you come talk to me. Half up front and half on delivery. Cash. Used twenties."

"No. That's not— No!"

Judy picked up his menu. "I think I'll have the bacon cheeseburger. What about you?"

"Maybe a plain hamburger."

Judy nodded and waited patiently for the waiter.

When they had finished their greaseburgers and were drinking a cup of coffee, Albright said, "If I pay you fifty tonight, fifty on Monday, when could you have the disks?"

"When will you have the rest of the money?"

"A week from Monday."

"Then that's when you get the disks."

At seven o'clock Luis Camacho called his in-laws. Sally answered.

"Hey. You made it."

"Oh, Luis. It's going to be a nice visit. The folks are a little baffled, but they're delighted to have us."

"Great. It'll go okay."

"What did you do this afternoon? What did you have for dinner?"

They discussed the condition of the larder for three or four minutes, then Camacho wished her good night.

An hour and a half later the phone rang. "He's headed home," Dreyfus reported.

"Who was with him?"

"Don't know. We got an infrared photo as they crossed the Chesapeake Bay Bridge. The photographer isn't very optimistic. They came on into the metro area and stopped at a storage place in Bladensburg for a bit. Then the subject dropped the passenger at a Metro station and he was gone by the time we could get a man into the station. Subject is heading your way now. He'll be there in about five minutes."

"Get someone over to Smoke Judy's place. See if they can spot him coming home. And get a list of the license numbers of the cars parked around that bar where the subject picked up his passenger. Run them through the computer."

"Okay, boss. Anything else?"

"When will the photo be ready?"

"Tomorrow."

"Okay."

"And I put a stakeout on the storage lot. Thought we might get a warrant tomorrow and search it."

"The subject will be making some phone calls tonight or tomorrow. Be ready."

"You really think he's going to move?"

"He's got to. He's got to go for checkmate or concede."

"Keep your gun handy."

On Sunday morning Luis Camacho was painting the yard furniture when Harlan Albright hailed him across the back fence. He came through the gate and settled himself on one of the chairs waiting for its spring coat.

"I have another brush in the garage if you want to help."

Albright grinned and sipped his coffee. "Who said Tom Sawyer is dead? Sorry. I gotta go run some errands this morning." He looked at the house. "Where's Sally?"

"Went to visit her mother." Camacho was working on a table leg and didn't look up.

"Oh."

"Women," Luis muttered.

"Yeah. Gonna stay a week or two?"

"Dunno."

"Like that, huh?"

"Yeah."

"And the boy?"

"He went too. It's been years since he spent time with his grand-parents. He didn't want to go, of course."

Albright watched Camacho work on the table. The paint ran down the brush onto his fingers, which he wiped on the grass. "May rain this afternoon, you know," Albright said.

"Just my luck."

"What would you say to packing it in and going home?"

Camacho put the paintbrush in the can and stood up. He looked carefully at Albright, trying to read his expression.

"You mean Russia?"

"Yeah. You been here what? Twenty-eight or -nine years?"

"Thirty-one."

"Yeah. Are you ready to go home?"

"I can't even speak the language anymore. When I hear it I have to concentrate real hard to get the drift, and then I can't think of the proper response. I been dreaming in English for over twenty-five years. Want some more coffee?"

"Okay."

Luis took his cup and went inside. He returned in a moment with Albright's coffee and a cup for himself. They both sampled the brew, then sat in silence. Birds were squawking vigorously in the tree behind them. Camacho took a deep breath and exhaled slowly. How could he leave? He liked this place and these people.

Albright broke the silence. "You really think Caplinger is the Minotaur?"

Luis considered. "He could be," he said at last. "It fits. He has the necessary access, he was on the official guest list of that party three years ago when the first letter was stuck in the ambassador's coat. He's an egomaniac, likes the power trip. It's possible."

"But why?"

Camacho shrugged. "List all the possibilities and look at them. Pick the one you like."

"I've done that. And you know what? I got the sneaking suspicion that the real reason wasn't on my list."

"Why does a happily married man start buying tricks on a street corner? Why does a man in his fifties steal a few hundred from the petty-cash drawer?"

"That was the shortest reason on the list. Nut case. But I don't think so."

"Happens all the time." Camacho drained his cup, set it out of the way and got back to the painting.

"Royce Allen Caplinger," Albright said, pronouncing the name slowly. "Sixty-three years old. Estimated net worth, $132 million. Son of a druggist. Grew up in St. Paul. Married twice. Second wife died of a heart attack six years ago. Hasn't remarried, though he's screwing his secretary who's worked for him for fifteen years. He's been doing that about once a month for ten years. She's forty-two, never married, modestly attractive, had a hysterectomy eight years ago. Caplinger collects American Indian art, pays too much, sometimes gets good stuff, sometimes bad. Buys what he likes and to hell with the experts. Has a copy of every book ever written about MacArthur and the best MacArthur memorabilia collection in existence. *Time* said he has every piece of old junk Mrs. MacArthur ever threw out. What else? Oh yeah. He has two grown children, two dogs, and drives a fifteen-year-old Jaguar. Owns an estate in Virginia near Middleburg. Gives his entire government salary to charity."

"Was involved in a panty raid when he was in college and was suspended for a semester," Camacho said without taking his eyes from his work.

"That too. The rattling bones from his youth." Albright tossed the dregs of his coffee into the grass and laid the cup on his lap. "So, Dr. Freud, has Caplinger gone over the edge? Is he copulating with Mother Russia?"

Albright rose and, dangling the cup from a finger, ambled through the gate. Thirty minutes later Camacho heard his car start out front and drive away.

Albright drove to a Wal-Mart store near Laurel. After browsing for ten minutes, he used the pay phone in the entryway. No one answered at the number he tried. He waited exactly one minute and tried again. The third time someone picked up the phone.

Albright talked for almost a minute. The other party never spoke. Then Albright hung up and went back into the store, where he wandered the aisles and handled merchandise for another half hour.

When he left the store he drove aimlessly for an hour. At Burtonsville he stopped for gas and bought a can of soda pop, a Dr Pepper. He drank the contents as he drove north on Route 29 and used a rag in the car to carefully wipe the fingerprints from the can.

Approaching the outskirts of Columbia, he took the off-ramp for Route 32, made an illegal left turn at the top and a sweeping right down onto Route 29 headed south as he scanned the mirrors. No one followed. No choppers or light planes in sight. At Route 216 he turned right from the through lane at the very last instant, just as the stoplight turned green.

He was on two-lane blacktop now, a local county road. He watched the mirror. A car turned from 29 onto this road, but it had been traveling north. He didn't recognize it. Local traffic passed him going the other way.

Fulton was a tiny village—just a few farms, a church and a small post office with a few nearby shops—1.1 miles west of Route 29. Albright angled left onto Lime Kiln Road. This asphalt ribbon was more narrow and twisty as it followed the natural descent of a creek. He was in an area of beautiful homes set in huge meadows well back from the road. Trees lined the fences and horses grazed on the lush grass. The car that had followed him from Route 29 turned left at Reservoir Road and went up a little hill into a sprawling subdivision.

A half mile past Reservoir Road Albright slowed the car. There it was, right beside the road—a stone drinking fountain fed by a pipe from a spring. He eased to a stop and slammed the gear shift lever into park. From the floor of the backseat he selected a 7-Up can, grasping it with a rag. He slid across the seat, opened the passenger door and set the can at the base of the fountain so it was visible from the road. Back into the car, door shut, and rolling again. Twenty seconds.

He glanced left, up a long sloping meadow at a huge house set on top of the hill in a grove of trees. No one in sight.

Three hundred yards farther on he came to a T intersection. This was Brown Bridge Road, another strip of two-lane asphalt with a double yellow line down the center and no berms. He sat at the intersection and looked both ways. No traffic. Nothing in the rearview mirror.

He turned right. The road wound up a wooded draw and came out into rolling, open country. A mile from Lime Kiln Road he came to another stop sign at a T intersection. This was Route 216 again. To the right, east, was Fulton; 1.1 miles to the west was Highland Junction. He knew, because he had spent many a Sunday driving these suburban county roads, learning their twists and turns, looking for likely drop sites. Directly across the road was a Methodist church. Three or four cars in the lot, no people in sight.

He turned right, toward Fulton. He went through the village and out to Route 29, which he crossed and continued on through Skaggsville, across I-95, and into Laurel, where he turned around in the parking lot of a convenience store and began retracing his route as he watched for vehicles he had seen before and scanned the sky for airplanes.

Exactly thirty minutes later, at 2:47 P.M., he again passed Reservoir Road on Lime Kiln. Someone was changing a flat tire on a van fifty yards up the hill on Reservoir. He hadn't seen that van before. Maybe. It could be the FBI. Or it could be anybody. He continued past and slowed for the stone fountain.

The 7-Up can was still there. No vehicles in sight. No people on the hills that he could see. No choppers or planes overhead. He kept rolling past the fountain and dropped down to the Brown Bridge Road intersection.

He stopped at the stop sign and looked both ways. No traffic. He looked back over his shoulder, thinking about the van with the flat tire, weighing it.

He turned left. The road ran along a creek that was dropping toward the Patuxent River. The little valley was heavily wooded. Houses sat amid the trees off to his left, but the steep bank on his right was a forest.

Two-tenths of a mile from the intersection a gravel road branched off to the right. "Schooley Mill Road," the sign read. He took it.

The road was narrow, no more than ten feet wide. It ran just along the north side of the creek, parallel to the asphalt road, which was twenty-five feet or so above him at the top of a steep embankment on his left. This was a secluded lovers' lane, for a few hundred yards invisible from the paved road above. Apparently, when the teenagers weren't screwing here, the locals used this lane as a trash depository. Green garbage bags, beer and soda-pop cans lay abandoned alongside the gravel.

There was one paved driveway leading north from this road, and it had a mailbox on a wooden post. He passed the box and stopped at the first large tree. He bolted out the passenger door, set the Dr Pepper can at the base of the tree and jumped back in the car.

A tenth of a mile later Schooley Mill Road rejoined Brown

Bridge Road. Two-tenths of a mile after he was back on the asphalt he crossed Brown Bridge, a modern low concrete highway bridge across the Patuxent River, which was several hundred yards wide here. Now this highway became Ednor Road. He continued the two miles to New Hampshire Avenue, Maryland Route 650, and turned left. He had to be back at the drop in twenty-five minutes. He checked his watch.

Eight thousand feet overhead in a Cessna 172, Agent Clarence Brown laid his binoculars in his lap and rubbed his eyes as he keyed the mike. "Subject went down that Schooley Mill fuck road and was hidden by the trees for about two minutes. He might have stopped in there. You better check it."

Sitting in the van with the wheel off on Reservoir Road, Lloyd Dreyfus turned to the man beside him. "That can down at the spring wasn't the drop. The subject was just testing the water."

"You sure?"

"Hell no." But Dreyfus felt it in his gut. He looked at his map. The drops were close together, too close really. Albright should have been more careful. He's getting careless.

"Think he's spotted the plane?"

"No," Dreyfus said. "Brown's too high. He flew right over us a couple minutes ago. You can't hear him at that altitude and you can't see him unless you know where to look."

Dreyfus keyed the radio mike. "Stay on him, Clarence. I want to know when he's coming back."

"Roger."

To the man beside him Dreyfus said, "Have the guys get the wheel back on. Get ready to roll fast." Then he switched frequencies and began moving his agents.

Ten minutes later when Vasily Pochinkov passed the Methodist church on Route 216 and turned onto Brown Bridge Road, he was photographed from a station wagon parked in the church parking lot amid four other cars. He never noticed. His eye was captured by the svelte figure of a woman in shorts walking toward the church door.

He glanced at his wife in the passenger seat as she hunted for a glove on the floor. She had dropped it and was feeling blindly. She was too fat to bend over and look for it.

Why is it, he wondered, not for the first time, that all Russian women have figures like potato sacks while American women keep their figures well past middle age? You wouldn't know it to look at her, but this potato bag was only thirty-four years old and had had the figure of a ballerina when he married her just twelve years ago. It took a lot of vodka these days to prime himself for an expedition between those padded pillars she called thighs.

"Get ready, Nadya. Get the gloves on."

The road began to twist and descend as it dropped toward Brown Bridge. Pochinkov slowed to twenty-five miles per hour, watched the odometer and looked for Schooley Mill Road.

There!

He saw the Dr Pepper can when he was fifty yards away. He glanced around as he braked to a stop. The glen was empty. Nadya stepped out, a green garbage bag in hand, and placed it fifteen feet west of the tree. While she was doing that, Pochinkov walked over to the Dr Pepper can, glanced around once and placed a second one beside it.

They got back in the car, closed the door and rolled.

The Buick was climbing the hill on the south side of the river when the van shot out of Lime Kiln Road and roared the thousand feet to the entrance to Schooley Mill. The driver braked to a halt and two men wearing gloves jumped out. One opened the green trash bag while the other took flash photos.

Inside the van Lloyd Dreyfus was listening to Agent Brown in the Cessna. "Subject is about a half mile south of Ednor Road, northbound on New Hampshire. I'd say you have no more than six or seven minutes . . . He just passed the drop car, which was southbound."

The two men piled back into the van within a minute. The agent at the wheel fed gas when he heard the rear door slam. When he reached the asphalt of Brown Bridge, he made a hard left and headed east, back up the road, toward Lime Kiln.

The lane was empty when Harlan Albright entered four minutes later. He didn't even get out of the car. After a glance at the soda cans, he merely braked to a stop beside the trash bag and picked it up. He set it on the floor in front of the empty passenger seat as he pulled the door shut with his left hand and took his foot off the brake.

Glancing in he could see trash: a wadded-up bread wrapper, a couple empty vegetable cans, three squashed soda-pop cans and an old meat wrapper. They had, he knew, been carefully washed so they would not attract dogs. Under the trash was the money, $200,000 in used twenties, one hundred bundles of a hundred twenties each.

It was 5 P.M. when he pulled into his driveway in Silver Spring. The Sunday *Post* was still lying by the mailbox. He took it into the house with him, turned on the television, and settled back with the newspaper.

26

Toad Tarkington awoke at four-thirty Monday and went to the bathroom. He got back into bed, but he wasn't sleepy. Still dark outside. Wide awake and irritated because he couldn't sleep, he went to the window and peered out. Some clouds with stars visible between them. Not too many stars, though. Funny, but early in the morning, just before dawn, the stars seem to fade, almost as if the weaker ones grow tired of shining and are sent home early.

He prowled the little room, restless. He pulled on jeans and a sweatshirt and was sitting in the easy chair when the light began to spread on the eastern horizon.

The telephone rang.

"Tarkington."

"Lieutenant, this is the shift supervisor at the hospital. Your wife is awake and she asked for you."

"I'll be right over. You tell her!" He dropped the instrument onto the hook and grabbed for his shoes.

The sedan refused to start. He jabbed at the accelerator and held the key over. The engine ground and ground and didn't fire. Too late he realized he had probably flooded it.

Heck. It was only three-quarters of a mile or so over there. He slammed the door behind him and began to trot. Awake! Asking for him! He picked up the pace.

The sun was about ready to come over the earth's rim. The clouds above were blue, turning pink. Above them was blue sky.

The last three blocks he sprinted, down the street and across the windswept dirt that would someday be a lawn and across the empty parking lot with its tumbleweeds and right through the front door.

The nurse at the desk was grinning as he charged by. He skidded around the corner and lunged down the hall for the ICU.

A doctor was there beside her bed, talking to her as a nurse took her pulse. The doctor stepped back as Toad skidded to a halt inside the door and walked forward, into Rita's line of sight.

She tried to grin.

"Hey, babe." He bent over and kissed her.

"Yeah, Mrs. Moravia, she's out of the coma. And she recognizes me! She's asleep right now, real tired, but she's out of the coma!"

"Oh, *thank God!*"

"I really think she's gonna be okay, Mrs. Moravia. It's like a miracle. She doesn't remember anything about the flight or the ejection, but she remembers me and being in Nevada and the other flights, and she kept asking how long she's been in the hospital. The doctor and the nurses are excited! I'm excited!" That was an understatement of major proportions. He was so worked up he felt like he could fly by merely flapping his arms.

After promising to call again after his next visit with Rita, Toad called his parents. He called his sister to give her the news. He called Harriet, Rita's best friend. Due to the time difference on the East Coast, Harriet was at work. And he called Jake Grafton.

Captain Grafton was also at the office and he could hear the activity in the background, but Toad could almost see Grafton leaning back in his chair and propping his feet on his middle desk drawer as if he had all the time in the world. The captain kept him on the phone almost twenty minutes, making him tell of Rita's every word and gesture, listening as long as Toad wanted to talk. Finally Toad realized the captain must have something else to do, and said a reluctant goodbye.

"You tell her I said to get well quick."

"I will, sir."

"And tell her Amy asks about her every day. Amy and Callie have been pulling real hard for her."

"I'll tell her."

"Keep the faith, shipmate," Jake Grafton said, and was gone.

"Yeah," said Toad Tarkington, hanging up the receiver and wiping his eyes. The tears wouldn't stop. So he laughed and cried at the very same time.

Monday evening after work Commander Smoke Judy went home, changed clothes, then drove to a bar in Georgetown. He had trouble finding the place, then he had to park six blocks away and hike back. The streets were packed with the trendy and the chic. Poodles anointed lampposts and fire hydrants as their ladies gazed away with a studied casualness.

Judy had to stand by the door until a stool opened at the bar. He perched there and studied the beer list. The bartender paused across the polished mahogany bar and said, "On draft we have Guinness, Watney's, Steinlager—"

"Gimme a Bud. In a bottle."

He saw Harlan Albright come in about fifteen minutes later and grab an empty stool on the far end. Albright was carrying a gym bag.

Nice touch that, Judy decided. Half the people in the place, men and women, had a gym bag with them or were wearing exercise clothes. Not sweaty tank tops and grungy shorts, mind you, but stuff that looked like it came from Saks and routinely visited a dry-cleaning plant.

When the man beside Judy left to visit a woman who had just slipped into a booth, Albright came over and sat on the vacant stool.

"Ever been here before?"

"Nope. Gonna come back, though. This is a real meat market. And on a Monday evening too!"

"Next Monday. A week from today, same time, right here." Albright signaled the bartender, laid a five on the wood and left.

Smoke nursed his second beer. The mirror behind the bar gave him an excellent view of the Lycra thighs and hungry eyes of the female patrons, most of whom seemed to be drinking white wine or Perrier with a twist.

Smoke Judy, fighter pilot, took a last swallow and counted his change. He left a dollar tip. With a final glance around, he hoisted the gym bag and walked out, right past some sweet little piece in spandex on her way in.

* * *

Tuesday evening Rita grinned as Toad entered her room. She had been moved from the ICU and was in a semiprivate room, but the other bed was empty. The respirator and heart monitor had not accompanied her.

Toad closed the door behind him and kissed her. "How you feeling?"

"Like I got hit by a truck." Her voice was soft, almost a whisper.

"I've been talking to the doctor. They're going to medevac you to Bethesda on Thursday if you keep improving. Being as how I'm next of kin, I get to ride along."

"Good," she said, and continued to grin with her eyes on him.

"So," he said, returning her smile. "So."

"I've read a little bit." Her grin broadened.

"I thought you couldn't focus very well yet."

"I can't. Read a little here, a little there. *The Adventures of Tarkington.* You're a pretty good writer."

"You're a poor critic."

"I'm glad I married you."

"I'm damn glad you did."

The air force medevac plane, a C-141, landed at Andrews AFB. Rita traveled the rest of the way to Bethesda in an ambulance. That evening, when she awoke from her nap, Toad was waiting with her parents, whom he had driven straight to the hospital from National Airport.

Mrs. Moravia was teary but determined to maintain a stiff upper lip. Five minutes after she arrived she launched into a speech that she had apparently been rehearsing for weeks:

"It's time, Rita. It's *time.* You've got a fine husband and it's time you stopped this flying business. Why, Sarah Barnes—you remember Sarah, the cheerleader who went to Bryn Mawr? Such a sweet girl! I can't think of her new married name . . . Sarah just had her second baby, a perfectly darling little boy. Her husband's a med student who's going into pediatrics. And Nancy Stroh, who married that new dentist from Newport—you knew about that, a perfectly gorgeous wedding in May—her mother told me just last week that Nancy's practically pregnant. And Kimberly Hyer . . ."

Mr. Moravia slipped out into the hallway and Toad followed.

"She looks very tired."

"She's had a long day," Toad said.

"Is she going to recover completely?"

"No way to tell. The physical therapy will start in a few weeks and we'll know more then. Right now she's pretty desperate to get out of that lower-body cast. The itching and all is driving her nuts. That's a good sign, I think."

Ten minutes later, as they finished coffees from a vending machine, Toad suggested, "Maybe we'd better go get your wife and say good night to Rita. She wears down pretty quickly and she'll need some sleep."

"We can visit some more in the morning," the older man agreed.

Walking back toward the room, Toad said, "Rita turned out a little different than her mom."

"Different generations." Mr. Moravia shrugged. He was a philosopher.

"They want different things," Toad said, probing gently.

"Every generation does."

"Rita'll keep flying if the doctors let her."

"I believe you. Madeline's just blowing off steam. Rita knows that. Where are we going to eat tonight?"

The next morning, a Friday, Toad accompanied the Moravias to the hospital, then had Mr. Moravia drop him at a Metro station. They were going to the National Gallery. Toad went to the office.

Even the subways were stifling in the August heat. Toad's white uniform shirt threatened to melt before he reached the air-conditioned sanctuary of the lobby in Crystal City.

The elevator took forever to respond to the call button. He waited impatiently. For seven weeks now he had been speculating on the cause of the accident, and Jake Grafton and Helmut Fritsche and Smoke Judy had all refused to enlighten him on the telephone. They had been noncommittal. "We're investigating." That was the party line. Toad jabbed the up button again. He wanted some answers.

He gave the secretary the hi sign and marched straight for Grafton's office. The door was closed, so he knocked, then opened it and stuck his head in. " 'Lo, Captain." Two men he didn't know were sitting in the guest chairs.

"Be with you in a few minutes, Toad. Good to see you back."

Tarkington went to his desk and impatiently pawed the stuff in his in basket. Routine read-and-initial crap. He threw his hat on his desk and sat staring at Grafton's closed door.

The secretary came over to his desk. "How's Rita?"

"She's up at Bethesda. I think she's gonna be okay."

"It was big news around here that you two were married." She grinned and leaned forward conspiratorially. "None of us had any idea! It's so romantic."

"Yeah," said Toad Tarkington.

"We're all just delighted that she's doing so well. We've had her in our thoughts and prayers every day."

"Thank you," Toad said, finally pulling his eyes from Grafton's door and giving the woman a smile. "Know anything about that accident? Why it happened?"

"It's all very hush-hush," she confided, her voice low. She glanced around. "I just haven't seen anything on it, but it was *so terrible!*"

After he assured her he would convey her good wishes to Rita, she went back to her desk. She was sitting there sorting the mail when Smoke Judy came in. Toad went over to him. "Commander, good to see you."

"Hey, Tarkington. How's your wife?"

"Gonna be okay, I think, Commander. Say"—Toad drew the senior officer away from the secretary's desk—"what can you tell me about the accident investigation? What went wrong?"

"Toad, all that is classified special access, and I don't know if you have access. All I've seen is the confidential section of the report. You'll have to talk to Captain Grafton."

"Sorta off the record, it was the E-PROMs, wasn't it? I figure EMI dicked them up." EMI was Electromagnetic Interference.

Judy grinned. "Ask Grafton. Give my best to your wife. And congratulations!"

"Thanks."

Grafton's door opened and Toad stood. He watched the two men in civilian clothes who came out. Their eyes swept the office as they exited, casually, taking in everything at a glance. Toad forgot about them as soon as they were out of sight. He was walking toward the door when Jake Grafton stuck his head out and motioned to him.

"How's Rita?"

"Settled in at Bethesda, sir. The reason I wanted to see you"—

Toad carefully closed the door—"is that I want to know why that plane went out of control. What have you guys found out?"

Jake Grafton stood with his back to Toad, facing the window. In a moment he rubbed his nose, then tugged at an earlobe.

"What have you found out, sir?" Toad asked again.

"Huh? Oh. Sorry. The E-PROMs were defective."

"EMI, I'll bet."

"No. The chips were defective. Won't happen, can't happen, not a chance in a zillion, but it did." Grafton shoved both hands into his pockets and turned around slowly. He stared at a corner of his desk. "Defective when installed."

Something was amiss. "When did you learn this?" Toad said.

"Uh, we knew something was wrong with the chips when we saw the telemetry, but . . . ah . . ." He gestured vaguely at the door. "Those guys who were just here . . ."

"Who were they?"

"Uh . . ." Suddenly the wrinkles disappeared from Jake Grafton's brow and he looked straight at Toad's face, as if seeing him for the first time. "Can't tell you that," he said curtly. "Classified."

"CAG, I've got a wife who may be crippled for life. I *need* to know."

"You *want* to know. There's a hell of a difference. Glad you're back."

Toad tried to approach the subject from another angle, only to be rebuffed and shown the door.

Jake Grafton went back to the window and stared without seeing. Agents Camacho and Dreyfus had been informative, to a point. No doubt it was a rare experience for them, answering the questions instead of asking them. And all those looks and pauses, searching for words! A performance! That's what it had been—a performance. Produced and acted because Vice Admiral Henry demanded it. Well, as little satisfaction as they gave, they were still virgins.

So what did he know? The E-PROMs were defective. The data on the chips was that of preliminary engineering work done several years ago. Somehow . . . No. Someone in this office or at TRX had given that data to the manufacturer. The agents had skated around that conclusion, but they didn't challenge it. They couldn't. "Who?" was the question they had refused to answer. He had run through names to see if he could get a reaction, but no. They had just stared at him.

"Does this have anything to do with Captain Strong's death?" He had asked them that and they had discussed the possibilities, in the end saying nothing of substance. They should have been politicians, not federal agents.

The only fact he now had that he hadn't had before was that the data on the chips matched preliminary engineering work. For *that* they had come at Henry's insistence?

"Why in hell," Jake muttered, "does everything have to be so damned complicated?"

At 2 P.M. Smoke Judy decided to do it. The desk beside him was empty. Les Richards was at a meeting and would be for another hour, at least. Most of the people in the office were busy on Captain Grafton's report or were in a meeting somewhere.

He inserted a formatted disk in the a-drive of his terminal and started tapping. The code word for the file he wanted was "kilderkin." He didn't legally have access to this file. The code word that Albright had supplied was a word he had never heard before. Before he typed it, he wiped his hands on his trousers and adjusted the brightness level of the screen.

He had been debating this all week. He had a hundred grand of Albright's money plus the bucks he already had. He could walk out of here this evening, jump a plane at Dulles tomorrow and by 7 A.M. Monday be so far from Washington these clowns would never find him. Not in fifty years, even if he lived to be ninety-three.

He would be stiffing Albright, of course, but the man was a spy and wasn't going to squeal very loudly. And what the hey, in the big wide world of espionage, a hundred thousand bucks must be small change.

Or he could copy this file and give it to Albright on Monday night. Roll the dice, pass Go and collect another hundred and fifty. Then he would have a total of almost three hundred thousand green American dollars, in cash. Now, for that kind of money you could live pretty damn good in one of those little beach villages out on the edge of nowhere. Get yourself a firm, warm something to take to bed at night. Live modestly but well, loose and relaxed, as light as it's possible to get and keep breathing.

If he copied this file he would not be able to ever come back. If he walked without it, the heat would dissipate sooner or later over that E-PROM chip flap and he could slip back into the country.

Do you pay a hundred and fifty grand to keep your options open? Without the money he would eventually go broke and have to come back.

He typed the word. "Kilderkin." There was the list. Three dozen documents. He looked at the list carefully. Something caught his eye. He studied the column of numbers that listed how many bytes each file was composed of. Boy, these were short files.

Then he understood.

He opened one of the files. The title page came up. He hit the page advance key. The second page was blank. Nothing!

The title page was the whole document! He tried a second document. Just a title page.

The Athena file was empty!

Smoke Judy stared at the screen, trying to think. Possibility Three leaped into his mind. It hadn't even occurred to him until this moment. No wonder you never went up the ladder, Smoke. You just don't think like those snake charmers, those greasy dream merchants who slice off a couple million before they're thirty and spend the rest of their lives pretending they are somebody. Okay, my slow, dim-witted son, this is your chance to butcher the fat hog. Albright isn't going to have a computer in that singles bar to check the disk. Give him an empty disk, take his fucking money, and run.

But no. The joke will be on him. He'll get exactly what he paid for. It's Albright's tough luck the file is empty, not yours.

Judy punched the keys. The disk whirled and whirred.

The file was quickly copied. No wonder, short as it was. Judy put the disk in a side pocket of his gym bag, exited the program and turned off the terminal. He spent another ten minutes cleaning up his desk, locking the drawers, watching the other people in the office.

At the door he used the grease pencil to annotate the personnel board hanging on the wall. Back at 4:30. "I'm going to work out," he called to the secretary, snagged his cover from the hat rack and logged out with the security guards. That easy. *Sayonara,* mothers.

The elevator took a while to arrive. It always did. The navy had a dirt-cheap lease on this space, so the building owner refused to update the elevators. The thought made Smoke Judy smile. This was the very last time he would ever have to put up with all the petty irritations that came with the uniform. He was through. When he took this uniform off tonight, that would be the very last time.

Thank you, Commander Judy. Thank you for your twenty-one years of faithful service to the navy and the nation. Thank you for eight cruises, three of them to the Indian Ocean. Thank you for your devotion, which ruined your marriage and cost you your kids. Thank you for accepting a mediocre salary and a family move every two years and the prospect of a pissy little pension. Thank you for groveling before the tyrannical god of the fitness report, your fate dependent upon his every whim. Commander Smoke Judy, *you* are a great American.

The signal above the elevators dinged. Judy glanced at it. The up light illuminated on the elevator at the far left.

The door of that elevator opened. Vice Admiral Tyler Henry stepped out. Automatically the commander straightened.

"Good afternoon, Ad—"

The look on Henry's face stopped him.

"You!" the admiral roared. He turned to the civilian who had accompanied him on the elevator as he pointed a rigid finger at Judy. "That's *him! That's* the fucking traitor!"

Judy turned and banged open the door to the stairs. With his last glimpse over his shoulder he saw the civilian reaching under his jacket for something on his belt.

He went down the staircase like a rabbit descending a hole, taking them three at a time.

"Stop! NIS!" The shout came from above, a hollow sound, reverberating in the stairwell.

Your luck's running true to form, Smoke.

He groped into the gym bag as he ran. The pistol was under the gym clothes.

Seventh floor. Sixth. Noises from above. They were after him. Fourth.

He kept going down.

Second floor. As he rounded the landing Vice Admiral Henry came through the fireproof door on the first floor. He rode the damn elevator!

Smoke shot at the man behind Henry through the door opening and threw his weight against the door, slamming it shut. In this enclosed space the report deafened him. The admiral grabbed for him, so he chopped at his head with the gun barrel.

Tyler Henry went to his knees. Smoke reversed the gun in his hand and hit him in the head with the butt, using all his strength. The admiral collapsed.

With ears ringing, he wiped his forehead, trying to think. If he could get into the parking garages under the building quickly enough, he might have a chance. He could hear running feet above. Galvanized, he leaped over the admiral's body and charged downward.

Level G1. Smoke went out the door and looked wildly around as he ran for the nearest row of cars. No one in sight. He had beaten them down here, but he had mere seconds.

He ran along looking for keys dangling in the ignition, frustration and panic welling in him.

Hang tough, Smoke. You've been in tight spots before and you've always gotten yourself out in one piece.

He loped down the row, searching desperately.

Ah, there ahead, some guy was unlocking his door. A civilian. Smoke went for him on a dead run.

The man heard Judy coming at the last moment and looked back over his shoulder, just in time to see the gun barrel chopping down.

Smoke picked up the keys from the concrete and tossed his gym bag through the open driver's door. He pulled the man out of the way and got behind the wheel. As he started the car he could see men pouring out of the elevator and stairwell. They were searching, spreading out, hunting for him.

The engine caught. Smoke backed out carefully, snicked the transmission into drive and headed for the exit. Someone was coming this way, shouting.

A shot!

He stepped on the gas.

He went around the last pillar with tires squalling and shot up the exit ramp.

The street at the top of the ramp was one-way, from right to left. Smoke looked right. One car coming. He swerved that way and jammed the accelerator down. The driver of that sedan swerved to avoid him, then decided to try to ram. Too late!

Down the street a half block to the intersection, then left

through a hole in traffic, almost grazing an oncoming truck, which skidded to avoid him with its horn roaring.

Right again, then left. He ran a red light and swung right onto the bus-only ramp, which led up onto the freeway. Merged with traffic and scanning the rearview mirror, only then did Smoke Judy begin to try to sort out what had happened.

"He's dead." The ambulance attendant covered the body of Vice Admiral Tyler Henry with a sheet. "You people give us some room."

Jake Grafton walked out into the elevator lobby, dazed. A half dozen FBI agents were talking on their hand-held radios and listening to the words coming back. There was still a bloody spot on the floor where one agent had gone down with a bullet in his shoulder. Who would have believed . . . Smoke Judy?

Toad Tarkington blocked his path.

"Judy. He's the guy who sold the E-PROM data, wasn't he?"

Jake nodded.

Toad turned and walked away.

"Tarkington! Tarkington!"

Jake caught up with the lieutenant in the plaza. "Where do you think you're going?"

Tarkington didn't look at him. "For a few lousy bucks that bastard damn near killed my wife. She'll never fully recover. She'll carry the scars *all her life.*"

"The FBI'll get him. They're the pros at this."

"They'd better," Toad muttered. "If I get to the cocksucker before they do, they can quit looking."

Tarkington walked away and Jake stood and watched him go. What the hell, he needs some time off anyway. He'll never find Judy. The FBI will scoop him up in a day or two. And maybe the time off will do Toad some good.

Back inside he ran into an agent he recognized, Lloyd Dreyfus. "What the hell happened, Dreyfus?"

"Well, Captain, it seems that the National Security Agency was monitoring the terminals, and when Judy got into the Athena file, they called Vice Admiral Henry right after they called us. Henry beat us here by about a minute."

Jake started to speak and Dreyfus held up a hand. "I know, I know. They shouldn't have done that. And now some poor schnook will probably lose his job. But Tyler Henry was Tyler

Henry. Very few people ever managed to say no to him and make it stick."

"That's true," Jake acknowledged. "Who was the civilian upstairs with Henry?"

"Guy from the Naval Investigative Service. We got all this from him."

"Where's Luis Camacho?"

"Working."

"I want to talk to him."

"I'll pass that along."

"No. You tell him he'll talk with me or I'm going to raise holy hell. When somebody kills a vice admiral in a navy building, the lid is gonna get ripped off pretty damned quick. Right now I know a lot more than my boss, and I don't know much. When I start answering his questions he is not going to be a happy camper. He's a vice admiral too, by the way. I *will* answer his questions. He's another one of those guys who doesn't take no for an answer. George Ludlow, the Secretary of the Navy, he hasn't even heard the word since he got out of diapers. And CNO . . ." Jake snorted.

"Camacho—"

"He won't be able to wave his badge over on the E-Ring and stuff this shit back into the goose . . . *You tell him!*"

As Commander Smoke Judy drove across the George Mason Memorial Bridge into Washington, he stripped off his white uniform shirt with the black shoulder boards and threw it onto the floor of the backseat. He was still wearing a white T-shirt, but that would attract less attention than the uniform. His cover was gone, lost somewhere back in the stairwell.

He needed a change of clothes, he needed to get rid of this car and he needed a place to hide.

He took the Fourteenth Street exit on the east side of the bridge and went north, rolling slowly with the traffic between tour buses and out-of-state cars laden with tourists. A motel? No—they would be checking motels and hotels and bus stations and . . .

He crossed Constitution Avenue and continued north into the business district.

Three blocks north of New York Avenue he was stopped in traffic inching through a single-lane construction choke point when he saw a drunk stagger into an alley, a derelict, or in the language of the social reformers, a "homeless person."

It took five minutes to go halfway around the block and enter the alley from the other end. There was just room to get the car by a delivery truck. The drunk was collapsed beside a metal Dumpster, his wine bottle beside him. His head lay on a blanket roll. Beside him sat a green trash bag. After checking to make sure there was no one in sight, Smoke stopped the car and stepped out.

The drunk was semiconscious. Smoke examined the trash bag. It contained an old coat, some filthy shirts.

"Sorry, buddy. This is the end of the line." Judy throttled him with both hands. The bum, who looked to be in his sixties, with a two-week growth of beard, kicked some and struggled ineffectually. In less than a minute he was gone.

Judy stripped the shirt from the dead man and put it on over his T-shirt. The trousers were next. Sheltered between the Dumpster and the delivery truck, Smoke took off his white trousers and white shoes and socks and pulled the derelict's grime-encrusted trousers on. Perhaps this garment had once been gray, but now it was just dark, blotchy. And a little big. All the better. He even took the dead man's shoes. They were too small, but he put them on anyway.

Judy loaded the trash bag and blanket roll in the car. He helped himself to the wine bottle too, wedging it between the stuff on the backseat so it wouldn't fall over and spill.

He rolled out of the alley and, with the help of a courteous tourist, managed to get back into traffic. He discarded all his white uniform items in a Dumpster near RFK Memorial Stadium, then parked the car in the lot at D.C. General Hospital.

With his blanket roll over one shoulder and the trash bag—which now contained his gym bag—dangling across the other, he shuffled across the parking lot toward the Burke Street Metro stop. He didn't get far. His feet were killing him. The shoes were impossibly small. He sat on a curb with a little hedge behind it and put on his running shoes from his gym bag. The car keys he buried in the soft dirt. He stuffed the drunk's shoes under the hedge, sprinkled some wine on himself and smeared it on his face and left the bottle beside the shoes after wiping it of prints. There was an old cap in the trash bag, which he donned.

He sat there on the curb, considering. A car drove into the lot. A

woman and her two teenage youngsters. She glanced at him, then
ignored him. The teenagers scowled.

This just might work, Judy told himself. He shouldered his load
and set off again for the Metro stop.

Harlan Albright was in the car dealer's snack area, feeding quarters into the coffee machine, when FBI agents arrived at 4:30 to
arrest him. He extracted the paper cup from the little door in the
front of the machine and sipped it experimentally as he glanced
idly through the picture windows at the service desk. Three men in
business suits, one of them black, short haircuts, their coats hanging open. One of them had a word with Joe Talley, the other
service rep, while the other two scanned the area.

As he looked at them, Albright knew. They weren't here about a
car. When Talley pointed in this direction, Albright moved.

On the back wall of the snack area was a door marked "Employees Only." It was locked. Albright used his key and went through
into the parts storeroom. The door automatically locked behind
him.

He walked between the shelves and passed the man at the
counter with a greeting. Out in the corridor he walked ten feet,
then turned left and went through an unmarked door into the
service bay.

Halfway down the bay, one of the mechanics was lowering a car
on the hoist. "You about finished with that LTD, Jimmy?"

"All done, Mr. Albright. Was gonna take it out of here."

"I'll do that. The owner is out at the service desk now. She's
impatient, as usual."

"Starter wire was loose," the mechanic said. "That was the
whole problem. Keys are in it. But what about the paperwork?"

"Go ahead and walk it over to the office."

"Sure." As Albright started the car, the mechanic raised the
garage door and kicked the lifting blocks out of the way of the
tires.

Albright backed out carefully and drove down the alley toward
the area where customers' cars were parked.

Yep, another guy in a business suit hustling this way, and another going around the building toward the front entrance. Albright turned left and drove by the agent walking toward the main
showroom. That agent looked at him with surprise. As Albright

paused at the street, he glanced in the rearview mirror. The agent was talking on a hand-held radio and looking this way.

Albright fed gas and slipped the car into traffic.

They would be right behind him. He jammed the accelerator down and shot across the next intersection just as the light turned red.

He went straight for three more blocks, then turned right for a block, then right again.

He entered the dealership lot from the back and coasted the car toward the service parking area, watching carefully for agents. His trip around town had taken five minutes. Yes, they all seemed to be gone.

He parked the car and walked back inside.

Joe Talley saw him coming. "Hey, Harlan, some guys were here looking for you."

" 'S'at right?"

"Yeah. Didn't say, but they were cops. Had those little radios and charged outta here like their tails were on fire. Just a couple minutes ago. Say, what've you done anyway? Robbed a bank?"

"Nah." Albright quickly sorted through the rack of keys of cars that were awaiting service. "Forgot to put a quarter in the meter." This one, a new Taurus. In for its first oil change.

"Sons of bitches came after me two years ago," Talley said. "My ex swore out a warrant."

"I sent her the fucking check last week," Albright growled. He walked back toward the parking area. "They come back, you tell 'em I went out to feed the meter," he called. "See you after a while."

"Yeah, sure, Harlan." Talley laughed.

"Do my time card too, will ya, Joe?"

"You're covered." Talley went back to annotating a service form.

Albright never returned to the dealership, of course. Less than two hours later he abandoned the Taurus in a parking garage in downtown Washington and walked four blocks to a KGB safe house.

"Just like that, cool as ice, he went back and traded cars?"

"Yessir." Dreyfus tried to keep his eyes on Camacho's face. It was difficult.

"Two guys in two hours go through our fingers! What is this,

Keystone Kops?" Camacho sighed heavily. "Well, what are we doing to round up these public enemies?"

"Warrants for them both, Murder One for Judy and Accessory Before the Fact for Albright. Stakeouts. Briefings for the D.C., federal, airport and suburban police—every pistol-packer within fifty miles of the Washington Monument. Photos on the eleven o'clock news and in tomorrow's papers. The cover story is drugs."

"We really needed Albright, Lloyd."

"I know, sir." Dreyfus was stunned. Luis Camacho had never before called him by his first name in the five years they had known each other.

Camacho sat rubbing his forehead with the first two fingers of his left hand.

"Drugs in the Pentagon is going to get a lot of press," Dreyfus volunteered. "Already Ted Koppel wants the Director for *Nightline*. Some nitwit on the Hill is promising a congressional investigation. Everybody on the west side of the Potomac is probably going to have to pee in a bottle on Monday morning."

If Camacho heard, he gave no sign. After a moment he said softly, "We'll never get him unless he comes to us."

27

A Saturday in August is a terrible time to be in Washington. The heat and humidity make any trip outdoors an endurance trek. The summer haze diffuses the sunlight, but doesn't soften it. Perspiration oozes from every square inch of hide and clothes become sodden rags.

By eleven o'clock Saturday morning, Smoke Judy felt as if he had lived on the street for six months. He had managed only two hours' sleep the night before, most of it in fifteen-minute spurts. The alley he now called home housed three other derelicts, all of whom were comatose drunk by 9 P.M. They had no trouble at all sleeping.

At 7 A.M., or thereabouts—Judy had stowed his watch in his gym bag—his companions stirred themselves and collected their traps. He followed them as they staggered the five blocks to a mission. Two of them vomited along the way. The little neon sign over the door proclaimed: "Jesus Saves."

Breakfast was scrambled eggs, toast and black coffee. Judy carefully observed the men and four women, maybe five—he wasn't sure about one—who ate listlessly or not at all. The alcoholics in the final stages of their disease drank coffee but didn't touch the food. Almost everyone smoked cigarettes. A man across from him offered him an unfiltered Pall Mall, which Smoke Judy accepted. He hadn't smoked a cigarette since he was twenty-four, but when in Rome . . .

"I see you been to the barber college," his benefactor said as he blew out his match.

"Yeah."

"Go there myself from time to time."

Judy concentrated on smoking the cigarette until the man beside him lost interest in conversation. Behind the screen of rising smoke he studied the people around him. He was apparently the only one who showed any interest in his companions. Most of them sat with vacant eyes, or stared at their plates, or the wall, or the smoke rising from their cigarettes.

By eight o'clock he was back on the street. The humidity was bad and the heat was building. Already the concrete sidewalks had become griddles. His companions wandered off in twos and threes, looking for shady spots to snooze, spots near areas of heavy pedestrian traffic that later in the day could be mined by panhandling for enough money to purchase the daily bottle.

Deciding the street was too dangerous for a man with only a day's growth of beard, Judy ambled back toward the alley where he had spent the night. He concentrated on the derelict's shuffle, the head-down, stoop-shouldered, eyes-averted gait that characterized so many of the defeated wanderers.

His eye caught a headline in a newspaper rack. The photo—that was him! He walked along, wondering. Up ahead was a trash bin with a paper sticking out. He snagged it and took it back to the alley.

Drugs. Cocaine trafficking. The photo of him in uniform was that service-record shot he had submitted last year. The picture of Harlan Albright was a candid street shot, almost as if he had been unaware of the camera. Still, it was a good likeness. With his back to the Dumpster, sitting on the asphalt, Smoke Judy read the stories carefully. Vice Admiral Henry was dead, according to the *Post,* killed by a drug dealer resisting arrest. Well, was the *Post* ever wrong?

When he finished the story he threw the paper in the Dumpster.

Now he lay in the heat, his head on his blanket roll, watching an old dog search for edible garbage. A slight breeze wafted down the alley, but it wasn't much. The place was a sauna. After the dog left, the only creatures vigorously stirring were the flies.

Jesus, who would have believed things could go so wrong so fast? The feds must have been monitoring access to that file, and the instant he opened it, jumped in the car to drive over and arrest him. From commander in the U.S. Navy to hunted fugitive killer all in one fifteen-minute period—that had to be a new record for the fastest fall in the history of the navy.

As he thought about it, Smoke Judy did not agonize over the split-second decisions he had made or torture himself with what-ifs. He had spent his adult life in a discipline composed of split-second decisions, and he had long ago learned to live with them. You made the best choice you could on the information you had and never wasted time later regretting the choice. He didn't now.

Still, as he looked back, he couldn't really pinpoint any specific decision that he could say had been the perfect choice to make when he made it. So here he was, lying in an alley ten blocks northeast of the White House. Hell must be like this, dirty and hot, all the sinners baking slowly, desperate for a beer. God, a cold beer would taste so good!

The money. After that phone call from Homer T. Wiggins, he had felt it unsafe to leave the money in his apartment when he wasn't there, so he had put it in a duffel bag in the trunk of his car. His passport was in the bag too. The car was undoubtedly in the police impound lot by this time and the money and passport were in the evidence safe. He had been tempted yesterday to try to get it, but that temptation he had easily resisted. Smoke Judy, fighter pilot, knew all about what happened to guys who went back to a heavily defended target for one more run.

Man, the bumper sticker is right—shit happens. And it happens fast. The real crazy thing is it all happened to him. The great sewer in the sky dumped it all on him. Fuck! He said it aloud: "Fuck."

"Fuck!" He shouted it, liking the sound of his voice booming the obscenity at the alley walls. The word seemed to gain weight and substance as it echoed toward the street. He filled his lungs with air and roared, *"Fuck fuck fuck fuck fuck!"*

"Hey, you down there." He looked up. Some guy was leaning out a window. "You stop that damn shouting or I'll call a cop to run you out of there. You hear?"

"Yeah. Sorry."

"Goddamn fucking drunk psychos," the man said as he closed the window, probably to keep in the cool, conditioned air.

Okay, Judy told himself, going through the whole thing one more time. He was in the smelly stuff to his eyes. Okay. How was he going to get the hell out of this mess?

Well, this alley was as good a place as any to spend the weekend.

If he tried to check into a motel or hotel, or tried to buy clothes or steal a car, he might be recognized. The cops wouldn't be looking for him in an alley, at least not for a few days. No doubt they were watching the airports, train station and bus depot. And looking for that car he drove away from Crystal City.

So sitting here in this shithole for a few days looked like a pretty good idea. Of course, selling the E-PROM data to Homer T. Wiggins had looked good too, as did killing Harold Strong, copying the Athena file . . .

Ah me.

Well, he still had a card. One chance. $150,000. Boy, did he ever need that money now. Monday evening, Harlan Albright, that meat market in Georgetown. One way or the other, Albright was parting with the cash, he told himself grimly. There were still five live cartridges left in the pistol.

Jake Grafton sent his family to the beach Friday evening. Saturday he was back at the office finishing his report on the testing of the prototypes. He had already circulated a draft to his superiors and now he was incorporating their comments.

The senior secretary had volunteered to work on Saturday, and she was making the changes on the computer when the telephone rang. "Jake, this is Admiral Dunedin. I have a couple FBI agents here with me. Could you come up to my office?"

"Yessir. Be right there."

The agents turned out to be Camacho and Dreyfus. They shook his hand politely. Jake sat in a chair against the wall, facing the side of the admiral's desk.

"Captain," the admiral said to get the ball rolling, "these gentlemen said you had some concerns that you wished to discuss."

Jake snorted and rearranged his fanny on the chair. "I suspect my concerns are minor and worlds away from the FBI's, but they're real enough. I've read the morning papers. Apparently the ATA program is some kind of cover for drug dealers who are supplying all the addicts in the Pentagon, and one of them went bug-fuck crazy yesterday and beat an admiral to death."

"Now, Captain—" Camacho began.

"Let me finish. Presumably this boondoggle operation is run by some airhead who is unable to recognize the nefarious character of his subordinates, who have been engaged in subverting the national defense establishment from within. Moral rot and all that. And who is the airhead who commands this collection of criminals in uniform? Why, it's the navy's very own Jake Grafton, who next week is going to be testifying before various committees of Congress about the necessity to fund a new all-weather, carrier-based, stealth attack plane. No doubt this Captain Bligh will be questioned closely by concerned congressmen about his inability to see beyond the end of his nose. So my question is this—just what the hell do you gentlemen suggest I tell the congressmen?"

The agents looked at each other, then the admiral.

"We need this airplane," said the admiral. "Any suggestions?"

"This would be a great place for the truth," Jake observed.

It was Camacho who spoke. "The truth is this is a national security matter. Any additional comment will jeopardize an ongoing investigation."

"You expect me to go over to the Hill and say that?" Jake asked incredulously. "See this uniform? I'm a naval officer, not a spook. How about the directors of the FBI and CIA go over there and make a little statement behind closed doors, ahead of time?"

Camacho considered it.

"They can swear on Bibles or cross their hearts, or whatever it is you spooks do on those rare occasions when you're really going to come clean."

"I suppose we could ask the Director," Camacho said with a glance at Dreyfus.

"While you're mulling that, how about explaining to me and the admiral just what is going on? I'd like to know enough to avoid stepping on my crank, and I don't think that's asking too much."

"This matter should be resolved in the next few weeks," Camacho murmured.

Grafton just stared. The admiral looked equally frosty.

"Judy was selling information to defense contractors. He—"

"We *know* that," the admiral said testily. "Tell us something we don't know."

"He was recruited by a Soviet agent to copy the Athena file. Apparently he agreed to do so. He attempted it Friday afternoon, NSA called us and Henry, Henry beat us here." He shrugged.

"How did Admiral Henry learn that there might be an attempt to copy the Athena file?" Dunedin wanted to know.

"I told him," Camacho said.

"Oh."

"Yes."

"Why?"

"I can't go into that. Obviously, I had authority to tell him."

"Did Henry know that?"

"Know what?"

"Know that you had authority to tell him."

"I don't know what he knew. Or thought or suspected. Perhaps."

Dunedin's eyebrow was up. He looked skeptical.

"What do you want to hear, Admiral? That Henry thought he was getting unauthorized information from a confidential source? Okay, that's what he thought. Henry was Mr. Naval Aviation. Honest, loyal, brilliant, he had an immense ego. Perhaps that's why he was Assistant Chief of Naval Operations for Air. He had the habit of sticking his nose in where it didn't belong, of wanting to know more than the law allowed. For example, we found this notebook in his desk drawer yesterday afternoon." Camacho took a small spiral notebook from an inside coat pocket and tossed it on the desk.

Dunedin examined it for a moment, turning the pages slowly. He glanced up at Camacho several times, but each time his eyes quickly returned to the pages before him. Without comment, he slowly closed the book and passed it across the table to Captain Grafton.

"A, B, C . . . who are these people?"

"The letters stand for people that Henry wanted information about. Some of the information was supplied by psychotherapists, some by police agencies, some by people in government in sensitive positions who talked out of school. One of those letters apparently stands for Callie Grafton. I believe she was seeing a psychologist, wasn't she, Captain?"

Jake Grafton began ripping pages from the notebook. A handful at a time, he deposited them in the classified burn bag by Dunedin's desk.

As he watched, Camacho continued. "Henry was very worried about the Minotaur. He feared the unknown. So he did what he could to protect his trust. It's hard to condemn him."

"These little pieces of the cloth that you let us see, they're tantalizing." The admiral leaned back in his chair and made a tent of his fingers.

That comment drew no response from the agents. Dreyfus examined his fingernails as Camacho watched Grafton complete his job of destruction.

"Why did this Soviet agent approach Judy?" the admiral asked. "Why did he single him out?"

"I told him about the commander's troubles," Camacho replied.

"You told *him?"* The admiral's eyes widened. "Good God! Who are *you* working for, anyway?"

"I'm on your side, Admiral."

"Hallelujah! I hate to think of the mess we'd be in if you weren't."

"Why my wife?" Jake asked.

"You'd been given guardianship of the holy grail, Athena. You, a captain. Smoke Judy worked for you. Admiral Henry knew Judy was a bad apple, and he knew I knew."

"It's a wonder he slept nights," Dunedin muttered.

"Are you saying he didn't trust me?" Jake said doggedly.

"Tyler Henry didn't trust anyone. He didn't just cut the cards; he insisted on shuffling every time. But I don't think it was you he was really worried about. It was me. He didn't want you corrupted by me."

"Say again?"

"He thought I might recruit you, so he was looking for clues in the only place he could." Camacho stood. Dreyfus got to his feet a second later. "Gentlemen, that's the crop. That's all you get."

"Not so fast, Camacho," the admiral said, pointing toward the chairs. "You can hike when I finish this interview. I have a few more questions to ask, and so you sit right there and I'll do the asking."

Camacho obeyed. Dreyfus remained erect. "You can wait outside," the admiral said.

"He can stay," Camacho said. Dreyfus sat.

"Who approved this operation?"

"My superiors."

"Who are?"

"The Assistant Director and the Director. And the committee."

"What I want to know is this: who gave you the green light to screw around with the U.S. Navy? As if we didn't have enough troubles."

"My superiors."

"I want *names*, mister! I want to know the names of the idiots who authorized a covert operation that resulted in the death of a vice admiral and jeopardized congressional approval of the A-12. I want some ass! The CNO is going to want blood. George Ludlow, Royce Caplinger, if they don't know about this—"

"Ask them. Any more questions?"

"Ludlow? Caplinger? *They* knew?"

"The people who have to know, know. You said those names; I didn't. Now if *you* will excuse me, I've said all I can say and I have work to do." Dreyfus reached the door before Camacho got completely out of his chair.

"The FBI Director better be there pouring oil on the water when I get to those hearings, Camacho," Jake said.

"And if he isn't?" Dreyfus asked with exaggerated politeness.

"Then you'd better be there with a warrant if you want me to keep quiet. I have this nasty little habit of answering questions by telling the truth."

Camacho just nodded and strolled for the door, which Dreyfus opened and held. "Thank you both," he told the naval officers, then stepped through.

When the door was shut behind them, Dunedin said, "Too bad we don't know any truth to answer questions with."

"We know a little."

"You've still got a lot to learn, Jake. Truth isn't something you can extrapolate from a tiny piece. And believe me, those two have given us the tiniest piece they could. If it was a piece of the truth at all, which is debatable."

On Monday morning Jake signed his report, which recommended the TRX prototype as the plane the navy should buy, and hand-carried it to Admiral Dunedin's office. The admiral flipped through it to see that the changes he wanted were made, then he signed the prepared endorsement. From there Jake carried it over to the program coordinator's office. Commander Rob Knight was tapping a letter on his word processor when Jake came in.

"This is it, huh?"

"Yep." Jake pulled up a chair. Knight reviewed the changes, then signed the routing slip. "Congratulations. Another milestone passed."

"Think we'll get this plane?"

"Looks good. Looks good." Knight grinned. He spent a large portion of his time talking to congressional staffers on behalf of the CNO's office. "They know we need it. They know it's a good buy.

The only really iffy thing is the choice of prototypes. Duquesne knows this is coming and he's loading his guns."

"What's he going to come at me with?"

"I'll know more by tomorrow. I'll be over at nine with a guy from the Office of Legislative Affairs to brief you on expected questions, suggested answers, how to keep your cool—all the good stuff. You'll be testifying with Admiral Dunedin and he'll go first. But you're the guy they'll try to rip. You originated the recommendation. If they can get you to admit you're an incompetent, lying idiot, then Dunedin, CNO, SECNAV, SECDEF, they all have to reconsider. So wear your steel underwear."

Jake's next stop was CNO's office. He had to talk to the executive assistant—the EA—and wait an hour, but with the CNO's blessing on his document, he walked it down to the Secretary of the Navy's office. After the obligatory half hour wait while the EA reviewed the document, Ludlow invited him in.

"How close is this to the draft I saw?"

"Pretty close, sir. Vice Admiral Dunedin and CNO wanted some changes, and they're incorporated."

"Are you prepared to defend this report on the Hill?"

"Yessir."

Ludlow quizzed him for an hour on the technical aspects of the report. Apparently satisfied, he accompanied Jake to the door. "Just don't get cute with the elected ones. Be open, aboveboard, a good little sailor."

Smoke Judy changed into his running clothes and stowed his rags behind a Dumpster in a Georgetown alley. God, he smelled ripe. But what the hell—they sold this stink in a bottle now, didn't they? He would probably have women crawling all over him. Everyone would think he just ran five miles and dropped by for a tall, cool Perrier. Just as trendy as a pair of Gucci shoes.

He walked the four blocks to the bar carrying the gym bag in his right hand. The place was packed, just like last week. If anyone noticed his aroma, they didn't show it.

He made his way through the crowd and into the men's room, where he washed his face and neck and arms as thoroughly as possible. He even used a paper towel on his armpits without taking his shirt off.

Whew! He felt better.

He stepped out of the men's room and stood looking. A two-person booth opened up at the back of the room, so he immediately slipped into it. Holding the gym bag under the table, he extracted the pistol from the bag and laid it on his lap.

The waitress didn't give his four-day beard a second glance. "Gimme a Bud."

He drank the first one quickly, then nursed the second. Twenty minutes passed, then thirty.

What if Albright doesn't show?

Judy got a sick feeling in the pit of his stomach. The beer felt like it was going to come up. He stared at the door, scrutinizing every face.

When Albright came in, Judy almost shouted.

He walked the length of the room and slid into the booth. Only then did Judy realize his hands were empty.

"Jesus," Albright said. "You look bad."

"Had a little trouble."

"I guess you did. I read about it. Dealing, are you?"

"A crock."

"Yeah." Albright ordered a Corona. He sat looking around.

"Where'd you spend the weekend?"

"In an alley."

"Smart."

"They haven't caught me yet."

"You wired?"

"What?"

"Are you wearing a wire?"

"Hell no. Where's the fucking money?"

"You got it?"

"Yeah, right here. You wanta see it?"

"Okay. Show me."

Judy passed him the gym bag. "The side pocket. Look but don't take it out." Albright did as requested.

"So, you got it?"

"What's it look like?"

"What it looks like, my friend, is a five-and-a-quarter-inch floppy disk, which could have anything under the sun on it. It could even be empty. You didn't think I was just going to take it on faith that you're an honorable gentleman and hand you all that lettuce, did you?"

"Something like that."

The Corona came. Albright took his time squeezing the lime

slice and dropping it down the neck of the bottle. "Your good health," he said, and took a sip.

"Where is it?"

"Where is what?"

"The bread, asshole."

"Out in my car."

"You want the disk, you go get it."

"I need to see what's on the disk first. What say we both go out there and I'll check the disk on my laptop. I brought it along, just in case."

"Uh-uh. No money, no disk."

"You make me very suspicious, my friend. Your refusal to come outside indicates there is a very good possibility you are wearing a wire. The possibility is even higher that the file I want is not on this disk." Albright grinned. "You see how it is."

"What I see is this: I've got it and you aren't leaving here with it until I see the money."

"When did you copy this disk?"

"Friday afternoon."

"When did the admiral come by?"

"About ten minutes later."

Albright looked at the faces around him, then turned back to Judy. "Even if you think you have the file—I will grant you your good faith—I doubt seriously if it is the information I want. Not on Friday afternoon, with NIS and the FBI just ten minutes away. They were waiting for you. It was a trap."

"I got the file," Judy insisted.

"No. I think not." Albright started to slide out of the booth. Something hard hit his leg, and he stopped.

"Is that what I think it is?"

"I don't know what you think. Use your hand, gently, and feel."

Albright did so. "I see."

"Turn back around. Face me."

Albright obeyed. He took another sip of beer. "Now what?"

"Now I want that money."

"How do you propose to get it?"

"You had better think of something I like real fucking quick or you aren't walking out of here. I'm going to blow your cock off with the first one, then I'm going to put one right in your solar plexus. Who knows, an ambulance could get here so fast you might live. But you'll be in a wheelchair for the rest of your life and you're going to do all your peeing sitting down."

Albright wasn't fazed. "Do you have any suggestions?"

"You do the suggestions. You have one minute."

"Hmmm."

"I got nothing to lose, Albright. I *will* pull this trigger. Believe it!"

"You'll be caught."

"Probably, but they're going to try me for killing a vice admiral, not for blowing the cock off a commie spy. Who knows, with you on my record, I may get probation. You got forty seconds."

"Who knows. Indeed, who knows." Albright considered.

"Thirty seconds."

"Quiet. I'm thinking." He took a deep breath, then exhaled slowly. "Look to your left. Against the bar. There is a man there wearing a UCLA sweatshirt. Look at his hand."

Warily, Smoke glanced left, then back at Albright. The man across the booth was watching him with an amused look. Judy looked again. The man at the bar had a pistol, and it was pointed straight at him.

"I didn't come alone. You pull that trigger and he will kill you before you pull it again."

In spite of himself, Judy looked again. It sure looked like a real pistol, an automatic, held low, shielded by the body of the man beside him. The gunman was looking straight into his eyes.

"So," said Harlan Albright. "Here is how it will be. You will put your gun back in the gym bag. We will walk out to my car—oh yes, I do have a car. We will put the disk in the laptop and check it. If indeed it contains the Athena file, I will give you the money. If not, we'll shake hands, and you'll go your way, I mine."

"I oughta just shoot you, here and now."

"As you say, I may live. You most certainly won't. Your choice."

"I'm busted. I got nothing. They—" He swallowed hard. Tears were obstructing his vision. "They emptied the file. It was a setup. Nothing there but the title pages of thirty documents, each document just one page. Honest. I got what you wanted to buy. I'm desperate! I *need* the money."

Albright nodded. "I'm sorry."

"C'mon, mister," he pleaded. "I'll do you a deal. The title pages must be worth something. I got fifteen bucks to my name. That's it! Fifteen lousy bucks." He was sobbing.

"I think not." Albright looked around. Spectators were watching Judy. It was past time to go. Albright took out his wallet and tossed all the currency he had on the table. "There's something over a hundred and forty there. You take it."

Judy seized the bills. He scooped them up with his left hand, then fumbled below the table with the gun. "I need the gym bag. Here"—he held out the disk. "You take it. I don't want it."

"Good luck," Albright said, and then rose and walked toward the entrance, leaving Judy holding the disk and staring after him. When Albright was through the door, the gunman on Smoke's left followed him.

Judy lowered his head to the table.

"Mister," he heard someone saying. "Mister, you're going to have to leave. Please, mister," urged the hard, insistent voice, "you can't stay here."

28

Senator Duquesne has a copy of your service record."

"What? How'd he get that?"

Commander Rob Knight shrugged. "God only knows, and he won't tell. What's in your service record that would do him any good?"

"I don't know," Jake Grafton said.

"He may not use any part of it. Probably won't. But he told some colleague's aide, figuring you'd hear about it and get worried."

"What a guy."

"This is major-league hardball, Grafton. And he's got that crackpot Samuel Dodgers scheduled to testify before you get on the stand, after SECDEF and Dunedin finish."

"He's playing Russian roulette. Dodgers is a genius with the personality of a warthog."

"His strategy, apparently, is to get the A-12 defeated. The story I hear from a couple aides is that Athena is such a revolutionary new technology, it needs to be produced and evaluated before the navy buys any stealth airplanes—i.e., neither prototype will be purchased. Then Consolidated can participate in another competition for a more conventional design that makes full use of Athena's capabilities. The argument is that a more conventional airplane that uses Athena exclusively for stealth protection will save the government several billions."

"Is he going to try this out on Caplinger?"

"Nope. He's going to let Caplinger and Dunedin testify, then wring the juice out of Dodgers and dump it all in your lap in the hope you'll blow it."

"Has he got the votes?"

"Not yet. There are enough fence sitters so that the issue is very much up in the air. We had the A-12 sold to the Senate and the House committees until Athena came along, but with the headlines lately—and the budget deficit—any way they can save money looks better and better."

Jake knew the headlines Knight was referring to. The Soviets under Mikhail Gorbachev had renounced world domination, and the aftershocks were being felt in capitals around the world. Gorbachev was well on his way to becoming the most popular and overexposed human on the planet, eclipsing rock stars, athletes, and, in some places, even God. The Cold War was over, according to some commentators and politicians with their own agendas. True or not, the perception of great change taking place in the "evil empire" had profound consequences for the foreign and domestic policy of every Western democracy, and none more so than the United States.

The two officers spent the morning going over the cost projections of the A-12, which were based on an optimum purchase schedule. Any proposal that kept the A-6 in service for more years than already planned would also have to include the escalating costs of maintaining and repairing this aging airframe. These costs were also calculated. Finally, any new proposal for another design would incur huge upfront costs, as the A-12 program had, and to kill the A-12 now would mean all the money spent to date would be wasted.

After lunch Knight, an officer from the Office of Legislative Affairs, and Jake's staff gathered in the conference room and pretended to be a congressional panel. They spent the afternoon grilling him. By five o'clock he was drained and hoarse.

Callie was reading Amy a bedtime story when the telephone rang. The girl leaped for the phone, then held it out to Jake.

"Captain Grafton."

"This is Luis Camacho. Do you have a Robert E. Tarkington working for you?"

"What's he done now?" Tarkington had been on the mock panel this afternoon and had done a terrible job. His heart had obviously not been in it.

"Well, he's not at home, for one thing. His car is sitting outside an apartment building in Morningside and we think he's in it. It's the building that Commander Judy lives in. He's right smack-dab in the middle of our surveillance."

"So run him off."

"Well, that might produce sticky complications. I understand he has reason to bear Judy a grudge concerning his wife's injuries a couple months ago. He might be armed. If so, he might be arrested on a concealed weapons charge, which I suppose wouldn't do his navy career much good."

"It wouldn't. What if I ran him off?"

"Would you? Here's the address." Camacho gave it, said good-bye, then hung up.

Callie looked at Jake with raised eyebrows. "Would you ladies like to go for a ride before bedtime? Maybe get some frozen yogurt?"

After five minutes of furious activity, the females were ready. Jake drove through the heart of monumental Washington and ended up on the Suitland Parkway. Callie gave him directions with the aid of a map. They got lost once but eventually found the right street.

Although it was after 9 P.M., it had been totally dark less than half an hour. Heat still rose from the streets and children still ran through yards. Here and there stickball games were being conducted under streetlights. "This is the best time of the day," Jake told Callie as they sat at a stoplight listening to pop music pouring from the open windows of a car full of teenagers.

Six blocks later Callie said, "That's the building, I think, up there on the left."

"Keep your eyes peeled for Toad," Jake advised Amy. "He's sitting in one of these cars."

"Why?" Amy asked.

"You'll have to ask him. Now look."

His car was parked a half block beyond the apartment building. Only the top of his head was visible as Jake drove by with Amy squealing and pointing. Jake turned around again and this time double-parked just past his car. With the engine running and the transmission in park, he got out and walked back.

Toad's window was down. He stared blankly up at Jake's face.

"We're going out for a frozen yogurt. Wanta come?"

"How'd you—"

"Lock your car and climb in with us."

"Jesus, CAG, I—"

Jake opened the driver's door and held it. "Come on. That's an order."

Toad rolled up the windows and locked the car. "You can ride in back." Toad obediently slipped in beside Amy. She greeted him like a long-lost friend. "How's Rita?" she demanded.

"Doing okay," Toad said. "And how are you, Mrs. Grafton?"

"Just fine, Toad. What kind of frozen yogurt do you like?"

"Any kind," Tarkington said, still bewildered.

"Why were you parked out here?" Amy asked, hanging her arms around Toad's neck. "You don't live here, do you?"

"Waiting on a man. He hasn't shown up."

"Oh!" Amy thought about it. "When can we see Rita?"

"Anytime you want."

"Well, it's only nine o'clock," Jake said to Callie. "No school tomorrow for you aristocrats. What say we drive over to Bethesda and see if Rita's still awake? That okay with you, Toad?"

"Sure, Captain, sure."

They stopped at a mall near the beltway entrance and bought cones of frozen yogurt. Everyone got one. As Amy skipped back toward the car and the adults followed, Toad asked Jake. "How'd you know where I was?"

"FBI called me. They don't want you there."

The younger man bristled. "It's a public street. And I didn't see them lurking around waiting on anybody."

"Oh, they're there. They saw you, got your license number, ran the plate and called me. They really didn't want to arrest you on a felony weapons charge."

Toad's shoulders sagged.

"You must get on with your life," Callie said gently, "yours and Rita's, for you are part of her."

"Let's go see her," Jake suggested, and led the way toward the car.

Tarkington rode silently as Amy chattered between licks on her cone. He put his tongue in motion in the hospital reception room after the woman at the desk said, "It's after visiting hours, Lieutenant."

"I know, but I'm her husband. These are my folks, just in from the Coast. We'll be quiet and not stay long." Toad winked at her and gave her his most sincere lying smile.

"I don't suppose a short visit after hours will do any real harm. For such close relatives."

"Toad," Amy asked in the elevator, "why did you tell that lady a lie?"

"I didn't *really* lie," Toad explained. "See, I winked at her and she knew you weren't my relatives, that I was just giving her a good reason to bend the rules a tiny bit. If I tell you a story about fairies and frogs and passionate princesses, you know it isn't true and so it isn't a lie, is it? It's a story."

"Well . . ." Amy said as she scrunched up her brows and tried to follow Toad's logic.

"I knew you'd understand, sis," Toad said as the elevator door opened. He led them off and along the corridor toward Rita's room.

Rita was asleep when they tiptoed into the room. "Maybe we should let her sleep," Callie suggested.

Toad bent over and whispered her name. Her eyes fluttered. Then he kissed her cheek. "You've got company, dearest."

"Oh, Callie! Amy! Captain Grafton. What a pleasant surprise. How nice of you to come by."

"Toad brought us," Amy said. "He lied to the lady downstairs. Said we were his family." She winked hugely while Callie rolled her eyes.

Thirty minutes later Jake insisted they had to go. He led his family down the corridor while Toad said a private goodbye to Rita. Amy was tiring and talking too loud, so Callie tried to hush her, which made her whine. Jake picked her up and carried her.

In the car Callie chided Toad. "You sitting in that car in Morningside while your in-laws are at your house. You should be ashamed."

"Well . . ."

"When Rita gets out of the hospital, you must bring her over to the beach some weekend."

"Sure. You bet, Mrs. Grafton. I will."

Back in Morningside, Jake double-parked across the street and walked with Toad over to his car. Jake waited until Tarkington had the car unlocked, then said, "You have a beautiful wife, a good job, and all of life before you. Don't fuck it up by sitting here waiting to kill a man."

"You saw what he did to Rita."

"Yeah. And if you get lucky and get a bullet into him, the stuff that will happen to you afterwards will hurt her a lot worse than the airplane crash did. You'll be the one who twisted the knife. *Don't do that to her.*"

"Yessir." Toad shook Jake's hand, then climbed into the car and cranked the window down.

"Thanks, CAG . . ."

"It's a good life, kid. Don't throw it away."

". . . for the frozen yogurt." Tarkington started his car and snapped on the headlights.

"Night, Toad."

"Good night, sir."

As soon as Jake got his car rolling, Amy stretched out in the backseat. In a few minutes he checked that she was asleep, then said to Callie, "Admiral Henry had a notebook." He told her what he had learned from Camacho, that Callie's psychologist was telling Henry what she said in her therapy sessions.

"Oh, Jake." She bit her lip. "I've half a mind to write a letter to the Medical Board."

"He was just trying to help Henry."

"Damn him." He looked at her. She was rigid, with both fists clenched.

He began to talk. He told her about the Minotaur, about Smoke Judy and Luis Camacho and the Russian spy. Crossing the Anacostia River, going north on South Capitol Street, creeping through the cooling evening along Independence Avenue by the Air and Space Museum, he told her everything he knew.

She listened carefully. They were parked facing the Lincoln Memorial on Twenty-third Street and watching the crowd still going to and from the Wall when she said, "Camacho told the spy about Judy?"

"That Judy was corrupt? Yes. So he says."

"He wanted something to happen."

"What do you mean?"

"He was trying to make something happen."

"Something *has* happened. Judy tried to steal the Athena file and killed Henry getting away."

"That wasn't it," she said, speaking with conviction. "Henry had ordered the file changed, the documents moved. You knew—everyone with access knew. Camacho must have warned Henry."

"But if Camacho knows a Soviet spy and talks to him, why doesn't he arrest him?"

"Something is *supposed* to happen. Something involving the spy and the Minotaur. And it hasn't happened yet."

On Friday morning at 7 A.M. Jake met Rob Knight in a bagel joint on Independence Avenue, two blocks east of the Capitol. As they huddled at a tiny table in a corner munching bagels smeared with cream cheese and sipping coffee, Knight filled Jake in on the testimony of Royce Caplinger and Vice Admiral Dunedin before the joint subcommittee of the Senate and House Armed Services Committees the previous day. Neither had been asked about Vice Admiral Henry's death or Smoke Judy, perhaps because the Director of the FBI had spent thirty minutes with the committee before Caplinger went on.

"Dodgers will go first this morning. Duquesne will be done with him in an hour or so. He's going to question him very lightly on just the technical aspects of Athena, then praise him to the skies as the intellectual heir of Edison, Bell, and Einstein. That's his plan, anyway." Knight grinned impishly.

"You really enjoy this, don't you?"

"It's the ultimate theater. The stakes are money, the mother's milk of politics, great heaping mountains of it. And the actors are politicians, without a doubt the lowest form of animate life. Charlatans, mountebanks, liars, hypocrites—they'd cut off your nuts for another term in office, or even a favorable article in a hometown newspaper. If you rendered the whole lot of 'em, you couldn't skim enough scruples to fill a thimble."

"They're not all like that," Jake protested.

Knight made a gesture of frustration. "I suppose not."

"When do they want me there?"

"Well, you're going to watch Dodger's performance. You go after him. Normally these things are closed-door, but I got some members to sign two passes." He displayed them, then handed one to Jake.

They wandered outside, then across to the Library of Congress. On the second floor of the giant anteroom they found a wooden bench in a corner and reviewed the documents Jake would refer to if necessary during his testimony.

After thirty minutes, Jake announced he was ready and stowed the documents in the briefcase he had chained to his wrist.

"Nervous?"

"Yeah. My stomach feels like . . ."

"Well, that's normal. I've seen vice admirals preparing for these soirees sweat like they were going to the gallows."

"Too bad about Admiral Henry."

"Yeah. Think they'll ever catch Judy?"

"Oh, he'll turn up, sooner or later."

"What are you going to say if they ask you about him?"

"The truth. Just watch."

"Don't get rattled. If you can't remember something, just say so. And don't feel bad about fumbling for a document. I'll be right there with you, and I'll help you find it."

They chatted for another five minutes about this and that, about their careers, about mutual friends, about ships they had been on. Finally Knight announced that it was time.

They crossed the street and walked past the limos and congressmen's cars parked in the Capitol's back lot. They went up the marble steps and into the rotunda.

The place was packed with tourists standing in knots of thirty or more, cameras clicking, guides roaring their patter over the hubbub, the noise echoing in the huge open space above. The two naval officers in service-dress blue uniforms threaded their way through and turned right, passing between the statues into the main corridor.

They went up one flight of stairs and stopped finally beside a door manned by armed security guards, where they showed their passes. The guards consulted a list and said they could go in.

"You ready?" Knight asked again.

"Let's go to the head first."

"Good idea." Knight asked a guard for directions to the nearest men's.

Standing shoulder to shoulder at the urinals, Knight said, "Think of all the great men who have relieved themselves here— senators, congressmen, generals, tycoons, kings. Makes you humble, doesn't it?"

The hearing room was a disappointment to Jake. He had expected some spacious room richly decorated in a courtroom motif, but what they got was another drab, windowless hearing room that needed paint and more lights. He and Knight took a seat against the back wall and watched the elected persons make their way in. They conferred with one another and found chairs on the dais that dominated the room. Duquesne came in, nodded at Jake and placed his briefcase at the speaker's stand in the center of the dais. Then he went from political person to political person shaking hands, murmuring softly.

"It never stops, does it?" Knight whispered.

"They'll be shaking hands and kissing babies at their own funerals," Jake agreed.

Dodgers didn't even glance around when he was led in by two men that Jake assumed were senatorial aides. They placed him at the little witness table and sat down on either side of him.

With a glance at the clock, Duquesne took his seat. "By mutual agreement, this is a meeting of the Senate and House Armed Services Committees' joint subcommittee on stealth projects. Dr. Dodgers, I understand you are here by subpoena. Please pass it to the clerk, and state your full name."

"Samuel Brooklyn Dodgers."

"Is that his real name?" one of the congresswomen asked Duquesne, who repeated the question to Dodgers.

"Yes. I had it legally changed some years back."

"Do you wish to make a statement to the subcommittee?"

"Yes, I do."

Duquesne looked surprised. "Is it written? Do you have copies with you?"

"No, sir. I just have a few preliminary remarks."

"Go ahead then. You have five minutes."

"As you know, I am the inventor of a radar suppression device that the U.S. Navy has licensed and is putting into production under the code name Athena. I have been working closely with the navy on my invention, and I must say, they are very enthusiastic, as I am. My invention renders radar obsolete, makes it useless, which will revolutionize warfare as we know it. I feel my invention is the greatest instrument for God's peace ever invented. It will give the United States an insurmountable military advantage that will allow us to lead the world to God's new kingdom here on earth. We can once and for all demand that the heathen nations—"

Senator Duquesne interrupted as his colleagues began whispering among themselves. "Please limit your remarks to the subject at hand, Dr. Dodgers."

"Yessir. Athena will allow us to convert the Jews and Moslems and pagans to God-fearing, righteous Christians who won't start wars or—"

"Dr. Dodgers," Duquesne said, "I must insist. Your invention is not the only matter before this joint subcommittee. We are short of time. We have another witness to follow you." Duquesne gestured at Jake. For the first time Dodgers turned and saw him. "We could get right to the questions, if you don't mind."

"One more point, sir. The naval officer who is in charge of Athena is here today, Captain Jake Grafton. I see him sitting back there against the wall. I wish to say here and now that he is a godless sinner, a mouther of obscene blasphemies, an agent of Satan. I have complained to the navy and various members of Congress to no avail. I am a man of God and a man of peace. I cannot continue to work with this—"

Duquesne whacked his gavel. "Time! Thank you, Dr. Dodgers. We'll get right to the questions."

The aides whispered fervently in Dodgers' ear. Duquesne gave them the time. When Dodgers seemed to be settled down, Duquesne led him through a set of simple questions about Athena: what it was, how it worked, what Dodgers projected its capabilities as being.

"Dr. Dodgers, does the Athena device have to go on a stealth airplane?"

"No, sir. It would work on any airplane, stealth or not. It would work on a ship, on a building, on a tank, a truck—anything that has a fixed set of radar-reflective properties that the computer can be programmed to nullify."

When Duquesne had finished, he opened the floor to questions from other members. The chairman of the House Armed Services Committee, Representative Delman Richardson, from California, went first.

"I take it, Doctor, that you are convinced your device can be put into production cheaply and in a timely manner?"

"Yessir."

"And it will work? It will do what you and the navy say it will do?"

"Yes. That is correct. It will prevent the object that it is placed upon from being detected by radar."

"Yet, if I understand your earlier statement correctly, you think we should use this military advantage to convert the peoples of the world to Christianity?"

An uproar ensued as Duquesne tried to rule the question out of order and various members all tried to talk at once. The issue seemed to be whether the members from the House could ask the questions they could have asked had they not agreed to a joint hearing to save time. While all this was going on Rob Knight nudged Jake. "Best show in town," he whispered.

On the threat of being abandoned by the House subcommittee members, Duquesne caved in. Dodgers was given free rein to state his views on religion, sin, and conspiracies by each and every minority he could readily recall. Duquesne took it like a man, Jake thought. He should have known better. Other committee members took it less well, seeming to take offense that they had to sit through a recitation of Dodgers' poisonous inanities.

Dodgers was finally silenced by mutual consent and shown the door. After a ten-minute recess, it was Jake's turn. Gazing upward at the legislators on the dais, he immediately understood the psychological advantage the raised platform conferred on his interrogators.

"Do *you* have a statement to make?" Duquesne asked him when the preliminaries were completed.

"No, sir."

A chuckle swept the room. That's a good start, Jake thought.

A committee staffer passed out copies of Jake's report and led him through it, page by page, conclusion by conclusion. It took the rest of the morning. When Duquesne announced a lunch break, Jake was surprised at how much time had passed.

He and Knight walked back to the bagel place for a tuna salad sandwich.

"How am I doing?"

"They haven't even started on you yet. Ask me at five o'clock."

"Are we going to be here that long?"

"Maybe. Depends on Duquesne."

After lunch the senator resumed his questioning. "Tell me, Captain, just what were your orders when you were given your present assignment?"

"I was told to evaluate the two prototypes and prepare a recommendation as to which one I believed the navy should select for production as the A-12 medium attack bomber."

"Did Vice Admiral Henry or Secretary Ludlow tell you—let me rephrase that—did either of them suggest which prototype you should recommend?"

"No. They didn't."

"They didn't even hint at which one they wanted?"

"They discussed the navy's requirements for a new medium attack bomber on numerous occasions with me, sir, and they did make it clear to me that the plane had to be able to meet the needs of the navy. But they did not tell me which plane they thought would best meet those needs. Determining that was the whole purpose of the fly-off."

"So the conclusions stated in this report and the recommendations made are yours?"

"Yessir. And the admirals wrote endorsements, and the Secretary of the Navy wrote one when he forwarded the report to SECDEF."

"Did you tell your superiors what the substance of your report would be before you wrote it?"

"Yessir. I kept them fully informed about my activities and my opinions as I reached them."

"Did they suggest changes to the draft document."

"Yessir. That is normal practice. We were under a time crunch, and I circulated a summary of the report and they commented upon it and I made certain changes to the report that I felt were necessary based on their comments. But this is *my* report. I could have refused to make a suggested change and they could have commented on the matter in their endorsement. That, too, would be normal practice."

"Did you refuse to make any changes?"

"No, sir."

"So this report is now the way your superiors in the chain of command want it to be?"

"I believe the endorsements speak for themselves, sir."

"You recommended the navy purchase the TRX plane in spite of the fact that the prototype crashed during evaluation and you failed to complete all the tests you had planned?"

"That is correct."

"Why?"

"Senator, I think the report addresses that point much better than I could orally. I felt that the TRX plane had fewer technical problems than the Consolidated prototype and was a better compromise of mission capability and stealthiness. I also felt it was better suited to carrier operations. I thought that it would require less preproduction modifications to achieve the performance goals. All this is in the report. In short, I thought this plane gave the navy the most bang for its bucks."

"Did you personally fly either plane?"

"No, sir. A test pilot did."

"How much experience did this test pilot have?"

"I believe she has about sixteen hundred hours total flight time."

"That isn't much, is it?"

"Everything is relative."

"How much flight time do you have, Captain?"

"About forty-five hundred hours."

"Do you have any previous experience testing prototypes?"

"No, sir."

"Did your test pilot have any previous prototype testing experience?"

"No, sir."

"Yet you used her anyway. Why is that?"

"She had an outstanding record at the Test Pilot School at Patuxent River. She finished first in her class. My predecessor was on the staff at TPS and picked her for this project. I saw no reason to fire her and get someone else."

"Yet she crashed the TRX prototype?"

"It crashed while she was flying it. The E-PROM chips in the fly-by-wire system were defective."

"Would the plane have crashed with a more experienced pilot at the controls?"

"Well, that's impossible to say, really."

"You, for instance?"

"Senator, any answer I gave to that question would be pure speculation. I feel Lieutenant Moravia did a fine job handling that plane before and after it went out of control. There may be a pilot somewhere on this planet who could have saved it, but I don't know."

Duquesne led him into the buy-rate and cost projections for the A-12. "I see here that you recommend a total buy of three hundred sixty planes: a dozen the first year, twenty-four the second, then forty-eight each year subsequently."

"That's correct." Jake went into the cost equations. Before he could get very deep into the subject, Duquesne moved on.

Finally Duquesne got down to it.

"Captain, you have also been in charge of the Athena program, have you not?"

"Yes, sir."

"This morning Dr. Dodgers testified that this device would be cheap to build"—he gave the figures—"could be in production in a year or fifteen months and could protect any object it was placed upon. In view of that, why does the navy want a stealth attack plane?"

"Athena can be made to work, with enough research, time and money. But it's not going to be easy. Right now the only way to determine the radar-reflective characteristics of an object is to test the entire object on a specially constructed range. And these characteristics change based on the frequency of the radar doing the looking. So every frequency must be tested. Consequently the data base that the Athena computer must use is very, very large. That's why we need a superconductive computer to perform all the calculations required in a minimum amount of time. Still, it is impossible to build a system that could effectively counter every conceivable frequency. Athena will counter every frequency the Soviets are known to use. Yet if they shift frequencies quickly enough, with a semi-stealthy aircraft design we would not lose all our airplanes before Athena could be modified.

"Secondly, Athena will *not* be ready for the fleet in a year. More like three or four. Third, new technology may be developed to counter Athena. We believe, based on what we know now, that we need an attack plane with at least A-6 performance and payload capabilities, state-of-the-art avionics, and stealthy characteristics. That's the A-12. The TRX plane is the best that American industry can give us now, and now is the time when we need to put this airplane into production."

"Why not kill the A-12 program and build a conventional attack plane that uses Athena to hide?"

"As I mentioned, Athena is added protection for our aircraft, but not the sole source, due to the limitations inherent in the technology. Quick change is the rule in electronic warfare, not the exception. The Israelis almost lost their 1973 war with Egypt due to advances in electronic warfare made by the Soviets and supplied to Egypt of which the West was not aware. The United States cannot afford to lose a war with the Soviets, Senator."

Jake reached for his briefcase. Knight had it ready. "My staff has done some calculations. To kill this program now and start all over again on another one, writing off all the development money spent to date and adding the inevitable inflationary factor, I figure it will cost just about the same per plane. Assuming Athena works well enough to become operational. If it doesn't, we'll have a brand-new, obsolete airplane. Regardless, in the interim we'll have to make do with the A-6, which is not aging gracefully. We may even need to fund the A-6G program, just to keep the A-6s in the air until the follow-on airplane arrives."

An aide passed a copy of Jake's figures to every member. Jake spent the next hour defending the methodology and the numbers.

Duquesne opened the floor to questions from other members, who had a variety of concerns. One of them asked, "I understand you were awarded the Medal of Honor by this Congress, Captain?"

"That's correct, sir."

"Why aren't you wearing it now?"

"It's a little gaudy, don't you think?"

Another congressman asked, "Why is the navy going to name the A-12 the Avenger?" The propeller-driven Grumman TBF Avenger was the plane the President flew during World War II.

"In a survey of A-6 flight crews conducted navy-wide, that was the most popular suggestion. The people in the navy are very proud of the navy's tradition and history."

"The choice of that name looks a little like bootlicking, don't you think?"

"Sir, I happen to like that name. The Avenger torpedo-bomber was a fine airplane in its day, with a proud name and a great combat record. We've named other jets after prop planes—Phantom and Corsair are two—so it's a choice popular with the people in naval aviation. Should Avenger get derailed somewhere along the way, my personal second choice would be Hellcat, another good old navy name."

"That choice wouldn't be popular with Dr. Dodgers," the congressman said dryly.

"I doubt if it would," Jake agreed.

And then it was over. He was excused. It was 4 P.M. Out on the steps Knight said, "One down, two to go."

That was right. Assuming the Armed Services Committees authorized some airplanes and the full House and Senate agreed, then the battle would begin to convince the appropriations committees to provide the dollars to pay for them.

Jake groaned.

"Relax. You did very well."

"C'mon. Let's go get a beer somewhere. I'm dying of thirst."

On Sunday morning as they walked on the beach and Amy played in the surf, Jake and Callie talked again about the Minotaur. "As I understand it," Jake said, "he's not a mole in the usual sense of the word. He's not a Russian who slipped in years ago and worked his way into a position of trust. He's an American. A traitor."

"This world of espionage and counterespionage," Callie said, "it reminds me of Alice in Wonderland. Nothing is ever as it seems."

"What made you think of that?"

"If you lose something and look for it in all the usual places and you don't find it, what conclusion do you reach?"

"It isn't in a usual place."

"Precisely. And if the FBI has been looking for a mole for three years, then the mole is not in the usual place."

"But the usual places are positions where a person would have access to the information being passed."

"Perhaps the mole was never there at all."

Jake stared at her.

"How do you know the FBI has been looking?" she asked.

"Henry said so. Camacho said so."

"Henry merely repeated what he was told. Camacho told you what he wanted you to hear. What if there is no mole at all? What if the Minotaur is merely a character, an actor assigned to play a part?"

Amy called her to look at something that had washed up on the beach during the night, and she went. Jake stood and watched them. The surf broke and swirled around their ankles as the sea-birds circled and called.

"You are a very smart woman," he told her when she rejoined him.

"Oh, I'm glad you noticed. What did I say that was smart?"

On Monday morning at the office Jake stopped by the copy machine and helped himself to twenty or so sheets of paper. In his office he closed the door and pulled on a pair of gloves he had brought from home. Spreading the pile of paper gingerly, he selected a sheet from the middle of the pile and slid it away from the others. It should be free of fingerprints. From his pocket he took a black government pen. He clicked the point in and out a few times as he stared thoughtfully at the paper.

In block letters in the center of the page he wrote: "I KNOW WHO YOU ARE." He put the words all on one line.

He inspected it carefully, then folded the sheet and placed it in a blank letter-sized envelope he had removed from a box at home this morning.

There was a pair of tweezers in his desk, in that vanity case Callie got him for Christmas a year or so ago. He found them and dropped them in his pocket.

He took the gloves off. With the envelope inside his shirt, he went to the men's head. There he used the tweezers to put the envelope on the counter. Holding his shirt pocket open, he used the tweezers again to fish a stamp from the interior. He moistened it on a damp place on the sink, then affixed it to the envelope.

Back in the office, trying very hard not to touch the envelope at all, he dug through the classified Department of Defense directory until he found the address he wanted. This he copied onto the face of the envelope in block letters.

He put the envelope back into his shirt, put on his hat and told the secretary in the outer office he would be back in ten minutes.

He dropped the envelope in a mailbox on the plaza near the entrance to his building, then retraced his steps back to the office.

29

Vice Admiral Henry's funeral was on Wednesday in Arlington National Cemetery, held outdoors on the grass at the request of his eldest daughter. Everyone who was anyone in the Department of Defense was on hand, so Jake Grafton ended up seated among the rank and file. The politicians who ruled the armed forces sat on the right-hand side of the aisle, while on the left were the admirals and generals, who had been carefully seated in order of seniority as protocol demanded. A band played funeral airs and Royce Caplinger, George Ludlow, and CNO delivered short eulogies.

From where he sat Jake could see the backs of the heads of some of the heavyweights. Off to his left were the rows and rows of white monuments, marching across the green rolling terrain with faultless precision.

To his right was the low bulk of the Pentagon, only the top of it visible between the heads of the people and the uniformed ushers at parade rest.

Tyler Henry had spent his adult life in uniform, and Jake had no doubt that interment at this cemetery, with all those who had also served, would have met with Henry's approval. After all, Henry had died in combat, fighting for something he believed in.

Half listening to the speeches, Jake Grafton once again considered all he knew about the Minotaur affair. It was precious little, yet it seemed to him he could see the underlying structure. Perhaps, he mused, even that was an illusion.

The funeral was real enough. Henry was truly dead. The people involved were real, the information passed to the Soviets was real, Smoke Judy's attempt to steal the Athena file was real. And yet . . .

When he got back to the office, he made another trip to the copy machine for paper. This time he wrote: "I KNOW YOU ARE THE MINOTAUR."

He addressed the envelope as before and deposited it in the plaza mailbox when he went down to catch the shuttle to the Pentagon for another round of meetings.

On Thursday the announcement was made that the various committees of congress had authorized the navy to purchase the TRX plane as the A-12. Although the buy schedule was lower than planned, which would raise the cost of each plane by five million dollars, a general celebration was in order. That afternoon Jake and Admiral Dunedin treated everyone in the office to a beer bash at Gus's Place, a beanery on the lower floor of Jefferson Plaza 1.

"If you had any class, Grafton," Rob Knight told him, "you'd have taken us to Amelia's in the Underground."

"No class. You got that right."

"Two more hearings to go," Rob said. "Without an appropriation of money, all we have is a piece of paper to frame."

Dunedin was in a cheerful mood. He laughed and joked with the troops, seemingly glad to once again, if only for a little while, be just one of the guys. He never could be, of course. The officers he had spent his career with were all retired, except for those precious few who were also vice admirals. All the others were playing golf in Phoenix and Orlando, selling insurance in Virginia Beach or boats in San Diego, or were working for defense contractors.

At one point Dunedin ended up at Jake's table. When they were temporarily alone, he said, "Really a shame about Tyler Henry. He was going to retire in three months, you know."

No, Jake didn't know.

"Had a little cottage up in Maine, right near the beach. Owned it for years. Was going to spend the rest of his life there, he told me, and if he never heard the sound of freedom again he thought he could live with that." "The sound of freedom" was a public relations euphemism for jet noise.

"I guess you burn out after a while," Jake said.

"I guess. You win some, lose some, hope for the best. Even the politicians, they try to do that."

Jake remembered that comment the following week after he watched Royce Caplinger sweat in front of a Senate Appropriations subcommittee. They kept him going over numbers for most of the day. Although he was subpoenaed, Jake never took the stand. He was delighted.

Caplinger stayed afterwards for private conversations with the senators. Jake left with Toad Tarkington, who had accompanied him. As they were leaving, Caplinger and Senator Duquesne were shaking hands. It was then that Jake remembered Dunedin's comment.

A week later the House Appropriations Committee held their closed-door hearing. Caplinger spent three hours on the stand, Ludlow two hours. After lunch came Jake's turn on the hot seat. Three hours later Congresswoman Samantha Strader cleared her throat.

Strader was in her early fifties, her hair permed, her eyes screwed up in a characteristic squint. One of only two Democrats in her state's congressional delegation, she represented a district carved from the core of her state's capital city, the only area of the state with a significant minority population. She had one of the safest Democratic seats in the country and had been elected pro forma a dozen times, yet until the last election she had been almost unknown outside her state. Prior to that election she had publicly entertained the idea of entering the presidential primaries as the only woman in the field. Her short-lived quest came to grief on the shoals of political and financial reality, but not before her name and face had been splashed coast to coast by the media. She had jabbed and pricked the real contenders during her moment in the spotlight, had a delightful time, and squinted all the while.

Sam Strader's avowed passion was the military. Every officer in the Pentagon knew what that meant. She hated them. With an excellent mind, a quick wit, and a tongue to match, she was a formidable opponent.

Today, at this closed hearing of the black projects subcommittee of the House Appropriations Committee, she adjusted the microphone in front of her and gazed at Jake Grafton as though looking through a dense smoke screen. "Captain, please justify, if you can, the acquisition of another very expensive major weapons system by the U.S. Navy when Chairman Gorbachev is cutting the Soviet military budget drastically, reducing manpower levels by ten percent, slashing new ship construction, cutting navy steaming time."

"Congresswoman," Jake said, trying to digest the question. "I don't think I'm qualified to address that. I'm here to testify about the merits of the prototypes evaluated by the Advanced Tactical Aircraft program for production as the A-12."

"Didn't Secretary Ludlow send you over here to testify?"

"Yes, ma'am. He did. And this panel questioned him for two hours this morning."

"Now it's your turn. Answer the question, if you can."

"As I've already said, we need the A-12 because the A-6 is wearing out. The A-6 has an airframe designed in the 1950s and is already past the end of its service life. The carriers must have a viable all-weather attack capability or they are obsolete and—"

"But what about the Soviet initiative?"

"Congresswoman, he's trying to answer your question." The chairman of the House Appropriations Committee was a Texas Democrat. Just now he looked bored. No doubt he was faking. Rumor had it he had underestimated Sam Strader once too often in the past. That was a mistake Jake Grafton had no intention of making. He was sitting at attention, listening carefully.

Strader ignored the chairman. "Captain Grafton, I want to know when the navy is going to realize that the Soviet threat is diminishing and accordingly lower its requests for funds from this Congress."

"The navy doesn't make budget requests of Congress. The administration does. Be that as it may, you assume the Soviet threat is diminishing significantly. I disagree. And the Soviets are only one of our possible adversaries. They still have four million men under arms. They have a formidable, capable navy. We are buying the A-12 to provide an all-weather attack capability for our aircraft carriers for the next thirty years. We must provide a strong Sunday punch for our fleet regardless of the twists and turns of Soviet policy or the ups and downs of this or that communist politician."

"If the threat is diminishing, can we then scrap a carrier or two and cut back the A-12 buy order?"

"Congresswoman, the Warsaw Pact still has over fifty thousand tanks, four times as much artillery, and twice as many planes as NATO can muster. The Soviet army is three times larger than ours. We are a sea power. Over fifty percent of our oil is imported. I think any reduction of our naval capability when faced with these realities would be very unwise."

"Captain, it seems to me that both we and the Soviets have spent more money on the military than either nation can afford, and now we have a perfect opportunity to reduce that expenditure. If we deterred them with what we had before they made a ten percent reduction, we can deter them just as well in the future if we make a ten percent reduction."

"You persist in assuming the Soviet Union is our only possible opponent in a world in which we have global commitments. In the last forty years the navy has seen action in Korea, Vietnam, Grenada, and Libya and Lebanon several times. We've had to meet those commitments and deter the Soviets *too.*"

"And more gadgets are going to enable the navy to continue to do that?"

"I wouldn't characterize the A-12 as a—"

"I would! You people are gadget-happy. The attitude in the Pentagon seems to be that gadgets will keep us free. In the meantime our schools are atrocious and our bridges and highways are disintegrating. We desperately need a nationwide child-care system for working mothers and a long-term healthcare system for the elderly. The damage that drugs are doing to the children of America is a national disgrace. We need to greatly expand our drug education and law enforcement efforts. Yet we can afford none of this because we keep borrowing money to buy grotesque gadgets to kill people with. And this at a time when the Cold War is *over!*"

"I'm not testifying to that," Jake said tartly, and felt Toad Tarkington kick him under the table. "The choices are difficult," he added. "I don't envy you your responsibilities."

"Congresswoman Strader," the chairman rumbled. "This is a closed hearing. Your remarks will not leave this room, so I am at a loss as to why you are making a stump speech to Captain Grafton, who, unless I am mistaken, doesn't vote in your district."

Strader shifted her squint back to Grafton. "Just when will the navy's budget requests reflect the new geopolitical realities?"

Jake answered carefully. "The navy's budget requests *to the administration* are based on the needs of the navy in light of the commitments the government has assigned the navy. As for geopolitical realities, I think the political ferment that is occurring in the Soviet Union is the most hopeful development in that nation in this century. But who knows if Gorbachev will prevail? He may be assassinated. There may be a coup. He may just be booted out by his colleagues. We can't sink the U.S. Navy this year and hope for the best."

"Time will tell. Is that your testimony? We should let the real human needs of our citizens go unmet so we can continue to fund a military establishment that is a travesty in a world seeking real peace?"

"Your admiration for Chairman Gorbachev is in many ways reminiscent of Neville Chamberlain's warm regard for Adolf Hitler. I hope you don't have reason later on to regret your enthusiasm, as Chamberlain did."

Toad's shoe smacked on his shin again as Strader snarled, "I deeply resent that remark, Captain. I—"

The chairman cut her off. "Congresswoman Strader, this is not the time and place for a political colloquy with Captain Grafton. Please address your questions to the issue at hand. I must insist."

Strader stared at Grafton. She was furious. "Why is the A-12 a black project?"

"The technology involved is—"

"No! I reject that. The air force used that explanation for the B-2 bomber—$516 million each—and going higher—and the F-117A —$62 million each. They've acquired unproven airplanes with limited capabilities, airplanes that must be operated from paved runways that will be the Soviets' first nuclear targets in the event of war. No, Captain Grafton. *Public debate* is what the administration and the Pentagon seek to avoid." Her gaze shifted to the chairman. "Public debate is what you wish to avoid, Mr. Chairman, so that your state can secure another bloated, outrageous defense contract for technology that may well not do what those hogs at the Pentagon—"

"Time's up." The chairman smacked his gavel.

Strader was just getting up steam. ". . . that those money-hungry swine at the Pentagon have carefully steered to your state so that—"

"You're out of *time,* Congresswoman," the chairman said, his voice rising, "and out of *order.* Thank you for your testimony, Captain Grafton. You're excused."

Strader kept talking. Jake packed his briefcase and handcuffed it to his wrist. ". . . these machines are being purchased to fight wars that everyone knows will *never* occur. Billions of dollars down the sewer! It's *obscene*."

Jake rose and walked for the door with Tarkington at his elbow. Behind him Strader and the chairman were shouting at each other.

"You ever kick me again, Tarkington, and you'll need a proctologist to surgically remove that shoe."

"Yes, sir."

When the door closed behind them and they were walking down the corridor, Jake said, "I really lost it in there, didn't I?"

"Yes, sir. You did."

"Well, if they'll just vote the funds now, we've done the navy a pretty good job."

"I suppose."

As they went down the outside steps of the Capitol, Jake said, "I hope she's right. I hope the wars never occur."

"Yeah. And I hope I live forever," Toad Tarkington said, and signaled to the transportation pool driver, who was standing beside the car a hundred yards away.

As the car pulled up, Toad climbed into the front seat, Jake into the back. They had just pulled the doors shut when the rear door opened again. Jake looked up. The man standing there had a pistol pointed at him. "Slide over, Captain."

Jake hesitated for just a second and glanced into the front seat. The driver had a gun pointed at Toad. Jake scooted.

The man outside took a seat and pulled the door shut.

"Gentlemen, as you can see, we are both armed. You are going to be our guests for a little while. Mr. Tarkington?"

When Toad didn't respond, the man beside Jake nudged Toad in the neck with the barrel of his gun. "Mr. Tarkington?"

"Yeah."

"I have a gun too, and it is pointed at Captain Grafton. The gentleman behind the wheel is going to put his gun in his pocket and drive. If you twitch, if you shout, if you open your door or reach for the wheel or ignition key, I will first shoot Captain Grafton, then I will shoot you. Do you understand?"

"Yeah."

"Do you feel heroic?"

"Not especially."

"That is very good. You and your captain may live through this experience if you do exactly as I say, when I say it."

Tarkington said nothing.

"Put on your seat belts and lock your doors."

Jake and Toad obeyed.

"Okay, if everyone understands the ground rules, we go."

The driver put the transmission in drive and fed gas.

The gunman in the backseat was in his fifties, with short hair. He was tanned, stocky, and wore a well-fitting dark suit.

"Where is the sailor who was driving this car?"

"Captain, I warn you for the last time. You will sit absolutely quiet. One word, just one more word, and I will hurt you very badly."

Jake Grafton looked at the gunman, then at the back of the driver's head. Toad sat rigid, staring straight ahead.

The car went out onto Independence Avenue and crept west in stop-and-go traffic. Jake eased the briefcase on his lap and felt the gun dig into his side. He sat very still and eventually the gun went away.

Okay, so he wasn't going to whack this guy with the briefcase and bail out of the car. That stuff only works in movies. He was going to sit very still and hope this guy didn't blow his brains out, or Tarkington's.

In spite of the air conditioning, Jake was perspiring profusely. He felt the moisture form rivulets on his face.

He tried to think. Here he was in the backseat of a navy Ford Fairmont sedan rolling through the streets of Washington. At the curbs buses were loading and unloading tourists, hordes of people from Nashville and Little Rock and Tokyo. People in cars with plates from the Midwest and South rubbernecked, and the drivers ignored the traffic signs, seeming to delight in suicidal lane changes and illegal turns onto one-way streets. Kids were running and shoving and demanding pop, mothers were calming squealing infants, and everyone was waiting in line or looking for a restroom. Yet in the middle of it all Jake Grafton and Toad Tarkington had guns in their ribs.

Maybe this guy was the Minotaur. Maybe he was an Ivy League political appointee who had sold out for some reason only a psychiatrist would understand. Yet the way he handled that pistol—Jake knew competence with a weapon when he saw it.

The driver swung left on Fourteenth Street and began to accelerate as he jockeyed with traffic. He crossed the Potomac on the George Mason Memorial Bridge and took the ramp down onto George Washington Parkway northbound.

"You can drop us anywhere along here," Toad said, "and we'll walk back to the office."

Jake winced at the sound of his voice. The gunman beside him paid no attention.

"Glad we could give you guys a—" The driver's right hand flicked into Toad's face with a sickening smack, which knocked his hat off. The car didn't even swerve.

Toad sagged against the window, then slowly raised his head.

The car continued up the parkway. The river was visible between the trees on the right. They passed the entrance to the CIA complex at Langley and continued on at fifty-five miles per hour, the traffic flowing around them at least ten miles over the speed limit.

Traffic on the beltway was thickening as the first surge of rush hour emptied from the city. The man at the wheel kept the car in the middle lane. On and on they rolled, past the Frederick cutoff, east now across the northern edges of the city.

Jake Grafton was bitterly regretting the impulse that had made him mail two letters to the Minotaur when the driver finally edged into a gap in the right lane and took the ramp down to New Hampshire Avenue, where he caught the green light and turned left, northward. They passed the Naval Surface Weapons Center and turned left, into a residential area. After four or five turns down shady streets with cars parked at the curbs and in driveways, the man at the wheel slowed. From a pocket he produced a garage-door opener. He aimed it as he swung left into a driveway. The door rose obediently. The car coasted to a stop inside the garage and the driver triggered the remote-control device again. The garage got very dark as the closing door shut out the light.

"Okay, gentlemen. We are here. We will sit here very quiet and still while the driver checks out the house." The driver was already out of the car. He fiddled with the knob on the inside door, used a key or pick, and had it open in a few seconds. Before he entered he took out his pistol. In about a minute he was back. He nodded.

Toad went first, walking around the car while the driver in the doorway held a pistol on him.

Then it was Jake's turn. From the garage he entered a kitchen. Through the sliding glass door he could see a backyard swing.

"The basement."

Jake went down the stairs. The slanted ceiling was so low he had to tilt his head.

The older of the two men, the man who had ridden in the backseat with Jake, held out his hand toward Toad. "The handcuff key."

Toad extracted it from his pocket and passed it across. The man used it to unlock the briefcase from Jake's wrist and cuff him to a chair. The driver produced a set of cuffs from a trouser pocket and cuffed Tarkington to a table.

As the driver sat on the couch with his pistol on his lap and lit a cigarette, the older man examined the lock on the briefcase. He glanced at Jake. "The combination?"

"Fuck you."

"Ah, Captain. Do you honestly think I couldn't open the case without it? I merely wished to save myself several minutes of effort."

Jake told him the combination. The man had it open in thirty seconds, scooped out the documents, and after glancing at his watch, sat down on the couch to read them.

"Who are you?" Toad asked.

"Does it matter?" the reader asked without looking up.

"Not right now. But I'd like a name to give to the FBI."

The man just chuckled dryly and continued reading.

After a while—Jake wasn't sure how long, since he couldn't see his watch—the man said, "This Athena device, a superconductive computer with multiple CPUs, do you think it can be successfully produced in three years?"

Jake said nothing. His stomach felt like he had swallowed a stone.

"Oh well, I don't have the time to get the answers, and I doubt that you would be forthright in any event. But it certainly is an interesting technological development. You Americans! A nation of tinkerers. What will you think of next?"

He went back through the documents slowly, taking his time, studying them. His pistol lay on the table beside him, within easy reach. Twice he glanced at his watch.

Jake looked around the room. The driver kept his eyes on him or Toad all the time. His pistol lay in his lap. Toad had both wrists cuffed together around the leg of a rather large table. Still, given a few seconds, he could lift the leg and be free of the table. Obviously that possibility did not concern the two gunmen very much. If Toad tried it, he would be shot or pistol-whipped within seconds.

Jake's cuffs went through the arm of a chair. Beside the chair sat a floor lamp, but to reach it with his right hand, he would need to stick his left hand under this chair arm. It was temptingly close, but he would need an opportunity. And if he got it, what then?

What did those instructors always say at SERE—Survival, Evasion, Resistance, and Escape—school? Never give up. Stay ready. Your chance will come.

These guys were waiting for someone. That much was obvious. Who? The Minotaur?

They had been in the basement for almost an hour when the stocky man spoke to the driver. "Upstairs now, I think. Be sure to unplug the garage-door opener."

"Yes, sir." The driver went.

"Are you the Minotaur?" Toad asked.

The stocky man threw back his head and laughed. "That is good. Very good. You are a real comedian."

"He's not the Minotaur," Jake said.

"Ah, Captain. What makes you say that?"

Jake didn't answer.

"A captain in the U.S. Navy knows the identity of the Minotaur. Or at least knows who he is not. Interesting. Instructive. I'll bet you are a fount of interesting information, Captain. No doubt we'll have time later this evening to elicit some of it."

He walked toward Jake with his back toward Toad. Jake tried to keep his eyes on the gunman, yet still he saw Toad bend down and grasp the table leg. It came off the floor. Even as it did the gunman whirled with his pistol at arm's length, leveled in both hands, pointed straight at Toad's face. "What makes you think," he asked easily, "that I need you alive?"

Toad let the table leg go back down to the floor. "Oh," he said lightly, trying to smile and not succeeding, "I thought you liked my witty repartee."

"I *do* like you. With a mouth like yours you should be in Hollywood in the movies, not pushing paper at the Pentagon." The gunman lowered the gun and took the seat on the couch that the driver had vacated, a place where he could watch both men with a minimum of effort. "Now I think we will sit silently, not saying a word. Like mice."

"You're a cocksucker," Toad said.

The gunman looked at him and pursed his lips slightly.

"A genuine cocksucker. A cheap dick-sucking spook with a gun, a man who thinks everybody should faint dead away when he pulls out his weapon. Is that what they do when you whip out your dick? Is that—"

The gunman was very quick. He was moving and chopping with the pistol all in one motion.

Toad Tarkington was just as quick. He came off the chair and kicked mightily with his right leg. It caught the man in the knee and he lost his balance. Toad was erect now, the table hanging from his cuffs, his leg swinging again. This kick hit the gunman in the arm. The pistol went flying.

Jake leaped from the chair, dragging it. The lamp fell over. He dragged the heavy chair toward the pistol on the floor. Toad was still kicking.

He was almost to the gun when he heard the shot and saw a chunk fly from the carpet just in front of him.

He froze. The driver came down the stairs with the gun leveled. "Get back." He gestured threateningly at Toad, who seemed to shrink as his muscles relaxed. Tarkington exhaled convulsively, then turned slightly to find the chair he had been sitting on. At that moment the driver hit him a vicious blow in the back of the head with the gun and he fell heavily, overturning the table.

The second man helped the stocky man to the couch. He was still holding his stomach. He had blood on the corner of his mouth. Apparently one of Toad's kicks had taken him in the face.

"Upstairs. Get back upstairs. Get me my gun first."

The second man obeyed, then went back up the stairs.

"Sit in the chair, Captain, right where you are. Sit! One move, just one, and I'll kill you and the lieutenant. Understand?"

Jake made the smallest of head nods. He sat.

Time passed. Minute by minute. The gunman on the couch massaged his arm and leg. Toad had really connected. Twice the man wiped the sweat from his face with his shirttail.

Toad stirred once. The table was on end beside him. He lay amid the magazines and newspapers that had gone flying when he jerked the table off the floor. Toad seemed to be breathing easily.

Jake heard the shuffling on the floor above him, and faintly the sound of a door closing. In seconds he heard someone walking above, then steps on the stair. He turned his head. Legs descending.

Luis Camacho walked into the room with the driver behind him, his gun in Camacho's back. "Hi, Harlan. Didn't know if I was going to see you again."

Camacho walked over to the couch and seated himself next to Albright. "Jesus, what have you idiots done to my basement?"

Albright gestured at Tarkington, who was stirring again. "That fucker thought he was a hero."

"Looks like that table has a busted leg. My wife isn't going to be happy."

The driver stood near the bottom of the stairs where he could watch everyone. He kept the pistol leveled at Camacho.

"Well, Captain," Camacho said. "You've had an eventful afternoon."

"Yeah," Jake replied. "Who are these guys?"

"Well, the man beside me goes by the name of Harlan Albright. His real name is Peter Aleksandrovich Chistyakov. And this gentleman with the pistol at the bottom of the stairs—though I have never before had the pleasure—is, I think, Major Arkady Yakov of the Soviet Army."

"Okay," Albright said, "thanks for the introductions." He rose from the couch and turned Toad's table upright, then pulled a chair around and sat on it, facing Camacho.

"You know why I'm here. I thought since I was going to drop by, I might as well help myself to some Athena information on the way. It was very interesting. But it is you I want."

"How droll. I wanted to talk to you too. You should have called."

"You're going to give me some answers, Luis. Now. If you don't, I'm going to kill the lieutenant. Then the captain. Then you. I want answers."

"What will you do with them if you get them?"

Albright's eyes widened. He took three steps across to the telephone at the end of the couch, picked it up and held it to his ear. He jiggled the button on the cradle, then replaced the instrument. "Upstairs, Yakov. Check the front and back."

The major took the stairs two at a time.

In about a minute he was back. He spoke to Albright in a foreign language, one that sounded to Jake like Russian.

"This is a setup."

Camacho shrugged. "My people saw you drive in. I thought you might be by to see me sooner or later. Didn't know who you brought with you, though. Sorry, Captain."

Jake nodded.

Camacho stood and shook out his trousers. "Tell you what,

Harlan. Let's you and I go downtown. We can talk there. No sense keeping these fellows any longer."

Albright took his pistol from his pocket. "Sit."

When Camacho obeyed, Albright followed suit, back at the table. He rubbed his eyes. "So." He spoke a sentence in Russian.

Camacho waved a hand irritably. "You know I can't handle that language anymore. English or nothing."

"You've been stringing me right along, haven't you, Luis?"

Camacho's shoulders moved a quarter inch up, then subsided.

"That name you gave me. That was bullshit, wasn't it?"

"No. That was the name."

"Why?"

"You have something we want. At least, we think you have it. You're going to give it to me, Harlan. Hard or easy, you're going to give it to me."

"Tell me what you want and maybe I'll give it to you now."

Camacho threw back his head and laughed. "You want to defect?"

Albright's eyebrows went up. "Maybe."

"Then shoot the major."

"Just like that?"

"Then we'll talk. That would be the easy way. The hard way will be more strenuous, but equally productive, I think."

Albright glanced at the major, who was looking straight at Camacho. Still, Jake saw the major's eyes flick sideways to catch Albright's glance.

"You can't get out of here, Harlan," Camacho said, and stretched lazily. "The place is completely surrounded, with helicopters and light planes overhead. Why don't you two give me the guns and we'll go upstairs and wave at Dreyfus. Then you and I can go downtown to the office. I'm sure the two of us can work something out."

"I may not know the fact you want, Luis."

"I think you do."

"You've gone to an extraordinary lot of trouble for nothing if I don't know it."

"Life's like that."

"Maybe I could just give it to you here and now. If I know it."

Camacho sat silently looking at Albright. "Three names," he said at last.

Albright laughed, a long, loud guffaw. "All of this—for that?"

"Yes."

"My hat is off to you. I salute you. Never did I suspect. Not even once." Albright shook his head and chuckled silently as he examined his pistol.

Camacho sat motionless, watching Albright.

"You do know," the FBI agent said finally, when all the laughing had stopped.

"You found the bomb?"

"Yes."

"It was a warning. I needed that name."

"I know. Hard or easy. Your choice."

"You mean it?"

"Yes."

"We'll take you and Captain Grafton as hostages," Albright said, rising from the chair. He glanced toward Yakov and jerked his head at Jake. As Yakov stepped in that direction Albright shot him.

Yakov spun, firing at Albright. The bullet hit Albright square in the chest and his pistol sagged, exploding again pointed at the floor. At almost the same instant Toad Tarkington lashed out with his feet, and Albright went sideways as a foot was kicked out from under him. Yakov's second shot hit his shoulder and he spun from the impact as he fell.

Yakov's third shot came as he was falling. It was aimed at Camacho, who was still sitting on the couch. He hadn't moved.

Camacho doubled over as Yakov hit the floor.

Jake toppled his chair going for Yakov's pistol. He wrestled the gun from the major's weak grasp and crouched beside the chair, on top of the Russian major as he watched Albright.

The whole sequence hadn't taken five seconds.

Toad got to his feet. He was free of the table. He bent down shakily and retrieved the pistol that Albright had dropped. "This one's still alive."

"Quick," Jake said. "Check Camacho."

Jake held the gun on the major's head as Toad stretched Camacho on the couch. "He's hit lower down," Toad said. "Dead center. Still alive, though."

"Go upstairs. Get the agents." Toad made for the stairs. "Put the gun in your pocket," Jake called after him. "Don't let them shoot you."

Camacho sat up on one elbow.

"Is he dead?" he whispered hoarsely, looking at the major.

"No," Jake said. "He's hit in the right side, but he isn't dead. He may make it."

"Kill him."

"Why?"

"He heard too much. Kill him!" Camacho coughed, a bubbly gurgle.

Jake moved toward Camacho, dragging the chair. Behind him Major Yakov began to crawl.

"Give me the gun," Camacho said.

"No."

"This isn't a game, Grafton! *Give me the gun!*"

Jake tossed it.

The pistol landed on the couch. Camacho groped for it while Yakov struggled for the stairs.

Yakov jerked as the first shot hit him. He tried again to crawl. Taking his time, Camacho shot him four more times. A red stain spread across the back of Yakov's shirt and he lay still.

Camacho dropped the pistol and sagged down onto the couch.

"Albright! Albright, can you hear me?"

"Yeah."

"Give—me—the—names." Camacho dragged himself along the couch so he could see the Russian's face.

"I—" Albright's lips were moving but no sound came out. Then he ceased to move at all.

Camacho's head went down to rest on the couch.

"Who is the Minotaur?" Jake demanded. With a heave he got the chair over to the couch and shook Camacho. "Tell me! *Who is the Minotaur?*"

"You don't want— No! It's not what you—he's not . . ."

Camacho went limp. Jake turned his head so he could see his face. His eyes were open, staring fixedly at nothing.

Jake sagged down beside the bloody couch. He heard the sound of running feet upstairs.

30

The sky was crystal-clear, a pleasant change from the late-summer haze. From this infinite sky a bright sun shone down on a day not hot and not yet cold, a perfect late-September Sunday. The trees along the roads where Jake Grafton drove had just begun to lose their green and don their autumn colors. Their leaves shimmered and glistened in the brilliant sun.

Most of the radio stations were broadcasting music, but it was public-service time on the others. He listened a few moments to two women discussing the nuances of breast-feeding, then twirled the selector knob. The next station had a preacher asking for donations for his radio ministry. Send the money to a P.O. box in Arkansas. He left the dial there. The fulminations filled the car and drifted out the open window. Samuel Dodgers would have liked this guy: hellfire for sinners, damnation for the tempters.

Toad Tarkington was leaning against the side of his car at the Denny's restaurant when Jake pulled into the lot.

"Been waiting long?"

"Five minutes." Toad walked around the front of Jake's car and climbed in. In spite of the sun and seventy-five-degree temperature, he was wearing a windbreaker.

"How's Rita?"

"Doing okay."

Jake got the car in motion.

"Where're we going?"

"I told you on the phone. To see the Minotaur."

"Yessir. But where is that?"

"You'll see."

Toad lapsed into silence. He sat with his hands in his lap and stared straight ahead at the road. On the radio the preacher expounded on how Bible prophecy had predicted the popularity of rock music.

Passing through Middleburg Toad said, "I think we ought to kill him."

Jake held out his right hand, palm up. Toad just looked at it.

"Let me have it."

"What?"

"Your gun. The one you have under that jacket."

Toad reached under the left side of his jacket and extracted a pistol from his beltline, which he laid in the captain's hand. It was a navy-issue nine-millimeter automatic, well oiled but worn. Jake pushed the button and the clip fell out in his hand. This he pocketed. Holding the gun with his right hand, he worked the slide with his left. A shiny cartridge flipped out and went over his shoulder into the backseat. The gun he slipped under the driver's seat.

"Who is he?"

"You'll see."

"Why are we going if we aren't going to kill him?"

"You've been watching too many Clint Eastwood movies. And you ask too many questions."

"So why did you call me?"

"I didn't want to go alone. I wanted a witness. The witness had to be someone who is basically incorruptible, someone beyond his reach."

"I'm not beyond anyone's reach."

"Oh, I think you are, Tarkington. Not physical reach. I'm talking about moral reach. None of his weapons will get to you."

"You make me sound retarded. How do you know this guy we're going to see is the Minotaur?"

"I wrote him three letters. Notes. Then this morning I called him and said I was dropping by to chat."

"Just friendly as fucking shit." Toad thought about it. Jake waited for him to ask how Jake learned the Minotaur's identity, but the lieutenant had other things on his mind. "If it weren't for this turd, Camacho would have arrested Judy months ago and Rita wouldn't have got whacked up. Camacho would still be alive." He reached for the radio and snapped it off. "Goddamnit, Captain, this man is *guilty*."

"You don't *know* anything, Toad. You don't know who, you don't know why. Since Rita did get hurt, since that little mess in Camacho's basement, I thought you had a right to know. That's why I called you. So you're going to find out this afternoon."

"Do you know?"

"Why, you mean?"

Toad nodded.

Jake thought about it. "I've made some guesses. But they're only that. Guesses are three for a quarter. Facts I don't have. Camacho, though, he knew."

"And he's dead."

"Yes." Jake turned the radio back on.

"Are we going to turn him in, call the cops?"

"You ask too many questions."

In a moment Toad said, "Why do you listen to this crap?" He gestured toward the radio.

"It's refreshing to hear a man who knows precisely where he stands. Even if I don't share his perch."

The leaves of the trees alongside the road had the deep green hues of late summer. Cattle and horses grazing, an occasional female rider on a groomed horse in the manicured meadows, glimpses of huge two- or three-story mansions set back well away from the public road at the end of long drives; this countryside was fat. The contrast between this rich and verdant world of moneyed indolence and the baked, potholed streets of Washington jarred Jake Grafton. He could feel his confidence in his assessment of the situation ebbing away as the car took them farther and farther from the Pentagon and the navy.

Five miles north of Middleburg he began to watch the left side of the road. He found the tree and mailbox he had heard about. The box merely had a number, no name. He turned into the hard-packed gravel drive and drove along it. Huge old trees lined the north side of the road, a row that ended in a small grove around a large brick house almost covered with ivy.

Jake Grafton parked right in front.

"Ring the bell," he muttered at Toad, who gave several tugs on a pull. The sound of chimes or something was just audible through the door.

Tarkington's eyes darted around.

The door opened.

"Did you get lost?" Royce Caplinger asked, and stood aside to let the two men enter.

"Little longer drive than I figured, Mr. Secretary."

Toad gaped.

"Close your mouth, son. People'll think you're a politician," Caplinger muttered and led the way down the hall. They passed through a dining room furnished with massive antique tables and chairs and accented with pewter tankards and plates, and on through a kitchen with brick walls and a huge fireplace with an iron kettle hanging in it. A refrigerator, sink, and conventional stove sat against the far wall, on the other side of a work island.

"Nice place you have here," Jake Grafton said.

"Rustic as hell. I like it. Makes me feel like Thomas Jefferson."

"He's real dead," Toad said.

"Yeah. Sometimes I feel that way too, out here without the traffic and airplane noise and five million people all scurrying . . ." They were in the study now, a corner room with high windows and ceilings. The walls were covered with books. Newspapers scattered on the carpet, some kind of a red-and-blue Oriental thing.

Caplinger waved his hand toward chairs and sank into a large stuffed chair with visibly cracked leather.

He stared at them. Toad avoided his gaze and looked at the books and the bric-a-brac tucked between them. By Toad's chair was a pipe stand. In it was a corncob pipe, blackened from many fires.

"I wasn't sure, but I thought it might be you, Captain," Caplinger said. "Didn't recognize your voice on the phone this morning."

Jake Grafton rubbed his face with his hands and crossed his legs.

"We were just driving through the neighborhood, Royce," Toad said, "and thought we'd drop by and ask why you turned traitor and gave all those secrets to the Russians. Why did you?"

Jake caught Toad's eye. He moved his head ever-so-slightly from side to side.

Jake addressed Caplinger. "Mr. Secretary, we have a problem. We know you're the Minotaur and we have some ideas, probably erroneous, about the events of the last few months. Four or five people have died violently. Mr. Tarkington's wife, Rita Moravia, is a navy test pilot who was seriously injured, almost killed, because various law enforcement agencies failed to properly investigate and make arrests on information they had had for some time. To make a long story short, we came here to ask if you would like to discuss this matter with us before we go to the authorities and the press. Do you?"

"Are you going to the press?"

"That depends."

"You notice I didn't ask about the authorities. That doesn't worry me, but for reasons—well!"

Caplinger slapped his knees and stood suddenly. Toad started. "Relax, son. I only eat lieutenants at the office. Come on, let's make some coffee." He led the way into the kitchen.

He filled a pot with water. The pot went on the stove, after he lit the gas jet with a match. He put a paper filter in a drip pot and ladled three spoonfuls of coffee in. "You two are entitled to an explanation. Not legally, but morally. I'm sorry about your wife, Lieutenant. So was Luis Camacho. We had too much at stake to move prematurely." He shrugged. "Life is complicated."

Caplinger pulled a stool from under the counter and perched on it.

"Three years ago, no, four, a KGB colonel defected to the United States. It wasn't in the papers, so I won't tell you his name. He thought he was brimming with useful information that we would be delighted to have in return for a ton of money and a new life in the West. The money he got and the new identity he got. But the information wasn't worth much. He did, however, have one piece of information that he didn't think much of but we found most interesting."

Caplinger checked the water on the stove.

"It seems that one day about three years before he defected he paid a visit to the Aquarium, the Moscow headquarters of the GRU, which is Soviet military intelligence. His errand doesn't really matter. During his two or three hours there he was taken into the office of a general who was not expecting company. On the desk was a sheet of paper with four names. The colonel read the names upside down before the general covered the paper with a handy file."

The water began to rumble. Caplinger checked the pot as he continued. "Under hypnosis the defector could remember three of the four names. We recognized one of them. V. Y. Tsybov."

The coffeepot began to whistle. As he reached for it Caplinger said, "Vladimir Yakovich Tsybov was the real name of Luis Camacho."

He poured the hot water into the drip cone and watched the black fluid run out the bottom. "Luis Camacho was a Soviet mole, a deep illegal sent to this country when he was twenty years old. He was half Russian and half Armenian, and with his olive skin and facial characteristics, he seemed a natural to play the role of a Mexican-American. He knew just a smattering of Spanish, but what the hey. His forefathers, so said his bio, had been in this country since Texas became a state.

"Tsybov, now Camacho, attended a university in Texas and graduated with honors. He obtained a law degree at night while he worked days. The FBI recruited him.

"It's funny"—Caplinger shook his head—"that J. Edgar Hoover's lily-white FBI needed a smart Mexican-American. But at the time Hoover was casting suspicious eyes on the farm-labor movement in California, which was just being organized, and needed some Chicanos to use as undercover agents. So Luis Camacho was investigated and approved and recruited."

Caplinger laughed. "Hoover, the paranoid anti-communist, recruited a deep Soviet plant! Oh, they tried to check Camacho's past, and the reports to Washington certainly looked thorough. But the agents in the field—all good, white Anglo Protestants with dark suits and short haircuts—couldn't get much cooperation from the Chicano population of Dallas and San Antonio. So rather than admit failure to the Great One, they sort of filled in the gaps and sent the usual reports to Washington. And the FBI got themselves a new agent."

"How do you like your coffee?"

Royce Caplinger got milk from the refrigerator and let Toad add some to his coffee. They carried their cups back to the study.

"Where was I?"

"Camacho was a deep plant."

"Yes. Anyway, being smart and competent, he rose as far as the racial politics of the FBI would allow, which really wasn't very far. Still, amazingly enough, Luis Camacho liked America. But that is another story." Caplinger set his coffee beside him. "Maybe I should fill it in, though. Luis was a very special human being. Luis—"

"There were three other names on the list," Toad said irritably. His whole manner told what he thought of Caplinger's tale.

"Ah yes," Caplinger said, looking at the lieutenant thoughtfully. "Three more names, two of which the defector could remember, one which he could not. The problem was we didn't know who any of the other three were. Tsybov was Camacho, whom the Soviets thought was still a plant under deep cover, a sleeper, available for use if the need arose. They didn't know that Camacho had revealed himself to us voluntarily almost ten years before."

Caplinger looked from face to face. "You see the problem. The Soviets had three more agents in America planted deep. And we didn't know who they were!

"Naturally the intelligence coordinating committee took this matter up. What could be done?"

"So you became the Minotaur." Jake Grafton made it a statement, not a question.

"We needed bait, good bait. We wanted those three deep agents. Or two or one. Whatever we could get. Someone had to become the Minotaur, so the President chose me."

"The President?" Toad said, incredulously.

"Of course. Who better to choose what military secrets the Soviets would find interesting? Who better to reveal the aces?" Caplinger sipped his coffee.

"So you . . ." Jake began. "You wrote the letters and mailed them?"

"Yes. The National Security Agency gave me the computer codes I needed and helped with the encryptions. But I had to sit down and write each letter. The human touch, you see. Each letter would reveal something of the man who wrote it, so they all had to be written by one man.

"Much to our dismay, the instrument the Soviets chose to exploit the gifts of the Minotaur was a traitor-for-hire who had already approached their embassy a year or so before. Terry Franklin. What Terry Franklin didn't know was that the National Security Agency has special programs that reveal when each selected classified document is accessed. He wrote a trapdoor program that got him by the first security layer, but there was another that he didn't know about. So we were immediately on to him. And immediately faced with a dilemma."

"If you arrested him too soon, the Soviets might just ignore the Minotaur."

"Precisely, Captain. For this to work, the information had to be very good stuff, the best. And we had to give them enough so that they would become addicted to it. Then, and only then, would they feel the potential profit was enough to risk deep plants that had been in place for twenty to thirty years." The secretary looked from face to face. "Don't you see? These sleepers were assets! They belonged to someone in the GRU who had built his career on the fact that he had these assets, which would someday, at the right moment, be of incalculable value. Our task was to convince him or his superiors that *now* was that moment."

"So you let Franklin do his thing."

"Precisely. And we gave them excellent information. We let them see the best stuff that we had. We got them addicted, and curious. So one day Franklin's control approached Camacho, Tsybov." He lifted a finger skyward for dramatic effect. "That was a very important event. *The Soviets had gone to one of the names on the list.* Now we knew we were on the right track. We were heartened."

Caplinger rose quickly from his chair and began to pace. He explained that Harlan Albright, the control, was a GRU colonel. He made contact with Camacho, moved into the house beside him, insisted on biweekly briefings. "What the Soviets wanted, of course, was the identity of the Minotaur. So the game began for Luis Camacho. We didn't authorize him to reveal the Minotaur's identity. But he knew. He had to know. He knew from the first. He was the man who was actually going to uncover the sleepers."

He was silent for a moment, thinking it over yet again. "Once Camacho was in the game, he became the key player. It was inevitable. He had to appear to be a double agent and yet he had to force the Soviets to act. *To act* as we wanted them to. He was playing a dangerous role. And to appreciate how good he was at it, you would have to have known Luis Camacho very, very well. I didn't, but I got the flavor of the man. In his own way, in his own field, he was a master."

Caplinger stopped at the window and looked out at the meadows and distant blue mountains, which were a thin line on the western horizon. "Inevitably, and I do not use that word lightly, people were going to get hurt. Smoke Judy was an information peddler. He killed Harold Strong—your predecessor, Captain—when Strong found out about his activities. Camacho learned his identity, but we thought he might be of use later, so the committee ordered him left alone. Certainly no one could foresee that an indirect result of that decision would be the loss of the TRX prototype and your wife's injuries, Lieutenant, but . . . there were reasons that looked good at the time why it was handled the way it was." He finished lamely and turned to face Tarkington. "I am sorry."

Tarkington was examining his running shoes. He retied one of the laces.

"Anyway, there were several other deaths. A woman was killed who witnessed a drop set up by the Soviets to give Terry Franklin information, a Mrs. Matilda Jackson. Harlan Albright killed her, after *we* ordered Camacho to reveal her identity to Albright as proof of his bona fides, his commitment. Camacho refused at first, but we convinced him. This was the way it *had* to be. Better to sacrifice one to save the many." The secretary went back to his chair and sat heavily. He shook his head slowly. "Too often," he said softly, "we must assume some of God's burden. It is not light."

"Too bad," said Toad Tarkington, now staring at the secretary, "that after you gave an innocent civilian the chop, this whole thing fizzled."

"Did it?" Caplinger's voice assumed an edge, a hard flinty edge. "Did it now?"

When Toad didn't respond, Caplinger went on, his voice back to normal. "So after three years and some damn tragic risks, the stage was set. After a few carefully chosen facts were fed to Albright, he killed Terry Franklin. That was a masterpiece of cunning, well set up by Camacho. Of course Luis didn't like it, not he, but he played his part to perfection. Albright personally eliminated the Soviets' only access to the Pentagon computer. He had to find another. Because now the Minotaur offered the richest gift of all: Athena."

"Smoke Judy," said Jake Grafton, unable to keep silent.

"Yes. Smoke Judy, a bitter little man who had killed once and found how easy it is. Of course, that was the crisis. When Judy failed, as fail he surely would with Luis Camacho watching him, Albright would have no other choice. He would have to go to another deep plant on the list! And he would make this inevitable choice of his own free will, unpressured by anyone. That was our thinking, at least. Didn't work out that way. Camacho thought Albright was onto him and made a decision on his own to warn Vice Admiral Henry about the risk to Athena." He gestured to the heavens. "It was all downhill from there. Henry took it upon himself to apprehend Judy. You know how that turned out. The jig was up. Camacho had no choice. He sent men to arrest Albright."

"You were willing to give away Athena?" Jake's horror was in his voice.

"We on the committee were willing to take the risk Albright would get it, which isn't precisely the same thing, Captain. By now the Minotaur's credentials were impeccable. We thought that surely, for this exquisite technical jewel, the Soviets would brush the dirt off one or two deep agents."

"But they didn't?"

"No. Perhaps Albright was suspicious. Probably was. Camacho knew that Albright saw the whole operation too clearly, so he revealed the Minotaur's actual identity to save the game. It wasn't enough. With Judy and Albright in hiding, the Minotaur wrote one more letter, giving the access codes for the *new* Athena file. Then we waited for the Soviets to activate one of the sleepers. They didn't. What happened next was Albright kidnapped you, swiped all the Athena information he could readily lay hands on, then went to Camacho's house to kill him. Camacho had been expecting Albright to try something, but we didn't know exactly what it would be. When Luis Camacho came down those stairs and saw you there that afternoon—then he knew. The Soviets weren't going to invest any more major assets in this operation. His sole hope of getting the sleepers' names was Harlan Albright, who *might* know."

Jake said, "I wondered why the Athena file was suddenly renamed, all the access codes changed."

"Henry shouldn't have done that. Camacho shouldn't have warned him. But Camacho was worried he didn't have all the possible holes covered and he knew Athena's real value. Still, it would have worked if Henry hadn't interfered." Caplinger sounded as if he was trying to convince himself.

"We had to let the Russians work at it. If they succeeded too easily, they would have smelled the setup. No, our mistake was giving them the real Minotaur. Perhaps they found his identity too troublesome once they knew."

Caplinger shrugged. "After Judy failed, we wanted Albright badly. Our thinking then was that perhaps we could get the names from him, willingly or with hypnosis and drugs. We thought the odds about three to one that he knew the names *then*. If the GRU was even contemplating using a sleeper, the controller had to be briefed in advance, before the possibility became the necessity. Yet Albright evaded the clowns sent to pick him up. The agents thought they were going to arrest a mail-fraud suspect." Caplinger spread his hands, a gesture of frustration. "So we waited, hoping against hope a sleeping mole would awaken. It didn't happen."

"So you failed," Toad said.

"Oh no, Mr. Tarkington. The Minotaur succeeded beyond our wildest dreams. Not exactly in the way we expected, of course, but the benefits are real and tangible. This operation was one of the most successful covert intelligence operations ever undertaken by any nation. Ever."

"Please explain, sir."

"I see the disbelief written all over your face, Captain."

"My impression is that you people gave away the ranch, sir. Just how many top secret programs *did* you compromise?"

"We showed them the crown jewels, Captain. We had to. They would never have taken the bait otherwise. The three buried moles are very valuable."

"Pooh." Tarkington shook his head. "I'm not buying it. Those three agents may have turned, exactly like Camacho. If the Soviets ever try to use them, those guys may run straight to the FBI. The Russians may not even know where they are now."

"You are a very young man, *Lieutenant.*" Caplinger was scathing. "You have a *lot* to learn. The deep plants are valuable to the Soviets as chips in the Cold War poker games, at home and abroad. They are valuable in exactly the same way that thermonuclear weapons are valuable, ICBMs, boomer submarines—I could go on. Those three buried agents are *hole cards,* Lieutenant. They may even be dead. *Yet we can never afford to ignore them.* Do you begin to understand?"

"Yessir." Toad looked miserable. "But—"

"There are layers and layers and layers."

"But listen," Toad objected reasonably. "We didn't even know these men existed until four years ago. What if they don't?"

"*Aha!* The light becomes a glow!"

Caplinger leaped from his chair, galvanized. "Perhaps they don't exist! Perhaps the defection of a mid-level KGB officer was a ploy, and the list was bait to make us think they had three agents. They write the list, they leave it where a man of dubious professional accomplishments, a man of dubious loyalty and dubious value, will see it. Very convenient, you must admit! And in the fullness of time he is given an opportunity to defect, which he, no fool, takes as the best of a poor range of options."

Caplinger's voice rose to a shout. "And he gets here and tells us his little tale. We give it credence. *We must!* We have no other choice."

"I'm slightly baffled, Mr. Secretary," Jake said dryly. "Just how did the Minotaur succeed, if that word can even be used in these kinds of—what the hell are they?—games?"

Royce Caplinger began to walk back and forth, lost in thought. "The Soviet Union today is a nation in transition. Their system is against the wall. The Soviet people want good wages and housing and food to eat. The generals want to maintain their privileged positions. The politicians want to stay in power. (That's human enough. Ours will sell their soul for another term in office.) To do all of this the Soviets need money, vast quantities of it, money that does not exist.

"So the government is scrambling for money. What the Minotaur did was prove beyond a shadow of a doubt that the amount they have been spending for defense was nowhere near enough. The Soviets have spent as much money in real terms as we have for defense over the years, but it's a much larger percentage of their Gross National Product. Only a dictatorship can maintain that level of defense spending." He stopped his pacing and spread his arms. "The Minotaur put the spotlight on the Soviet system's failings. The Soviet economy, if it can be called that, is an abject debacle: food must be purchased from abroad, there is nothing in the stores to buy, the prosperity of the other industrial nations has eluded them. And now the military needs many more billions to replace hardware it has spent billions to obtain which is now obsolete, years and years before the Soviets planned to replace it."

He examined the faces of his listeners. "Don't you read newspapers? Where have you been? Gorbachev has been talking *perestroika* and *glasnost* for years. Why? The threat of Star Wars technology was a major impetus. There was no way they could match it. Under no conceivable circumstances could enough rubles be printed or squeezed from the people to fund such a program. The generals lost power. The politicians gained it. Through diplomacy the threat of Star Wars could be blunted, perhaps even eliminated. Soviet foreign policy changed course dramatically; arms reduction treaties were agreed to and signed, mutual verification was at last swallowed with good grace. Then came the Minotaur's revelations."

"I see," Jake said, rubbing his chin and glancing at Toad.

"Yes, Captain. We are having a major technological revolution in America just now. The research of the space programs has borne fruit. Ever smaller, ever more powerful computers, lasers, missiles, fiber optics, new manufacturing techniques that allow us to build structures and engines with capabilities undreamed of ten years ago: *last year's cutting-edge designs are obsolete before we can get them into production!* It's like something out of science fiction. This must have struck you these past six months?"

"Yes."

Caplinger nodded as he seated himself behind the desk. He just couldn't stay still for any length of time, Jake thought. "It struck me five years ago when I became SECDEF. I listened to the briefings in awe. This black magic was *real.* It's not just Star Wars; it's everything. Jet engines with over three times the thrust per pound of Soviet engines are *real,* ready for deployment. Stealth obsoletes their radar systems. America is preparing to deploy a new generation of weaponry that will make obsolete everything the Russian generals have bled the Soviet Union to get for the last forty years. They have reached the end of their string. If this is table stakes, they have bet their last ruble, and we have raised."

"The Minotaur," Jake said slowly, "gave them the awful truth."

"Chapter and verse. Imagine the horror in Moscow as the true dimensions of their dilemma sank in. The rumors and hints they had heard were *all true!* The United States was even farther ahead technologically than the worst pessimists predicted. It was a nightmare."

"They could have ordered a first strike," Tarkington said. "Started World War III before their military situation became hopeless."

"Yes. But they didn't. They are, after all, sane."

"Jee-sus!" Tarkington came out of his chair like a coiled spring. He planted himself in front of Caplinger's desk. "What if they *had*?"

"Then none of us would be alive now, would we, Lieutenant? Please sit down."

"Who commissioned you to play God with the universe, Caplinger? Where does it say in the Constitution that you have the right to bet the existence of every living thing on this planet, for whatever reason?"

Caplinger rose from his chair and leaned across the desk, until his face was only a foot from Toad's. "What ivory tower did you crawl down from? You think we should just strum our banjos and sing folk songs and *pray* that nuclear war never happens? Sit down and *shut the fuck up!*"

Tarkington obeyed. The cords in his neck were plainly visible.

"What is he, Captain?" Caplinger jerked a thumb at Toad. "Your conscience that you drag around?"

"He's a man who cares," Jake Grafton said slowly. "He sincerely cares."

"We all do," Caplinger replied, cooling down and taking his seat again. He rubbed his hand across his balding dome several times. "We all care, Tarkington. You think I enjoy this?"

"Yep. That's precisely what I think."

Caplinger rubbed his face. "Maybe you're right." He toyed with a pen on his desk. "Yeah. I guess 'enjoy' isn't the right word. But I do get satisfaction from it. Yes, I do." He looked at Tarkington. "This is my contribution. Is that so terrible?"

"That retired woman that Albright killed—I'll bet she enjoyed her little walk-on role in your drama. Didn't she have any rights?"

Caplinger looked away.

Toad pressed. "You just chopped her like she was nothing. Is that what we are to you? Pawns? Rita—you have the right to stuff my wife through the meat grinder for the greater good? You asshole!"

After a while Caplinger said, "We took big risks, but the reward was worth it." He set his jaw. "It was worth it," he insisted.

Neither officer replied.

Caplinger examined both their faces. "Come, gentlemen. Let's have another cup of coffee." Toad didn't get out of his chair. He had the corncob pipe in his hands as the other two men left the room.

In the kitchen Jake said, "Somebody's liable to shoot Gorbachev, you know. He's threatening to break a lot of rice bowls. Revolutions from the top rarely work."

"Even if Gorbachev dies, the Soviet Union will never be the same. If the old guard tries to clamp down, sooner or later there'll be another Russian Revolution, from the bottom next time. There's going to be another revolution in China, sooner or later. The communists can't go backwards, though they can sure try."

"Why were they so concerned about the Minotaur's identity?"

" 'They' is a very broad term. The GRU wanted evidence that the Minotaur's revelations were false, to discredit them. When Camacho gave them the name of the Secretary of Defense, they were left with an empty bag. The men in the Politburo realized that it was entirely possible the United States government was providing the information as a matter of policy. That possibility had to be weighed.

"The implications are difficult," he added, searching for words. "Perhaps the best way to say it is this: Some of the Soviet decision makers saw America, maybe for the first time, as we see ourselves —strong and confident, with excellent reasons for being confident. Frightened men start wars, and we aren't frightened."

Back in the den, Jake asked, "So we still don't know the identity of the three deep moles, the sleepers?"

"Let's say we're resigned to the fact that, if the agents exist, they will probably not be revealed. But we achieved so much! The changes in the Soviet Union the last three years have been profound."

"You play your fucking games," Toad murmured, "and the little guys get left holding the bag. Like Camacho."

"Ah, I hear the voice of the eternal private complaining because the generals are willing to sacrifice him to achieve a military objective."

"Sorry, I didn't read about your little war in the papers. And I didn't volunteer to fight it."

"America was Luis Camacho's adopted home. He loved this country and he loved its people. He knew exactly what he was doing every step of the way. Like you and your wife when you fly, he knew the risks. You think his job was *easy*? Having Albright right next door? Camacho had a wife and kid. You think he had no nerves?"

Toad sat silently with his arms folded across his chest, staring out the window. Jake and Caplinger talked a while longer. It was almost 4 P.M. when Caplinger said, "By the way, Captain, you did an excellent job presenting the TRX plane and Athena to Congress. I'm looking forward to getting a ride in an A-12 someday."

"That makes two of us."

Toad picked up the corncob pipe from the pipe stand again and examined it idly. "Why did Camacho admit his past?"

Caplinger smiled. "Who knows the human heart? His explanation, which I read very carefully after Albright approached him a year or so ago, was that America is a country that cares about people. You see, he was a cop. A cop in J. Edgar Hoover's FBI. But in spite of Hoover's paranoid insanities, Luis saw that the vast majority of the agents there were trying their best to enforce the laws in an even, fair manner, with due regard to the rights of their fellow citizens. Camacho came from a country where the police have no such mission. The police there are *not* honest, honorable men." He shrugged. "Luis Camacho instinctively understood Hoover. He had grown up in a nation ruled by such men. But Camacho came to see himself as a public servant. He became an American."

"Thanks for your time today, Mr. Secretary."

"I'll walk you to your car."

He led them through the kitchen to the door that led to the parking area. As he walked, he asked Jake, "How'd you learn I was the Minotaur?"

"I didn't. I guessed. Your seeing us today was the proof."

"You guessed?"

"Yes, sir. My wife suggested that perhaps the Minotaur was a role played by an actor, an intuitive insight which seemed to me to explain a great deal. Then I remembered that comment you made one evening at dinner in China Lake this past summer, something to the effect that the perception of reality is more important than the facts. Camacho had said that the people who had to know about this operation did know. By implication that comment included you. So I decided you were probably the Minotaur."

"I thought your notes meant blackmail, until I saw you this afternoon."

"I thought you might."

Jake stepped to the car ten feet away and opened the door.

"All our scheming," Caplinger mused. "So transparent. No wonder Camacho thought Albright saw through it. Albright was no fool."

Royce Caplinger stopped at the end of the walk to look at the clouds building above the mountains to the west. He started as something hard dug into his back.

In his ear Toad said, "You miscalculated once too often, Caplinger."

Catching the tone but not the words, Jake Grafton turned with a puzzled look on his face.

The lieutenant had his arm on Caplinger's shoulder. He jerked the older man sideways until he was between him and Grafton. "Don't move, Captain! I swear I'll shoot him if I have to."

"What—?"

"That's right, Caplinger," Toad hissed in the secretary's ear. "I'll pull this trigger and blow your spine clean in half. This time it isn't Matilda Jackson or Rita Moravia or Luis Camacho. It's you! You thought you had everything figured, didn't you? Minotaur! *You were wrong!* The decision has been made. It's time for you to die."

The secretary tried to turn. "Now listen—"

"Tarkington!" Jake Grafton roared.

Toad twisted the man's arm, squeezing as hard as he could. "The decision has been made! *They* decided. It's over for *you*."

"Please *listen*—" Caplinger began as Jake strode toward the two men, his face a mask of livid fury.

"Tarkington!"

"So long, asshole!" Toad stepped to one side, raised his arm and pointed right into Caplinger's face. "Bang," he said, and let the corncob pipe fall from his hand.

Caplinger stood staring at it.

"Tarkington," Jake said softly, his voice as ominous as a gathering storm.

Toad walked away down the drive. He stumbled once, caught himself and kept walking. He didn't look back.

Caplinger lowered himself into the gravel. He put his head on his knees. After a bit he whispered, "I really . . . I really thought . . ."

"His wife . . ."

"He's right, you know."

Jake turned and looked down the long, straight driveway. Tarkington was still going, marching for the road, his head up and shoulders back. "Yeah."

"Go. Take him with you. Go."

"You going to be okay?"

"Yes. Just go."

Jake started the car, turned it around and went down the driveway. He slowed to a crawl alongside Toad, who kept walking. "Get in."

Tarkington ignored him. He was chewing on his lower lip.

"Get in the car, Lieutenant, or I will court-martial you, so help me God!"

Tarkington stopped and looked at Grafton behind the wheel. He hesitated, then opened the passenger door and climbed in.

As Jake started the car rolling again he glanced in the rearview mirror. In front of the huge mansion covered with ivy, Caplinger was still sitting in the gravel with his head down.

Three miles down the road Toad spoke. "Why did you stay in the navy?"

"Some things are worth fighting for."

Toad sat silently, his eyes on the road, for a long time. Finally he said, "I'm sorry."

"Everyone's sorry." *We're born sorry, we spend our life apologizing, and we die sorry. Sorry for all the guys with their names on the Wall. Sorry for the silly bastards who sent them there and stayed home and aren't sorry themselves. Sorry for the 230 grunts killed in Lebanon by a truck bomb. Sorry for the simple sonuvabitch who wouldn't let the sentry load his rifle. We're sorry for them all.*

"Forget it," Jake added.

"I should've killed the bastard."

"Wouldn't have done any good."

"I suppose not."

31

Rita was released from the hospital on a Wednesday in November. She wore a cervical collar and a blue uniform that Toad had had dry-cleaned. He picked her up at noon. "Where to, beautiful?"

"Straight to the beauty shop, James. I'm going to treat myself to a cut, shampoo and perm, then home to bed."

She was very tired when he got her home to their apartment. After a nap, that evening she walked around slowly, looking at this, touching that. Harriet came over for a gabfest and left at nine when Rita visibly wilted.

On Friday, Rita insisted on going to the office with Toad. The crowd paraded by the desk one at a time to welcome her back. She greeted each of them joyfully, with genuine enthusiasm. Her delightful exhilaration was contagious. She seemed the incarnation of the promise and hope of life. Yet by noon she was tired, so Toad drove her home, then he returned to the office alone.

Saturday morning arrived crisp and clear. "How do you feel today?" Toad asked as he helped her into the collar.

"Good. I'll need a nap this afternoon, though."

"Want to go on an expedition? I promise a nap."

"Where?"

He wouldn't tell. So, suitably dressed, they went down to the car, where Toad announced he had forgotten something upstairs.

He rode the elevator back up to the third floor and made several quick phone calls, then returned smiling.

He drove out to a small civilian airport in Reston, all the while refusing to answer questions, parked the car in front of the flying service's little building, and came around to help her out.

" 'Just as lovely a morning as ever was seen, for a nice little trip in a flying machine,' " quoteth Toad.

"What is this? Toad! I can't fly!"

"I can. You can watch me."

"You? You've been taking lessons?"

"Got my license too. Last weekend. Now we're both pilots." He grinned broadly and hugged her gently.

Toad took her inside and introduced her to the owner of the flying service, who visited with her while Toad preflighted the plane and taxied it to the front, where he killed the engine. The machine was a Cessna 172, white with a red stripe extending horizontally along the fuselage, back from the prop spinner. Toad thought it looked racy.

Rita was standing in the door, watching him. He couldn't resist. He bowed deeply from the waist. "Come," he said. "Come fly with me."

He helped her strap into the right seat, then walked around the machine and strapped himself into the left.

"This feels funny," she giggled.

"Come fly with me, darling Rita. We'll fly the halls of heaven, watch the angel choir. We'll soar with the eagles and see where the storms are born. Fly with me, Rita, all your life."

"Start the engine, Toad-man."

With a half inch of throttle, the engine spluttered to life again. He pulled the throttle back to idle and the Lycoming ran smoothly, the propeller a blurred disk. Out they went down the narrow asphalt taxiway with Toad monitoring the Unicom frequency and checking the sky. He paused at the end of the taxiway, ran the engine up to 1,700 RPM and checked the mags, carb heat and mixture control, all the while acutely aware of Rita's scrutiny.

He was trying very hard to do everything right and not to laugh at the incongruity of the situation. When he glanced at Rita, she quickly averted her gaze. She was biting her lip, no doubt to keep from smiling. She had that scrunched-up look around her eyes. Trying hard to keep a straight face himself, Toad got back to the business at hand.

He wiped the controls through a cycle and ran the flaps out and in with an eye on the voltage needle. Satisfied, he announced his intentions on Unicom and took the runway.

The engine snarled as he smoothly pushed the throttle knob in all the way. With his feet dancing on the rudder pedals, the plane swerved only a little as it accelerated. At fifty-five knots he pulled back on the yoke and the plane came willingly off the runway. He trimmed the plane for a seventy-knot climb and said, "You've got it."

She took the wheel gingerly and waggled it experimentally. "Oh, Toad! It's *terrific!* It flies great."

"Anything that gets you off the ground is a great airplane." He gave her the course he wanted and checked that the IFF was properly set.

Upward they climbed. They circled south of the metropolitan Washington area and headed eastward across the Chesapeake at 5,500 feet, 105 knots indicated. The engine was loud, but not unpleasantly so.

Rita flew with a smile, occasionally waggling the wings or kicking the rudder, just to see how it felt. She made gentle coordinated climbing and descending turns as Toad monitored the engine instruments, swept the sky for other airplanes, and kept track of their position with the VOR needles. Still, 105 knots was not warp speed, so between all these tasks he had time to watch the boats on the Chesapeake a mile below. They were small, trailing short wakes on the great blue water, under the great blue sky.

The wind helped the plane eastward. About fifteen knots of wind from the northwest, Toad figured. Approaching the eastern shore of Maryland, he could see smoke rising skyward from odd smokestacks and bending with the wind as it drifted aloft.

Rita signaled that he should take the controls, and he did. She sat back in her seat and watched him fly. Somewhere over eastern Maryland she began to laugh.

What began as a giggle quickly became an eye-watering gut buster. Toad joined in. Together they laughed until they had tears in their eyes. When they had melted themselves down to wide grins, she ran her fingers through his hair as he continued his impersonation of Orville Wright, Glenn Curtiss and Eddie Rickenbacker, Douglas McCampbell and Randy Cunningham, Jake Grafton and Rita Moravia and all the rest, all those who were only truly alive when they had a stick in their hand and the airplane was a part of them.

Finally she devoted her attention to the sky and the green earth spread out below. When he next looked at her she wore a gentle, contented smile. She seemed very much at peace.

I must always remember her this way, he thought, with the sun on her face and the blue sky behind her, happy and content.

The field at Rehoboth was grass. Toad held the plane off until the stall warning sounded, and after the main mounts kissed, he held the weight off the nose with full back elevator until he had slowed to the speed of a man walking.

Jake Grafton was leaning on the fence, watching them taxi in. Toad flapped a hand. The captain waved back.

"Have a good flight?" Jake asked after Toad killed the engine and climbed out.

"The best. No lie, sir, this was the finest flight of my life."

" 'Lo, Rita. Was he safe?"

She laughed and grasped Toad's hand. "I'll fly with him anytime."

At the Graftons' house Callie led Rita upstairs, where she stretched out in Amy's bed, at Amy's proud insistence. Callie seized the girl's hand and led her from the room, closing the door behind them. "You can visit with her all you want when she wakes. She's very tired right now."

"I'm going to be just like her when I grow up," Amy announced, not for the first time.

"You already are, Amy. I think you're sisters at heart."

They had finished dinner and rinsed the dishes and arranged them in the dishwasher when the phone rang. Callie answered it in the kitchen, then stuck her head around the corner and said, "It's for you, Jake."

He took the call on the phone in the living room.

"Captain, this is George Ludlow. Sorry to disturb you at home."

"Quite all right, sir."

"Just wanted you to know. We have a new man ordered in as the prospective program manager. Rear Admiral Harry Church. He'll arrive Wednesday. I want you to do the turnover by December 15."

"Aye aye, sir. But this is pretty quick, isn't it? I've only been at

this job nine months or so and am not due for orders for another—"

"You're going to the staff of the Chairman of the Joint Chiefs.
From your record, it looks as if you've never had a joint staff tour.
CNO wants you to get one now so they can send you to a task
group when you make rear admiral."

"Rear admiral? I thought—"

"CNO thinks you're flag material. For what it's worth, two senators and three congressmen have mentioned you to me this past
month. They want to see your name on the flag list next year or the
year after. I concur. Wholeheartedly. So does Royce Caplinger.
The CNO personally picked this billet for you."

After a few pleasantries, they said goodbye. Jake hung up,
slightly stunned. Callie glanced at him and raised an inquisitive
eyebrow, but he shrugged and grinned. He would tell her later,
when they were alone.

The phone rang again. "Is Amy there?" The voice was high, well
modulated. David, from down the street.

"Amy, it's for you."

Jake resumed his seat at the table. He was only half listening
when he heard Amy say, "I'll have to ask my dad." She held the
phone at arm's length and said loudly, "Jake, can I go over to
David's?"

"Sure. Be back in about an hour or so and you can go with us
when we take Rita and Toad back to the airport."

"Can David come too?"

"Yep."

She held the phone to her ear. "My dad says I can come over.
And you can go with us to the airport. See you in a sec." She threw
the instrument roughly onto its cradle and bolted, elbows flying.

"Wear your coat," Callie called.

The youngster snagged the garment from the peg and charged
for the door, yelling over her shoulder, "See you later, Rita." The
door slammed shut behind her.

"You get that?" Toad asked Jake with a grin. "Dad?"

"Yeah," said Jake Grafton. He stretched hugely. "It's a nice
sound, isn't it?"

One Thursday in February, Admiral Church, the new project manager, called Toad to his office. Tarkington was one of only three
officers in the office this day: everyone else was somewhere in Texas

or Nevada or over at the Pentagon. The first production A-12 was due to roll out next week and everyone was swamped with work. Although Washington was suffering one of its rare blizzards, the navy was steaming as before. The Metro wasn't running and all nonessential government employees had the day off. Only one of the civil service secretaries had made it to the office.

"You wanted to see me, sir?"

"Yes, Lieutenant. We got a call from the D.C. police. They would like one of the officers to drop by D.C. General this afternoon. If you can spare the time, would you go, please."

"Yes, sir. Did they say what this is all about?"

"No, they didn't. But they wanted an officer from this unit. Ask for a Dr. Wagner. And brief me in the morning, will you?"

"Aye aye, sir."

As Toad approached the reception desk at D.C. General Hospital, he brushed the snow from his coat and shook the moisture from his cover. He explained his errand to the receptionist. She busied herself with the telephone buttons and he watched the flakes fall outside the front door while he absently pulled off his black leather gloves and placed them in the left pocket of his navy-blue bridge coat. The white scarf around his neck he folded and tucked into the other pocket. Finally he removed the coat and hung it over his arm. His hat he retrieved from the counter and held in his left hand.

"A navy officer . . ." the receptionist was telling someone. ". . . Dr. Wagner."

The snow had been falling for two days. The sailor from Minnesota who had driven him here had had numerous pithy comments about the locals' ability to drive on icy, snow-packed streets. The hospital staff, Toad noted with a trace of satisfaction, was apparently as indifferent to the edicts of the transportation authorities as Admiral Church was.

"Take the elevator on that wall. Third floor, turn left, then left again, fourth or fifth door on the right. I think."

"I'll find it."

She smiled and fielded another phone call. Toad went to the bank of elevators and jabbed a button.

Wagner was in his early fifties, with thin, iron-gray hair and an air of nervous energy. He seemed fit and agile in spite of the rather prominent tummy he sported.

"You from the A-12 program?"

"Yessir."

"Know why we asked you to come over?"

"Haven't the foggiest."

"Put your coat and hat on this chair. And do sit down." Dr. Wagner hefted a pile of files to make room, then quickly surveyed the office for an empty spot. He placed the files on a corner of his desk, then took the remaining unoccupied seat. The chair behind the desk already contained a heap of paper a foot thick.

Wagner glanced at Toad's uniform, then spoke. "Terrible weather. Plays havoc with the street people. Police and charities are scooping them up as fast as they can and bringing the ones in need of medical attention here."

Toad nodded politely, wondering what this had to do with the navy.

"Got a case in last week during that terrible cold snap, those nights when it got down almost to zero. Just terrible." He shook his head. "Wreck of a man. Had to amputate all his fingers and toes. Did save the stump of one thumb. He was dying of hypothermia, gangrene, and alcohol poisoning when the police found him. And we had to amputate his ears, the tip of his nose, and a portion of his lower lip. They were gangrenous when we got him, probably from damage during that storm at the end of January."

Seeing the look on Toad's face, the doctor added, "Amazingly enough, I think he's out of danger now. His liver—well, usually these alcoholics have a liver the size and consistency of a football, but this one doesn't. Damaged, of course, but not yet fatally so."

"Amazing."

"Yep. Anyway, this man is, of course, incoherent most of the time, but he has lucid moments occasionally. We thought you might be able to identify him."

Toad smiled his doubt. "We have our share of party animals in the navy, but we haven't misplaced any from our office lately."

"No fingerprints to match, of course," the doctor said. "No fingers. No wallet, no ID, no jewelry, but he is *somebody*. It's a long shot, I know."

"Has he given a name?"

"No. He keeps talking about a woman, probably a wife or daughter. Judy. Never gives her last name. And this only during coherent moments. There aren't all that many of those."

Toad Tarkington felt hot. He tugged at his tie.

"You must see quite a few of these folks," he managed.

"Yes. Schizophrenics, most of them. Mental illness complicated by alcoholism and drug addiction. What say we go look? You're busy and I don't want to keep you. Not a chance in a thousand, I know."

Toad lurched to his feet and arranged his coat and hat on his arm.

"How do you know," he asked as they walked the corridor, "that these derelicts aren't criminals?"

"No doubt some of them are. Petty thieves and whatnot. But the prosecutors have bigger fish to fry. And even if we found a man they wanted to prosecute, he'd probably be incompetent to stand trial."

"I see."

"We'd have to send them to St. Elizabeth's for treatment and evaluation, hoping they could get well enough to understand the charges against them and assist in their defense."

"Very civilized," Toad said.

"I detect a note of irony there." The medical man paused at the fire door of a staircase with his hand on the knob. "Actually all these derelicts should be in an institution. They are completely incapable of looking after themselves. The lawyers and judges— they are such asses."

"What d'ya mean?"

"Unless someone is being held for trial, we must go to the courts and seek an involuntary commitment order. We must prove the person we wish to commit is a danger to himself or others. Assuming the judge agrees, we can hold the man for six months. Then there is another hearing on precisely the same issue. And a group of public-interest lawyers have dedicated themselves to representing these people for nothing. The attorneys, all with the best of intentions, do their absolute damnedest to get these sick people out of the institutional setting and right back onto the streets, where they can drink and starve themselves to death."

"What a great country," Toad muttered.

The doctor opened the door and led the way down the stairs. "In America these days, freedom for those who are functionally disabled, incapable of keeping body and soul together, means the freedom to commit suicide with a bottle on a public sidewalk while the world walks around them. The politicians ignore the problem: these people don't vote. There is no problem, the lawyers say.

Vagrancy and alcoholism aren't crimes, the judges say. Nothing can be done."

"This man we're going to see—is he dangerous?"

"Only to himself. And the lawyers and judges would disagree."

They were in a corridor now, proceeding past double swinging doors with little windows that opened onto wards. Toad could see the patients in the beds, smell the disinfectant. Nurses hustled by. He could hear people moaning, and from somewhere a man roaring common obscenities in a mindless chant, the mantra of the insane.

"What will become of him?"

"When the bandages come off? Oh, we'll ship him over to St. Elizabeth's and they'll try for an involuntary commitment, and who knows, they may get lucky. But in six months, or a year, or a year and a half, the judge will turn him loose. He'll drink himself to death in an alley. Or die some winter night when the police are late coming by."

The doctor turned left and went through a door.

The patient was staring at a spot on the ceiling over the bed. Both arms were bandaged to the elbows. Lumps, bandages probably, under the covers where his feet were.

A chunk of his lower lip was missing. The cavity had stitches at the bottom of it. Bandages on both ears and nose; a strip of tape went completely around his head to hold them in place. He was secured to the bed by a cloth harness.

"You have to get over here, where he will see you. I think the alcohol has destroyed a lot of his peripheral vision." The doctor led the hesitant lieutenant to where he wanted him, then waved his hand in front of the patient's eyes.

The eyes moved. They traveled up the hand to the doctor's face. Then they moved to Toad, focusing on the dark, navy-blue uniform.

The man in the bed tried to speak.

"Take your time," the doctor said. "Tell us who you are."

"Uh . . . uh . . ."

"What is your name? Please tell us your name."

"Uh . . ." He stared at the uniform, at the ribbons, at the wings, at the brass buttons, at the gold rings on the sleeves. "Ju-dee. Ju-dee." His gaze was fixated on the gleaming wings.

"There he goes again," the doctor said to Toad. "Sometimes he mumbles about A-12. That could be an apartment, of course, but I remembered seeing all that stuff in the papers about the navy's new airplane, so I decided to call you. A long shot." The doctor sighed. "I do wish I knew who his Judy is. Maybe a daughter who'd like to take care of him, or at least know where he is. She's obviously someone he cares about." His voice became brisk, business-like: "So, do you recognize him?"

Toad Tarkington stared at the man in the bed as he weighed it: three squares a day in a nice warm cell for thirty or forty years, or an alcoholic's death in a frozen alley.

At last he said, "I never saw him before in my life."

ABOUT THE AUTHOR

STEPHEN COONTS graduated from West Virginia University with a degree in political science and a commission in the navy, where he flew A-6 bombers in Vietnam and accumulated over two thousand hours in the air. He is the author of *Flight of the Intruder* and *Final Flight,* both major best sellers. He now lives in Boulder, Colorado.